MEMENTO MORI

THE GIRLS OF SLENDER MEANS

Books by Muriel Spark

★

THE COMFORTERS

THE GO-AWAY BIRD WITH OTHER STORIES

ROBINSON

THE BALLAD OF PECKHAM RYE

THE BACHELORS

VOICES AT PLAY

THE PRIME OF MISS JEAN BRODIE

DOCTORS OF PHILOSOPHY

MEMENTO MORI

THE GIRLS
OF SLENDER MEANS

BY

MURIEL SPARK

THE REPRINT SOCIETY LONDON

THIS EDITION PUBLISHED BY THE REPRINT SOCIETY 1965
BY ARRANGEMENT WITH MESSRS. MACMILLAN & CO. LTD.

The verses from 'Moonlit Apples',
The Collected Poems of John Drinkwater,
are quoted by permission of
Sidgwick and Jackson, Ltd.

*Printed in Great Britain by Richard Clay (The Chaucer Press), Ltd.,
Bungay, Suffolk*

MEMENTO MORI

For
TERESA WALSHE
with love

What shall I do with this absurdity—
O heart, O troubled heart—this caricature,
Decrepit age that has been tied to me
As to a dog's tail?

W. B. YEATS
(*The Tower*)

O what Venerable and Reverend Creatures
did the Aged seem! Immortal Cherubims!

THOMAS TRAHERNE
(*Centuries of Meditation*)

Q. What are the four last things to be ever
   remembered?
A. The four last things to be ever remembered are Death, Judgment, Hell, and
   Heaven.

The Penny Catechism

Chapter One

Dame Lettie Colston refilled her fountain pen and continued her letter:

One of these days I hope you will write as brilliantly on a happier theme. In these days of cold war I *do* feel we should soar above the murk & smog & get into the clear crystal.

The telephone rang. She lifted the receiver. As she had feared, the man spoke before she could say a word. When he had spoken the familiar sentence she said, 'Who is that speaking, who is it?'

But the voice, as on eight previous occasions, had rung off.

Dame Lettie telephoned to the Assistant Inspector as she had been requested to do. 'It has occurred again,' she said.

'I see. Did you notice the time?'

'It was only a moment ago.'

'The same thing?'

'Yes,' she said, 'the same. Surely you have some means of tracing——'

'Yes, Dame Lettie, we will get him, of course.'

A few moments later Dame Lettie telephoned to her brother Godfrey.

'Godfrey, it has happened again.'

'I'll come and fetch you, Lettie,' he said. 'You must spend the night with us.'

'Nonsense. There is no danger. It is merely a disturbance.'

'What did he say?'

'The same thing. And quite matter-of-fact, not really threatening. Of course the man's mad. I don't know what the police are thinking of, they must be sleeping. It's been going on for six weeks now.'

'Just those words?'

'Just the same words—*Remember you must die*—nothing more.'

'He must be a maniac,' said Godfrey.

*   *   *

Godfrey's wife Charmian sat with her eyes closed, attempting to put her thoughts into alphabetical order which Godfrey had told her was better than no order at all, since she now had grasp of neither logic nor chronology. Charmian was eighty-five. The other day a journalist from a weekly paper had been to see her. Godfrey had subsequently read aloud to her the young man's article:

> . . . By the fire sat a frail old lady, a lady who once set the whole of the literary world (if not the Thames) on fire . . . Despite her age, this legendary figure is still abundantly alive . . .

Charmian felt herself dropping off, and so she said to the maid who was arranging the magazines on the long oak table by the window, 'Taylor, I am dropping off to sleep for five minutes. Telephone to St. Mark's and say I am coming.'

Just at that moment Godfrey entered the room holding his hat and wearing his outdoor coat. 'What's that you say?' he said.

'Oh, Godfrey, you made me start.'

'*Taylor* . . .' he repeated, 'St. Mark's . . . Don't you realise there is no maid in this room, and furthermore, you are not in Venice?'

'Come and get warm by the fire,' she said, 'and take your coat off'; for she thought he had just come in from the street.

'I am about to go *out*,' he said. 'I am going to fetch Lettie who is to stop with us tonight. She has been troubled by another of those anonymous calls.'

'That was a pleasant young man who called the other day,' said Charmian.

'Which young man?'

'From the paper. The one who wrote——'

'That was five years and two months ago,' said Godfrey.

'Why can't one be kind to her?' he asked himself as he drove to Lettie's house in Hampstead. 'Why can't one be more gentle?' He himself was eighty-seven, and in charge of all his faculties. Whenever he considered his own behaviour he thought of himself not as 'I' but as 'one'.

'One has one's difficulties with Charmian,' he told himself.

*   *   *

'Nonsense,' said Lettie. 'I have no enemies.'

'*Think*,' said Godfrey. 'Think hard.'

'The red lights,' said Lettie. 'And don't talk to me as if I were Charmian.'

'Lettie, if you please, I do not need to be told how to drive. I observed the lights.' He had braked hard, and Dame Lettie was jerked forward.

She gave a meaningful sigh which, when the green lights came on, made him drive all the faster.

'You know, Godfrey,' she said, 'you are wonderful for your age.'

'So everyone says.' His driving pace became moderate; her sigh of relief was inaudible, her patting herself on the back, invisible.

'In your position,' he said, 'you must have enemies.'

'Nonsense.'

'I say *yes*.' He accelerated.

'Well, perhaps you're right.' He slowed down again, but Dame Lettie thought, I wish I hadn't come.

They were at Knightsbridge. It was only a matter of keeping him happy till they reached Kensington Church Street and turned into Vicarage Gardens, where Godfrey and Charmian lived.

'I have written to Eric,' she said, 'about his book. Of course, he has something of his mother's former brilliance, but it did seem to me that the subject-matter lacked the joy and hope which was the mark of a good novel in those days.'

'I couldn't *read* the book,' said Godfrey. 'I simply could not go on with it. A motor salesman in Leeds and his wife spending a night in a hotel with that communist librarian. . . . Where does it all lead you?'

Eric was his son. Eric was fifty-six and had recently published his second novel.

'He'll never do as well as Charmian did,' Godfrey said. 'Try as he may.'

'Well, I can't quite agree with that,' said Lettie, seeing that they had now pulled up in front of the house. 'Eric has a hard streak of realism which Charmian never——'

Godfrey had got out and slammed the door. Dame Lettie
sighed and followed him into the house, wishing she hadn't
come.

*   *   *

'Did you have a nice evening at the pictures, Taylor?' said
Charmian.

'I am not Taylor,' said Dame Lettie, 'and in any case, you
always called Taylor "Jean" during her last twenty or so years
in your service.'

Mrs. Anthony, their daily housekeeper, brought in the milky
coffee and placed it on the breakfast table.

'Did you have a nice evening at the pictures, Taylor?'
Charmian asked her.

'Yes, thanks, Mrs. Colston,' said the housekeeper.

'Mrs. Anthony is not Taylor,' said Lettie. 'There is no one
by name of Taylor here. And anyway you used to call her Jean
latterly. It was only when you were a girl that you called Taylor
Taylor. And, in any event, Mrs. Anthony is not Taylor.'

Godfrey came in. He kissed Charmian. She said, 'Good
morning, Eric.'

'He is not Eric,' said Dame Lettie.

Godfrey frowned at his sister. Her resemblance to himself
irritated him. He opened *The Times*.

'Are there lots of obituaries today?' said Charmian.

'Oh, don't be gruesome,' said Lettie.

'Would you like me to read you the obituaries, dear?' Godfrey
said, turning the pages to find the place in defiance of his
sister.

'Well, I should like the war news,' Charmian said.

'The war has been over since nineteen forty-five,' Dame
Lettie said. 'If indeed it is the last war you are referring to.
Perhaps, however, you mean the First World War? The
Crimean perhaps . . . ?'

'Lettie, please,' said Godfrey. He noticed that Lettie's hand
was unsteady as she raised her cup, and the twitch on her large
left cheek was pronounced. He thought in how much better
form he himself was than his sister, though she was the younger,
only seventy-nine.

Mrs. Anthony looked round the door. 'Someone on the phone for Dame Lettie.'

'Oh, who is it?'

'Wouldn't give a name.'

'Ask who it is, please.'

'Did ask. Wouldn't give——'

'I'll go,' said Godfrey.

Dame Lettie followed him to the telephone and overheard the male voice. 'Tell Dame Lettie,' it said, 'to remember she must die.'

'Who's there?' said Godfrey. But the man had hung up.

'We must have been followed,' said Lettie. 'I told no one I was coming over here last night.'

She telephoned to report the occurrence to the Assistant Inspector.

He said, 'Sure you didn't mention to anyone that you intended to stay at your brother's home?'

'Of course I'm sure.'

'Your brother actually heard the voice? Heard it himself?'

'Yes, as I say, he took the call.'

She told Godfrey, 'I'm glad you took the call. It corroborates my story. I have just realised that the police have been doubting it.'

'Doubting your word?'

'Well, I suppose they thought I might have imagined it. Now, perhaps, they will be more active.'

Charmian said, 'The police . . . what are you saying about the police? Have we been robbed?'

'I am being molested,' said Dame Lettie.

Mrs. Anthony came in to clear the table.

'Ah, Taylor, how old are you?' said Charmian.

'Sixty-nine, Mrs. Colston,' said Mrs. Anthony.

'When will you be seventy?'

'Twenty-eighth November.'

'That will be splendid, Taylor. You will then be one of us,' said Charmian.

Chapter Two

THERE were twelve occupants of the Maud Long Medical Ward (aged people, female). The ward sister called them the Baker's Dozen, not knowing that this is thirteen, but having only heard the phrase; and thus it is that a good many old sayings lose their force.

First came a Mrs. Emmeline Roberts, seventy-six, who had been a cashier at the Odeon in the days when it *was* the Odeon. Next came Miss or Mrs. Lydia Reewes-Duncan, seventy-eight, whose past career was uncertain, but who was visited fortnightly by a middle-aged niece, very bossy towards the doctors and staff, very uppish. After that came Miss Jean Taylor, eighty-two, who had been a companion-maid to the famous authoress Charmian Piper after her marriage into the Colston Brewery family. Next again lay Miss Jessie Barnacle who had no birth certificate but was put down as eighty-one, and who for forty-eight years had been a newsvendor at Holborn Circus. There was also a Madame Trotsky, a Mrs. Fanny Green, a Miss Doreen Valvona, and five others, all of known and various careers, and of ages ranging from seventy to ninety-three. These twelve old women were known variously as Granny Roberts, Granny Duncan, Granny Taylor, Grannies Barnacle, Trotsky, Green, Valvona, and so on.

Sometimes, on first being received into her bed, the patient would be shocked and feel rather let down by being called Granny. Miss or Mrs. Reewes-Duncan threatened for a whole week to report anyone who called her Granny Duncan. She threatened to cut them out of her will and to write to her M.P. The nurses provided writing-paper and a pencil at her urgent request. However, she changed her mind about informing her M.P. when they promised not to call her Granny any more. 'But,' she said, 'you shall never go back into my will.'

'In the name of God that's real awful of you,' said the ward sister as she bustled about. 'I thought you was going to leave us all a packet.'

'Not now,' said Granny Duncan. 'Not now, I won't. You don't catch me for a fool.'

Tough Granny Barnacle, she who had sold the evening paper for forty-eight years at Holborn Circus, and who always said, 'Actions speak louder than words,' would send out to Woolworth's for a will-form about once a week; this would occupy her for two or three days. She would ask the nurse how to spell words like 'hundred' and 'ermine'.

'Goin' to leave me a hundred quid, Granny?' said the nurse. 'Goin' to leave me your ermine cape?'

The doctor on his rounds would say, 'Well, Granny Barnacle, am I to be remembered or not?'

'You're down for a thousand, Doc.'

'My word, I must stick in with you, Granny. I'll bet you've got a long stocking, my girl.'

Miss Jean Taylor mused upon her condition and upon old age in general. Why do some people lose their memories, some their hearing? Why do some talk of their youth and others of their wills? She thought of Dame Lettie Colston who had all her senses intact, and yet played a real will-game, attempting to keep the two nephews in suspense, enemies of each other. And Charmian. . . . Poor Charmian, since her stroke. How muddled she was about most things, and yet perfectly sensible when she discussed the books she had written. Quite clear on just that one thing, the subject of her books.

A year ago, when Miss Taylor had been admitted to the ward, she had suffered misery when addressed as Granny Taylor, and she thought she would rather die in a ditch than be kept alive under such conditions. But she was a woman practised in restraint; she never displayed her resentment. The lacerating familiarity of the nurses' treatment merged in with her arthritis, and she bore them both as long as she could without complaint. Then she was forced to cry out with pain during a long haunted night when the dim ward lamp made the beds into grey-white lumps like terrible bundles of laundry which muttered and snored occasionally. A nurse brought her an injection.

'You'll be better now, Granny Taylor.'

'Thank you, nurse.'

'Turn over, Granny, that's a good girl.'

'Very well, nurse.'

The arthritic pain subsided, leaving the pain of desolate humiliation, so that she wished rather to endure the physical nagging again.

After the first year she resolved to make her suffering a voluntary affair. If this is God's will then it is mine. She gained from this state of mind a decided and visible dignity, at the same time as she lost her stoical resistance to pain. She complained more, called often for the bed-pan, and did not hesitate, on one occasion when the nurse was dilatory, to wet the bed as the other grannies did so frequently.

Miss Taylor spent much time considering her position. The doctor's 'Well, how's Granny Taylor this morning? Have *you* been making your last will and test——' would falter when he saw her eyes, the intelligence. She could not help hating these visits, and the nurses giving her a hair-do, telling her she looked like sixteen, but she volunteered mentally for them, as it were, regarding them as the Will of God. She reflected that everything could be worse, and was sorry for the youngest generation now being born into the world, who in their old age, whether of good family or no, educated or no, would be forced by law into Chronic Wards; she dared say every citizen in the Kingdom would take it for granted; and the time would surely come for everyone to be a government granny or grandpa, unless they were mercifully laid to rest in their prime.

Miss Doreen Valvona was a good reader, she had the best eyes in the ward. Each morning at eleven she read aloud everyone's horoscopes from the newspaper, holding it close to her brown nose and—behind her glasses—to the black eyes which came from her Italian father. She knew by heart everyone's Zodiacal sign. 'Granny Green—Virgo,' she would say. '*A day for bold measures. Close partnerships are beneficial. A wonderful period for entertaining.*'

'Read us it again. My hearing aid wasn't fixed.'

'No, you'll have to wait. Granny Duncan's next. Granny Duncan—Scorpio. *Go all out for what you want today. Plenty of variety and gaiety to keep you on your toes.*'

Granny Valvona remembered everyone's horoscope all the day, checking up to see the points where it came true, so that, after Dame Lettie Colston had been to visit Granny Taylor the old family servant, a cry arose from Granny Valvona: 'What did I tell you in your horoscope? Listen while I read it out again. Granny Taylor—Gemini. *You are in wonderful form today. Exceptionally bright social potents are indicated.*'

'*Portents*,' said Miss Taylor. 'Not potents.'

Granny Valvona looked again. She spelt it out. 'Potents,' she said. Miss Taylor gave it up, murmuring, 'I see.'

'Well?' said Granny Valvona. 'Wasn't that a remarkable forecast? *You are in wonderful form today. Exceptionally bright social. . . .* Now isn't that your visitor foretold, Granny Taylor?'

'Yes, indeed, Granny Valvona.'

'Some dame!' said the littlest nurse, who could not make out why Granny Taylor had so seriously called her visitor 'Dame Lettie'. She had heard of dames as jokes, and at the pictures.

'Wait, nurse, I'll read your horoscope. What's your month?'

'I've to go, Granny Valvoni. Sister's on the hunt.'

'Don't call my name Valvoni, it's Valvon*a*. It ends with an *ah*.'

'*Ah*,' said the little nurse, and disappeared with a hop and a skip.

*   *   *

'Taylor was in wonderful form today,' Dame Lettie told her brother.

'You've been to see Taylor? You are really very good,' said Godfrey. 'But you look tired, I hope you haven't tired yourself.'

'Indeed, I felt I could have changed places with Taylor. These people are so fortunate these days. Central heating, everything they want, plenty of company.'

'Is she in with nice people?'

'Who—Taylor? Well, they all look splendid and clean. Taylor always says she is perfectly satisfied with everything. So she should be.'

'Got all her faculties still?' Godfrey was obsessed by the question of old people and their faculties.

'Certainly. She asked for you and Charmian. She cries a little of course at the mention of Charmian. Of course she was fond of Charmian.'

Godfrey looked at her closely. 'You look ill, Lettie.'

'Utter nonsense. I'm in wonderful form today. I've never felt more fit in my life.'

'I don't think you should return to Hampstead,' he said.

'After tea. I've arranged to go home after tea, and after tea I'm going.'

'There was a telephone call for you,' said Godfrey.

'Who was it?'

'That chap again.'

'Really? Have you rung the C.I.D.?'

'Yes. In fact, they're coming round tonight to have a talk with us. They are rather puzzled about some aspects of the case.'

'What did the man say? What did he say?'

'Lettie, don't upset yourself. You know very well what he said.'

'I go back to Hampstead after tea,' said Lettie.

'But the C.I.D.——'

'Tell them I have returned to Hampstead.'

Charmian came unsteadily in. 'Ah, Taylor, have you enjoyed your walk? You look in wonderful form today.'

'Mrs. Anthony is late with tea,' said Dame Lettie, moving her chair so that her back was turned to Charmian.

'You must not sleep alone at Hampstead,' said Godfrey. 'Call on Lisa Brooke and ask her to stop with you for a few days. The police will soon get the man.'

'Lisa Brooke be damned,' said Dame Lettie, which would have been an alarming statement if intended seriously, for Lisa Brooke was not many moments dead, as Godfrey discovered in *The Times* obituary the next morning.

Chapter Three

LISA BROOKE died in her seventy-third year after her second stroke. She had taken nine months to die, and in fact it was only a year before her death that, feeling rather ill, she had decided to reform her life, and reminding herself how attractive she still was, offered up the new idea, her celibacy to the Lord to whom no gift whatsoever is unacceptable.

It did not occur to Godfrey as he marched into a pew in the crematorium chapel that anyone else present had ever been Lisa's lover except himself. It did not even come to mind that he had been Lisa's lover, for he had never been her lover in any part of England, only Spain and Belgium, and at the moment he was busy with statistics. There were sixteen people present. On first analysis it emerged that five were relatives of Lisa. Next, among the remaining eleven, Godfrey elicited Lisa's lawyer, her housekeeper, the bank manager. Lettie had just arrived. Then there was himself. That left six, only one of whom he recognised, but all of whom were presumably Lisa's hangers-on, and he was glad their fountain of ready cash had dried up. All those years of daylight robbery; and many a time he had told Lisa, 'A child of six could do better than that,' when she displayed one of the paintings, outrages, committed by one of her pets. 'If he hasn't made his way in the world by now,' he had said, time and again, of old Percy Mannering the poet, 'he never will. You are a fool, Lisa, letting him drink your gin and shout his poetry in your ears.'

Percy Mannering, almost eighty, stood with his lean stoop as the coffin was borne up the aisle. Godfrey stared hard at the poet's red-veined hatchet cheekbones and thin nose. He thought, 'I bet he's regretting the termination of his income. They've all bled poor Lisa white. . . .' The poet was, in fact, in a state of excitement. Lisa's death had filled him with thrilling awe, for though he knew the general axiom that death was everyone's lot, he could never realise the particular case; each new death gave him something fresh to feel. It came to him as the service began that within a few minutes Lisa's coffin would start sliding down into the furnace, and he saw as in a fiery vision her flame-tinted hair aglow as always, competing with the angry tresses of the fire below. He grinned like an elated wolf and shed tears of human grief as if he were half-beast, half-man, instead of half-poet, half-man. Godfrey watched him and thought, 'He must be senile. He has probably lost his faculties.'

The coffin began to slide slowly down the slope towards a gap in the wall while the organ played something soft and religious. Godfrey, who was not a believer, was profoundly touched by this ensemble, and decided once and for all to be cremated when his time came. 'There goes Lisa Brooke,' he said to himself as he saw the last tilt of the coffin. The prow, thought the poet, lifts, and the ship goes under with the skipper on board. . . . No, that's too banal, Lisa herself as the ship is a better idea. Godfrey looked round him and thought, 'She should have been good for another ten years, but what can you expect with all that drink and all these spongers?' So furiously did he glare about him that he startled the faces which caught his eye.

Tubby Dame Lettie caught up with her brother in the aisle as he moved with the others to the porch. 'What's the matter with you, Godfrey?' Lettie breathed.

The chaplain was shaking doleful hands with everyone at the door. As Godfrey gave his hand he said over his shoulder to Lettie, 'The matter with *me*? What d'you mean what's the matter with me? What's the matter with *you*?'

Lettie, as she dabbed her eyes, whispered, 'Don't talk so loud. Don't glare so. Everyone's looking at you.'

On the floor of the long porch was a muster of flowers done up, some in tasteful bunches, one or two in old-fashioned wreaths. These were being inspected by Lisa's relatives, her middle-aged nephew and his wife, her parched elder sister Janet Sidebottome, who had been a missionary in India at a time when it *was* India, her brother Ronald Sidebottome, who had long since retired from the City, and Ronald's Australian wife, who had been christened Tempest. Godfrey did not immediately identify them, for he saw only the row of their several

behinds as they stooped to examine the cards attached to each
tribute.

'Look, Ronald, isn't this sweet? A tiny bunch of violets—oh,
see, it says, "Thank you, Lisa dear, for all those wonderful
times, with love from Tony." '

'Rather odd words. Are you sure——'

'Who's Tony, I wonder?'

'See, Janet, this huge yellow rose wreath here from Mrs.
Pettigrew. It must have cost her a fortune.'

'What did you say?' said Janet who did not hear well.

'A wreath from Mrs. Pettigrew. It must have cost a fortune.'

'Sh-sh-sh,' said Janet, looking round. True enough, Mrs.
Pettigrew, Lisa's old housekeeper, was approaching in her well-
dressed confident manner. Janet, cramped from the card-in-
spection, straightened painfully and turned to meet Mrs.
Pettigrew. She let the woman grip her hand.

'Thank you for all you have done for my sister,' said Janet
sternly.

'It was a pleasure.' Mrs. Pettigrew spoke in a surprisingly soft
voice. It was understood Janet was thinking of the will. 'I loved
Mrs. Brooke, poor soul.'

Janet inclined her head graciously, firmly withdrew her hand,
and rudely turned her back.

'Can we see the ashes?' loudly enquired Percy Mannering as
he emerged from the chapel. 'Is there any hope of *seeing* them?'
At the noise he made, Lisa's nephew and his wife jumped
nervily and looked round.

'I want to see those ashes if possible.' The poet had cornered
Dame Lettie, pressing his hungry demand. Lettie felt there was
something unhealthy about the man. She moved away.

'That's one of Lisa's artists,' she whispered to John Sidebottome, not meaning to prompt him to say 'Oh!' and lift his
hat in Percy's direction, as he did.

Godfrey stepped backwards and stood on a spray of pink
carnations. 'Oh—sorry,' he said to the carnations, stepping off
them quickly, and then was vexed at his folly, and knew that in
any case no one had seen him after all. He ambled away from the
trampled flowers.

'What's that fellow want with the ashes?' he said to Lettie.

'He wants to see them. Wants to see if they've gone grey. He is quite disgusting.'

'Of course they will be grey. The fellow must have lost his faculties. *If* he ever had any.'

'I don't know about faculties,' said Lettie. 'Certainly he has no feelings.'

Tempest Sidebottome, blue-haired and well corseted, was saying in a voice which carried away out to the Garden of Remembrance, 'To some people there's just nothing that's sacred.'

'Madam,' said Percy, baring his sparse green teeth in a smile, 'the ashes of Lisa Brooke will always be sacred to me. I desire to see them, kiss them if they are cool enough. Where's that cleric?—He'll have the ashes.'

'Do you see over there—Lisa's housekeeper?' Lettie said to Godfrey.

'Yes, yes, I wonder——'

'That's what *I'm* wondering,' said Lettie, who was wondering if Mrs. Pettigrew wanted a job, and if so would agree to undertake the personal care of Charmian.

'But I think we would need a younger woman. That one must be getting on,' said Godfrey, 'if I remember aright.'

'Mrs. Pettigrew has a constitution like a horse,' said Dame Lettie, casting a horse-dealer's glance over Mrs. Pettigrew's upright form. 'And it is impossible to get younger women.'

'Has she got all her faculties?'

'Of course. She had poor Lisa right under her thumb.'

'I hardly think Charmian would want——'

'Charmian needs to be bullied. What Charmian needs is a firm hand. She will simply go to pieces if you don't keep at her. Charmian needs a firm hand. It's the only way.'

'But what about Mrs. Anthony?' said Godfrey. 'The woman might not get on with Mrs. Anthony. It would be tragic if we lost her.'

'If you don't find someone soon to look after Charmian you will certainly lose Mrs. Anthony. Charmian is too much of a handful for Mrs. Anthony. You will lose Mrs. Anthony.

Charmian keeps calling her Taylor. She is bound to resent it. Who are you staring at?'

Godfrey was staring at a short bent man walking with the aid of two sticks round a corner of the chapel. 'Who is that man?' said Godfrey. 'He looks familiar.'

Tempest Sidebottome fussed over to the little man, who beamed up at her with a fresh face under his wide black hat. He spoke in a shrill boyish tone. 'Afraid I'm late,' he said. 'Is the party over? Are you all Lisa's sinisters and bothers?'

'That's Guy Leet,' said Godfrey, at once recognising him, for Guy had always used to call sisters and brothers sinisters and bothers. 'The little rotter,' said Godfrey, 'he used to be after Charmian. It must be thirty-odd years since last I saw him. He can't be more than seventy-five and just see what he's come to.'

*   *   *

Tables at a tea-shop near Golders Green had been reserved for Lisa's post-crematorial party. Godfrey had intended to miss the tea party, but the arrival of Guy Leet had changed his mind. He was magnetised by the sight of the clever little man doubled over his sticks, and could not keep his eyes off the arthritic hobbling of Guy making his way among the funeral flowers.

'Better join them for tea,' he said to Lettie, 'hadn't we?'

'What for?' said Lettie, looking round the company. 'We can have tea at home. Come back with me for tea, we can have it at home.'

'I think we'd better join them,' said Godfrey. 'We might have a word with Mrs. Pettigrew about her taking on Charmian.'

Lettie saw Godfrey's gaze following the hunched figure of Guy Leet, who, on his sticks, had now reached the door of his taxi. Several of the party helped Guy inside, then joined him. As they drove off, Godfrey said, 'Little rotter. Supposed to be a critic. Tried to take liberties with all the lady novelists, and then he was a theatre critic and he was after the actresses. You'll remember him, I daresay.'

'Vaguely,' said Lettie. 'He never got much change out of *me*.'

'He was never after you,' said Godfrey.

*   *   *

At the tea-shop Dame Lettie and Godfrey found the mourners being organised into their places by Tempest Sidebottome, big and firm in her corsets, aged seventy-five, with that accumulated energy which strikes despair in the hearts of jaded youth, and which now fairly intimidated even the two comparative young-sters in the group, Lisa's nephew and his wife, who were not long past fifty.

'Ronald, sit down here and stay put,' Tempest said to her husband, who put on his glasses and sat down.

Godfrey was casting about for Guy Leet, but in the course of doing so his sight was waylaid by the tables on which were set silver-plate cakestands with thin bread and butter on the bottom tier, cut fruit cake above that, and on the top, a pile of iced cakes wrapped in Cellophane paper. Godfrey began to feel a passionate longing for his tea, and he pushed past Dame Lettie to stand conspicuously near the organiser, Tempest. She did notice him right away and allotted him a seat at a table. 'Lettie,' he called then, 'come over here. We're sitting here.'

'Dame Lettie,' said Tempest over his head, 'you must come and sit with us, my dear. Over here beside Ronald.'

'Damned snob,' thought Godfrey. 'I suppose she thinks Lettie is somebody.'

Someone leant over to offer him a cigarette which was a filter-tip. However, he said, 'Thanks, I'll keep it for after tea.' Then, looking up, he saw the wolf grin on the face of the man who was offering him the packet with a trembling hand. Godfrey plucked out a cigarette and placed it beside his plate. He was angry at being put beside Percy Mannering, not only because Percy had been one of Lisa's spongers but also because he must surely be senile with that grin and frightful teeth, and Godfrey felt the poet would not be able to manage his teacup with those shaking hands.

He was right, for Percy spilled a lot of his tea on the cloth. 'He ought to be in a home,' thought Godfrey. Tempest glanced at their table every now and then and tut-tutted a lot, but she did this all round, as if it were a children's beanfeast. Percy was oblivious of the mess he was making or of anyone's disapproval.

Two others sat at their table, Janet Sidebottome and Mrs. Pettigrew. The poet had taken it for granted that he was the most distinguished and therefore the leader of conversation.

'One time I fell out with Lisa,' he roared, 'was when she took up Dylan Thomas.' He pronounced the first name Dye-lan. 'Dylan Thomas,' he said, 'and Lisa was good to him. Do you know, if I was to go to Heaven and find Dylan Thomas there, I'd prefer to go to HELL. *And* I wouldn't be surprised if Lisa hasn't gone to Hell for aiding and abetting him in his poetry so-called.'

Janet Sidebottome bent her ear closer to Percy. 'What did you say about poor Lisa? I don't hear well.'

'I say,' he said, 'I wonder if Lisa's gone to Hell because of her——'

'From respect to my dear sister,' said Janet with a hostile look, 'I don't think we will discuss——'

'Dye-lan Thomas died from D.T.,' said the old poet, becoming gleeful. 'You see the coincidence?—His initials were D. T. and he *died* from D.T. Hah!'

'In respect for my late sister——'

'Poetry!' said Percy. 'Dylan Thomas didn't know the meaning of the word. As I said to Lisa, I said, "You're making a bloody fool of yourself supporting that charlatan. It isn't poetry, it's a leg-pull." She didn't see it, nobody saw it, but I'm telling you his verse was all a HOAX.'

Tempest turned round in her chair. 'Hush, Mr. Mannering,' she said, tapping Percy on the shoulder.

Percy looked at her and roared, 'Ha! Do you know what you can tell Satan to do with Dye-lan Thomas's poetry?' He sat back to observe, with his two-fanged gloat, the effect of this question, which he next answered in unprintable terms, causing Mrs. Pettigrew to say, 'Gracious!' and to wipe the corners of her mouth with her handkerchief. Meanwhile various commotions arose at the other tables and the senior waitress said, 'Not in *here*, sir!'

Godfrey's disgust was arrested by fear that the party might now break up. While everyone's attention was still on Percy he hastily took a couple of the Cellophane-wrapped cakes from the top tier of the cakestand and stuffed them into his pocket. He looked round and felt sure no one had noticed the action.

Janet Sidebottome leaned over to Mrs. Pettigrew. 'What did he say?' she said.

'Well, Miss Sidebottome,' said Mrs. Pettigrew, meanwhile glancing at herself sideways in a glass on the wall, 'as far as I could comprehend, he was talking about some gentleman indelicately.'

'Poor Lisa,' said Janet. Tears came to her eyes. She kissed her relatives and departed. Lisa's nephew and his wife sidled away, though before they had reached the door they were summoned back by Tempest because the nephew had left his scarf. Eventually, the couple were permitted to go. Percy Mannering remained grinning in his seat.

To Godfrey's relief Mrs. Pettigrew refilled his cup. She also poured one for herself, but when Percy passed his shaking cup she ignored it. Percy said, 'Hah! That was strong meat for you ladies, wasn't it?' He reached for the teapot. 'I hope it wasn't me made Lisa's sister cry,' he said solemnly. 'I'd be sorry to have made her cry.' The teapot was too heavy for his quivering fingers and fell from them on to its side, while a leafy brown sea spread from the open lid over the tablecloth and on to Godfrey's trousers.

Tempest rose, pushing back her chair as if she meant business. She was followed to the calamitous table by Dame Lettie and a waitress. While Godfrey was being sponged, Lettie took the poet by the arm and said, 'Please go.' Tempest, busy with Godfrey's trousers, called over her shoulder to her husband, 'Ronald, you're a man. Give Dame Lettie a hand.'

'What? Who?' said Ronald.

'Wake up, Ronald. Can't you see what has to be done? Help Dame Lettie to take Mr. Mannering outside.'

'Oh,' said Ronald, 'why, someone's spilt their tea!' He ogled the swimming tablecloth.

Percy shook off Dame Lettie's hand from his arm, and grinning to right and left, buttoning up his thin coat, departed.

A place was made for Godfrey and Mrs. Pettigrew at the Sidebottomes' table. 'Now we shall have a fresh pot of tea,' said

Tempest. Everyone gave deep sighs. The waitresses cleaned up the mess. The room was noticeably quiet.

Dame Lettie started to question Mrs. Pettigrew about her future plans. Godfrey was anxious to overhear this conversation. He was not sure that he wanted Lisa Brooke's housekeeper to look after Charmian. She might be too old or too expensive. She looked a smart woman, she might have expensive ideas. And he was not sure that Charmian would not have to go into a home.

'There's no definite offer, of course,' he interposed.

'Well, Mr. Colston, as I was saying,' said Mrs. Pettigrew, 'I can't make any plans, myself, until things are settled.'

'What things?' said Godfrey.

'Godfrey, please,' said Lettie, 'Mrs. Pettigrew and I are having a chat.' She slumped her elbow on the table and turned to Mrs. Pettigrew, cutting off her brother from view.

'What is your feeling about the service?' said Tempest.

Godfrey looked round at the waitresses. 'Very satisfactory,' he said. 'That older one handled that Mannering very well, I thought.'

Tempest closed her eyes as one who prays for grace. 'I mean,' she said, 'poor Lisa's last rites at the crematorium.'

'Oh,' said Godfrey, 'you should have said funeral service. When you said the service, naturally I thought——'

'What do you feel about the cremation service?'

'First rate,' said Godfrey. 'I've quite decided to be cremated when my time comes. Cleanest way. Dead bodies under the ground only contaminate our water supplies. You should have said cremation service in the first place.'

'I thought it was cold,' said Tempest. 'I do wish the minister had read out poor Lisa's obituary. The last cremation I was at—that was Ronald's poor brother Henry—they read out his obituary from the *Nottingham Guardian*, all about his war service and his work for S.S.A.F.A. and Road Safety. It was so very moving. Now why couldn't they have read out Lisa's? All that in the papers about what she did for the Arts, he should have read it out to us.'

'I quite agree,' said Godfrey. 'It was the least he could have done. Did you make a special request for it?'

'No,' she sighed. 'I left the arrangements to Ronald. Unless you do everything yourself. . . .'

'They always get very violent about other poets,' said Ronald. 'You see, they feel very personal about poetry.'

'Whatever is he talking about?' said Tempest. 'He's talking about Mr. Mannering, that's what he's on about. We aren't talking about Mr. Mannering, Ronald. Mr. Mannering's left, it's a thing of the past. We've gone on to something else.'

As they rose to leave Godfrey felt a touch on his arm. Turning round, he saw Guy Leet behind him, his body crouched over his sticks and his baby face raised askew to Godfrey's.

'Got your funeral baked meats all right?' said Guy.

'What?' said Godfrey.

Guy nodded his head towards Godfrey's pocket which bulged with the cakes. 'Taking them home to Charmian?'

'Yes,' said Godfrey.

'And how is Charmian?'

Godfrey had partly regained his poise. 'She's in wonderful form,' he said. 'I'm sorry,' he said, 'to see you having such a difficult time. Must be terrible not being able to get about on your own pins.'

Guy gave a high laugh. He came close to Godfrey and breathed into his waistcoat, 'But I *did* get about, dear fellow. At least I did.'

On the way home Godfrey threw the cakes out of his car window. Why did one pocket those damned things? he thought. One doesn't need them, one could buy up every cake-shop in London and never miss the money. Why did one do it? It doesn't make sense.

'I have been to Lisa Brooke's funeral,' he said to Charmian when he got home, 'or rather, cremation.'

Charmian remembered Lisa Brooke, she had cause to remember her. 'Personally, I'm afraid,' said Charmian, 'that Lisa was a little spiteful to me sometimes, but she had her better side. A generous nature when dealing with the right person, but——'

'Guy Leet was there,' said Godfrey. 'He's nearly finished now, bent over two sticks.'

Charmian said, 'Oh, and what a clever man he was!'

'Clever?' said Godfrey.

Charmian, when she saw Godfrey's face, giggled squeakily through her nose.

'I have quite decided to be cremated when my time comes,' said Godfrey. 'It is the cleanest way. The cemeteries only pollute our water supplies. Cremation is best.'

'I do so agree with you,' said Charmian sleepily.

'No, you do *not* agree with me,' he said. 'R.C.'s are not allowed to be cremated.'

'I mean, I'm sure you are right, Eric dear.'

'I am not Eric,' said Godfrey. 'You are not sure I'm right. Ask Mrs. Anthony, she'll tell you that R.C.'s are against cremation.' He opened the door and bawled for Mrs. Anthony. She came in with a sigh.

'Mrs. Anthony, you're a Roman Catholic, aren't you?' said Godfrey.

'That's right. I've got something on the stove.'

'Do you believe in cremation?'

'Well,' she said, 'I don't really much like the idea of being shoved away quick like that. I feel somehow it's sort of——'

'It isn't a matter of how you feel, it's a question of what your Church says you've not got to do. Your Church says you must not be cremated, that's the point.'

'Well, as I say, Mr. Colston, I don't really fancy the idea——'

'*Fancy the idea* . . . It is not a question of what you fancy. You have no choice in the matter, do you see?'

'Well, I always like to see a proper burial, I always like——'

'It's a point of discipline in your Church,' he said, 'that you mustn't be cremated. You women don't know your own system.'

'I see, Mr. Colston. I've got something on the stove.'

'*I* believe in cremation, but you don't—Charmian, you disapprove of cremation, you understand.'

'Very well, Godfrey.'

'And you too, Mrs. Anthony.'

'O.K., Mr. Colston.'

'On principle,' said Godfrey.

'That's right,' said Mrs. Anthony and disappeared.

Godfrey poured himself a stout whisky and soda. He took from a drawer a box of matches and a razor blade and set to work, carefully splitting the slim length of each match, so that from one box of matches he would eventually make two boxfuls. And while he worked he sipped his drink with satisfaction.

Chapter Four

THE reason Lisa Brooke's family arranged her post-funeral party at a tea-shop rather than at her small brick studio-house at Hampstead was this. Mrs. Pettigrew, her housekeeper, was still in residence there. The family had meanwhile discovered that Lisa had bequeathed most of her fortune to Mrs. Pettigrew, whom they had long conceived as an unfortunate element in Lisa's life. They held this idea in the way that people often are obscurely right, though the suspicions that lead up to their conclusions are faulty. Whatever they suspected was the form that Mrs. Pettigrew's influence over Lisa took, they hoped to contest Lisa's will if possible, on the grounds that Lisa, when she made it, was not in her right mind, and probably under undue influence of Mrs. Pettigrew.

The very form of the will, they argued, proved that Lisa had been unbalanced when she made it. The will had not been drafted by a lawyer. It was a mere sheet of writing paper, witnessed by the charwoman and her daughter a year before Lisa's death, bequeathing her entire fortune 'to my husband if he survives me and thereafter to my housekeeper, Mabel Pettigrew'. Now Lisa, so her relatives believed, had no husband alive. Old Brooke was long dead, and, moreover, Lisa had been divorced from him during the Great War. She must have been dotty, they argued, even to mention a husband. The sheet of paper, they insisted, must be invalid. Alarmingly, their lawyers saw nothing invalid on the face of it; Mrs. Pettigrew was apparently the sole beneficiary.

Tempest Sidebottome was furious. 'Ronald and Janet,' she said, 'should inherit by rights. We'll fight it. Lisa would never have mentioned a husband had she been in her right mind. Mrs. Pettigrew must have had a hold on Lisa.'

'Lisa was always liable to say foolish things,' Ronald Sidebottome remarked.

'You're a born obstructionist,' Tempest said.

Hence, they had felt it cautious to avoid the threshold of Harmony Studio for the time being, and had felt it equally cautious to invite Mrs. Pettigrew to the tea-shop.

Dame Lettie was explaining this to Miss Taylor, who had seen much in her long service with Charmian. Dame Lettie had, unawares, in the past few months, slipped into the habit of confiding in Miss Taylor. So many of Lettie's contemporaries, those who knew her world and its past, had lost their memories or their lives, or were away in private homes in the country; it was handy having Miss Taylor available in London to discuss things with.

'You see, Taylor,' said Dame Lettie, 'they never did like Mrs. Pettigrew. Now, Mrs. Pettigrew is an admirable woman. I was hoping to persuade her to take on Charmian. But of course with Lisa's money in prospect, she does not intend to work any longer. She must be over seventy, although of course she says . . . Well, you see, with Lisa's money——'

'She would never do for Charmian,' said Miss Taylor.

'Oh really, I feel Charmian needs a firm hand if we are to keep her at home. Otherwise she will have to go into a nursing home. Taylor, you have no conception how irritated poor Godfrey gets. He tries his best.' Dame Lettie lowered her voice. 'And then, Taylor, there is the lavatory question. Mrs. Anthony can't be expected to take her every time. As it is, Godfrey attends to the chamber pots in the morning. He isn't used to it, Taylor, he's not used to that sort of thing.'

In view of the warm September afternoon Miss Taylor had been put out on the balcony of the Maud Long Ward where she sat with a blanket round her knees.

'Poor Charmian,' she said, 'darling Charmian. As we get older these affairs of the bladder and kidneys do become so important to us. I hope she has a commode by her bedside, you know how difficult it is for old bones to manage a pot.'

'She has a commode,' said Dame Lettie. 'But that doesn't solve the daytime problem. Now Mrs. Pettigrew would have been admirable in that respect. Think what she did for poor Lisa after the first stroke. However, Mrs. Pettigrew is out of the question because of this inheritance from Lisa. It was ridiculous of Lisa.'

Miss Taylor looked distressed. 'It would be tragic,' she said, 'for Mrs. Pettigrew to go to the Colstons. Charmian would be most unhappy with the woman. You must not think of such a thing, Dame Lettie. You don't know Mrs. Pettigrew as I do.'

Dame Lettie's yellow-brown eyes focused as upon an exciting scene as she bent close to Miss Taylor. 'Do you think,' she enquired, 'there was anything peculiar, I mean not right, between Mrs. Pettigrew and Lisa Brooke?'

Miss Taylor did not pretend not to know what she meant. 'I cannot say,' she said, 'what were the habits of their relationship in former years. I only know this, and you yourself know, Dame Lettie, Mrs. Pettigrew was very domineering towards Mrs. Brooke in the last eight or nine years. She is not suitable for Charmian.'

'It is precisely because she is domineering,' said Lettie, 'that I wanted her for Charmian. Charmian *needs* a bully. For her own good. But anyway, that's beside the point, Mrs. Pettigrew does not desire the job. I understand Lisa has left her practically everything. Now Lisa was very comfortable as you know, and——'

'I would not be sure that Mrs. Pettigrew will in fact inherit,' insisted Miss Taylor.

'No, Taylor,' said Dame Lettie, 'I'm afraid Lisa's family do not stand a chance. I doubt if their advisers will let them take it to court. There is no case. Lisa was perfectly sane to the day she died. It is true Mrs. Pettigrew had an undesirable influence over Lisa, but Lisa was in her right mind to the end.'

'Yes, it is true Mrs. Pettigrew had a hold on her.'

'I wouldn't say a hold, I would say an influence. If Lisa was fool enough——'

'Quite, Dame Lettie. Was Mr. Leet at the funeral, by any chance?'

'Oh, Guy Leet was there. I shouldn't think he will last long. Rheumatoid arthritis with complications.' Dame Lettie recalled, as she spoke, that rheumatoid arthritis was one of Miss Taylor's afflictions, but, she thought, after all she must face the facts. 'Very advanced case,' said Dame Lettie, 'he was managing with great difficulty on two sticks.'

'It is like wartime,' Miss Taylor remarked.

'What do you say?'

'Being over seventy is like being engaged in a war. All our friends are going or gone and we survive among the dead and the dying as on a battlefield.'

She is wandering in her mind and becoming morbid, thought Dame Lettie.

'Or suffering from war nerves,' Miss Taylor said.

Dame Lettie was annoyed, because she had intended to gain some advice from Miss Taylor.

'Come now, Taylor,' she said. 'You are talking like Charmian.'

'I must,' said Miss Taylor, 'have caught a lot of her ways of thought and speech.'

'Taylor,' Lettie said, 'I want to ask your advice.' She looked at the other woman to see if she was alert. 'Four months ago,' she said, 'I began to receive anonymous telephone calls from a man. I have been receiving them ever since. On one occasion when I was staying with Godfrey, the man, who must have traced me there, gave a message for me to Godfrey.'

'What does he say?' said Miss Taylor.

Dame Lettie leant to Miss Taylor's ear and, in a low tone, informed her.

'Have you told the police?'

'Of course we have told the police. They are useless. Godfrey had an interview with them too. Useless. They seem to think we are making it up.'

'You will have thought of consulting Chief Inspector Mortimer, who was such a fan of Charmian's?'

'Of course I have not consulted Mortimer. Mortimer is

retired, he is close on seventy. Time passes, you know. You are living in the past, Taylor.'

'I only thought,' said Miss Taylor, 'that Inspector Mortimer might act privately. He might at least be helpful in some way. He always struck me as a most unusual——'

'Mortimer is out of the question. We want a young, active detective on this job. There is a dangerous lunatic at large. I know not how many people besides myself are endangered.'

'I should not answer the telephone, Dame Lettie, if I were you.'

'My dear Taylor, one can't be cut off perpetually. I still have my Homes to consider, I am not entirely a back number, Taylor. One must be on the phone. But I confess, I am feeling the strain. Imagine for yourself every time one answers the telephone. One never knows if one is going to hear that distressing sentence. It *is* distressing.'

'Remember you must die,' said Miss Taylor.

'Hush,' said Dame Lettie, looking warily over her shoulder.

'Can you not ignore it, Dame Lettie?'

'No, I can not. I have tried, but it troubles me deeply. It *is* a troublesome remark.'

'Perhaps you might obey it,' said Miss Taylor.

'What's that you say?'

'You might, perhaps, try to remember you must die.'

She is wandering again, thought Lettie. 'Taylor,' she said, 'I do not wish to be advised how to think. What I hoped you could suggest is some way of apprehending the criminal, for I see that I must take matters into my own hands. Do you understand telephone wires? Can you follow the system of calls made from private telephone boxes?'

'It's difficult,' said Miss Taylor, 'for people of advanced years to start remembering they must die. It is best to form the habit while young. I shall think of some plan, Dame Lettie, for tracing the man. I did once know something about the telephone system, I will try to recall what I knew.'

'I must go.' Lettie rose, and added, 'I expect you are keeping pretty well, Taylor?'

'We have a new ward sister here,' said Miss Taylor. 'She is not so pleasant as the last. I have no complaint personally, but

some of my companions are inclined to be touchy, to imagine
things.'

Lettie cast her eye along the sunny verandah of the Maud
Long Ward where a row of old women sat out in their chairs.

'They are fortunate,' said Dame Lettie and uttered a sigh.

'I know it,' said Miss Taylor. 'But they are discontented and
afraid.'

'Afraid of what?'

'The sister in charge,' said Miss Taylor.

'But what's wrong with her?'

'Nothing,' said Miss Taylor, 'except that she is afraid of these
old people.'

'*She* is afraid? I thought you said the patients were afraid of
her.'

'It comes to the same thing,' said Miss Taylor.

She is wandering, thought Lettie, and she said, 'In the Balkan
countries, the peasants turn their aged parents out of doors
every summer to beg their keep for the winter.'

'Indeed?' said Miss Taylor. 'That is an interesting system.'
Her hand, when Dame Lettie lifted it to say goodbye, was
painful at the distorted joints.

'I hope,' said Miss Taylor, 'you will think no more of employing Mrs. Pettigrew.'

Dame Lettie thought, She is jealous of anyone else's having
to do with Charmian.

Perhaps I am, thought Miss Taylor who could read Dame
Lettie's idea.

And as usual after Dame Lettie had left, she pondered and
understood more and more why Lettie came so frequently to
visit her and seemed to find it pleasant, and at the same time
seldom spoke or behaved pleasantly. It was the old enmity
about Miss Taylor's love affair in 1907 which in fact Dame
Lettie had forgotten—had dangerously forgotten; so that she
retained in her mind a vague fascinating enmity for Jean Taylor
without any salutary definition. Whereas Miss Taylor herself,
until quite recently, had remembered the details of her love
affair, and Dame Lettie's subsequent engagement to marry the
man, which came to nothing after all. But recently, thought

Miss Taylor, I am beginning to feel as she does. Enmity is
catching. Miss Taylor closed her eyes and laid her hands loosely
on the rug which covered her knees. Soon the nurses would
come in to put the grannies to bed. Meanwhile she thought
with a sleepy pleasure, I enjoy Dame Lettie's visits, I look forward to them, in spite of which I treat her with my asperity.
Perhaps it is because I have now so little to lose. Perhaps it is
because these encounters have an exhilarating quality. I might
sink into a torpor were it not for fat old Lettie. And perhaps,
into the bargain, I might use her in the matter of the ward sister,
although that is unlikely.

*   *   *

'Granny Taylor—Gemini. *Evening festivities may give you all
the excitement you want. A brisk day for business enter-prises,*'
Granny Valvona read out for the second time that day.

'There,' said Miss Taylor.

The Maud Long Ward had been put to bed and was now
awaiting supper.

'It comes near the mark,' said Miss Valvona. 'You can
always know by your horoscope when your visitors are coming
to see you, Granny Taylor. Either your Dame or that gentleman that comes; you can always tell by the stars.'

Granny Trotsky lifted her wizened head with low brow and
pug nose, and said something. Her health had been degenerating
for some weeks. It was no longer possible to hear exactly what
she said. Miss Taylor was the quickest in the ward at guessing
what Granny Trotsky's remarks might be, but Miss Barnacle
was the most inventive.

Granny Trotsky repeated her words, whatever they were.

Miss Taylor replied, 'All right, Granny.'

'What did she say?' demanded Granny Valvona.

'I am not sure,' said Miss Taylor.

Mrs. Reewes-Duncan, who claimed to have lived in a bunga-
low in former days, addressed Miss Valvona. 'Are you aware
that the horoscope you have just read out to us specifies evening
festivities, whereas Granny Taylor's visitor came at three-fifteen
this afternoon?'

Granny Trotsky again raised her curiously shaped head and spoke, emphasising her statement with vehement nods of this head which was so fearfully and wonderfully made. Whereupon Granny Barnacle ventured, 'She says festivities my backside. What's the use of the stars foretell with that murderous bitch of a sister outside there, she says, waiting to finish off the whole ward in the winter when the lot goes down with pneumonia. You'll be reading your stars, she says, all right when they need the beds for the next lot. That's what she says—don't you, Granny Trotsky?'

Granny Trotsky, raising her head, made one more, and very voluble effort, then drooped exhausted on her pillow, closing her eyes.

'That's what she said,' said Granny Barnacle. 'And right she is, too. Come the winter them that's made nuisances of their-selves don't last long under that sort.'

A ripple of murmurs ran up the rows of beds. It ceased as a nurse walked through the ward, and started again when she had gone.

Miss Valvona's strong eyes stared through her spectacles into the past, as they frequently did in the autumn, and she saw the shop door open on a Sunday afternoon, and the perfect ices her father manufactured, and heard the beautiful bellow of his accordion after night had fallen, on and on till closing time. 'Oh, the parlour and the sundaes and white ladies we used to serve,' she said, 'and my father with the Box. The white ladies stiff on your plate, they were hard, and made from the best-quality products. And the fellows would say to me, "How do, Doreen," even if they had another girl with them after the pictures. And my father got down the Box and played like a champion. It cost him fifty pounds, in those days, mind you, it was a lot.'

Granny Duncan addressed Miss Taylor, 'Did you ask that Dame to do something for us, at all?'

'Not exactly,' said Miss Taylor, 'but I mentioned that we were not so comfortable now as we have been previously.'

'She goin' to *do* something for us?' demanded Granny Barnacle.

'She is not herself on the management committee,' Miss Taylor explained. 'It is a friend of hers who is on the committee. Now, it will take time. I can't, you know, press her. She is very easily put off. And then, you know, in the meantime, we must try to make the best of this.' The nurse walked back through the ward among the grannies, all sullen and silent but for Granny Trotsky who had now fallen noisily asleep with her mouth open.

It was true, thought Miss Taylor, that the young nurses were less jolly since Sister Burstead had taken over the ward. Of course it was but two seconds before she had become 'Sister Bastard' on the lips of Granny Barnacle. The associations of her name, perhaps, in addition to her age—Sister Burstead was well over fifty—had affected Granny Barnacle with immediate hostile feelings. 'Over fifty they got the workhouse mind. You can't never trust a ward sister over fifty. They don't study that there's new ways of goin' on since the war by law.' These sentiments in turn had affected the other occupants of the ward. But the ground had been prepared the week before by their knowledge of the departure of the younger sister: 'A change, hear that?—there's to be a change. What's the stars say, Granny Valvona?' Then, on the morning that Sister Burstead took over, she being wiry, bespectacled and middle-aged with a bad-tempered twitch at one side of her face between lip and jaw, Granny Barnacle declared she had absolutely placed her. 'The workhouse mind. You see what'll happen now. Anyone that's a nuisance or can't contain themselves like me with Bright's disease, they won't last long in this ward. You get pneumonia in the winter, can't help but do, and that's her chance.'

'What you think she'll do, Granny Barnacle?'

'Do? It's what she won't do. You wait to the winter, you'll be lyin' there and nothin' done for you. Specially if you got no relations or that to raise enquiries.'

'The other nurses is all right, Granny, though.'

'You'll see a difference in *them*.'

There had been a difference. The nurses were terrified of their new superior, that was all. But as they became more brisk and efficient so did the majority of the grannies behold them with hostile thoughts and deadly suspicions. When the night staff came on duty the ward relaxed, and this took the form of much shouting throughout the night. The grannies shouted in their sleep and half-waking restlessness. They accepted their sedative pills fearfully, and in the morning would ask each other, 'Was I all right last night?' not quite remembering whether they or another had made the noise.

'It all goes down in the book,' said Granny Barnacle. 'Nothing happens during the night but what it goes into the book. And Sister Bastard sees it in the morning. You know what that'll mean, don't you, when the winter comes?'

At first, Miss Taylor took a frivolous view of these sayings. It was true the new sister was jittery and strict, and over fifty years of age, and frightened. It will all blow over, thought Miss Taylor, when both sides get used to the change. She was sorry for Sister Burstead and her fifty-odd years. Thirty years ago, thought Miss Taylor, I was into my fifties, and getting old. How nerve-racking it is to be getting old, how much better to be old! It had been touch and go, in those days, whether she would leave the Colstons and settle down with her brother in Coventry while she had the chance. It was such a temptation to leave them, she having been cultivated by twenty-five years' association with Charmian. By the time she was fifty it really seemed absurd for her to continue her service with Charmian, her habits and tastes were so superior to those of the maids she met on her travels with Charmian, so much more intelligent. She had been all on edge for the first two years of her fifties, not knowing whether to go to look after the widowed brother in Coventry and enjoy some status or whether to continue waking Charmian up every morning, and observing in silence Godfrey's infidelities. For two years while she made up her mind she had given Charmian hell, threatening to leave every month, folding Charmian's dresses in the trunk so that they were horribly creased, going off to art galleries while Charmian rang for her in vain.

'You're far worse now,' Charmian would tell her, 'than when you were going through the menopause.'

Charmian plied her with bottles of tonic medicine which she

had poured down the lavatory with a weird joy. At last, after a month's holiday with her brother in Coventry, she found she could never stand life with him and his ways, the getting off to his office in the morning, the keeping him in clean shirts, and the avaricious whist parties in the evening. At the Colstons' there was always some exotic company, and Charmian's sitting-room had been done out in black and orange. All the time she was at Coventry Miss Taylor had missed the exciting scraps of conversation which she had been used to hearing on Charmian's afternoons.

'Charmian darling, don't you think, honestly, I should have Boris bumped off?'

'No, I rather like Boris.'

And those telephone messages far into the nights.

'Is that you, Taylor darling? Get Charmian to the phone, will you? Tell her I'm in a state. Tell her I want to read her my new poem.' That was thirty years ago.

Ten years before that, the telephone messages had been different again, 'Taylor, tell Mrs. Colston I'm in London. Guy Leet. Not a word, Taylor, to *Mr.* Colston.' These were messages which Miss Taylor sometimes did not deliver. Charmian herself was going through her difficult age at that time, and was apt to fly like a cat at any man who made approaches to her, even Guy who had previously been her lover.

At the age of fifty-three Miss Taylor had settled down. She could even meet Alec Warner without any of the old feelings. She went everywhere with Charmian, sat for hours while Charmian read aloud her books, while still in manuscript, gave judgment. As gradually the other servants became difficult and left, so Jean Taylor took charge. When Charmian had her hair bobbed so did Miss Taylor. When Charmian entered the Catholic Church Miss Taylor was received, really just to please Charmian.

She rarely saw her brother from Coventry, and when she did, counted herself lucky to have escaped him. On one occasion she told Godfrey Colston to watch his step. The disappointed twitch at the side of her mouth which had appeared during her forties, now gradually disappeared.

So it will be, thought Miss Taylor, in the case of Sister Burstead, once she settles down. The twitch will go.

Presently, however, Miss Taylor began to feel there was very little chance of the new sister's twitch disappearing. The grannies were so worked up about her, it would not be surprising if she did indeed let them die of pneumonia should she ever get the chance.

'You must speak to the doctor, Granny Barnacle,' said Miss Taylor, 'if you really feel you aren't getting the right treatment.'

'The doctor my backside. They're hand-in-glove. What's a old woman to them I ask you?'

The only good that could be discerned in the arrival of the new sister was the fact that the ward was now more alert. Everyone's wits had improved, as if the sister were a sort of shock treatment. The grannies had forgotten their will-making, and no longer threatened to disinherit each other or the nurses.

Mrs. Reewes-Duncan, however, made the great mistake of threatening the sister with her solicitor one dinner-time when the meat was tough or off, Miss Taylor could not recall which. 'Fetch the ward sister to me,' Mrs. Reewes-Duncan demanded. 'Fetch her here to me.'

The sister marched in purposefully when thus summoned.

'Well, Granny Duncan, what's the matter? Hurry up now, I'm busy. What's the matter?'

'This meat, my good woman. . . .' The ward felt at once that Granny Duncan was making a great mistake. 'My niece will be informed. . . . My solicitor. . . .'

For some reason, the word 'solicitor' set fire to Sister Burstead. That one word did the trick. You could evidently threaten the doctor, the matron, or your relations, and she would merely stand there glaring angrily with her twitch, she would say no more than, 'You people don't know you're born,' and, 'Fire ahead, tell your niece, *my dear*.' But the word solicitor fairly turned her, as Granny Barnacle recounted next day, arse over tip. She gripped the bedrail and yelled at Granny Duncan for a long time, it might have been ten minutes. Words, in isolation and grouped in phrases, detached themselves like sparks from the fiery scream proceeding from Sister Burstead's mouth.

'Old beast . . . dirty old beast . . . food . . . grumble and grouse . . . I've been on since eight o'clock this morning . . . I've been on and on . . . work, work, work, day after day, for a lot of useless old, filthy old. . . .'

Sister Burstead went off duty immediately assisted by a nurse. If only, thought Miss Taylor, we could try to be sweet old ladies, she would be all right. It's because we aren't sweet old things. . . .'

'Scorpio,' Granny Valvona had declared four hours later, although like everyone else in the ward she was shaken-up. 'Granny Duncan—Scorpio. *You can sail ahead with confidence. The success of another person could affect you closely.*' Granny Valvona put down the paper. 'You see what I mean?' she said. 'The stars never let you down. *The success of another person.* . . . A remarkable forecast.'

The incident was reported to the matron and the doctor. The former made enquiries next morning of a kind which clearly indicated she was hoping against hope Sister Burstead could be exonerated, for she would be difficult to replace.

The matron bent over Miss Taylor and spoke quietly and exclusively. 'Sister Burstead is having a rest for a few days. She has been overworking.'

'Evidently,' said Miss Taylor, whose head ached horribly.

'Tell me what you know of the affair. Sister Burstead was provoked, I believe?'

'Evidently,' said Miss Taylor, eyeing the bland face above her and desiring it to withdraw.

'Sister Burstead was cross with Granny Duncan?' said the matron.

'She was nothing,' said Miss Taylor, 'if not cross. I suggest the sister might be transferred to another ward where there are younger people and the work is lighter.'

'All the work in this hospital,' said the matron, 'is heavy.'

Most of the grannies felt too upset to enjoy the few days' absence from duty of Sister Burstead, for whenever the general hysteria showed signs of waning, Granny Barnacle applied the bellows: 'Wait till the winter. When you get pneumonia. . . .'

During those days it happened that Granny Trotsky had her

second stroke. An aged male cousin was summoned to her bedside, and a screen was put round her bed. He emerged after an
hour still wearing the greenish-black hat in which he had
arrived, shaking his head and hat, and crying all over his blotchy
foreign face.

Granny Barnacle, who was up in her chair that day, called to
him, 'Pssst!'

Obediently he came to her side.

Granny Barnacle flicked her head towards the screened-in bed.
'She gone?'

'Nah. She breathe, but not speak.'

'D'you know who done it?' said Granny Barnacle. 'It was the
sister that brought it on.'

'She have no sister. I am next of kin.'

A nurse came and hurried him away.

Granny Barnacle declared once more to the ward, 'Sister
Bastard done for Granny Trotsky.'

'Ah but Granny, it was her second stroke. There's always a
second, you know.'

'Sister done it with her bad temper.'

On learning that Sister Burstead had neither been dismissed
nor transferred to another ward but was to return on the following
day, Granny Barnacle gave notice to the doctor that she refused
further treatment, was discharging herself next day, and that
she would tell the world why.

'I know my bloody rights as a patient,' she said. 'Don't think
I don't know the law. *And* what's more, I can get the phone
number of the newspaper. I only got to ring up and they come
along and want to know what's what.'

'Take it easy, Granny,' said the doctor.

'If Sister Bastard comes back, I go,' said Granny Barnacle.

'Where to?' said the nurse.

Granny Barnacle glared. She felt that the nurse was being
sarcastic, must know that she had spent three months in Holloway prison thirty-six years ago, six months twenty-two years
ago, and subsequently various months. Granny Barnacle felt
the nurse was referring to her record when she said 'Where to?'
in that voice of hers.

The doctor frowned at the nurse and said to Granny Barnacle, 'Take it easy, Granny. Your blood pressure isn't too good this morning. What sort of a night did you have? Pretty restless?'

This speech unnerved Granny Barnacle who had indeed had a bad night.

Granny Trotsky, who had so far recovered that the bedscreen had been removed, had been uttering slobbery mutters. The very sight of Granny Trotsky, the very sound of her trying to talk as she did at this moment, took away Granny Barnacle's nerve entirely.

She looked at the doctor's face, to read it. 'Ah, doc, I don't feel too bloody good,' she said. 'And I just don't feel easy with that bitch in charge. I just feel anything might happen.'

'Come, come, the poor woman's overworked,' he recited. 'We all like to be of help if we can and in any way we can. We are trying to help you, Granny.'

When he had gone Granny Barnacle whispered over to Miss Taylor, 'Do I look bad, love?'

'No, Granny, you look fine.' In fact, Granny Barnacle's face was blotched with dark red.

'Did you hear what the doc said about my blood pressure? Do you think it was a lie, just so's I wouldn't make a fuss?'

'Perhaps not.'

'For two pins, Granny Taylor, I'd be out of that door and down them stairs if it was the last thing I did and——'

'I shouldn't do that,' said Miss Taylor.

'Could they certify me, love?'

'I don't know,' said Miss Taylor.

'I'll tell the priest.'

'You know what he'll say to you,' said Miss Taylor.

'Offer it bloodywell up for the Holy Souls.'

'I daresay.'

'It's a hard religion, Granny Taylor. If it wasn't that my mother was R.C. I would never of——'

'I know a lady——' It was then Miss Taylor had said, rashly, 'I know a lady who knows another lady who is on the management committee of this hospital. It may take some time but I will see what I can do to get them to transfer Sister Burstead.'

'God bless you, Granny Taylor.'

'I can't promise. But I'll try. I shall have to be tactful.'

'You hear that?' said Granny Barnacle to everyone in the ward. 'You hear what Granny Taylor's goin' to do?'

Miss Taylor was not very disappointed with her first effort at sounding Dame Lettie. It was a beginning. She would keep on at Dame Lettie. There was also, possibly, Alec Warner. He might be induced to speak to Tempest Sidebottome who sat on the management committee of the hospital. It might even be arranged without blame to dreary Sister Burstead.

*   *   *

'Didn't your Dame promise nothing definite then?' said Granny Barnacle.

'No, it will take time.'

'Will it be done before the winter?'

'I hope so.'

'Did you tell her what she done to Granny Duncan?'

'Not exactly.'

'You should of. Strikes me you're not on our side entirely, Granny Taylor. I seem to remember that face somehow.'

'Whose face?'

'That Dame's face.'

The difficulty was, Miss Taylor reflected, she could not feel the affair to be pre-eminently important. Sometimes she would have liked to say to the grannies, 'What if your fears were correct? What if we died next winter?' Sometimes she did say to them, 'Some of us may die next winter in any case. It is highly probable.' Granny Valvona would reply, 'I'm ready to meet my God, any time.' And Granny Barnacle would stoutly add, 'But not before time.'

'You must keep on at your friend, Granny Taylor,' said Granny Duncan, who, among all the grannies, most irritated Sister Burstead. Granny Duncan had cancer. Miss Taylor often wondered if the sister was afraid of cancer.

'I seem to remember that Dame's face,' Granny Barnacle kept on. 'Was she ever much round Holborn way of an evening?'

'I don't think so,' said Miss Taylor.

'She might be an old customer of mine,' said Granny Barnacle. 'I think she had her papers sent.'

'Did she go out to work, this Dame?'

'Well, not to a job. But she did various kinds of committee work. That sort of thing.'

Granny Barnacle turned over the face of Dame Lettie in her mind. 'Was it charity work you said she did?'

'That kind of thing,' said Miss Taylor. 'Nothing special.'

Granny Barnacle looked at her suspiciously, but Miss Taylor would not be drawn, nor say that Dame Lettie had been a Prison Visitor at Holloway from her thirtieth year until it became too difficult for her, with her great weight and breathlessness, to climb the stairs.

'I will keep on at Dame Lettie,' she promised.

It was Sister Burstead's day off, and a nurse whistled as she brought in the first supper tray.

Granny Barnacle commented in a hearty voice,

'A whistling woman, a crowing hen,
Is neither fit for God nor man.'

The nurse stopped whistling and gave Granny Barnacle a close look, dumped the tray and went to fetch another.

Granny Trotsky attempted to raise her head and say something.

'Granny Trotsky wants something,' said Granny Duncan.

'What you want, Granny?'

'She is saying,' said Miss Taylor, 'that we shouldn't be unkind to the nurses just because——'

'Unkind to the nurses! What they goin' to do when the winter——'

Miss Taylor prayed for grace. Is there no way, she thought, for them to forget the winter? Can't they go back to making their wills every week?

In the course of the night Granny Trotsky died as the result of the bursting of a small blood-vessel in her brain, and her spirit returned to God who gave it.

Chapter Five

MRS. ANTHONY knew instinctively that Mrs. Pettigrew was a kindly woman. Her instinct was wrong. But the first few weeks after Mrs. Pettigrew came to the Colstons to look after Charmian she sat in the kitchen and told Mrs. Anthony of her troubles.

'Have a fag,' said Mrs. Anthony, indicating with her elbow the packet on the table while she poured strong tea. 'Everything might be worse.'

Mrs. Pettigrew said, 'It couldn't very well be worse. Thirty years of my life I gave to Mrs. Lisa Brooke. Everyone knew I was to get that money. Then this Guy Leet turns up to claim. It wasn't any marriage, that wasn't. Not a proper marriage.' She pulled her cup of tea towards her and, thrusting her head close to Mrs. Anthony's, told her in what atrocious manner and for what long-ago reason Guy Leet had been incapable of consummating his marriage with Lisa Brooke.

Mrs. Anthony swallowed a large sip of her tea, the cup of which she held in both hands, and breathed back into the cup while the warm-smelling steam spread comfortingly over her nose. 'Still,' she said, 'a husband's a husband. By law.'

'Lisa never recognised him as such,' said Mrs. Pettigrew. 'No-one knew about the marriage with Guy Leet, until she died, the little swine.'

'I thought you says she was all right,' said Mrs. Anthony.

'Guy Leet,' said Mrs. Pettigrew. 'He's the little swine.'

'Oh, I see. Well, the courts will have something to say to that, dear, when it comes up. Have a fag.'

'You're making me into a smoker, Mrs. Anthony. Thanks, I will. But you should try to cut them down, they aren't too good for you.'

'Twenty a day since I was twenty-five and seventy yesterday,' said Mrs. Anthony.

'Seventy! Gracious, you'll be——'

'Seventy years of age yesterday.'

'Oh, seventy. Isn't it time you had a rest then? I don't envy you with this lot,' Mrs. Pettigrew indicated with her head the kitchen door, meaning the Colstons residing beyond it.

'Not so bad,' said Mrs. Anthony. '*He's* a bit tight, but *she's* nice. I like *her*.'

'He's tight with the money?' said Mrs. Pettigrew.

Mrs. Anthony said, 'Oh very,' swivelling her eyes towards her companion to fix the remark.

Mrs. Pettigrew patted her hair which was thick, dyed black and well cut, as Lisa had made her wear it. 'How old,' she said, 'would you say I was, Mrs. Anthony?'

Mrs. Anthony, still sitting, pushed back in her chair the better to view Mrs. Pettigrew. She looked at the woman's feet in their suède black shoes, her tight good legs—no veins, her encased hips, and good bust. Mrs. Anthony then put her head sideways to regard, from an angle of fifteen degrees, Mrs. Pettigrew's face. There were lines from nose to mouth, a small cherry-painted mouth. Only the beginnings of one extra chin. Two lines across the brow. The eyes were dark and clear, the nose firm and broad. 'I should say,' said Mrs. Anthony, folding her arms, 'you was sixty-four abouts.'

The unexpectedness of Mrs. Pettigrew's gentle voice was due to her heavily-marked appearance. It was gentler still as she said to Mrs. Anthony, 'Add five years.'

'Sixty-nine. You don't look it,' said Mrs. Anthony. 'Of course you've had the time and money to look after yourself and powder your face. You should of been in business.'

In fact, Mrs. Pettigrew was seventy-three, but she did not at all look the age under her makeup.

She drew her hand across her forehead, however, and shook her head slowly. She was worried about the money, the court case which would probably drag on and on. Lisa's family were claiming their rights too.

Mrs. Anthony had started washing up.

'Old Warner still in with *her*,' she said, 'I suppose?'

'Yes,' said Mrs. Pettigrew. 'He is.'

'It takes her off my hands for a while,' said Mrs. Anthony.

'I must say,' Mrs. Pettigrew said, 'when I was with Lisa

Brooke I used to be asked in to meet the callers. I mixed with everyone.'

Mrs. Anthony started peeling potatoes and singing.

'I'm going in,' said Mrs. Pettigrew, rising and brushing down her neat skirt. 'Whether she likes it or whether she doesn't, I'd better keep my eye on her in any case, that's what I'm here for.'

* * *

When Mrs. Pettigrew entered the drawing-room she said, 'Oh, Mrs. Colston, I was just wondering if you were tired.'

'You may take the tea-things away,' said Charmian.

Instead Mrs. Pettigrew rang for Mrs. Anthony, and, as she piled plates on the tray for the housekeeper to take away, she knew Charmian's guest was looking at her.

Charmian said to Mrs. Anthony, 'Thank you, Taylor.'

Mrs. Pettigrew had met Alec Warner sometimes at Lisa Brooke's. He smiled at her and nodded. She sat down and took a cigarette out of her black suède bag. Alec lit it. The clatter of Mrs. Anthony's tray faded out as she receded to the kitchen.

'You were telling me . . .?' Charmian said to her guest.

'Oh yes.' He turned his white head and grey face to Mrs. Pettigrew. 'I was explaining the rise of democracy in the British Isles. Do you miss Mrs. Brooke?'

'Very much,' said Mabel Pettigrew, blowing out a long puff of smoke. She had put on her social manner. 'Do continue about democracy,' she said.

'When I went to Russia,' said Charmian, 'the Tsarina sent an escort to——'

'Now, Mrs. Colston, just a moment, while Mr. Alec Warner tells us about democracy.'

Charmian looked about her strangely for a moment, then said, 'Yes, continue about democracy, Eric.'

'Not Eric—Alec,' said Mrs. Pettigrew.

Alec Warner soothed the air with his old, old steady hand.

'The real rise of democracy in the British Isles occurred in Scotland by means of Queen Victoria's bladder,' he said. 'There had, you know, existed an idea of democracy, but the real thing occurred through this little weakness of Queen Victoria's.'

Mabel Pettigrew laughed with a backward throw of her head. Charmian looked vague. Alec Warner continued slowly as one filling in the time with his voice. His eyes were watchful.

'Queen Victoria had a little trouble with the bladder, you see. When she went to stay at Balmoral in her latter years a number of privies were caused to be built at the backs of little cottages which had not previously possessed privies. This was to enable the Queen to go on her morning drive round the countryside in comfort, and to descend from her carriage from time to time, ostensibly to visit the humble cottagers in their dwellings. Eventually, word went round that Queen Victoria was exceedingly democratic. Of course it was all due to her little weakness. But everyone copied the Queen and the idea spread, and now you see we have a great democracy.'

Mrs. Pettigrew laughed for a long time. Alec Warner was gazing like a bird-watcher at Charmian, who plucked at the rug round her knees, waiting to tell her own story.

'When I went to Russia,' said Charmian, looking up at him like a child, 'the Tsarina sent an escort to meet me at the frontier, but did not send an escort to take me back. That is so like Russia, they make resolutions then get bored. The male peasants lie on the stove all winter. All the way to Russia my fellow-passengers were opening their boxes and going over their belongings. It was spring and . . .'

Mrs. Pettigrew winked at Alec Warner. Charmian stopped and smiled at him. 'Have you seen Jean Taylor lately?' she said.

'Not for a week or two. I have been away to Folkestone on my research work. I shall go to see her next week.'

'Lettie goes regularly. She says Jean is very happy and fortunate.'

'Lettie is——' He was going to say she was a selfish fool, then remembered Mrs. Pettigrew's presence. 'Well, you know what I think of Lettie's opinions,' he said and waved away the topic with his hand.

And as if the topic had landed on Charmian's lap, she stared at her lap and continued, 'If only you had discovered Lettie's character a little sooner. If only . . .'

He rose to leave, for he knew how Charmian's memory was

inclined to wake up in the past, in some arbitrary year. She would likely fix on those events, that year 1907, and bring them close up to her, as one might bring a book close to one's eyes. The time of his love-affair with Jean Taylor when she was a parlourmaid at the Pipers' before Charmian's marriage, would be like last week to Charmian. And her novelist's mind by sheer habit still gave to those disjointed happenings a shape which he could not accept, and in a way which he thought dishonest. He had been in love with Jean Taylor, he had decided after all to take everyone's advice. He had therefore engaged himself to Lettie. He had broken the engagement when he came to know Lettie better. These were the facts in 1907. By 1912 he had been able to contemplate them without emotion. But dear Charmian made the most of them. She saw the facts as a dramatic sequence reaching its fingers into all his life's work. This interested him so far as it reflected Charmian, though not at all so far as it affected himself. He would, nevertheless, have liked to linger in his chair on that afternoon, in his seventy-ninth year, and listen to Charmian recalling her youth. But he was embarrassed by Mrs. Pettigrew's presence. Her intrusion had irritated him, and he could not, like Charmian, talk on as if she were not present. He looked at Mrs. Pettigrew as she helped him on with his coat in the hall, and thought, 'An irritating woman.' Then he thought, 'A fine-looking woman,' and this was associated with her career at Lisa's as he had glimpsed it at intervals over twenty-six years. He thought about Mabel Pettigrew all the way home across two parks, though he had meant to think about Charmian on that walk. And he reflected upon himself, amazed, since he was nearly eighty and Mrs. Pettigrew a good, he supposed, sixty-five. 'Oh,' he said to himself, 'these erotic throes that come like thieves in the night to steal my High Churchmanship!' Only, he was not a High Churchman—it was no more than a manner of speaking to himself.

He returned to his rooms—which, since they were officially described as 'gentlemen's chambers', he always denied were a flat—off St. James's Street. He hung his coat, put away his hat and gloves, then stood at the large bow window gazing out as at an imposing prospect, though in reality the window looked

down only on the side entrance to a club. He noted the comings
and goings of the club porter. The porter of his own chambers
came up the narrow street intently reading the back page of an
evening paper. With his inward eye, Dr. Warner, the old
sociologist, at the same time contemplated Old Age which had
been his study since he had turned seventy. Nearly ten years of
inquisitive work had gone into the card indexes and files encased in two oak cabinets, one on either side of the window.
His approach to the subject was unique; few gerontologists had
the ingenuity or the freedom to conduct their investigations on
the lines he had adopted. He got about a good deal; he employed agents; his work was, he hoped, valuable; or would be,
one day.

His wide desk was bare, but from a drawer he took a thick
bound notebook and sat down to write.

Presently he rose to fetch the two boxes of index cards which
he used constantly when working at his desk. One of these contained the names of those of his friends and acquaintances who
were over seventy, with details of his relationship to them, and
in the case of chance encounters, the circumstances of their
meeting. Special sections were devoted to St. Aubrey's Home
for mental cases in Folkestone where, for ten years, he had
been visiting certain elderly patients by way of unofficial research.

Much of the information on this first set of cards was an
aid to memory, for, although his memory was still fairly good,
he wished to ensure against his losing it: he had envisaged the
day when he might take up a card, read the name and wonder,
for instance, 'Colston—Charmian,—who is Charmian Colston?
Charmian Colston . . . I know the name but I can't for the
moment think who . . .' Against this possibility was inscribed
'Nee Piper. Met 1907. Vide Ww page . . .' 'Ww,' stood for
Who's Who. The page number was inserted in pencil, to be
changed every four years when he acquired a new *Who's Who*.
Most of the cards in this category were filled in with small
writing on both sides. All of them were, by his instruction, to
be destroyed at his death. At the top left-hand corner of each
card was a reference letter and number in red ink. These cross-

referred to a second set of cards which bore pseudonyms invented by Dr. Warner for each person. (Thus, Charmian was, in the second set of cards, 'Gladys'.) All these cards in the second set were his real working cards, for these bore the clues to the case-histories. On each was marked a neat network of codes and numbers relating to various passages in the books around the walls, on the subjects of gerontology and senescence, and to the ten years' accumulation of his thick notebooks.

Alec Warner lifted the house phone and ordered grilled turbot. He sat to his desk, opened a drawer and extracted a notebook; this was his current diary which would also be destroyed at his death. In it he noted his afternoon observations of Charmian, Mrs. Pettigrew, and himself. 'Her mind,' he wrote, 'has by no means ceased to function, as her husband makes out. Her mind works associatively. At first she went off into a dream making plucking movements at the rug on her knees. She appeared to be impatient. She did not follow my story at all, but apparently the words "Queen Victoria" had evoked some other regal figure. As soon as I had finished she embarked upon a reminiscence (which is likely to be true in detail) of her visit to St. Petersburg to see her father in 1908. (As she spoke, I myself recalled, for the first time since 1908, Charmian's preparations for her journey to Russia. This has been dormant in my memory since then.) I observed that Charmian did not, however, mention the meeting with her father nor the other diplomat whose name I forgot, who later committed suicide on her account. Nor did she mention that she was accompanied by Jean Taylor. I have no reason to doubt the accuracy of her memory on the habits of Russian travellers. So far as I recall her actual words were . . .'

He wrote on till his turbot came up.

My Aunt Marcia, he reflected as he ate, was ninety-two, that is seven years older than Charmian, and was still playing a brilliant game of chess to the time of her death. Mrs. Flaxman, wife of the former Rector of Pineville, was seventy-three when she lost her memory completely; twelve years younger than Charmian. Charmian's memory is not completely gone, it is only erratic. He rose from the table and went to his desk to make a

note in the margin of his diary where he had written his day's
account of Charmian: 'Vide Mrs. Flaxman.'

He returned to his turbot. Ninon de Lenclos of the seven-
teenth century died at ninety-nine, in full reason and reputed for
wit, he reflected.

His wine-glass rested a moment on his lip. Goethe, he mused,
was older than me when he was writing love poems to young
girls. Renoir at eighty-six . . . Titian, Voltaire. Verdi composed
Falstaff at the age of eighty. But artists are perhaps exceptions.

He thought of the Maud Long Ward where Jean Taylor lay,
and wondered what Cicero would make of it. He looked round
his shelves. The great Germans on the subject: they were either
visionaries or pathologists, largely. To understand the subject,
one had to befriend the people, one had to use spies and win
allies.

He ate half of what he had been sent. He drank part of half
a bottle of wine. He read over what he had written, the account
of the afternoon from the time of his arrival at the Colstons' to
his walk back across the park with the thoughts, which had
taken him by surprise, of Mrs. Pettigrew whose intrusive
presence, as he had noted in his diary, had excited him with both
moral irritability and erotic feelings. The diary would go into
the fire, but his every morning's work was to analyse and
abstract from it the data for his case-histories, entering them in
the various methodical notebooks. There Charmian would
become an impersonal, almost homeless, 'Gladys', Mabel
Pettigrew 'Joan', and he himself 'George'.

Meantime he put away his cards and his journal and read, for
an hour, from one of the fat volumes of Newman's *Life and
Letters*. Before he put it down he marked a passage with a
pencil:

I wonder, in old times what people died of. We read, 'After
this, it was told Joseph that his father was sick.' 'And the
days of David drew nigh that he should die.' What were they
sick, what did they die, of? And so of the great Fathers. St.
Athanasius died past seventy—was his a paralytic seizure?
We cannot imitate the Martyrs in their death—but I some-

times feel it would be a comfort if we could associate ourselves with the great Confessor Saints in their illnesses and
decline: Pope St. Gregory had the gout, St. Basil had a liver
complaint, but St. Gregory Nazianzen? St. Ambrose? St.
Augustine and St. Martin died of fevers, proper to old age . . .

*   *   *

At half past nine he took a packet of ten cigarettes from a
drawer and went out. He turned into Pall Mall where the road
was up and a nightwatchman on duty whom Alec Warner had
been visiting each night for a week past. He hoped to get
sufficient consistent answers to construct a history. 'How old
are you? Where do you live? What do you eat? Do you believe
in God? Any religion? Did you ever go in for sport? How do you
get on with your wife? How old is she? Who? What? Why?
How do you feel?'

'Evening,' said the man as Alec approached. 'Thanks,' he
said, as he took the cigarettes. He shifted up on the plank by
the brazier to let Alec sit down beside him.

Alec warmed his hands.

'How you feeling tonight?' he said.

'Not so bad! How's yourself, guv?'

'Not so bad. How old did you say . . . ?'

'Seventy-five. Sixty-nine to the Council.'

'Of course,' said Alec.

'Doesn't do to let on too much.'

'I'm seventy-nine,' coaxed Alec.

'Don't look a day over sixty-five.'

Alec smiled into the fire knowing the remark was untrue, and
that he did not care how old he looked, and that most people
cared. 'Where were you born?' said Alec.

A policeman passed and swivelled his eyes towards the two
old men without changing the rhythm of his tread. He was not
surprised to see the nightwatchman's superior-looking companion. He had seen plenty of odd old birds.

'That young copper,' said Alec, 'is wondering what we're up to.'

The watchman reached for his bottle of tea, and pulled out
the cork.

'Got any tips for tomorrow?'

'Gunmetal for the two-thirty. They say Out of Reach for the four-fifteen. Tell me——'

'Gunmetal's even money,' said the watchman. 'Not worth your trouble.'

'How long,' said Alec, 'do you sleep during the day?'

*　　*　　*

Charmian had been put to bed. Rough physical handling made her mind more lucid in some ways, more cloudy in others. She knew quite well at this moment that Mrs. Anthony was not Taylor, and Mabel Pettigrew was Lisa Brooke's former house-keeper, whom she disliked.

She lay and resented, and decided against, Mrs. Pettigrew. The woman had had three weeks' trial and had proved unsatisfactory.

Charmian also lay and fancied Mrs. Pettigrew had wronged her, long ago in the past. This was not the case. In reality, it was Lisa Brooke who had blackmailed Charmian, so that she had been forced to pay and pay, although Lisa had not needed the money; she had been forced to lie awake worrying through-out long night hours, and in the end she had been forced to give up her lover Guy Leet, while Guy had secretly married Lisa to satisfy and silence her for Charmian's sake. All this Charmian blamed upon Mrs. Pettigrew, forgetting for the moment that her past tormentor had been Lisa; so bitter was the particular memory and so vicious was her new tormentor. For Mrs. Pettigrew had wrenched Charmian's arm while getting her dress off, had possibly bruised the arm with her hard impatient grasp. 'What you need,' Mrs. Pettigrew had said, 'is a nurse. I am not a nurse.'

Charmian felt indignant at the suggestion that she needed a nurse.

She decided to give Mrs. Pettigrew a month's money in the morning and tell her to go. Before Mrs. Pettigrew had switched out the light, Charmian had spoken sharply. 'I think, Mrs. Pettigrew——'

'Oh, do call me Mabel and be friendly.'

'I think, Mrs. Pettigrew, it will not be necessary for you to come in to the drawing-room when I have visitors unless I ring.'

'Good*night*,' said Mrs. Pettigrew and switched out the light.

Mrs. Pettigrew descended to her sitting-room and switched on the television which had been installed at her request. Mrs. Anthony had gone home. She took up her knitting and sat working at it while watching the screen. She wanted to loosen her stays but was not sure whether Godfrey would look in to see her. During the three weeks of her stay at the Colstons' he had been in to see her on five evenings. He had not come in the night. Perhaps he would come tonight, and she did not wish to be caught untidy-looking. There was indeed a knock at the door, and she bade him come in.

On the first occasion it had been necessary for him to indicate his requirements to her. But now, she perfectly understood. Godfrey, with his thin face outstanding in the dim lamplight, and his excited eyes, placed on the low coffee table a pound note. He then stood, arms dangling and legs apart, like a stage rustic, watching her. Without shifting her posture she raised the hem of her skirt at one side until the top of her stocking and the tip of her suspender were visible. Then she went on knitting and watching the television screen. Godfrey gazed at the stocking-top and the glittering steel of the suspender-tip for the space of two minutes' silence. Then he pulled back his shoulders as if recalling his propriety, and still in silence, walked out.

After the first occasion Mrs. Pettigrew had imagined, almost with alarm, that his request was merely the preliminary to more daring explorations on his part, but by now she knew with an old woman's relief that this was all he would ever desire, the top of her stocking and the tip of her suspender. She took the pound note off the table, put it in her black suède handbag and loosened her stays. She had plans for the future. Meantime a pound was a pound.

Chapter Six

MISS JEAN TAYLOR sat in the chair beside her bed. She never knew, when she sat in her chair, if it was the last time she would be able to sit out of bed. Her arthritis was gradually spreading and digging deep. She could turn her head slowly. So, and with difficulty, she did. Alec Warner shifted his upright chair a little to face her.

She said, 'Are you tormenting Dame Lettie?'

The thought crossed his mind, among other thoughts, that Jean's brain might be undergoing a softening process. He looked carefully at her eyes and saw the grey ring round the edge of the cornea, the *arcus senilis*. Nevertheless, it surrounded the main thing, a continuing intelligence among the ruins.

Miss Taylor perceived his scrutiny and thought, it is true he is a student of the subject but he is in many ways the same as the rest. How we all watch each other for signs of failure!

'Come, Alec,' she said, 'tell me.'

'Tormenting Lettie?' he said.

She told him about the anonymous telephone calls, then said, 'Stop *studying* me, Alec. I am not soft in the brain as yet.'

'Lettie must be so,' he said.

'No, she isn't, Alec.'

'And supposing,' he said, 'she really has been receiving these telephone calls. Why do you suggest I am the culprit? I ask as a matter of interest.'

'It seems to me likely, Alec. I may be wrong, but it is the sort of thing, isn't it, that you would do for purposes of study? An experiment——'

'It is the sort of thing,' he said, 'but in this case I doubt if I am the culprit.'

'You *doubt*.'

'Of course, I doubt. In a court of law, my dear, I would with complete honesty deny the charge. But you know, I can't affirm or deny anything that is within the range of natural possibility.'

'Alec, are you the man, or not?'

'I don't know,' he said. 'If so, I am unaware of it. But I may be a Jekyll and Hyde, may I not? There was a recent case——'

'Because,' she said, 'if you are the culprit the police will get you.'

'They would have to prove the deed. And if they proved it to my satisfaction I should no longer be in doubt.'

'Alec,' she said, 'are you the man behind those phone calls?'

'Not to my knowledge,' he said.

'Then,' she said, 'you are not the man. Is it someone employed by you?'

He did not seem to hear the question, but was watching Granny Barnacle like a naturalist on holiday. Granny Barnacle accepted his attention with obliging submission, as she did when the doctor brought the medical students round her bed, or when the priest brought the Blessed Sacrament.

'Ask her how she is keeping,' said Miss Taylor, 'since you are staring at her.'

'How are you keeping?' said Alec.

'Not too good,' said Granny Barnacle. She jerked her head to indicate the ward dispensaries just beyond the door. 'Time there was a change of management,' she said.

'Indeed yes,' said Alec, and, inclining his head in final acknowledgment, which included the whole of the Maud Long Ward, returned his attention to Jean Taylor.

'Someone,' she said, 'in your employ?'

'I doubt it.'

'In that case,' she said, 'the man is neither you nor your agent.'

When she had first met him, nearly fifty years ago, she had been dismayed when he had expressed these curious 'doubts'. She had thought him perhaps a little mad. It had not occurred to her till many years later that this was a self-protective manner of speech which he used exclusively when talking to women whom he liked. He never spoke so to men. She had discerned, after these many years, that his whole approach to the female mind, his only way of coping with it, was to seem to derive amusement from it. When Miss Taylor had made this discovery she was glad they had never been married. He was too much masked behind his mocking, paternal attitude—now become a habit—for any proper relationship with a grown woman.

She recalled an afternoon years ago in 1928—long after the love affair—when she had been attending Charmian on a weekend party in the country and Alec Warner was a fellow-guest. One afternoon he had taken Jean Taylor off for a walk—Charmian had been amused—'to question her, as Jean was so reliable in her evidence'. Most of their conversation she had forgotten, but she recalled his first question.

'Do you think, Jean, that other people exist?'

She had not at once understood the nature of the question. For a moment she had wondered if his words might in some way refer to that love affair twenty-odd years earlier, and his further words, 'I mean, Jean, do you consider that people—the people around us—are real or illusory?' had possibly some personal bearing. But this did not fit with her knowledge of the man. Even at the time of their love relationship he was not the type to proffer the conceit: there is no-one in the world but we two; we alone exist. Besides, she who was now walking beside this middle-aged man was herself a woman in her early fifties.

'What do you mean?' she said.

'Only what I say.' They had come to a beech wood which was damp from a last night's storm. Every now and then a little succession of raindrops would pelt from the leaves on to his hat or her hat. He took her arm and led her off the main path, so that for all her sober sense, it rapidly crossed her mind that he might be a murderer, a maniac. But she had, the next instant, recalled her fifty years and more. Were they not usually young women who were strangled in woods by sexual maniacs? No, she thought again, sometimes they were women of fifty-odd. The leaves squelched beneath their feet. Her mind flashed messages to itself back and forth. But I know him well, he's Alec Warner. Do I know him, though?—he is odd. Even as a lover he was strange. But he is known everywhere, his reputation . . . Still, some eminent men have secret vices. No-one ever finds them out; their very eminence is a protection.

'Surely,' he was saying, as he continued to draw her into the narrow, dripping shadows, 'you see that here is a respectable question. Given that you believe in your own existence as self-evident, do you believe in that of others? Tell me, Jean, do you believe that I for instance, at this moment, exist?' He peered down at her face beneath the brim of her brown old hat.

'Where are you taking me?' she said, stopping still.

'Out of these wet woods,' he said, 'by a short cut. Tell me, now, surely you understood what I am asking? It's a plain question. . . .'

She looked ahead through the trees and saw that their path was indeed a short cut to the open fields. She realised at once that his question was entirely academic and he was not contemplating murder with indecent assault. And what reason, after all, had she to suspect this? How things do, she thought, come and go through a woman's mind. He was an unusual man.

'I agree,' she then said, 'that your question can be asked. One does sometimes wonder, perhaps only half-consciously, if other people are real.'

'Please,' he said, 'wonder more than half-consciously about this question. Wonder about it with as much consciousness as you have, and tell me what is your answer.'

'Oh,' she said, 'I think in that case, other people do exist. That's my answer. It's only common sense.'

'You have made up your mind too quickly,' he said. 'Take time and think about it.'

They had emerged from the wood and took a path skirting a ploughed field which led to the village. There the church with its steep sloping graveyard stood at the top of the street. Miss Taylor looked over the wall at the graveyard as they passed it. She was not sure now if his words had been frivolous or serious or both; for, even in their younger days—especially during that month of July 1907 at the farmhouse—she had never really known what to make of him, and had sometimes felt afraid.

She looked at the graveyard and he looked at her. He noted dispassionately that her jaw beneath the shade of the hat was more square than it had ever been. As a young woman she had been round-faced and soft; her voice had been extremely quiet, like the voice of an invalid. In middle age she had begun to reveal, in appearance, angular qualities; her voice was deeper; her jaw-line nearly masculine. He was interested in these factors; he supposed he approved of them; he liked Jean. She stopped and leaned over the low stone wall looking at the gravestones.

'This graveyard is a kind of evidence,' she said, 'that other people exist.'

'How do you mean?' he said.

She was not sure. Having said it, she was not sure why. The more she wondered what she had meant the less she knew.

He tried to climb over the wall, and failed. It was a low wall, but still he was not up to it. 'I am going on fifty,' he said to her without embarrassment, not even with a covering smile, and she remembered how, at the farmhouse in 1907, when he had chanced to comment that they were both past their prime, he being twenty-eight and she thirty-one, she had felt hurt and embarrassed till she realised he meant no harm by it, meaning only to point a fact. And she, catching this habit and tone, had been able to state quite levelly, 'We are not social equals,' before the month was over.

He brushed the dust of the graveyard wall from his trousers. 'I am going on fifty. I should like to look at the gravestones. Let's go in by the gate.'

And so they had walked among the graves, stooping to read the names on the stones.

'They are, I quite see, they are,' he said, 'an indication of the existence of others, for there are the names and times carved in stone. Not a proof, but at least a large testimony.'

'Of course,' she said, 'the gravestones might be hallucinations. But I think not.'

'There is that to be considered,' he said so courteously that she became angry.

'But the graves are at least reassuring,' she said, 'for why bother to bury people if they don't exist?'

'Yes, oh precisely,' he said.

They ambled up the short drive to the house where Lettie, who sat writing at the library window, glanced towards them and then away again. As they entered, Lisa Brooke with her flaming bobbed head came out. 'Hallo, you two,' she said, looking sweetly at Jean Taylor. Alec went straight to his room while Miss Taylor went in search of Charmian. On the way, various people encountered and said 'Hallo' to her. This party was composed of a progressive set; they would think nothing of her walk with Alec that summer of 1928 even though some remembered the farmhouse affair of 1907 which had been a little scandal in those days. Only a brigadier, a misfit in the party who had been invited because the host wanted his advice on dairy herds, and who had passed the couple on their walk, later enquired of Lettie in Miss Taylor's hearing, 'Who was that lady I passed with Alec? Has she just arrived?' And Lettie, loathing Jean as she did, but wishing to be broad-minded, replied, 'Oh, she's Charmian's maid.'

'Say what you like about that sort of thing, the other domestics won't like it,' commented the brigadier, which was, after all, true.

And yet, Jean Taylor reflected as she sat with Alec in the Maud Long Ward, perhaps it was not all mockery. He may have half-meant the question.

'Be serious,' she said, looking down at her twisted arthritic hands.

Alec Warner looked at his watch.

'Must you be going?' she said.

'Not for another ten minutes. But it'll take me three quarters of an hour across the parks. I have to keep fairly strictly to my times, you know. I am going on eighty.'

'I'm relieved it's not you, Alec—the telephone calls . . .'

'My dear, this has come from Lettie's imagination, surely that is obvious.'

'Oh no. The man has twice left a message with Godfrey. "Tell Dame Lettie," he said, "to remember she must die." '

'Godfrey heard it too?' he said. 'Well, I suppose, in that case, it must be a lunatic. How did Godfrey take it? Did he get a fright?'

'Dame Lettie didn't say.'

'Oh, do find out what their reactions were. I hope the police don't catch the fellow too soon. One might get some interesting reactions.' He rose to leave.

'Oh, Alec—before you go—there was something else I wanted to ask you.'

He sat down again and replaced his hat on her locker.

'Do you know Mrs. Sidebottome?'

'Tempest? Ronald's wife. Sister-in-law of Lisa Brooke. Now in her seventy-first year. I first met her on a boat entering the Bay of Biscay in 1930. She was——'

'That's right. She is on the Management Committee of this hospital. The sister in charge of this ward is unsuitable. We all here desire her to be transferred to another ward. Do you want me to go into details?'

'No,' he said. 'You wish me to talk to Tempest.'

'Yes. Make it plain that the nurse in question is simply overworked. There was a fuss about her some time ago, but nothing came of it.'

'I cannot speak to Tempest just yet. She went into a nursing home for an operation last week.'

'A serious one?'

'A tumour on the womb. But at her age it is, in itself, less serious than in a younger woman.'

'Oh well, then you can't do anything for us at present.'

'I shall think,' he said, 'if I know anyone else. Have you approached Lettie on the subject?'

'Oh, yes.'

He smiled, and said, 'Approach her no more. It is a waste of time. You must seriously think, Jean, of going to that home in Surrey. The cost is not high. Godfrey and I can manage it. I think Charmian would be joining you there soon. Jean, you should have a room of your own.'

'Not now,' said Miss Taylor. 'I shan't move from here. I've made friends here, it's my home.'

'See you next Wednesday, my dear,' he said, taking his hat and looking round the ward, sharply, at each of the grannies in turn.

'All being well,' she said.

Two years ago, when she first came to the ward, she had longed for the private nursing home in Surrey about which there had been too much talk. Godfrey had made a fuss about the cost, he had expostulated in her presence, and had quoted a number of their friends of the progressive set on the subject of the new free hospitals, how superior they were to the private affairs. Alec Warner had pointed out that these were days of transition, that a person of Jean Taylor's intelligence and habits might perhaps not feel at home among the general aged of a hospital.

'If only,' he said, 'because she is partly what we have made her, we should look after her.'

He had offered to bear half the cost of keeping Jean in Surrey. But Dame Lettie had finally put an end to these arguments by coming to Jean with a challenge, 'Would you not really, my dear, *prefer* to be independent? After all, you are the public. The hospitals are *yours*. You are entitled . . .' Miss Taylor had replied, 'I prefer to go to hospital, certainly.' She had made her own arrangements and had left them with the daily argument still in progress concerning her disposal.

Alec Warner had not liked to see her in this ward. The first week he had wanted her to move. In misery she had vacillated. Her pains were increasing, she was not yet resigned to them. There had been further consultations and talking things over. Should she be moved to Surrey? Might not Charmian join her there eventually?

Not now, she thought, after Alec Warner had departed. Granny Valvona had put on her glasses and was searching for the horoscopes. Not now, thought Miss Taylor. Not now that the worst is over.

*　　　*　　　*

At first, in the morning light, Charmian forgave Mrs. Pettigrew. She was able, slowly, to walk downstairs by herself. Other movements were difficult and Mrs. Pettigrew had helped her to dress quite gently.

'But,' said Mabel Pettigrew to her, 'you should get into the habit of breakfast in bed.'

'No,' said Charmian cheerfully as she tottered round the table, grasping the backs of chairs, to her place. 'That would be a bad habit. My morning cup of tea in bed is all that I desire. Good morning, Godfrey.'

'Lydia May,' said Godfrey, reading from the paper, 'died yesterday at her home in Knightsbridge six days before her ninety-second birthday.'

'A Gaiety Girl,' said Charmian. 'I well remember.'

'You're in good form this morning,' Mrs. Pettigrew remarked. 'Don't forget to take your pills.' She had put the bottle beside Charmian's plate. She now unscrewed the cap and extracted two pills which she laid before Charmian.

'I have had my pills already,' said Charmian. 'I had them with my morning tea, don't you remember?'

'No,' said Mrs. Pettigrew, 'you are mistaken, dear. Take your pills.'

'She made a fortune,' Godfrey remarked. 'Retired in 1893 and married money both times. I wonder what she has left?'

'She was before my time, of course,' said Mabel Pettigrew.

'Nonsense,' said Godfrey.

'I beg your pardon, Mr. Colston, she was before my time. If she retired in 1893 I was only a child in 1893.'

'*I* remember her,' said Charmian. 'She sang most expressively —in the convention of those times you know.'

'At the Gaiety?' said Mrs. Pettigrew. 'Surely——'

'No, I heard her at a private party.'

'Ah, you would be quite a grown girl, then. Take your pills, dear.' She pushed the two white tablets towards Charmian.

Charmian pushed them back and said, 'I have already taken my pills this morning. I recall quite clearly. I usually do take them with my early tea.'

'Not always,' said Mrs. Pettigrew. 'Sometimes you forget and leave them on your tray, as you did this morning, actually.'

'She was the youngest of fourteen children,' Godfrey read out from the paper, 'of a strict Baptist family. It was not till her father's death that, at the age of eighteen, she made her debut in a small part at the Lyceum. Trained by Ellen Terry and Sir Henry Irving, she left them however for the Gaiety where she became the principal dancer. The then Prince of Wales——'

'She was introduced to us at Cannes,' said Charmian, gaining confidence in her good memory that morning, 'wasn't she?'

'That's right,' said Godfrey, 'it would be about 1910.'

'And she stood up on a chair and looked round her and said, "Gad! The place is stinking with royalty." Remember we were terribly embarrassed, and——'

'No, Charmian, no. You've got it wrong there. It was one of the Lilley Sisters who stood on a chair. And that was much later. There was nothing like that about Lydia May, she was a different class of girl.'

Mrs. Pettigrew placed the two pills a little nearer to Charmian, but said no more about them. Charmian said, 'I mustn't exceed my dose,' and shakily replaced them in the bottle.

'Charmian, take your pills, my dear,' said Godfrey and took a noisy sip from his coffee.

'I have taken two pills already. I remember quite clearly doing so. Four might be dangerous.'

Mrs. Pettigrew cast her eyes to the ceiling and sighed.

'What is the use,' said Godfrey, 'of me paying big doctor's bills if you won't take his stuff?'

'Godfrey, I do not wish to be poisoned by an overdose. Moreover, my own money pays for the bills.'

'Poisoned,' said Mrs. Pettigrew, laying down her napkin as if tried beyond endurance. 'I ask you.'

'Or merely upset,' said Charmian. 'I do not wish to take the pills, Godfrey.'

'Oh well,' he said, 'if that's how you feel, I must say it makes life damned difficult for all of us, and we simply can't take responsibility if you have an attack through neglecting the doctor's instructions.'

Charmian began to cry. 'I know you want to put me away in a home.'

Mrs. Anthony had just come in to clear the table.

'There,' she said. 'Who wants to put you in a home?'

'We are a little upset, what with one thing and another,' said Mrs. Pettigrew.

Charmian stopped crying. She said to Mrs. Anthony, 'Taylor, did you see my early tea-tray when it came down?'

Mrs. Anthony seemed not to grasp the question, for though she had heard it, for some reason she felt it was more complicated than it really was.

Charmian repeated, 'Did you see——'

'Now, Charmian,' said Godfrey, foreseeing some possible contradiction between Mrs. Anthony's reply and Mrs. Pettigrew's previous assertion. In this, he was concerned overwhelmingly to prevent a conflict between the two women. His comfort, the whole routine of his life, depended on retaining Mrs. Anthony. Otherwise he might have to give up the house and go to some hotel. And Mrs. Pettigrew having been acquired, she must be retained; otherwise Charmian would have to go to a home. 'Now, Charmian, we don't want any more fuss about your pills,' he said.

'What did you say about the tea-tray, Mrs. Colston?'

'Was there anything on it when it came down from my room?'

Mrs. Pettigrew said, 'Of course there was nothing on the tray. I replaced the pills you had left on it in the bottle.'

'There was a cup and saucer on the tray. Mrs. Pettigrew brought it down,' said Mrs. Anthony, contributing what accuracy she could to questions which still confused her.

Mrs. Pettigrew started noisily loading the breakfast dishes on to Mrs. Anthony's tray. She said to Mrs. Anthony, 'Come, my dear, we've work to do.'

Mrs. Anthony felt she had somehow failed Charmian, and so, as she followed Mrs. Pettigrew out of the door, she pulled a face at her.

When they were gone Godfrey said, 'See the fuss you've caused. Mrs. Pettigrew was quite put out. If we lose her——'

'Ah,' said Charmian, 'you are taking your revenge, Eric.'

'I am not Eric,' he said.

'But you are taking your revenge.' Fifteen years ago, in her seventy-first year, when her memory had started slightly to fail, she had realised that Godfrey was turning upon her as one who had been awaiting his revenge. She did not think he was himself aware of this. It was an instinctive reaction to the years of being a talented, celebrated woman's husband, knowing himself to be reaping continually in her a harvest which he had not sown.

Throughout her seventies Charmian had not reproached him

with his bullying manner. She had accepted his new domina-
tion without comment until her weakness had become so marked
that she physically depended on him more and more. It was
then, in her eighties, that she started frequently to say what, in
the past, she would have considered unwise: 'You are taking
your revenge.'

And on this occasion, as always, he replied, 'What revenge for
what?' He really did not know. He saw only that she was beginning to look for persecution: poison, revenge; what next? 'You
are getting into a state of imagining that all those around you
are conspiring against you,' he said.

'Whose fault is it,' she said with a jolting sharpness, 'if I am
getting into such a state?'

This question exasperated him, partly because he sensed a
deeper sanity in it than in all her other accusations, and partly
because he could not answer it. He felt himself to be a heavily
burdened man.

Later in the morning, when the doctor called, Godfrey
stopped him in the hall.

'She is damn difficult today, Doctor.'

'Ah well,' said the doctor, 'it's a sign of life.'

'Have to see about a home if she goes on like this.'

'It might be a good idea, if only she can be brought round to
liking it,' said the doctor. 'The scope for regular attention is so
much better in a nursing-home, and I have known cases far
more advanced than your wife's which have improved tremendously once they have been moved to a really comfortable
home. How are you feeling yourself?'

'Me? Well, what can you expect with all the domestic worries
on my shoulders?' said Godfrey. He pointed to the door of the
garden-room where Charmian was waiting. 'You'd better go on
in,' he said, being disappointed of the sympathy and support
he had hoped for, and vaguely put out by the doctor's talk of
Charmian's possible improvement in health, should she be sent
to a home.

The doctor's hand was on the door knob. 'I shouldn't worry
too much about domestic matters,' he said. 'Go out as much as
possible. Your wife, as I say, may buck up tremendously if we

have to move her. It sometimes proves a stimulus. Of course, at
her age . . . her resistance . . . but there's a chance that she may
still get about again. It is largely neurasthenia. She has extraordinary powers of recovery, almost as if she had some secret
sources. . . .'

Godfrey thought: This is his smarm. Charmian has a secret
source, and I pay the bills. He said explosively, 'Well, sometimes I feel she deserves to be sent away. Take this morning for
instance——'

'Oh *deserves*,' said the doctor, 'we don't recommend nursing-
homes as a punishment, you know.'

'Bloody man,' said Godfrey in the doctor's hearing and before
he had properly got into the room where Charmian waited.

Immediately the doctor had entered through the door so did
Mrs. Pettigrew through the french windows. 'Pleasant for the
time of year,' she said.

'Yes,' said the doctor. 'Good morning, Mrs. Colston. How do
you feel today?'

'We wouldn't,' said Mrs. Pettigrew, 'take our pills this
morning, Doctor, I'm afraid.'

'Oh, that doesn't matter,' he said.

'I did take them,' said Charmian. 'I took them with my early
tea, and they tried to force me to take more at breakfast. I know
I took them with my early tea, and just suppose I had taken a
second dose——'

'It wouldn't really have mattered,' he said.

'But surely,' said Mrs. Pettigrew, 'it is always dangerous to
exceed a stated dose.'

'Just try to keep a careful check—a set routine for medicines
in future,' he said to Mrs. Pettigrew. 'Then neither of you will
make a mistake.'

'There was no mistake on my part,' said Mrs. Pettigrew.
'There is nothing wrong with my memory.'

'In that case,' said Charmian, 'we must question your *intentions* in trying to give me a second dose. Taylor knows I took
my pills as I always do. I did not leave them on the tray.'

The doctor said as he took her pulse, 'Mrs. Pettigrew, if you
would excuse us for a moment. . . .'

She went out with a deep loud weary sigh, and, in the kitchen, stood and berated Mrs. Anthony for 'taking that mad-woman's part this morning'.

'She isn't,' said Mrs. Anthony, 'a mad-woman. She's always been good to me.'

'No, she isn't mad,' said Mrs. Pettigrew, 'you are right. She's cunning and sly. She isn't as feeble as she makes out, let me tell you. I've watched her when she didn't know I was watching. She can move about quite easily when she likes.'

'Not when she likes,' said Mrs. Anthony, 'but when she feels up to it. After all, I've been here nine years, haven't I? Mrs. Colston is a person who needs a lot of understanding, she has her off days and her on days. No-one understands her like I do.'

'It's preposterous,' said Mrs. Pettigrew, 'a woman of my position being accused of attempts to poison. Why, if I was going to do that I should go about it a very different way, I assure you, to giving her overdoses in front of everybody.'

'I bet you would,' said Mrs. Anthony. 'Mind out my way,' she said, for she was sweeping the floor unnecessarily.

'Mind how you talk to me, Mrs. Anthony.'

'Look,' said Mrs. Anthony, 'my husband goes on at me about this job now he's at home all day, he doesn't like me being out. I only do it for that bit of independence and it's what I've always done my married life. But we can do on the pension now I'm seventy and the old man sixty-eight, and any trouble from you, let me tell you I'm leaving here. I managed *her* myself these nine years and we got on without you interfering and making trouble.'

'I shall speak to Mr. Colston,' said Mrs. Pettigrew, 'and inform him of what you say.'

'Him,' said Mrs. Anthony. 'Go on and speak to him. I don't reckon much of him. She's the one that I care for, not *him*.' Mrs. Anthony followed this with an insolent look.

'What do you mean by that exactly?' said Mrs. Pettigrew. 'What exactly do you mean?'

'You work it out for yourself,' said Mrs. Anthony. 'I'm busy with their luncheon.'

Mrs. Pettigrew went in search of Godfrey who was, however,

out. She went by way of the front door round to the french
windows, and through them. She saw that the doctor had left
and Charmian was reading a book. She was filled with a furious
envy at the thought that, if she herself were to take the vapours,
there would not be any expensive doctor to come and give her a
kind talk and an injection no doubt, and calm her down so that
she could sit and read a book after turning the household upside
down.

Mrs. Pettigrew went upstairs to look round the bedrooms,
to see if they were all right and tidy, and in reality to simmer
down and look round. She was annoyed with herself for letting
go at Mrs. Anthony. She should have kept aloof. But it had
always been the same—even when she had been with Lisa
Brooke—when she had to deal with lower domestics she became
too much one of them. It was kindness of heart, but it was weak.
She reflected that she had really started off on the wrong foot
with Mrs. Anthony; that, when she had first arrived, she should
have kept her distance with the woman and refrained from confidences. And now she had lowered herself to an argument with
Mrs. Anthony. These thoughts overwhelmed Mrs. Pettigrew
with that sense of having done a foolish thing against one's
interests, which in some people stands for guilt. And in this
frame of heart she repented, and decided, as she stood by
Charmian's neatly-made bed, to establish her position more
solidly in the household, and from now on to treat Mrs. Anthony
with remoteness.

A smell of burning food rose up the well of the stairs and into
Charmian's bedroom. Mrs. Pettigrew leaned over the banister
and sniffed. Then she listened. No sound came from the kitchen,
no sound of hurried removal of pots from the gas jets. Mrs.
Pettigrew came half-way down the stairs and listened. From the
small garden-room where Charmian had been sitting came
voices. Mrs. Anthony was in there, recounting her wrongs to
Charmian while the food was burning in the oven and the
potatoes burning dry and the kettle burning on the stove. Mrs.
Pettigrew turned back up the stairs, and up one more flight to
her own room. There she got from a drawer a box of keys. She
selected four and putting them in the black suède handbag

which, perhaps by virtue of her office, she always carried about the house, descended to Charmian's bedroom. Here, she tried the keys one by one in the lid of Charmian's bureau. The third fitted. She did not glance within the desk, but locked the lid again. With the same key she tried the drawers. It did not fit them. She placed the key carefully in a separate compartment of her handbag and tried the other keys. None fitted the drawers. She went to the landing, where the smell of burning had become alarming, and listened. Mrs. Anthony had not yet left Charmian, and it was clear to Mrs. Pettigrew that when she did, there would be enough to keep her busy for ten minutes more. She took from her bag a package of chewing gum, and unwrapped it. There were five strips of gum. She put the paper with three of the pieces back in her bag and two pieces of gum in her mouth. She sat on a chair near the open door and chewed for a few seconds. Then she wet the tips of her fingers with her tongue, took the soft gum from her mouth and flattened it. She next wet the surface of the gum with her tongue and applied it to the keyhole of one of the drawers. She withdrew it quickly and put it on Charmian's bedside table to set. She took two more pieces of gum, and having chewed them as before, moistened the lump and applied it to the keyhole of another drawer. She slung back her bag up to her wrist and holding the two pieces of gum, with their keyhole impressions, between the finger and thumb of each hand, walked up the flight of stairs to her bedroom. She placed the hardened gum carefully in a drawer, locked the drawer, and set off downstairs, through the houseful of smoke and smell.

Mrs. Anthony came rushing out of the garden-room just as Mrs. Pettigrew appeared on the first flight of stairs.

'Do I,' said Mrs. Pettigrew, 'smell burning?'

By the time she reached the foot of the stairs Mrs. Anthony was already in the kitchen holding the smoking raging saucepan under the tap. A steady blue cloud was pouring through the cracks of the oven door. Mrs. Pettigrew opened the door of the oven, and was driven back by a rush of smoke. Mrs. Anthony dropped her potato saucepan and ran to the oven.

'Turn off the gas,' she said to Mrs. Pettigrew. 'Oh, the pie!'

Mrs. Pettigrew, spluttering, approached the oven and turned off the gas taps, then she ran coughing from the kitchen and went in to Charmian.

'Do I smell burning?' said Charmian.

'The pie and potatoes are burned to cinders.'

'Oh, I shouldn't have kept Taylor talking,' said Charmian. 'The smell is quite bad, isn't it? Shall we open the windows?'

Mrs. Pettigrew opened the french windows and like a ghost a stream of blue smoke obligingly wafted out into the garden.

'Godfrey,' said Charmian, 'will be so cross. What is the time?'

'Twenty past,' said Mrs. Pettigrew.

'Eleven?'

'No, twelve.'

'Oh, dear. Do go and see how Mrs. Anthony is getting on. Godfrey will be in any moment.'

Mrs. Pettigrew remained by the french windows. 'I expect,' she said, 'Mrs. Anthony is losing her sense of smell. She is quite aged for seventy, isn't she? What I would call an *old* seventy. You would have thought she could have smelt the burning long before it got to this stage.' A sizzling sound came round the back of the house from the kitchen where Mrs. Anthony was drenching everything with water.

'*I* smelt nothing,' said Charmian. 'I'm afraid I kept her talking. Poor soul, she is——'

'There's Mr. Colston,' said Mrs. Pettigrew, 'just come in.' She went out to the hall to meet him.

'What the hell is burning?' he said. 'Have you had a fire?'

Mrs. Anthony came out of the kitchen and gave him an account of what had happened, together with accusations, complaints, and a fortnight's notice.

'I shall go and make an omelette,' said Mrs. Pettigrew, and casting her eyes to heaven behind Mrs. Anthony's back for Godfrey to see, disappeared into the kitchen to cope with the disorder.

But Godfrey would eat nothing. He told Charmian, 'This is all your fault. The household is upside down just because you argued about your pills this morning.'

'An overdose may have harmed me, Godfrey. I was not to know the pills were harmless.'

'There was no question of overdose. I should like to know *why* the pills were harmless. I mean to say, if the fellow prescribes two and you may just as well take four, what sort of a prescription is that, what good are the pills to you? I'm going to pay the bill and tell him not to come back. We'll get another doctor.'

'I shall refuse to see another doctor.'

'Mrs. Anthony has given notice, do you realise what that means?'

'I shall persuade her to stay,' said Charmian. 'She has been under great strain this morning.'

He said, 'Well, I'm going out again. This place is stinking.' He went to get his coat and returned to say, 'Be sure to get Mrs. Anthony to change her mind.' From past experience, he knew that only Charmian could do it. 'It's the least you can do after all the trouble. . . .'

Mrs. Pettigrew and Mrs. Anthony sat eating their omelette with their coats on, since it was necessary to have all windows open. In the course of the meal Mrs. Pettigrew quarrelled with Mrs. Anthony again, and was annoyed with herself afterwards for it. If only, she thought guiltily, I could keep a distance, that would be playing my cards.

Mrs. Anthony sat with Charmian all afternoon, while Mrs. Pettigrew, with the sense of performing an act of reparation, took her two pieces of chewing gum, each marked with a clear keyhole impression, to a person she knew at Camberwell Green.

Chapter Seven

THERE was a chill in the air, but Godfrey walked on the sunny side of the street. He had parked his car in a turning off King's Road outside a bombed building, so that anyone who recognised it would not be able to guess particularly why it was there. Godfrey had, for over three years now, been laboriously

telling any of his acquaintance who lived near Chelsea, that his
oculist was in Chelsea, his lawyer was in Chelsea, and that he
frequently visited a chiropodist in Chelsea. The more alert of
his acquaintance had sometimes wondered why he stated these
facts emphatically and so often—almost every time they met
him. But he was, after all, over eighty and, one supposed,
inclined to waffle about the merest coincidences.

Godfrey himself was of the feeling that one can never be too
careful. Having established an oculist, a lawyer, and a chiropodist
in the neighbourhood to account for his frequent appearances in
Chelsea, he still felt it necessary to park his car anonymously,
and walk the rest of the way, by routes expressly devious, to
Tite Street where, in a basement flat, Olive Mannering, grand-
daughter of Percy Mannering, the poet, resided.

He looked to right and left at the top of the area steps. The
coast was clear. He looked to right again, and descended. He
pushed the door open and called, 'Hello, there.'

'Mind the steps,' Olive called from the front room on the left.
There were three more steps to descend within the doorway.
Godfrey walked down carefully, and found his way along the
passage into a room of many lights. Olive's furnishings were
boxy and modern, coloured with a predominance of yellow. She
herself was fairly drab in comparison. She was twenty-four.
Her skin was pale with a touch of green. She had a Spanish
look, with slightly protruding large eyes. Her legs, full at the
calves, were bare. She sat on a stool and warmed these legs by a
large electric fire while reading the *Manchester Guardian*.

'Goodness, it's you,' she said, as Godfrey entered. 'Your
voice is exactly like Eric's. I thought it was Eric.'

'Is he in London, then?' said Godfrey, looking round the
room suspiciously, for there had been an afternoon when he
had called on Olive and met his son Eric there. Godfrey, however, had immediately said to Olive, 'I wonder if you have your
grandfather's address? I wish to get in touch with him.'

Olive had started to giggle. Eric had said 'Ha—hum' very
meaningly and, as Olive told him later, disrespectfully.

'I wish to get in touch with him in connection with,' said
Godfrey, glaring at his son, 'some poetry.'

Olive was a fair-minded girl in so far as she handed over to Eric most of the monthly allowances she obtained from Godfrey. She felt this was only Eric's due, since his father had allowed him nothing for nearly ten years past, Eric being now fifty-six.

'Is Eric in London?' said Godfrey again.

'He is,' said Olive.

'I'd better not stop,' said Godfrey.

'He won't be coming here today,' she said. 'I'll just go and put my stockings on,' she said. 'Would you like some tea?'

'Yes, all right,' said Godfrey. He folded his coat double and laid it on the divan-bed. On top of it he placed his hat. He looked to see if the curtains were properly drawn across the basement window. He sat down with a thump in one of the yellow chairs which were too low-built for his liking, and picked up the *Manchester Guardian*. Sometimes, while he waited, he looked at the clock.

Olive returned, wearing stockings and carrying a tea tray.

'Goodness, are you in a hurry?' she said as she saw Godfrey looking at the clock. He was not in a hurry, exactly. He was not yet sure of the cause of his impatience that afternoon.

Olive placed the tray on a low table and sat on her low stool. She lifted the hem of her skirt to the point where her suspenders met the top of her stockings, and with legs set together almost primly sideways, she poured out the tea.

Godfrey did not know what had come over him. He stared at the suspender-tips, but somehow did not experience his usual satisfaction at the sight. He looked at the clock.

Olive, passing him his tea, noticed that his attention was less fixed on her suspender-tips than was customary.

'Anything the matter, Godfrey?' she said.

'No,' he said, and took his tea. He sipped it, and stared again at the tops of her stockings, evidently trying hard to be mesmerised.

Olive lit a cigarette and watched him. His eyes did not possess their gleam.

'What's the matter?' she said.

He was wondering himself what was the matter. He sipped his tea.

'Running a car,' he remarked, 'is a great expense.'

She burst into a single laugh and said, 'Oh, go on.'

'Cost of living,' he muttered.

She covered up her suspender-tops with her skirt and sat hugging her knees, as one whose efforts are wasted. He did not seem to notice.

'Did you see in the paper,' she said, 'about the preacher giving a sermon on his hundredth birthday?'

'Which paper, where?' he said, reaching out for the *Manchester Guardian.*

'It was the *Mirror*,' she said. 'I wonder what I've done with it? He said anyone can live to a hundred if they keep God's laws and remain young in spirit. Goodness.'

'The government robbers,' he said, 'won't let you keep young in spirit. Sheer robbery.'

Olive was not listening, or she would not have chosen that moment to say, 'Eric's in a bad way, you know.'

'He's always in a bad way. What's the matter now?'

'The usual,' she said.

'What usual?'

'Money,' she said.

'I can't do more for Eric. I've done more than enough for Eric. Eric has ruined me.'

Then, as in a revelation, he realised what had put him off Olive's suspenders that afternoon. It was this money question, this standing arrangement with Olive. It had been going on for three years. Pleasant times, of course . . . One had possibly gained . . . but now, Mabel Pettigrew—what a find! Quite pleased with a mere tip, a pound, and a handsome woman, too. All this business of coming over to Chelsea. No wonder one was feeling put out, especially as one could not easily extricate oneself from an arrangement such as that with Olive. Moreover . . .

'I'm not so strong these days,' he commented. 'My doctor thinks I'm going about too much.'

'Oh?' said Olive.

'Yes. Must keep indoors more.'

'Goodness,' said Olive. 'You are wonderful for your age. A man like you could never stay indoors all day.'

'Well,' he admitted, 'there is that to it.' He was moved to look
longingly at her legs at the point where, beneath her dress, the
tip of her suspenders would meet the top of her stockings, but
she made no move to reveal them.

'You tell your doctor,' she said, 'to go to hell. What did you
see the doctor about, anyway?'

'Just aches and pains, my dear, nothing serious of course.'

'Many a younger man,' she said, 'is riddled with aches and
pains. Take Eric, for instance——'

'Feeling his age, is he?'

'I'll say he is. Goodness.'

Godfrey said, 'Only himself to blame. No, I'm wrong, I blame
his mother. From the moment that boy was born, she——'

He leaned back in his chair with his hands crossed above his
stomach. Olive closed her eyes and relaxed while his voice
proceeded into the late afternoon.

*   *   *

Godfrey reached his car outside the bomb site. He had felt
cramped when he rose from that frightful modern chair of
Olive's. One had talked on, and remained longer than one had
intended. He climbed stiffly into the car and slammed the door,
suddenly reproached by the more dignified personality he now
had to resume.

'Why does one behave like this, why?' he asked himself as he
drove into the King's Road and along it. 'Why does one do
these things?' he thought, never defining, however, exactly
what things. 'How did it start, at what point in one's life does
one find oneself doing things like this?' And he felt resentful
against Charmian who had been, all her life with him, regarded
by everyone as the angelic partner endowed with sensibility
and refined tastes. As for oneself, of Colston's Breweries, one
had been the crude fellow, tolerated for her sake, and thus
driven into carnality, as it were. He felt resentful against Charmian, and raced home to see if she had made everything all
right after upsetting Mrs. Anthony and Mrs. Pettigrew. He
took out his watch. It was seven and a half minutes to six. Home,
home, for a drink. Funny how Olive never seemed to have any

drinks in her flat. Couldn't afford it, she said. Funny she couldn't afford it; what did she do with her money, one wondered.

*   *   *

At half-past six Alec Warner arrived at Olive's. She poured him a gin and tonic which he placed on a table beside his chair. He took a hard-covered notebook from his briefcase. 'How are things?' he said, leaning his large white head against the yellow chairback.

'Guy Leet,' she said, 'has been diagnosed again for his neck. It's a rare type of rheumatism, it sounds like *tortoise*.'

'Torticollis?' said Alec Warner.

'That's it.'

Alec Warner made a note in his book. 'Trust him,' he said, 'to have a rare rheumatism. How are things otherwise?'

'Dame Lettie Colston has changed her will again.'

'Lovely,' he said, and made a note. 'What way has she changed it?'

'Eric is out again, for one. Martin is put in again. That's the other nephew in Africa.'

'She thinks Eric is responsible for the telephone calls, does she?'

'She suspects everyone. Goodness. This is her way of testing Eric. That ex-detective is out.'

'Chief Inspector Mortimer?'

'Yes. She thinks it might be him. Funny, it is. She has no sooner got him working privately on the case, than she thinks it might be him.'

'How old is Mortimer?' he asked.

'Nearly seventy.'

'I know. But when exactly will he be seventy? Did you enquire?'

'I'll find out exactly,' said Olive.

'Always find out exactly,' he said.

'I think,' said Olive, defending her lapse as best she could, he'll be seventy quite soon—early next year, I think.'

'Find out exactly, dear,' said Warner. 'Meantime he is not one of us. We'll come to *him* next year.'

'She thinks you may be the culprit,' said Olive. 'Are you?'

'I doubt it,' he said wearily. He had received a letter from Dame Lettie asking the same question.

'How you talk,' she said. 'Well, I wouldn't have put it past you.'

'Mrs. Anthony,' she said, 'had a row with Mrs. Pettigrew this morning and is threatening to leave. Charmian accused Mrs. Pettigrew of trying to poison her.'

'That's *very* hot news,' he said, 'Godfrey has been here today, I gather?'

'Oh yes. He was rather odd today. Something's put him off his stroke.'

'Not interested in suspenders today?'

'No, but he was trying hard. He said his doctor doesn't want him to go out and about so much. I didn't know whether to take that as a hint, or——'

'Mrs. Pettigrew—have you thought of *her*?'

'Oh goodness,' said Olive, 'I haven't.' She smiled widely and placed a hand over her mouth.

'Try to find out,' he said.

'Oh dear,' said Olive, 'no more fivers for poor old Eric. I can see it coming. Do you think Mrs. Pettigrew has it in her?'

'I do,' said Alec, writing his notes.

'There's a bit in the paper in the kitchen,' said Olive, 'about a preacher preaching on his hundredth birthday.'

'What paper?'

'The *Mirror*.'

'My press-cutting agency covers the *Mirror*. It's only the out-of-the-way papers they sometimes overlook. But thanks all the same. Always tell me of anything like that, just in case. Keep on the look-out.'

'O.K.,' said Olive, and sipped her drink, watching the old veined hand moving its pen steadily, in tiny writing, over the page.

He looked up. 'How frequently would you say,' he said, 'he passes water?'

'Oh goodness, it didn't say anything about that in the *Mirror*.'

'You know I mean Godfrey Colston.'

'Well, he was here about two hours and he went twice. Of course he had two cups of tea.'

'Is twice the average when he comes here?'

'I can't remember. I think——'

'You must try to remember everything exactly, my dear,' said Alec. 'You must watch, my dear, and pray. It is the only way to be a scholar, to watch and to pray.'

'Me a scholar, goodness. He had patches of red on the cheek-bones today, more so than usual.'

'Thank you,' said Alec, and made a note. 'Notice everything, Olive,' he looked up and said, 'for only you can observe him in relation to yourself. When I meet him, you understand, he is a different personality.'

'I'll bet,' she said, and laughed.

He did not laugh. 'Be sure to find out all you can on his next visit in case he deserts you for Mrs. Pettigrew. When do you expect to see him again?'

'Friday, I suppose.'

'There is someone,' he said, 'tapping at the window behind me.'

'Is there? It must be Granpa, he always does that.' She rose to go to the door.

Alec said quickly, 'Tell me, does he tap on the window of his own accord or have you asked him to announce himself in that way?'

'He does it of his own accord. He always has tapped at the window.'

'Why? Do you know?'

'No—no idea.'

Alec bent once more with his pen over his book, and recorded the facts which he would later analyse down to their last, stubborn elements.

Olive fetched in Percy Mannering who, on entering the room, addressed Alec Warner without preliminaries, waving in front of him a monthly magazine of a literary nature, on the cover of which was stamped in bold lettering, 'Kensington Public Libraries.'

'Guy Leet,' roared Percy, 'that moron has published part of

his memoirs in which he refers to Ernest Dowson, as "that weak-kneed wailer of Gallic weariness afflicted with an all-too-agonised afflatus". He is fantastically wrong about Dowson. Ernest Dowson was the spiritual and aesthetic child of Swinburne, Tennyson, and Verlaine. You can hear all their voices and Dowson was something of a French scholar and quite obviously under the spell of Verlaine as well as Tennyson and Swinburne, and very much in Arthur Symons' circle. He is fantastically wrong about Ernest Dowson.'

'How are you keeping?' said Alec, having risen from his chair.

'Guy Leet was never a good theatre critic, and he was a worse novel critic. He knows nothing about poetry, he has no right to touch the subject. Can't someone stop him?'

'What else,' said Alec, 'does he say in his memoir?'

'A lot of superficiality about how he attacked a novel of Henry James's and then met James outside the Athenaeum one day and James was talking about his conscience as an artist and Guy's conscience as a critic, and that whatever was actually committed to print——'

'Let the fire see the people, Granpa,' said Olive, for Percy was standing back-to-fire straddling and monopolising it. Alec Warner had closed and put away his notebook.

The poet did not move.

'That's because Henry James is fashionable today, that's why he writes about Henry James. Whereas he jeers at poor Ernest—— If you're pouring that brandy for me, Olive, it's too much. Half of that—Ernest Dowson, a supreme lyricist.' He took the glass, which he held with a shaky claw-like hand, and while taking his first sip seemed of a sudden to forget Ernest Dowson.

He said to Alec, 'I didn't see you at Lisa's funeral.'

'Sit down, Granpa,' said Olive. She worked him into a chair.

'I missed it,' said Alec, watching Percy's lean profile with concentration. 'I was in Folkestone at the time.'

'It was a fearful and thrilling experience,' said Percy.

'In what way?' said Alec.

The old poet smiled. He cackled from the depth of his throat, and the memory of Lisa's cremation seemed to be refracted from his mind's eye to the avid eyes in his head. As he talked, the eyes of Alec feasted on him, in turn.

*   *   *

Percy stayed on with his grand-daughter after Alec Warner had left. She prepared a supper of mushrooms and bacon which they ate off trays perched on their knees. She watched him while he ate. He gnawed with his few teeth at the toasted bread, but got through all of it, even the difficult crusts.

He looked up as he managed the last small rim of crust and saw her watching him. When he had finished all, he remarked, 'Final perseverance.'

'What you say, Granpa?'

'Final perseverance is the doctrine that wins the eternal victory in small things as in great.'

'I say, Granpa, did you ever read any books by Charmian Piper?'

'Oh rather, we all knew her books. She was a fine-looking woman. You should have heard her read poetry from a platform in the days of Poetry. Harold Monro always said——'

'Her son, Eric, has told me there's talk of her novels being reprinted. There's a revival of interest in her novels. There's been an article written, Eric says. But he says the novels all consist of people saying "touché" to each other, and it's all an affectation, the revival of interest, just because his mother is so old and still alive and was famous once.'

'She's still famous. Always has been. Your trouble is, you know nothing, Olive. Everyone knows Charmian Piper.'

'Oh no they don't. No-one's heard of her except a few old people, but there's going to be a revival. I say there's been an article——'

'You know nothing about literature.'

'Touché,' she snapped, for Percy himself was always pretending that nobody had forgotten his poetry, really. Then she gave him three pounds to make up for her cruelty, which in fact he had not noticed; he simply did not acknowledge the idea of revival in either case, since he did not recognise the interim death. However, he took the three pounds from Olive, of whose sideline activities he was unaware, for, besides having small private means from her mother's side, she also had occasional jobs as an actress on the B.B.C.

He carried the money by bus and underground to Leicester Square where the post office was open all night, and wrote out, on several telegraph forms, in large slow capitals, a wire to Guy Leet, The Old Stable, Stedrost, Surrey: 'You are fantastically wrong in your reference to Ernest Dowson that exceedingly poignant poet who only just steered clear of sentimentality and self-pity stop Ernest Dowson was the spiritual and aesthetic child of Swinburne Tennyson and especially Verlaine by whose verse he was veritably haunted Dowsons verse requires to be read aloud which is more than most verse by later hands can stand up to stop I cried for madder music and for stronger wine new line but when the feast is finished and the lamps expire new line then falls thy shadow Cynara the night is thine new line and I am desolate and sick of an old passion etcetera stop read it aloud man your cheap alliterative jibe carries no weight you are fantastically wrong—Percy Mannering.'

He handed in the sheaf of forms at the counter. The clerk looked closely at Percy, whereupon Percy made visible the three pound notes.

'Are you sure,' said the clerk then, 'you want to send all this?'

'I am,' bawled Percy Mannering. He handed over two of the notes, took his change and went out into the bright-lit night.

Chapter Eight

DAME LETTIE COLSTON had been happier without a resident maid, but the telephone incidents had now forced on her the necessity of having someone in the house to answer the dreadful calls. The mystery of it was, that the man never gave that terrible message to the girl. On the other hand, in the two weeks since her arrival, there had been a series of calls which proved to be someone getting the wrong number. When they had occurred three times in one day Dame Lettie began to bewilder the girl with questions.

'Who was it, Gwen, was it a man?'

'It was a wrong number.'

'Was it a man?'

'Yes, but it was a wrong number.'

'What did he say exactly? Do answer my question, please.'

'He said, "Sorry, it's a wrong number,"' shouted Gwen, 'that's what he said.'

'What kind of voice was it?'

'Oh mad-um. I said it was a man, didn't I? The lines must be crossed. I know phones like the back of my hand.'

'Yes, but was the voice young or old? Was it the same one as got the last wrong number?'

'Well, they're all the same to me, if they're wrong numbers. You better answer the phone yourself and then——'

'I was only asking,' said Dame Lettie, 'because we seem to be having such a lot of wrong numbers since you've been here. And it always seems to be a man.'

'What you mean? What exactly you mean by that, Mad-*um*?'

Dame Lettie had not meant whatever the girl thought she meant. It was Gwen's evening out, and Lettie was glad Godfrey was coming to dine with her.

At about eight o'clock, when they were at dinner, the telephone rang.

'Godfrey, you answer it, please.'

He marched out into the hall. She heard him lift the receiver and give the number. 'Yes, that's right,' he said next. 'Who's that, who is it?' Lettie heard him say. Then he replaced the receiver.

'Godfrey,' she said, 'that was the man?'

'Yes,' he shouted. ' "Tell Dame Lettie to remember she must die." Then he rang off. Damned peculiar.' He sat down and continued eating his soup.

'There is no need to shout, Godfrey. Keep calm.' Her own large body was trembling.

'Well, it's damned odd. I say you must have an enemy. Sounds a common little fellow, with his lisp.'

'Oh no, Godfrey, he is quite cultured. But sinister.'

'I say he's a common chap. This isn't the first time I've heard him.'

'There must be something wrong with your hearing, Godfrey. A middle-aged, cultivated man who should know better——'

'A barrow boy, I should say.'

'Nonsense. Go and ring the police. They said always to report——'

'What's the use?' he said. And seeing she would argue, he added, 'After dinner. I'll ring after dinner.'

'That is the first time he has left that message since I took on Gwen a fortnight ago. When Gwen answers the telephone the man says, "Sorry, wrong number." He does it two or three times a day.'

'It may *be* some fellow getting a wrong number. Your lines must be crossed with someone else's. Have you reported this nuisance to the Exchange?'

'I have,' she said. 'They tell me the lines are perfectly in order.'

'They must be crossed——'

'Oh,' she said, 'you are as bad as Gwen, going on about crossed lines. I have a good idea who it is. I think it is Chief Inspector Mortimer.'

'Nothing like Mortimer's voice.'

'Or his accomplice,' she said.

'Rubbish. A man in his position.'

'That is why the police don't find the culprit. They know, but they won't reveal his identity. He is their former Chief.'

'I say you have an enemy.'

'I say it is Mortimer.'

'Why then,' said Godfrey, 'do you continue to consult him about the case?'

'So that he shall not know I suspect him. He may then fall into a trap. Meantime, as I have told you, he is out of my will. He doesn't know *that*.'

'Oh, you are always changing your will. No wonder you have enemies.' Godfrey felt guilty at having gossiped to Olive about

Lettie's changes in her will. 'No wonder,' he said, 'you don't know the culprit.'

'I haven't heard from Eric lately,' Dame Lettie remarked, so that he felt more guilty, thinking of all he had told Olive.

Godfrey said, 'He has been in London the past six weeks. He returned to Cornwall last night.'

'But he hasn't been to see me. Why didn't you let me know before, Godfrey?'

'I myself did not know he was in London,' said Godfrey, 'until I learned of it from a mutual friend yesterday.'

'What mutual friend? What has Eric been up to? What friend?'

'I cannot recollect at the moment,' said Godfrey. 'I have long given up interest in Eric's affairs.'

'You should keep your memory in training,' she said. 'Try going over in your mind each night before retiring everything you have done during the day. I must say I am astonished that Eric did not call upon me.'

'He didn't come near us,' said Godfrey, 'so why should he come to see you?'

'At least,' she said, 'I should have thought he knew what side his bread's buttered.'

'Ha, you don't know Eric. Fifty-six years of age and an utter failure. You ought to know, Lettie, that men of that age and type can't bear the sight of old people. It reminds them that they are getting on. Ha, and he's feeling his age, I hear. You, Lettie, may yet see him under. We may both see him under.'

Lying in bed later that night, it seemed clear to Dame Lettie that Eric must really after all be the man behind the telephone calls. He would not ring himself lest she should recognise his voice. He must have an accomplice. She rose and switched on the light.

* * *

Dame Lettie sat in her dressing-gown at dead of night and re-filled her fountain pen. While she did so she glanced at the page she had just written. She thought, How shaky my writing looks! Immediately, as if slamming a door on it, she put the thought out of sight. She wiped the nib of her pen, turned over the sheet and continued, on the back, her letter to Eric:

> . . . and so, having heard of your having been in London these past six weeks, & your not having informed me, far less called, does, I admit, strike me as being, to say the least, discourteous. I had wished to consult you on certain matters relating to your Mother. There is every indication that we shall have to arrange for her to be sent to the nursing home in Surrey of which I told you when last I saw you.

She laid down her pen, withdrew one of the fine hairpins from her thin hair, and replaced it. Perhaps, she thought, I should take an even more subtle line with Eric. Her face puckered in folds under the desk-lamp. Two thoughts intruded simultaneously. One was: I am really very tired; and the other: I am not a bit tired, I am charging ahead with great energy. She lifted the pen again and continued to put the wavering marks across the page.

> I have recently been making some slight adjustments in my own affairs, about which I could have wished to consult you had you seen fit to inform me of your recent visit to London.

Was that subtle enough? No, it was too subtle, perhaps, for Eric.

> These *minor* adjustments, of course, have some bearing upon my Will. It has always seemed to me a pity that your cousin Martin, though doing so well in South Africa, should not be remembered in some small way. I would wish for no recriminations among the family after my passing. Your position is of course substantially unchanged, but I could wish you had made yourself available for consultation. You will recall the adjustments I made to existing arrangements after your cousin Alan fell on the field of battle. . . .

That is good, she thought, that is subtle. Eric had got out of the war somehow. She continued,

> I could have wished for discussions with you, but I am an old woman and quite realise that you, who are nearing the

end of your prime, must be full of affairs. Mr. Merrilees is now drawing up the amended Will and I would not wish to further interfere with existing arrangements. Nevertheless, I could have wished to discuss them with you had you seen fit to present yourself during the six weeks of your recent stay in London, of which I did not hear until after your return.

That ought to do it, she thought. He will come wheezing down from Cornwall as fast as the first train will carry him. If he is the guilty man he will know that I *know*. No-one, she thought, is going to kill me through fear. And she fell to wondering again who her enemy could be. She fell to doubting whether Eric had it in him . . . whether he had the financial means to employ an accomplice. Easier, she thought, for Mortimer. Anyway, she thought, it must be someone who is in my Will. And so she sealed and stamped her letter to Eric, placed it on the tray in the hall, took a tot of whisky and went to bed. Her head moved slowly from side to side on the pillow, for she could not sleep. She had caught a chill down there in the study. A cramp seized her leg. She had a longing for a strong friend, some major Strength from which to draw. Who can help me? she thought. Godfrey is selfish, Charmian feeble, Jean Taylor is bedridden. I can talk to Taylor, but she has not got the strength I need. Alec Warner . . . shall I go to see Alec Warner? I never got strength from him. Neither did Taylor. He has not got the strength one needs.

Suddenly she sprang up. Something had lightly touched her cheek. She switched on the light. A spider on her pillow, large as a penny, quite still, with its brown legs outspread! She looked at it feverishly then pulled herself together to try to pick it off the pillow. As she put forth her hand another, paler, spider-legged and fluffy creature on the pillow where the bed-lamp cast a shade caught her sight. 'Gwen!' she screams. 'Gwen!'

But Gwen is sleeping soundly. In a panic Dame Lettie plucks at the large spider. It proves to be a feather. So does the other object.

She dropped her head on her pillow once more. She thought: My old pillows, I shall get some new pillows.

She put out the light and the troubled movements of the head began again. Whom, she thought, can I draw Strength from? She considered her acquaintances one by one—who among them was tougher, stronger than she?

Tempest, she thought at last. I shall get Tempest Sidebottome to help me. Tempest, her opponent in forty years' committee-sitting, had frequently been a painful idea to Dame Lettie. Particularly had she resented Tempest's bossy activeness and physical agility at Lisa's funeral. Strangely, now, she drew strength from the thought of the woman. Tempest Sidebottome would settle the matter if anyone could. Tempest would hunt down the persecutor. Dame Lettie's head settled still on the pillow. She would go over to Richmond tomorrow and talk to Tempest. After all, Tempest was only seventy-odd. She hoped her idiotic husband Ronald would be out. But in any case, he was deaf. Dame Lettie turned at last to her sleep, deriving a half-dreamt success from the strength of Tempest Sidebottome as from some tremendous mother.

*   *   *

'Good morning, Eric,' said Charmian as she worked her way round the breakfast table to her place.

'*Not* Eric,' said Mrs. Pettigrew. 'We are a bit confused again this morning.'

'Are you, my dear? What has happened to confuse you?' said Charmian.

Godfrey sensed the start of bickering, so he looked up from his paper and said to his wife, 'Lettie was telling me last night that it is a great aid to memory to go through in one's mind each night the things which have happened in the course of the day.'

'Why,' said Charmian, 'that is a Catholic practice. We are always recommended to consider each night our actions of the past day. It is an admirable——'

'Not the same thing,' said Godfrey, 'at all. You are speaking exclusively of one's moral actions. What I'm talking about are things which have happened. It is a great aid to memory, as Lettie was saying last night, to memorise everything which has occurred in one's experience during the day. Your practice,

which you call Catholic, is, moreover, common to most religions.
To my mind, that type of examination of conscience is designed
to enslave the individual and inhibit his freedom of action.
Take yourself for example. You only have to appeal to
psychology——'

'To whom?' said Charmian cattily, as she took the cup which
Mrs. Pettigrew passed to her.

Godfrey turned back to his paper. Whereupon Charmian
continued the argument with Mrs. Pettigrew.

'I don't see that one can examine one's moral conduct without
memorising everything that's happened during the day. It is
the same thing. What Lettie advises is a form of——'

Godfrey put down his paper. 'I say it is not the same thing.'
He dipped an oblong of toast in his tea and put it in his mouth.

Mrs. Pettigrew rose to the opportunity of playing the peace-
maker. 'Now hush,' she said to Charmian. 'Eat your nice
scrambled egg which Taylor has prepared for you.'

'Taylor is not here,' stated Charmian.

'Taylor—what do you mean?' said Godfrey.

Mrs. Pettigrew winked at him.

Godfrey opened his mouth to retort, then shut it again.

'Taylor is in hospital,' said Charmian, pleased with her
clarity.

Godfrey read from the newspaper, ' "Motling"—are you
listening, Charmian?—"On 10th December at Zomba, Nyasa-
land; Major Cosmos Petwick Motling, G.C.V.O., husband of
the late Eugenie, beloved father of Patricia and Eugen, in his
91st year." Are you listening, Charmian?'

'Was he killed at the front, dear?'

'Ah, me!' said Mrs. Pettigrew.

Godfrey opened his mouth to say something to Mrs. Pettigrew, then stopped. He held up the paper again and from behind
it mumbled, 'No, Zomba. Motling's the name. He went out
there to retire. You won't remember him.'

'*I* recall him well,' said Mrs. Pettigrew; 'when his wife was
alive, Lisa used to——'

'Was he killed at the front?' said Charmian.

'The front,' said Mrs. Pettigrew.

' "Sidebottome," ' said Godfrey, '—are you listening, Charmian?—"On 18th December at the Mandeville Nursing Home, Richmond; Tempest Ethel, beloved wife of Ronald Charles Sidebottome. Funeral private." Doesn't give her age.'

'Tempest Sidebottome!' said Mrs. Pettigrew, reaching to take the paper from his hand. 'Let me see.'

Godfrey withdrew the paper and opened his mouth as if to protest, then closed it again. However, he said, 'I am not finished with the paper.'

'Well, fancy Tempest Sidebottome,' said Mrs. Pettigrew. 'Of course, cancer is cancer.'

'She always *was* a bitch,' said Godfrey, as if her death were the ultimate proof of it.

'I wonder,' said Mrs. Pettigrew, 'who will look after poor old Ronald now. He's so deaf.'

Godfrey looked at her to see more closely what she meant, but her short broad nose was hidden by her cup and her eyes stared appraisingly at the marmalade.

She was, in fact, quite shocked by Tempest's death. She had only a month ago agreed to join forces with the Sidebottomes in contesting Lisa Brooke's will. Tempest, when she had learnt of Guy Leet's hitherto secret marriage to Lisa, had been driven to approach Mrs. Pettigrew and attempt to make up their recent differences. Mrs. Pettigrew had rather worked alone, but the heavy costs deterred her. She had agreed to go in with Tempest against Guy Leet on the grounds that his marriage with Lisa Brooke had not been consummated. They had been warned that their case was a slender one, but Tempest had the money and the drive to go ahead, and Mrs. Pettigrew had in her possession the relevant correspondence. Ronald Sidebottome had been timid about the affair—didn't like raking up the scandal, but Tempest had seemed to have the drive. Tempest's death was a shock to Mrs. Pettigrew. She would have to work hard on Ronald. One got no rest. She stared at the marmalade pot as if to fathom its possibilities.

Godfrey had returned to his paper. 'Funeral private. That saves us a wreath.'

'You had better write to poor Ronald,' said Charmian, 'and

I will say a rosary for Tempest. Oh, I do remember her as a girl. She was newly out from Australia and her uncle was a rector in Dorset—as was also my uncle, Mrs. Pettigrew——'

'Your uncle was not in Dorset. He was up in Yorkshire,' said Godfrey.

'But he was a country rector, like Tempest's uncle. Leave me alone, Godfrey. I am just telling Mrs. Pettigrew.'

'Oh, do call me Mabel,' said Mrs. Pettigrew, winking at Godfrey.

'Her uncle, Mabel,' said Charmian, 'was a rector and so was mine. It was the thing we had in common. We had not a great deal in common, Mrs. Pettigrew, and of course as a girl she was considerably younger than me.'

'She is still younger than you,' said Godfrey.

'No, Godfrey, not now. Well, Mrs. Pettigrew, I do so remember our two uncles together and we were all staying down in Dorset. There was a bishop and a dean, and our two uncles. Oh, poor Tempest was bored. They were discussing the Scriptures and this manuscript called "Q". How Tempest was in a rage when she heard that "Q" was only a manuscript, because she had imagined them to be talking of a bishop and she said out loud *"Who* is Bishop Kew?" And of course everyone laughed heartily, and then they were sorry for Tempest. And they tried to console her by telling her that "Q" was nothing really, not even a manuscript, which indeed it wasn't, and I must confess I never understood how they could sit up so late at night fitting their ideas into this "Q" which is nothing really. As I say poor Tempest was in a rage, she could never bear to be made game of.'

Mrs. Pettigrew winked at Godfrey.

'Charmian,' said Godfrey, 'you are over-exciting yourself.' And true enough, she was tremulously crying.

Chapter Nine

PARTLY because of a reorganisation of the Maud Long Ward and partly because of Tempest Sidebottome's death, Sister Burstead was transferred to another ward.

She had been a protégée of Tempest's, and this had mostly accounted for the management committee's resistance to any previous suggestion that the sister could not cope with the old people's ward. The committee, though largely composed of recently empowered professional men and women, had been in many ways afraid of Tempest. Or rather, afraid to lose her lest they should get someone worse.

It was necessary for them to tolerate at least one or two remnants of the old-type committee people until they should die out. And they chiefly feared, in fact, that if Tempest should take offence and resign, she would be replaced by some more formidable, more subtle private welfare-worker and busybody. And whereas Tempest had many dramatic things to say in committee, whereas she was imperious with the matron, an opponent on principle of all occasions of expenditure, scornful in the extreme of physiotherapists and psychiatrists (everything beginning 'psycho-' or 'physio-' Tempest lumped together, believed to be the same thing, and dismissed)—although she was in reaction against the committee's ideals, she was so to the point of parody, and it was for precisely this reason, because she so much demonstrated the errors of her system, that she was retained, was propitiated from time to time, and allowed to have her way in such minor matters as that of Sister Burstead. Not that the committee were not afraid of Tempest for other, less evident reasons; but these were matters of instinct and not openly admitted. Her voice in committee had been strangely terrifying to many an eminent though small-boned specialist, even the bossy young heavily-qualified women had sometimes failed to outstare the little pale pebble-eyes of the great unself-questioning matriarch, Mrs. Sidebottome. 'Terrible woman,' everyone always agreed when she had left.

'After the fifties are over,' said the chairman, who was himself a man of seventy-three, 'everything will be easier. This transition period . . . the old brigade don't like change. They don't like loss of authority. By the middle-sixties everything will be easier. We will have things in working order.' Whereupon the committee surrendered themselves to putting up with Tempest, a rock of unchanging, until the middle-sixties of the century should arrive.

However, she had died, leaving behind her on the committee a Tempest-shaped vacuum which they immediately attempted, but had not yet been able to fill.

In the meantime, as if tempting Providence to send them another, avenging, Tempest, they transferred Sister Burstead, on the first of January, to another ward. That the old people's ward was being reorganised provided a reasonable excuse, and Sister Burstead made no further protest.

News of the transfer reached the grannies before the news of the reorganisation.

'I'll believe it when I see it,' said Granny Barnacle.

She saw it before that week-end. A new ward sister, fat and forceful with a huge untroubled faceful of flesh and brisk legs, was installed. 'That's how I like them,' said Granny Barnacle. 'Sister Bastard was too skinny.'

The new sister, when she caught Granny Green absent-mindedly scooping the scrambled egg off her plate into her locker, put her hands on her slab-like hips and said, 'What the hell do you think *you're* doing?'

'That's how I like them,' said Granny Barnacle. She closed her eyes on her pillow with contentment. She declared herself to feel safe for the first time for months. She declared herself ready to die now that she had seen the removal of Sister Bastard. She sprang up again from her pillow and with outstretched arm and pointing finger prophesied that the whole ward would now see the winter through.

Miss Valvona, who was always much affected by Miss Barnacle's feelings, consulted the stars: 'Granny Barnacle—Sagittarius. "*Noon period best for commencing long-distance travel. You can show your originality today*".'

'Ho!' said Granny Barnacle. 'Originality today, I'll wear me britches back to front.'

The nurses came on their daily round of washing, changing, combing, and prettifying the patients before the matron's inspection. They observed Granny Barnacle's excitement and decided to leave her to the last. She was usually excitable throughout this performance in any case. During Sister Burstead's term of office, especially, Granny Barnacle would screech when turned over for her back to be dusted with powder, or helped out of bed to sit on her chair.

'Nurse, I'll be covered with bruises,' she would shout.

'If you don't move, Gran, you'll be covered with bedsores.'

She would scream to God that the nurses were pulling her arms from their sockets, she would swear by the Almighty that she wasn't fit to be sat up. She moaned, whenever the physiotherapist made her move her fingers and toes, and declared that her joints would crack.

'Kill me off,' she would command, 'and be done with it.'

'Come on, Gran, you've got to get exercise.'

'Crack! Can't you hear the bones crack? Kill me off and——'

'Let's rub your legs, Gran. My, you've got beautiful legs.'

'Help, she's killing me.'

But at the best of times Granny Barnacle really liked an excuse for a bit of noise, it livened her up. In a sense, she gave vent to the whole ward's will to shout, so that the others did not make nearly so much noise as they might otherwise have done. It was true some of the other grannies were loud in complaints, but this was mostly for a few seconds when their hair was being combed. Granny Green would never fail to tell the nurses after her hair was done.

'I had a lovely head of hair till you cut it off,' although in reality there had been very little to cut off.

'It's hygiene, Granny. It would hurt far more when we combed it if your hair was long.'

'I had a lovely head. . . .'

'Me, too,' Granny Barnacle would declare, especially if Sister Burstead had been within hearing. 'You should have seen my head before they cut it off.'

'Oh, short hair is cooler when one is in bed,' Granny Taylor, whose hair had really been long and thick, and who actually preferred it short, would murmur to herself.

'Let's give you a nice wave today, Granny Barnacle.'

'Oh, you're killing me.'

On the day of the new sister's arrival, Granny Barnacle and her obvious excitement having been left to the last, it was found, when her turn came, that she was running a temperature.

'Get me out of bed, love,' she implored the nurse. 'Let's sit up today, seeing Bastard's gone.'

'No, you've got a temperature.'

'Nurse, I want to get up today. Get me a will-form, there's a bob in my locker, I want to make a new will and put in the new sister. What's her name?'

'Lucy.'

'Lucy Locket,' shrieked Granny Barnacle, 'lost her——'

'Lie still, Granny Barnacle, till we make you better.'

She submitted after a fuss. Next day, when they told her she must keep her bed she protested louder, even struggled a little, but Miss Taylor in the opposite bed noticed that Granny Barnacle's voice was unusually thin and high.

'Nurse, I'm going to get up today. Get me a will-form. I want to make a new will and put in the new sister. What's her name?'

'Lucy,' said the nurse. 'Your blood pressure's high, Gran.'

'Her last name, girl.'

'Lucy, Sister Lucy.'

'Sister Lousy,' screamed Granny Barnacle. 'Well, she's going in my will. Give me a hand. . . .'

When the doctor had gone she was given an injection and dozed off for a while.

At one o'clock, while everyone else was eating, she woke. Sister Lucy brought some milk custard to her bed and fed her with a spoon. The ward was quiet and the sound of grannies' spoons tinkling on their plates became more pronounced in the absence of voices.

About three o'clock Granny Barnacle woke again and started to rave in a piping voice, at first faintly, then growing higher and piercing. 'Noos, E'ning Noos,' fluted the old newsvendor. 'E'ning pap-*ar*, Noos, E'ning Stan-*ar*, E'ning Stah Noos *an* Stan-*ar*.'

She was given an injection and a sip of water. Her bed was wheeled to the end of the ward and a screen was put round it. In the course of the afternoon the doctor came, stayed behind the screen for a short while and went.

The new ward sister came and looked behind the screen from time to time. Towards five o'clock, when the few visitors were going home, Sister Lucy went behind the screen once more. She spoke to Granny Barnacle, who replied in a weak voice.

'She's conscious,' said Miss Valvona.

'Yes, she spoke.'

'Is she bad?' said Miss Valvona as the sister passed her bed.

'She's not too well,' said the sister.

Some of the patients kept looking expectantly and fearfully at the entrance to the ward whenever anyone was heard approaching, as if watching for the Angel of Death. Towards six o'clock came the sound of a man's footsteps. The patients, propped up with their supper trays, stopped eating and turned to see who had arrived.

Sure enough, it was the priest, carrying a small box. Miss Valvona and Miss Taylor crossed themselves as he passed. He went behind the screen accompanied by a nurse. Though the ward was silent, none of the patients had sharp enough ears, even with their hearing-aids, to catch more than an occasional humming sound from his recitations.

Miss Valvona's tears dropped into her supper. She was thinking of her father's Last Sacrament, after which he had recovered to live a further six months. The priest behind the screen would be committing Granny Barnacle to the sweet Lord, he would be anointing Granny Barnacle's eyes, ears, nose, mouth, hands, and feet, asking pardon for the sins she had committed by sight, by hearing, smell, taste, and speech, by the touch of her hands, and by her very footsteps.

The priest left. A few of the patients finished their supper. Those who did not were coaxed with Ovaltine. At seven the sister took a last look behind the screen before going off to the dining-room.

'How is she now?' said a granny.

'Sleeping nicely.'

About twenty minutes later a nurse looked behind the screen, went inside for a moment, then came out again. The patients watched her leave the ward. There she gave her message to the runner who went to the dining-room and, opening the door, caught the attention of the ward sister. The runner lifted up one finger to signify that one of the sister's patients had died.

It was the third death in the ward since Miss Taylor's admittance. She knew the routine. 'We leave the patient for an hour in respect for the dead,' a nurse had once explained to her, 'but no longer than an hour, because the body begins to set. Then we perform the last offices—that's washing them and making them right for burial.'

At five past nine, by the dim night-lamps of the ward, Granny Barnacle was wheeled away.

'I shan't sleep a wink,' said Mrs. Reewes-Duncan. Many said they would not sleep a wink, but in fact they slept more soundly and exhaustedly that night than on most nights. The ward lay till morning still and soundless, breathing like one body instead of eleven.

*   *   *

The reorganisation of the Maud Long Ward began next day, and all patients declared it a mercy for Granny Barnacle that she had been spared it.

Hitherto, the twelve beds in the Maud Long Ward had occupied only half of the space in the room; they had been a surplus from another, larger, medical ward, comprised mainly of elderly women. The new arrangement was designed to fill up the remaining half of the Maud Long Ward with a further nine elderly patients. These were to be put at the far end. Already, while the preparations were still in progress, this end of the ward was referred to among the nurses as the 'geriatric corner'.

'What's that word mean they keep saying?' Granny Roberts demanded of Miss Taylor.

'It's to do with old age. There must be some very old patients coming in.'

'We supposed to be teenagers, then?'

Granny Valvona said, 'Our new friends will probably be centenarians.'

'I didn't catch—just a minute till I get the trumpet right,' said Granny Roberts, who always referred to her small hearing fixture as the trumpet.

'See,' said Granny Green, 'what they're bringing in to the ward.'

A line of cots was being wheeled up the ward and arranged in the new geriatric corner. These cots were much the same as the other hospital beds, but with the startling difference that they had high railed sides like children's cots.

Granny Valvona crossed herself.

Next, the patients were wheeled in. Perhaps this was not the best introduction of the newcomers to the old established set. Being in varying advanced states of senility, and also being specially upset by the move, the new arrivals were making more noise and dribbling more from the mouth than usual.

Sister Lucy came round the grannies' beds, explaining that they would have to be patient with these advanced cases. Knitting needles must not be left lying about near the geriatric corner, in case any of the newcomers should hurt themselves. The patients were not to be alarmed if anything *funny* should occur. At this point the sister had to call a nurse's attention to one of the new patients, a frail, wizened, but rather pretty little woman, who was trying to climb over the side of her cot. The nurse rushed to settle the old woman back in bed. The patient set up an infant-like wail, yet not entirely that of a child—it was more like that of an old woman copying the cry of an infant.

The sisters continued addressing the grannies in confidential tones. 'You must try to remember,' she said, 'that these cases are very advanced, poor dears. And don't get upset, like good girls. Try and help the nurses by keeping quiet and tidy.'

'We'll soon be senile ourselves at this rate,' said Granny Green.

'Sh-sh,' said the sister. 'We don't use that word. They are geriatric cases.'

When she had gone Granny Duncan said, 'To think that I spent my middle years looking forward to my old age and a rest!'

Another geriatric case was trying to climb over the cot. A nurse bustled to the rescue.

'A mercy,' said Granny Duncan, 'poor Granny Barnacle didn't live to see it. Poor souls—— Don't you be rough with her, Nurse!'

The patient had, in fact, pulled the nurse's cap off and was now clamouring for a drink of water. The nurse replaced her cap, and while another nurse held a plastic beaker of water to the old woman's lips, assured the ward, 'They'll settle down. The moving's upset them.'

After a stormy night, the newcomers did seem quieter next morning, though one or two made a clamour in the ordinary course of conversation, and most, when they were helped out of bed to stand shakily upheld for a moment by the nurse, wet the floor. In the afternoon a specialist lady and an assistant came with draught-boards which she laid on the floor beside four of the new patients who were sitting up in chairs, but whose hands were crippled. They did not protest when their socks and slippers were removed and their feet manipulated and rubbed by the younger woman. Their socks and slippers were replaced and they seemed to know what to do when the draught-boards were set in front of their feet.

'Look, did you ever,' said Granny Valvona. 'They're playing draughts with their feet.'

'I ask you,' said Granny Roberts, 'is it a bloody circus we are here?'

'That's nothing to what you'll see in geriatrics,' said the nurse proudly.

'A blessing poor Granny Barnacle wasn't spared to see it.'

Miss Taylor absorbed as much of the new experience as she could, for the sake of Alec Warner. But the death of Granny

Barnacle, her own arthritic pains, and the noisy intrusion of the senile cases, had confused her. She was crying towards the end of the day, and worried lest the nurse should catch her at it, and perhaps report her too sick to be wheeled down next morning to the Mass which she and Miss Valvona had requested for the soul of Granny Barnacle who had no relatives to mourn her.

Miss Taylor dropped asleep, and waking in the middle of the night because of her painful limbs, still pretended to sleep on, and went without her injection. At eleven o'clock next morning Miss Valvona and Miss Taylor were wheeled into the hospital chapel. They were accompanied by three other grannies, not Catholics, from the Maud Long Ward who had been attached to Granny Barnacle in various ways, including those of love, scorn, resentment, and pity.

During the course of the Mass an irrational idea streaked through Miss Taylor's mind. She dismissed it and concentrated on her prayers. But this irrational idea, which related to the identity of Dame Lettie's tormentor, was to return to her later again and again.

Chapter Ten

'Is that Mr. Godfrey Colston?' said the man on the telephone.

'Yes, speaking.'

'Remember you must die,' said the man.

'Dame Lettie is not here,' he said, being flustered. 'Who is that speaking?'

'The message is for you, Mr. Colston.'

'Who is speaking?'

The man had hung up.

Though Godfrey was still tall, he had seemed to shrink during the winter to an extent that an actual tape-measure would perhaps not confirm. His bones were larger than ever; that is to say, they remained the same size as they had been throughout his adult life, but the ligaments between them had gradually shrunk, as they do with advancing age, so that the bones appeared huge-grown. This process had, in Godfrey, increased rapidly in the months between the autumn of Mrs. Pettigrew's joining his household and the March morning when he received the tele-phone call.

He put down the receiver and walked with short steps into the library. Mrs Pettigrew followed him. She herself was looking healthier and not much older.

'Who was that on the phone, Godfrey?' she said.

'A man . . . I can't understand. It should have been for Lettie but he definitely said it was for me. I thought the message——'

'What did he say?'

'That thing he says to Lettie. But he said "Mr Colston, it's for you, Mr. Colston." I don't understand. . . .'

'Look here,' said Mrs. Pettigrew, 'let's pull ourselves to-gether, shall we?'

'Have you got the key of the sideboard on you?'

'I have,' said Mabel Pettigrew. 'Want a drink?'

'I feel I need a little——'

'I'll bring one in to you. Sit down.'

'A stiff one.'

'Sit down. There's a boy.'

She came back, spritely in her black dress and the new white-streaked lock of hair among the very black, sweeping from her brow. Her hair had been cut shorter. She had painted her nails pink and wore two large rings which gave an appear-ance of opulent ancient majesty to the long wrinkled hand which held Godfrey's glass of brandy and soda.

'Thanks,' said Godfrey, taking the glass. 'Many thanks.' He sat back and drank his brandy, looking at her from time to time as if to see what she was going to do and say.

She sat opposite him. She said nothing till he had finished. Then she said, 'Now, look.'

She said, 'Now, look. This is all imagination.'

He muttered something about being in charge of his faculties.

'In that case,' she said—'in *that* case, have you seen your lawyer yet?'

He muttered something about next week.

'You have an appointment with him,' she said, 'this afternoon.'

'This afternoon? Who—how . . .?'

'I've made an appointment for you to see him at three this afternoon.'

'Not this afternoon,' said Godfrey. 'Don't feel up to it. Draughty office. Next week.'

'You can take a taxi if you don't feel up to driving. It's no distance.'

'Next week,' he shouted, for the brandy had restored him.

However, the effects wore off. At lunch Charmain said,

'Is there anything the matter, Godfrey?'

The telephone rang. Godfrey looked up, startled. He said to Mrs. Pettigrew, 'Don't answer.'

Mrs. Pettigrew merely said, 'I wonder if Mrs. Anthony has heard it? I bet she hasn't.'

Mrs. Anthony's hearing was beginning to fail, and she had obviously not heard the telephone.

Mrs. Pettigrew strode out into the hall and lifted the receiver. She came back presently and addressed Charmian.

'For you,' she said. 'The photographer wants to come tomorrow at four.'

'Very well,' said Charmian.

'I shan't be here, you know, tomorrow afternoon.'

'That's all right,' said Charmian. 'He does not wish to photograph *you*. Say that four o'clock will be splendid.'

While Mrs. Pettigrew went to give the message, Godfrey said, 'Another reporter?'

'No, a photographer.'

'I don't like the idea of all these strangers coming to the house. I had a nasty experience this morning. Put him off.' He rose from his seat and shouted through the door, 'I say, Mrs. Pettigrew, we don't want him coming here. Put him off, will you?'

'Too late,' said Mrs. Pettigrew, resuming her place.

Mrs. Anthony looked round the door.

'Was you wanting something?'

'We did hope,' said Mrs. Pettigrew very loudly, 'to have our meal without interruptions. However, I have answered the telephone.'

'Very good of you, I'm sure,' said Mrs. Anthony, and disappeared.

Godfrey was still protesting about the photographer. 'We'll have to put him off. Too many strangers.'

Charmian said, 'I shall not be here long, Godfrey.'

'Come, come,' said Mrs. Pettigrew. 'You may well last another ten years.'

'Quite,' said Charmian, 'and so I have decided to go away to the nursing home in Surrey, after all. I understand the arrangements there are almost perfect. One has every privacy. Oh, how one comes to appreciate privacy.'

Mrs. Pettigrew lit a cigarette and slowly blew the smoke in Charmian's face.

'No-one's interfering with your privacy,' Godfrey muttered.

'And freedom,' said Charmian. 'I shall have freedom at the nursing home to entertain whom I please. Photographers, strangers——'

'There is no need,' said Godfrey desperately, 'for you to go away to a home now that you are so much improved.'

Mrs. Pettigrew blew more smoke in Charmian's direction.

'Besides,' he said, glancing at Mrs. Pettigrew, 'we can't afford it.'

Charmian was silent, as one who need not reply. Indeed, her books were bringing in money, and her small capital at least was safe from Mrs. Pettigrew. The revival of her novels during the past winter had sharpened her brain. Her memory had improved, and her physical health was better than it had been for years in spite of that attack of bronchitis in January, when a day and a night nurse had been in attendance for a week. However, she still had to move slowly and was prone to kidney trouble.

She looked at Godfrey who was wolfing his rice pudding without, she was sure, noticing what he was eating, and she wondered what was on his mind. She wondered what new torment Mrs. Pettigrew was practising upon him. She wondered how much of his past life Mrs. Pettigrew had discovered, and why he felt it necessary to hush it all up at such costs. She wondered where her own duty to Godfrey lay—where does one's duty as a wife reach its limits? She longed to be away in the nursing home in Surrey, and was surprised at this longing of hers, since all her life she had suffered from apprehensions of being in the power of strangers, and Godfrey had always seemed better than the devil she did not know.

'To move from your home at the age of eighty-seven,' Godfrey was saying in an almost pleading voice, 'might kill you. There is no need.'

Mrs. Pettigrew, having pressed the bell in vain, said, 'Oh, Mrs. Anthony is quite deaf. She must get an Aid,' and went to tell Mrs. Anthony to fetch her tea and Charmian's milk.

When she had gone, Godfrey said,

'I had an unpleasant experience this morning.'

Charmian took refuge in a vague expression. She was terrified lest Godfrey was about to make some embarrassing confession concerning Mrs. Pettigrew.

'Are you listening, Charmian?' said Godfrey.

'Yes, oh yes. Anything you like.'

'There was a telephone call from Lettie's man.'

'Poor Lettie, I wonder he isn't tired of tormenting her.'

'The call was for me. He said, "The message is for you, Mr. Colston." I am not imagining anything, mind you. I heard it with my ears.'

'Really? What message?'

'You *know* what message,' he said.

'Well, I should treat it as it deserves to be treated.'

'What do you mean?'

'Neither more nor less,' said Charmian.

'I'd like to know who the fellow is. I'd like to know why the police haven't got him. It's preposterous, when we pay our rates and taxes, to be threatened like that by a stranger.'

'What did he threaten to do?' said Charmian. 'I thought he merely always said——'

'It's upsetting,' said Godfrey. 'One might easily take a stroke in consequence. If it occurs again I shall write to *The Times*.'

'Why not consult Mrs. Pettigrew?' said Charmian. 'She is a tower of strength.'

Then she felt suddenly sorry for him, huddled among his bones. She left him and climbed the stairs slowly, clinging to the banister, to take her afternoon rest. She considered whether she could bring herself to leave Godfrey in his plight with Mrs. Pettigrew. After all, she herself might have been in an awkward situation, if she had not taken care, long before her old age, to destroy all possibly embarrassing documents. She smiled as she looked at her little bureau with its secretive appearance, in which Mrs. Pettigrew had found no secret, although Charmian knew she had penetrated behind those locks. But Godfrey, after all, was not a clever man.

*   *   *

In the end Godfrey submitted, and agreed to keep the appointment with his lawyer. Mrs. Pettigrew would not absolutely have refused to let him put it off for another day, had she not been frightened by his report of the telephone call. Obviously, his mind was going funny. She had not looked for this. He had better see the lawyer before anyone could say he had been talked into anything.

He got out the car and drove off. About ten minutes later Mrs. Pettigrew got a taxi at the end of the street and followed him. She wanted just to make sure he was at the lawyer's, and she merely intended to drive past the offices to satisfy herself that Godfrey's car was outside.

His car was not outside. She made the driver take her round Sloane Square. There was still no sign of Godfrey's car. She got out and went into a café opposite the offices and sat where she could see him arrive. But by quarter to four there was still no sign of his car. It occurred to her that his memory had escaped him while on his way to the lawyer. He had sometimes remarked that his oculist and his chiropodist were in Chelsea. Perhaps he had gone, by mistake, to have his eyes tested or his feet done. She had trusted his faculties; he had always seemed all right until this morning; but after his silly talk this morning about that phone call anything could happen. It was to be remembered he was nearly eighty-eight.

Or was he cunning? Could the phone call have come from

the lawyer, perhaps to confirm the appointment, and Godfrey have cancelled it? After all, how could he have suddenly gone crazy like his sister without showing preliminary signs? Possibly he had decided to feign feebleness of mind merely to evade his obligations.

Mrs. Pettigrew paid for her coffee, resumed her brown squirrel coat, and set off along the King's Road. She saw no sign of his car outside the chiropodist. Anyway, he had probably gone home. She glanced up a side turning and thought she saw Godfrey's car in the blue half-light parked outside a bombed building. Yes indeed, on investigation, it proved to be Godfrey's Vauxhall.

Mrs. Pettigrew looked expertly around her. The houses opposite the bombed building were all occupied and afforded no concealment. The bombed building itself seemed to demand investigation. She walked up the dusty steps on which strangely there stood a collection of grimy milk bottles. The broken door was partly open. She creaked it further open and looked inside. She could see right through, over the decayed brick and plaster, to the windows at the back of the house. She heard a noise as of rustling paper—or could it be rats? She stepped back and stood once more outside the door considering whether and how long she could bear to stand in that desolate doorway and see, without being seen, from which direction Godfrey should return to his car.

*　　*　　*

Charmian woke at four and sensed the emptiness of the house. Mrs. Anthony now went home at two in the afternoons. Both Godfrey and Mrs. Pettigrew must be out. Charmian lay listening, to confirm her feeling of being alone in the house. She heard no sound. She rose slowly, tidied herself and, groping for one after another banister rail, descended the stairs. She had reached the first half-landing when the telephone rang. She did not hurry, but it was still ringing when she reached it.

'Is that Mrs. Colston?'

'Yes, speaking.'

'Charmian Piper—that's right, isn't it?'

'Yes. Are you a reporter?'

'Remember,' he said, 'you must die.'

'Oh, as to that,' she said, 'for the past thirty years and more I have thought of it from time to time. My memory is failing in certain respects. I am gone eighty-six. But somehow I do not forget my death, whenever that will be.'

'Delighted to hear it,' he said. 'Goodbye for now.'

'Goodbye,' she said. 'What paper do you represent?'

But he had rung off.

Charmian made her way to the library and cautiously built up the fire which had burnt low. The effort of stooping tired her and she sat for a moment in the big chair. After a while it was tea-time. She thought, for a space, about tea. Then she made her way to the kitchen where the tray had been set by Mrs. Anthony in readiness for Mrs. Pettigrew to make the tea. But Mrs. Pettigrew had gone out. Charmian felt overwhelmed suddenly with trepidation and pleasure. Could she make tea herself? Yes, she would try. The kettle was heavy as she held it under the tap. It was heavier still when it was half-filled with water. It rocked in her hand and her skinny, large-freckled wrist ached and wobbled with the strain. At last she had lifted the kettle safely on to the gas ring. She had seen Mrs. Anthony use the automatic lighter. She tried it but could not make it work. Matches. She looked everywhere for matches but could not find any. She went back to the library and took from a jar one of Godfrey's home-made tapers. She stooped dangerously and lit the taper at the fire. Then, cautiously, she bore the little quivering flame to the kitchen, holding it in one shaking hand, and holding that hand with her other hand to keep it as steady as possible. At last the gas was lit under the kettle. Charmian put the teapot on the stove to warm. She then sat down in Mrs. Anthony's chair to wait for the kettle to boil. She felt strong and fearless.

When the kettle had boiled she spooned tea into the pot and knew that the difficult part had come. She lifted the kettle a little and tilted its spout over the tea-pot. She stood as far back as she could. In went the hot water, and though it splashed quite a bit on the stove, she did not get any over her dress or her feet. She bore the tea-pot to the tray. It wafted to and fro, but she managed to place it down gently after all.

She looked at the hot-water jug. Should she bother with hot water? She had done so well up to now, it would be a pity to make any mistake and have an accident. But she felt strong and fearless. A pot of tea without the hot-water jug beside it was nonsense. She filled the jug, this time splashing her foot a little, but not enough to burn.

When all was set on the tray she was tempted to have her tea in the kitchen there in Mrs. Anthony's chair.

But she thought of her bright fire in the library. She looked at the tray. Plainly she could never carry it. She would take in the tea-things one by one, even if it took half-an-hour.

She did this, resting only once between her journeys. First the tea-pot, which she placed on the library hearth. Then the hot-water jug. These were the dangerous objects. Cup and saucer; another cup and saucer in case Godfrey or Mrs. Pettigrew should return and want tea; the buttered scones; jam; two plates, two knives, and two spoons. Another journey for the plate of Garibaldi biscuits which Charmian loved to dip in her tea. She could well remember, as she looked at them, the fuss about Garibaldi in her childhood, and her father's eloquent letters to *The Times* which were read aloud after morning prayers. Three of the Garibaldi biscuits slid off the plate and broke on the floor in the hall. She proceeded with the plate, laid it on a table, and then returned to pick up the broken biscuits, even the crumbs. It would be a pity if anyone said she had been careless. Still, she felt fearless that afternoon. Last of all she went to fetch the tray itself, with its pretty cloth. She stopped to mop up the water she had spilt by the stove. When she had brought everything into the room she closed the door, placed the tray on a low table by her chair and arranged her tea-things neatly upon it. The performance had taken twenty minutes. She dozed with gratitude in her chair for five more minutes, then carefully poured out her tea, splashing very little into the saucer. Even that little she eventually poured back into the cup. All was as usual, save that she was blissfully alone, and the tea was not altogether hot. She started to enjoy her tea.

*   *   *

Mrs. Pettigrew stood under the chipped stucco of the porch and looked at her watch. She could not see the dial in the gloom. She walked down the steps and consulted her watch under a lamp-post. It was twenty to five. She turned to resume her station in the bombed porch. She had mounted two steps, when, from nowhere, a policeman appeared.

'Anything you wanted, Madam?'

'Oh, I'm waiting for a friend.'

He went up the steps and pushing open the creaking door flashed his torch all over the interior, as if expecting her friend to be there. He gave her a curious look and walked away.

Mrs. Pettigrew thought, 'It's too bad, it really is, me being put in a predicament like this, standing in the cold, questioned by policemen; and I'm nearly seventy-four.' Something rustled on the ground behind the door. She looked; she could see nothing. But then she felt something, like the stroke of a hand over her instep. She shuffled backwards, and catching the last glimpse of a rat slithering through the railings down the area, screamed.

The policeman crossed over the street towards her, having apparently been watching her from some doorway on the other side.

'Anything wrong?' he said.

'A rat,' she said, 'ran across my feet.'

'I shouldn't stand here, Madam, please.'

'I'm waiting for my friend. Go away.'

'What's your name, Madam?'

She thought he said, 'What's your game?' and it occurred to her, too, that she probably looked years younger than she thought. 'You can have three guesses,' she replied pertly.

'I must ask you to move along, Madam. Where do you live?'

'Suppose you mind your own business?'

'Got anyone to look after you?' he said; and she realised he had not much underestimated her years, but probably suspected she was dotty.

'I'm waiting for my friend,' she said.

The policeman stood uncertainly before her, considering her face, and possibly what to do about her. There was a slight stir behind the door. Mrs. Pettigrew jumped nervously. 'Oh, is that a rat?'

Just then a car door slammed behind the policeman's bulk.

'That's my friend,' she said, trying to slip past him. 'Let me pass, please.'

The policeman turned to scrutinise the car. Godfrey was already driving off.

'Godfrey! Godfrey!' she called. But he was away.

'Your friend didn't stop long,' he observed.

'I've missed him through you talking to me.'

She started off down the steps.

'Think you'll get home all right?' The policeman seemed relieved to see her moving off.

She did not reply but got a taxi at King's Road, thinking how hard used she was.

Godfrey, on her arrival, was expostulating with Charmian. 'I say you *couldn't* have made the tea and brought it in here. How could you? Mrs. Pettigrew brought in your tea. Now think. You've been dreaming.'

Charmian turned to Mrs. Pettigrew. 'You have been out all afternoon, haven't you, Mrs. Pettigrew?'

'Mabel,' said Mrs. Pettigrew.

'Haven't you, Mabel? I made my tea myself and brought it in. Godfrey won't believe me, he's absurd.'

'I brought in your tea,' said Mrs. Pettigrew, 'before I went out for an airing. I must say I feel the need of it these days since Mrs. Anthony started leaving early.'

'You see what I mean?' said Godfrey to Charmian.

Charmian was silent.

'A whole long story,' said Godfrey, 'about getting up and making your own tea. I knew it was impossible.'

Charmian said, 'I am getting feeble in mind as well as body, Godfrey. I shall go to the nursing home in Surrey. I am quite decided.'

'Perhaps,' said Mrs. Pettigrew, 'that would be the best.'

'There's no need, my dear, for you to go into a home,' said Godfrey. 'No-one is suggesting it. All I was saying——'

'I'm going to bed, Godfrey.'

'Oh, dear, a supper tray,' said Mrs. Pettigrew.

'I don't want supper, thank you,' said Charmian. 'I enjoyed my tea.'

Mrs. Pettigrew moved towards Charmian as if to take her arm.

'I can manage quite well, thank you.'

'Come now, don't get into a tantrum. You must get your beauty sleep for the photographer tomorrow,' said Mrs. Pettigrew.

Charmian made her slow way out of the room and upstairs.

'See the lawyer?' said Mrs. Pettigrew.

'It's damn cold,' said Godfrey.

'You saw the solicitor?'

'No, in fact, he'd been called away on an urgent case. Have to see him some other time. I say I'll see him tomorrow, Mabel.'

'Urgent case,' she said. 'It was the lawyer you had an appointment with, not the doctor. You're worse than Charmian.'

'Yes, yes, Mabel, the lawyer. Don't let Mrs. Anthony hear you.'

'Mrs. Anthony has gone. And, anyway, she's deaf. Where have you been all afternoon?'

'Well, I called in,' he said, 'at the police.'

'What?'

'The police station. Kept me waiting a long time.'

'Look here, Godfrey, you have no evidence against me, you understand? You need proof. Just you try. What did you tell them? Come on, what did you say?'

'Can't remember exact words. Time they did something about it. I said, "My sister has been suffering from this man for over six months." I said, "Now he has started on me," I said, "and it's high time you did something about it," I said. I said——'

'Oh, your phone call. Is that all you have to think about? I ask you, Godfrey, is *that all* . . .?'

He huddled in his chair. 'Damn cold,' he said. 'Have we got any whisky there?'

'No,' she said, 'we haven't.'

He silently opened Charmian's door on his way to bed.

'Still awake?' he said in a whisper.

'Yes,' she said, waking up.

'Feeling all right? Want anything?'

'Nothing, thank you, Godfrey.'

'Don't go to the nursing home,' he said in a whisper.

'Godfrey, I made my own tea this afternoon.'

'All right,' he said, 'you did. But don't go——'

'Godfrey,' she said. 'If you will take my advice you will write to Eric. You will make it up with Eric.'

'Why? What makes you say that?'

But she would not say what made her say this, and he was puzzled by it, for he himself had been thinking of writing to Eric; he was uncertain whether Charmian knew more about him and his plight than he thought, or whether her words represented merely a stray idea.

*   *   *

'You must promise,' said Olive Mannering, 'that this is to be treated as a strictly professional matter.'

'I promise,' said Alec Warner.

'Because,' said Olive, 'it's dangerous stuff, and I got it in strictest confidence. And I wouldn't tell a soul.'

'Nor I,' said Alec.

'It's only for purposes of research,' said Olive.

'Quite.'

'How do you make your notes?' Olive enquired. 'Because there mustn't be names mentioned anywhere.'

'All documents referring to real names are to be destroyed at my death. No-one could possibly identify my case-histories.'

'O.K.,' said Olive. 'Well, goodness, he was in a terrible state this afternoon. I was really sorry for him. It's Mrs. Pettigrew, you see.'

'Suspenders and all that lark?'

'No, oh no. He's finished with that.'

'Blackmail.'

'That's right. She has apparently discovered a lot about his past life.'

'The affair with Lisa Brooke.'

'That and a lot more. Then there was some money scandal at the Colston Breweries which was hushed up at the time. Mrs. Pettigrew knows it all. She got at his private papers.'

'Has he been to the police?'

'No, he's afraid.'

'They would protect him. What is he afraid of? Did you ask?'

'His wife, mostly. He doesn't want his wife to know. It's his pride, I think. Of course, I haven't met her but it sounds to me that she's always been the religious one, and being famous as an author off and on, she gets all the sympathy for being more sensitive than him.'

Alec Warner wrote in his book.

'Charmian,' he remarked, 'would not be put out by anything she learnt about Godfrey. Now, you say he's *afraid* of her knowing?'

'Yes, he is, really.'

'Most people,' he said, 'would say she was afraid of him. He bullies her.'

'Well, I've only heard his side. He looks pretty bad just now.'

'Did you notice the complexion?'

'High-coloured. Goodness, he's lost weight.'

'Stooping more?'

'Oh, much more. The stuffing's knocked out of him. Mrs. Pettigrew keeps the whisky locked up.'

Alec made a note. 'Do him good in the long run,' he commented. 'He drank too much for his age. What is he going to do about Mrs. Pettigrew?'

'Well, he pays up. But she keeps demanding more. He hates paying up. And the latest thing, she wants him to make a new will in her favour. He was supposed to be at the lawyer's today, but he called in on me instead. He thought I might persuade Eric to come and frighten her. He says Eric wouldn't lose by it. But as you know, Eric feels very bitter about his family, and he's jealous of his mother, especially since her novels were in print again, and the fact is, Eric is entitled to a certain amount, it's only a question of time. . . .'

'Eric,' said Alec, 'is not one of us. Go on about Godfrey.'

'He says he'd like to make it up with Eric. I promised to write to Eric for him, and so I shall, but as I say——'

'Has Mrs. Pettigrew any money of her own?'

'Oh, I don't know. You never know with a woman like that, do you? I don't think she has much, because of something I heard yesterday.'

'What was that?'

'Well,' said Olive, 'I got the story from Ronald Sidebottome, he called yesterday. I didn't get it from Godfrey.'

'What was the story?' said Alec. 'You know, Olive, I always pay extra if it entails an extra interview on your part.'

'O.K.,' said Olive, 'keep your hair on. I just wanted you to know this makes another item.'

Alec smiled at her like an uncle.

'Ronald Sidebottome,' she said, 'has finally decided not to contest Lisa Brooke's will now that Tempest is dead. The case was really Tempest's idea. He said the whole thing would have been very distasteful. All about Lisa's marriage with Guy Leet not being consummated. Mrs. Pettigrew is awfully angry about the case being withdrawn, because she was working in with the Sidebottomes when Tempest died. And she hasn't managed to get her hold on Ronald, though she's been trying hard all winter. Ronald is a very independent type at heart. You don't know old Ronald. He's deaf, I admit, but——'

'I have known Ronald over forty years. How interesting he should strike you as an independent type.'

'He has a nice way with him on the quiet,' she said. She had met Ronald Sidebottome while strolling round a picture gallery with her grandfather shortly after Tempest's death, and had brought the two old men back to supper. 'But if you've known Ronald for forty years, then you don't want to hear any more from me.'

'My dear, I have known Ronald over forty years but I can't know him as you do.'

'He hates Mrs. Pettigrew,' Olive observed with an inward-musing smile. 'She won't get much of Lisa's bequest. All she has so far is Lisa's squirrel coat, that's all.'

'Does she think of contesting the will on her own account?'

'No, she's been advised her case is too weak. Mrs. Brooke paid her adequately all the time; there's no case. Anyway, I don't think she has the capital to finance it. She was depending on the Sidebottomes. Of course, under the will, the money goes to her when Guy Leet dies. But he's telling everyone how fit he feels. So you can be sure Mrs. P. is going to get all she can out of poor old Godfrey.'

Alec Warner finished his notes and closed the book. Olive passed him a drink.

'Poor old Godfrey,' said Olive. 'And he was upset by something else, too. He had an anonymous phone call from that man who worries his sister—or at least he thinks he had. It amounts to the same thing, doesn't it?'

Alec Warner opened his notebook again and got his pen from the pocket of his waistcoat. 'What did the man say?'

'The same thing. "You are going to die" or something.'

'Always be exact. Dame Lettie's man says, "Remember you must die"—was that what Godfrey heard?'

'I think so,' she said. 'This sort of work is very tiring.'

'I know, my dear. It must be. What time of day did he receive this call?'

'The morning. That I do know. He told me it was just after the doctor had left Charmian.'

Alec completed his notes and closed his book once more. He said to Olive, 'Has Guy Leet been informed of the withdrawal of the law-suit?'

'I don't know. The decision was only made yesterday afternoon.'

'Perhaps he does not know yet,' said Alec. 'Lisa's money will make a great difference to a man of Guy's tastes. He has been feeling the pinch lately.'

'He can't have long to live,' said Olive.

'Lisa's money will make his short time pleasanter. I take it this information is not particularly confidential?'

'No,' said Olive, 'only what I told you of Mrs. Pettigrew's hold on Godfrey—that's confidential.'

Alec Warner went home and wrote a letter to Guy Leet:

Dear Guy—I do not know if I am the first to inform you that neither Ronald Sidebottome nor Mrs. Pettigrew are now proceeding with their suit in contest of Lisa's will.

I offer you my congratulations, and trust you will long enjoy your good fortune.

Forgive me for thus attempting to anticipate an official notification. If I have been successful in being the first to convey this news to you, will you kindly oblige me by taking your pulse and your temperature immediately upon reading this letter, and again one hour afterwards, and again the following morning, and inform me of the same, together with your normal pulse-rate and temperature if you know it?

This will be invaluable for my records. I shall be so much obliged.

Yours, Alec Warner.

P.S. Any additional observations as to your reaction to the good news will of course be much appreciated.

Alec Warner went to post the letter and returned to write up his records. Twice, the telephone rang. The first call was from Godfrey Colston, whose record-card, as it happened, Alec held in his hand.

'Oh,' said Godfrey, 'you're in.'

'Yes. Have you been trying to get me?'

'No,' said Godfrey. 'Look here, I want to speak to you. Do you know anyone in the police?'

'Not well,' said Alec, 'since Mortimer retired.'

'Mortimer's no good,' said Godfrey. 'It's about these anonymous calls. Mortimer has been looking into them for months. Now the chap has started on me.'

'I have an hour to spare between nine and ten. Can you come round to the club?'

Alec returned to his notes. The second telephone call came a quarter of an hour later. It was from a man who said, 'Remember you must die.'

'Would you mind repeating that?' said Alec.

The speaker repeated it.

'Thank you,' said Alec, and replaced the receiver a fraction before the other had done so.

He got out his own card and made an entry. Then he made a cross-reference to another card which he duly annotated. Finally he wrote a passage in his diary, ending it with the words, 'Query: mass-hysteria.'

Chapter Eleven

IN the fine new sunshine of April which fell upon her through the window, Emmeline Mortimer adjusted her glasses and smoothed her blouse. She was grateful to be free of her winter jumpers and to wear a blouse and cardigan again.

She decided to sow parsley that morning and perhaps set out the young carnations and the sweet peas. Perhaps Henry would prune the roses. Henry was over the worst, but she must not let him hoe or weed or in any way strain or stoop. She must keep an eye on him without appearing to do so. This evening, when the people had gone he could spray the gooseberries with lime-sulphur in case of mildew and the pears with Bordeaux mixture in case of scab. And the blackcurrants in case of big bud again. There was so much to be done, and Henry must not overdo it. No, he must not spray the pears for he might over-reach and strain himself. The people would certainly exhaust him.

Her hearing was sharp that morning. Henry was moving about briskly upstairs. He was humming. The scent of her hyacinths on the window ledge came in brief irregular waves which she received with a sharp and pleasant pang. She sipped her warm and splendid tea and adjusted the cosy round the pot, keeping it hot for Henry. She touched her glasses into focus and turned to the morning paper.

Henry Mortimer came down in a few moments. His wife turned her head very slightly when he came in and returned to her paper.

He opened the french windows and stood there for a while satisfying his body with the new sun and air and his eyes with his garden. Then he closed the windows and took his place at the table. 'A bit of hoeing today,' he said.

She made no immediate objection, for she must bide her time. Not that Henry was touchy or difficult about his angina. It was more a matter of principle and habit; she had always waited her time before opposing any statement of Henry's.

He gestured with the back of his hand towards the sunny weather. 'What d'you think of it?' he said.

She looked up, smiled, and nodded once. Her face was a network of fine wrinkles except where the skin was stretched across her small sharp bones. Her back was straight, her figure neat, and her movements easy. One half of her mind was busy calculating the number of places she would have to set for the people this afternoon. She was four years older than Henry, who had turned seventy at the beginning of February. His first heart attack had followed soon after, and Henry, half-inclined to envisage his doctor as a personification of his illness, had declared himself much improved since the doctor had ceased to pay regular daily visits. He had been allowed up for afternoons, then for whole days. The doctor had bade him not to worry, always to carry his box of tablets, to stick to his diet, and to avoid any exertion. The doctor had told Emmeline to ring him any time if necessary. And then, to Henry's relief, the doctor had disappeared from the house.

Henry Mortimer, the former Chief Inspector, was long, lean, bald, and spritely. At the sides and back of his head his hair grew thick and grey. His eyebrows were thick and black. It would be accurate to say that his nose and lips were thick, his eyes small and his chin receding into his neck. And yet it would be inaccurate to say he was not a handsome man, such being the power of unity when it exists in a face.

He scraped butter sparingly on his toast in deference to the departed doctor, and remarked to his wife, 'I've got these people coming this afternoon.'

She said, 'There's another bit about them in the paper today.'

And she held her peace for the meantime about his having to take care not to wear himself out with them; for what was the point of his being retired from the Force if he continued to lay himself out on criminal cases?

He stretched out his hand and she put the paper into it. 'Hoax Caller Strikes Again,' he read aloud. Then he read on to himself:

Police are still mystified by continued complaints from a number of elderly people who have been receiving anonymous telephone calls from a male hoax-caller since August last year.

There may be more than one man behind the hoax. Reports on the type of voice vary from 'very young','middle-aged' to 'elderly,' etc.

The voice invariably warns the victim, 'You will die tonight.'

The aged victims' telephones are being tapped by the authorities, and police have requested them to keep the caller in conversation if possible. But this and all other methods of detecting hoax-callers have so far failed, the police admitted yesterday.

It was thought at first that the gang's activities were confined to the Central London area. But a recent report from former critic Mr. Guy Leet, 75, of Stedrost, Surrey, indicates that the net is spreading wider.

Among numerous others previously reported to be recipients of 'the Call' are Dame Lettie Colston, O.B.E., 79, pioneer penal reformer, and her sister-in-law Charmian Piper (Mrs. Godfrey Colston) the novelist, 85, author of *The Seventh Child*, etc.

Dame Lettie told reporters yesterday, 'I am not satisfied that the C.I.D. have taken these incidents seriously enough. I am employing a private agency. I consider it a great pity that flogging has been abolished. This vile creature ought to be taught a lesson.'

Charmian Piper, whose husband Mr. Godfrey Colston, 86, former Chairman of Colston Breweries, is also among the victims of the hoax, said yesterday, 'We are not in the least perturbed by the caller. He is a very civil young man.'

A C.I.D. spokesman said everything possible is being done to discover the offender.

Henry Mortimer put down the paper and took the cup his wife was passing him.

'An extraordinary sort of case,' she said.

'Embarrassing for the police,' he said, 'poor fellows.'

'Oh, they'll get the culprit, won't they?'

'I don't see,' he said, 'how they ever can, all evidence considered.'

'Well, you know the evidence, of course.'

'And considering the evidence,' he said, 'in my opinion the offender is Death himself.'

She was not really surprised to hear him say this. She had followed his mind all through its conforming life and late independence, so that nothing he said could surprise her very much. He had lived to see his children cease to take him seriously—his word carried more force in the outside world. Even his older grandchildren, though they loved him, would never now understand his value to others. He knew this; he did not care. Emmeline could never, however, regard Henry as a dear old thing who had taken to developing a philosophy, as other men, on their retirement, might cultivate a hobby. She did not entirely let her children see how she felt, for she liked to please them and seem solid and practical in their eyes. But she trusted Henry, and she could not help doing so.

She let him busy himself in the garden before she sent him indoors to rest. A few more weeks and he would be watching the post for that particular letter from his old friend in the country inviting him to come for a fortnight's fishing. It seemed miraculous that another spring had begun and that soon Henry would announce, 'I've heard from Harry. The may-fly's on the river. I'd better be off day after tomorrow.' Then she would be alone for a while, or perhaps one of the girls would come to stay after Easter and the younger children would roll over and over on the lawn if it was dry enough.

She sowed her parsley, and wondered excitedly what the deputation who were calling to see Henry this afternoon would look like.

*   *   *

The Mortimers' house at Kingston-on-Thames was not difficult to reach, if one followed Henry's directions. However, the deputation had found it a difficult place to find. They arrived shaken in nerve and body, half an hour late, in Godfrey's car and two taxis. In Godfrey's car, besides Godfrey himself, were Charmian, Dame Lettie, and Mrs. Pettigrew. The first taxi bore Alec Warner and Dame Lettie's maid, Gwen. In the second taxi came Janet Sidebottome, that missionary sister of Lisa Brooke; accompanying her were an elderly couple and an aged spinster who were strangers to the rest.

Mrs. Pettigrew, spruce and tailor-made, stepped out first. Henry Mortimer came beaming down the path and shook her hand. Godfrey emerged next, and meantime there was a general exit from the two taxis, and a fussy finding and counting of money for the fares.

Charmian, from the back of Godfrey's car, said, 'Oh, I have so enjoyed the drive. My first this year. The river is splendid today.'

'Wait a minute, wait a minute, Godfrey,' said Dame Lettie who was being pulled out. 'Don't pull me,' She had grown stouter and yet more fragile during the past winter. Her sight was failing, and it was obviously difficult for her to find the kerb with her foot. 'Wait, Godfrey.'

'We're late,' said Godfrey. 'Charmian, sit still, don't move till we've got Lettie out.'

Mrs. Pettigrew took Dame Lettie's other arm while Henry Mortimer stood holding the door. Lettie yanked her arm away from Mrs. Pettigrew, so that her handbag dropped to the pavement and the contents spilled out. The occupants of the taxis rushed to rescue Lettie's belongings, while Lettie herself drew back into the car and sank with a plump sound into her seat.

Young Gwen, whom Dame Lettie had brought as a witness, stood in the gateway and laughed aloud.

Mrs. Mortimer came briskly down the path and addressed

Gwen. 'Look lively, young person,' she said, 'and help your elders instead of standing there laughing.'

Gwen looked surprised and did not move.

'Go and pick up your aunt's belongings,' said Mrs. Mortimer.

Dame Lettie, fearful of losing her maid, called out from the car,

'I'm not her aunt, Mrs. Mortimer. It's all right, Gwen.'

Mrs. Mortimer, who was not normally an irate woman, took Gwen by the shoulders and propelled her over to the little group who were stiffly bending to retrieve the contents of the bag. 'Let the girl pick them up,' she said.

Most of the things were, however, by now collected, and while Alec Warner, directed by Henry Mortimer, stooped to fish with his umbrella under the car for Dame Lettie's spectacle-case, Gwen so far overcame her surprise as to say to Mrs. Mortimer, 'I got nothing to do with *you*.'

'All right, Gwen. It's all right,' said Dame Lettie from the car.

Mrs. Mortimer now kept her peace although it was clear she would have liked to say more to Gwen. She had been troubled, in the first place, by the sight of these infirm and agitated people arriving with such difficulty at her door. Where are their children? she had thought, or their nieces and nephews? Why are they left to their own resources like this?

She edged Gwen aside and reached into the car for Dame Lettie's arm. At the opposite door Henry Mortimer was reaching for Charmian's. Mrs. Mortimer as she assisted Dame Lettie, hoped he would not strain himself, and said to Dame Lettie, 'I see you have brought the spring weather.' As Lettie finally came to rest on the pavement Mrs. Mortimer looked up to see Alec Warner's eyes upon her. She thought: That man is studying me for some reason.

Charmian tottered gaily up the path on Henry Mortimer's arm. He was telling her he had just read, once more, her novel *The Gates of Grandella* in its fine new edition.

'It is over fifty years,' said Charmian, 'since *I* read it.'

'It captures the period,' said Mortimer. 'Oh, it brings everything back. I do recommend you to read it again.'

Charmian slid her eyes flirtatiously towards him—that gesture

which the young reporters who came to see her found so en-
chanting—and said, 'You are too young, Henry, to remember
when the book first came out.'

'No indeed,' he said, 'I was already a police constable. And a
constable never forgets.'

'What a charming house,' said Charmian, and she caught
sight of Godfrey waiting inside the hall, and felt she was, as
always when people made a fuss of her, making him sick.

The conference did not start for some time. Emmeline Mortimer consulted in low tones with the ladies of the deputation
in the hall, whether they would first like to go 'upstairs', or, if
the stairs were too much for them, there was a place downstairs,
straight through the kitchen, turn right. 'Charmian,' said Mrs.
Pettigrew out loud, 'come and make yourself comfortable. I'll
take you. Come along.'

Henry Mortimer piled the men's coats and hats neatly on a
chest, and, having shown the way upstairs to the male candi-
dates, ushered the rest of the men into the dining-room where,
at the long table, bare except for a vase of shining daffodils and,
at the top, a thick file of papers, Gwen was already seated, fum-
ing sulkily to herself.

When Godfrey came in he glanced round at the furnishings
with an enquiring air.

'Is this the right room?' he said.

Alec Warner thought: He is probably looking for signs of a
tea-tray. He probably thinks we are not going to get any tea.

'Yes, I think this is most suitable,' said Henry, as one taking
him into consultation. 'Don't you? We can sit round the table
and talk things over before tea.'

'Oh!' said Godfrey. Alec Warner congratulated himself.

At last they were settled round the table, the three strangers
having been introduced as a Miss Lottinville and a Mr. and Mrs.
Jack Rose. Mrs. Mortimer withdrew and the door clicked behind her like a signal for the start of business. The sunlight fell
mildly upon the table and the people round it, showing up
motes of dust in the air, specks of dust on the clothes of those
who wore black, the wrinkled cheeks and hands of the aged, and
the thick make-up of Gwen.

Charmian, who was enthroned in the most comfortable chair, spoke first, 'What a charming room.'

'It gets the afternoon sun,' Henry said. 'Is it too much for anyone? Charmian—another cushion.'

The three strangers looked uneasily at each other, simply because they were strangers and not, like the others, known to each other for forty, fifty years it might be.

Godfrey moved his arm to shoot back his sleeve, and said, 'This telephone man, Mortimer, I must say, it's a bit thick——'

'I have a copy of your statement here, Colston,' said Henry Mortimer, opening his file. 'I propose to read each one aloud by turn, and you may add any further comments after I have read it. Does that course meet with approval?'

No-one seriously disagreed with that course.

Gwen looked out of the window. Janet Sidebottome fiddled with the electric battery of her elaborate hearing-aid. Mrs. Pettigrew laid her arm on the table and her chin on her hand and looked intense. Charmian sat with her heart-shaped face composed beneath her new blue hat. Alec Warner looked carefully at the strangers, first at Mrs. Rose, then at Mr. Rose, and then at Miss Lottinville. Mrs. Rose had her eyebrows perpetually raised in resignation, furrowing deep lines into her forehead. Mr. Rose held his head sideways; he had enormous shoulders; his large mouth drooped downwards at the same degree of curvature as his chin, cheeks, and nose. The Roses must be nearly eighty, perhaps more. Miss Lottinville looked small and slight and angry. The left side of her mouth and her right eye kept twitching simultaneously.

Henry Mortimer's voice was not too official, but it was firm:

'. . . just after eleven in the morning . . . on three separate occasions. . . . It sounded like that of a common man. The tone was menacing. The words on each occasion were. . . .'

'. . . at various times throughout the day . . . the first occasion was on 12th March. The words were. . . . The tone was strictly factual. . . . He sounded young, like a Teddy-boy. . . .'

'. . . first thing in the morning . . . every week since the end of August last. It was the voice of a cultured, middle-aged man . . . the tone is sinister in the extreme. . . .'

'It was the voice of a very civil young man. . . .' This was Charmian's account. Godfrey broke in. 'How could he be a civil young man saying a thing like that? Use your head, Charmian.'

'He was,' said Charmian, 'most civil on all three occasions.'

'Perhaps,' said Henry, 'if I could continue . . .? Then Charmian can add her comments.'

He finished Charmian's statement. 'That is correct,' said Charmian.

'How could he be *civil*?' said Godfrey.

'Mr. Guy Leet,' Henry announced, taking up the next paper. 'Oh, Guy isn't here, of course——'

'Guy asked me to say,' said Alec, 'we could discuss his case as much as we like so long as we don't discuss his private life up to 1940.'

'Has to get about on two sticks,' commented Godfrey.

'Guy's account,' said Henry, 'is substantially the same as the others, with the most interesting exception that he gets Toll calls from London at between six and seven in the evening when the cheap rate is on. In his opinion the offender is a schoolboy.'

'Nonsense,' said Dame Lettie. 'A middle-aged man.'

'It is simple,' said Henry, 'to trace a Toll call from London to the country. And yet the police have not yet traced any caller to Guy Leet at Stedrost.'

'Quite,' said Dame Lettie. 'The police——'

'However, we will discuss these factors later,' said Henry. 'Next Mr. Ronald Sidebottome—Oh, Ronald's not here either. What's happened to Ronald, Janet?'

'He was a youth—a Teddy-boy, as I've said,' Janet Sidebottome replied.

'Ronald,' roared Godfrey into her ear. 'Why hasn't Ronald turned up? He said he was coming.'

'Oh, Ronald. Well, he was to call for me. I suppose he forgot. It was most annoying. I waited and then I rang him up but he wasn't at home. I really can't answer for Ronald these days. He is never at home.'

Alec Warner took out a small diary and scribbled something in pencil.

'Ronald's statement,' said Mortimer, 'describes the caller as a man well advanced in years with a cracked and rather shaky voice and a suppliant tone.'

'There must be something wrong with his phone,' said Dame Lettie. 'The man's voice is strong and sinister. A man of middle years. You must remember, Henry, that I have had far more experience of the creature than anyone else.'

'Yes, Lettie, my dear, I admit you have been greatly tried. Now Miss Lottinville, your statement. . . . 'At three o'clock in the morning. . . . A foreigner. . . .'

Mrs. Mortimer put her head round the door. 'Tea is ready, Henry, when you are. I have laid it in the breakfast room so that——'

'In five minutes, Emmeline.'

She disappeared and Godfrey looked yearningly after her.

'Finally Mr. Rose,' said Henry: "I received the call at my business premises at twelve noon on two days running . . . the man sounded like an official person . . . late middle age. . . ." '

'That sounds accurate,' said Dame Lettie. 'Only I would describe the voice as *sinister*.'

'Did he have a lisp?' said Godfrey.

'Mr. Rose has not mentioned a lisp in his statement—Had he a lisp, Mr. Rose?' said Henry.

'No, no. Like an official. My wife says an army man, but I would say a government chap.'

Everyone spoke at once.

'Oh no,' said Janet Sidebottome, 'he was——'

'A gang,' said Dame Lettie, 'there must be a gang.'

Miss Lottinville said: 'I assure you, Chief Inspector, he is a man of the Orient, I should say.'

Henry waited for a while till the noise subsided. He said to Mr. Rose, 'Are you satisfied with your account as I have read it?'

'A hundred per cent,' said Mr. Rose.

'Then let's continue the discussion after tea,' said Henry.

Miss Lottinville said: 'You have not read the statement of this lady on my left.' The lady on her left was Mrs. Pettigrew. '*I* haven't had any of your phone calls,' she said. 'I've made no statement.'

Alec Warner wondered, from the vehemence of her tone, if she were lying.

Mrs. Mortimer sat with her silver tea-pot poised at a well-spread table.

'Come and sit by me,' she said kindly to Gwen, 'and you can help to pass the cups.'

Gwen lit a cigarette and sat down sideways at the place indicated.

'Have you been afflicted with these phone calls?' Emmeline Mortimer asked her.

'Me? No, I get wrong numbers.'

Mrs. Pettigrew said confidentially to Mrs. Mortimer: 'I've had no trouble myself from any phone calls. Between ourselves, I think it's all made up. I don't believe a word of what they say. They're trying to draw attention to themselves. Like kids.'

'What a delightful garden,' said Charmian.

*   *   *

They were assembled once more in the dining-room where a fire sparkled weakly in the sunlight.

Henry Mortimer said: 'If I had my life over again I should form the habit of nightly composing myself to thoughts of death. I would practise, as it were, the remembrance of death. There is no other practice which so intensifies life. Death, when it approaches, ought not to take one by surprise. It should be part of the full expectancy of life. Without an ever-present sense of death life is insipid. You might as well live on the whites of eggs.'

Dame Lettie said suddenly and sharply, 'Who is the man, Henry?'

'My dear Lettie. I can't help you there.'

She looked so closely at him, he felt almost that she suspected himself.

'Lettie thinks you are the man,' said Alec wickedly.

'I hardly think,' said Henry, 'Lettie would attribute to me such energy and application as the culprit evidently possesses.'

'All we want,' said Godfrey, 'is to stop him. And to do that we've got to find the man.'

'I consider,' said Janet Sidebottome, 'that what Mr. Mortimer was saying just now about resigning ourselves to death is most uplifting and consoling. The religious point of view is too easily forgotten these days, and I thank you, Mr. Mortimer.'

'Why, thank you, Janet. Perhaps "resigning ourselves to death" doesn't quite convey what I mean. But of course, I don't attempt to express a specifically religious point of view. My observations were merely confined——'

'You sound most religious to me,' said Janet.

'Thank you, Janet.'

'Poor young man,' mused Charmian. 'He may be lonely, and simply wanting to talk to people and so he rings them up.'

'The police, of course, are hopeless. Really, Henry, it is time there was a question in the House,' said Lettie warningly.

'Considering the fairly wide discrepancies in your various reports,' said Henry, 'the police at one stage in their investigations assumed that not one man but a gang was at work. The police have, however, employed every method of detection known to criminology and science, so far without success. Now, one factor is constant in all your reports. The words, "Remember you must die." It is, you know, an excellent thing to remember this, for it is nothing more than the truth. To remember one's death is, in short, a way of life.'

'To come to the point——' said Godfrey.

'Godfrey,' said Charmian, 'I am sure everyone is fascinated by what Henry is saying.'

'Most consoling,' said Janet Sidebottome. 'Do continue, Mr. Mortimer, with your words.'

'Ah yes,' said Miss Lottinville who was also enjoying Henry's philosophising.

And Mrs. Rose, with her longanimous eyes and resignation, nodded her head in sad, wise, and ancient assent.

'Have you considered,' said Alec Warner, 'the possibility of mass hysteria?'

'Making telephones ring?' said Mr. Rose, spreading wide his palms.

'Absurd!' said Dame Lettie. 'We can eliminate mass hysteria.'

'Oh no,' said Mortimer. 'In a case like this we can't eliminate any possibility. That is just our difficulty.'

'Tell me,' Alec asked the Chief Inspector with his piercing look, 'would you describe yourself as a mystic?'

'Never having previously been called upon to describe myself, I really couldn't say.'

'The question is,' said Mr. Rose, 'who's the fellow that's trying to put the fear of God in us?'

'And what's the motive?' said Godfrey. 'That's what I ask.'

'The question of motive may prove to be different in each case, to judge by the evidence before us,' said Mortimer. 'I think we must all realise that the offender is, in each case, whoever we think he is ourselves.'

*   *   *

'Did you tell them,' said Emmeline Mortimer when they had gone, 'what your theory is?'

'No—oh no, my dear. I treated them to brief philosophical sermons instead. It helped to pass the time.'

'Did they like your little sermons?'

'Some of the women did. The young girl seemed less bored than at other times. Lettie objected.'

'Oh, Lettie.'

'She said the whole afternoon had been pointless.'

'How rude. After my lovely tea.'

'It was a lovely tea. It was my part that was pointless. I'm afraid it had to be.'

'How I wish,' said Emmeline, 'you could have told them outright, "Death is the culprit." And I should like to have seen their faces.'

'It's a personal opinion. One can't make up one's mind for others.'

'Can they make up their own minds, then?'

'No. I think I'll go and spray the pears.'

'Now, darling,' said Mrs. Mortimer. 'You know you've done enough for one day. I'm sure it's been quite enough for me.'

'The trouble with these people,' he said, 'they think that the

C.I.D. are God, understanding all mysteries and all knowledge. Whereas we are only policemen.'

He went to read by the fire in the dining-room. Before he sat
down he straightened the chairs round the table and put back
some of them in their places round the wall. He emptied the ash-
trays into the fire. He looked out of the window at the half-light
and hoped for a fine summer. He had not mentioned it to Emmeline yet, but this summer he hoped to sail that yacht of his for
which, in his retirement, he had sacrificed a car. Already he
could feel the bright wet wind about his ears.

The telephone rang. He went out to the hall, answered it.
Within a few seconds he put down the receiver. How strange, he
thought, that mine is always a woman. Everyone else gets a man
on the line to them, but mine is always this woman, gentle-
spoken and respectful.

Chapter Twelve

'I TOLD him straight what I feel,' said Mrs. Pettigrew to Mrs.
Anthony. 'I said, "It's all a lot of rot, Inspector. It started
with Dame Lettie Colston, then Godfrey feels he's got to be in
the picture and one sets off the other. To my dying day I'll swear
it's all make up." But he didn't side with me. Why? I'll tell you
why. He'd be put out of Dame Lettie's will if he agreed it was
all her imagination.'

Mrs. Pettigrew, though she had in fact, one quiet afternoon,
received the anonymous telephone call, had chosen to forget it.
She possessed a strong faculty for simply refusing to admit an
unpleasant situation, and going quite blank where it was concerned. If, for instance, you had asked her whether, eighteen
years before, she had undergone a face-lifting operation, she
would have denied it, and believed the denial, and moreover
would have supplied gratuitously, as a special joke, a list of people
who had 'really' had their faces lifted or undergone other re-
juvenating operations.

And so Mrs. Pettigrew continued to persuade herself she had
not heard the anonymous voice on the telephone; it was not a
plain ignoring of the incident; she omitted even to keep a mental record of it, but put down the receiver and blacked it out
from her life.

'A lot of imagination all round,' said Mrs. Pettigrew.

'Ah well,' said Mrs. Anthony, 'we all got to go some day.
But I shouldn't like to have that chap on the phone to me. I'd
give him something to get along with.'

'There isn't any chap,' said Mrs. Pettigrew. 'You hear what I
say?'

'I got my deaf-aid in, and I hear what you say. No need to
raise your voice.'

Mrs. Pettigrew was overcome by that guilt she felt whenever
she had lowered herself to the intimacy of shouting at Mrs.
Anthony, forgetting to play her cards. By way of recompense
she left the kitchen aloofly, and went to find Godfrey.

He was sitting by the fire, maddeningly, opposite Charmian.

'Please, Godfrey, let us not have all this over again. Ah, it's
you, Mrs. Pettigrew,' said Charmian.

'She is not Taylor,' said Godfrey, with automatic irritability.

'I know it,' said Charmian.

He looked unhappily at Mrs. Pettigrew. There was really no
consolation left in the house for a man. He was all the more
disturbed by Charmian's increasing composure. It was not that
he wished his wife any harm, but his spirits always seemed to
wither in proportion as hers bloomed. He thought, looking at
his wife, It is only for a time, this can't last, she will have a re-
lapse. He felt he was an old man in difficulties. Mrs. Pettigrew
had made another appointment for his lawyer that afternoon. He
did not feel up to keeping it. He supposed he would have to see
the lawyer some time, but that long fruitless going to and from
Kingston yesterday had left him exhausted. And that madman
Mortimer, making a fuss of Charmian—everyone making a fuss
of Charmian, as if she were still somebody and not a helpless
old invalid—roused within him all those resentments of the
long past; so that, having made the mistake of regarding Char-

mian's every success as his failure, now, by force of habit, he could never feel really well unless she were ill.

Charmian was saying to him, 'We did talk over the whole matter quite a lot last night. Let us leave the subject alone. I for one like Henry Mortimer, and I thoroughly enjoyed the drive.'

Mrs Pettigrew, too, was alarmed by this mental recovery of Charmian's, induced apparently by the revival of those old books. In reality it was also, in part, due to an effortful will to resist Mrs. Pettigrew's bullying. Mrs. Pettigrew felt that there might now even be some chance of Charmian's outliving Godfrey. Charmian should be in a home; and would be, if Godfrey were not weak-minded about it, trying to play on his wife's sympathy and keep her with him.

Godfrey looked across the fireplace at his ally and enemy, Charmian, and at Mabel Pettigrew, whom he so tremendously feared, sitting between them, and decided to give Mrs. Pettigrew the slip again this afternoon and go to see Olive.

Mabel Pettigrew thought: I can read him like a book. She had not read a book for over forty years, could never concentrate on reading, but this nevertheless was her thought; and she decided to accompany him to the solicitor.

After Charmian had gone to lie down after lunch Mrs. Pettigrew came in to her.

Charmian opened her eyes. 'I didn't hear you knock, Mabel,' she said.

'No,' said Mrs. Pettigrew. 'You didn't.'

'Always knock,' said Charmian.

'Mrs. Anthony,' said Mrs. Pettigrew, 'is getting too forgetful to manage the cooking. She has left out the salt three days running, as you know. There was a caterpillar cooked in yesterday's greens. She put all that garlic in the sweetbread casserole—said she thought it was celery, well, I mean to say. She boiled Godfrey's egg hard this morning, he couldn't touch it.'

'Keep an eye on her, Mabel. You have little else to do.'

Mrs. Pettigrew's feelings—those which prompted every action—rose to her throat at this independent attitude which Charmian had been gradually accumulating all winter. Mrs.

Pettigrew's breath, as she stood over Charmian's bed, became short and agitated.

'Sit down, Mabel. You are out of breath,' said Charmian.

Mrs. Pettigrew sat down. Charmian watched her, trying to sort out in her mind this new complaint about Mrs. Anthony, and what it could signify, apart from its plain meaning. Her thoughts drifted once more, for reassurance, to the nursing home in Surrey, in the same way that, as she knew, Jean Taylor's thoughts would, in the past, rest on her savings in the bank when from time to time her life with the Colstons had become too oppressive.

Mrs. Pettigrew's breathing was worse. She had been suddenly caught in a gust of resentment which had been stirring within her since Charmian's partial recovery. She felt a sense of great injustice at the evident power Charmian exerted over Godfrey—so strong that she did not seem conscious of it. It was a spell of her personality so mighty that, for fear of his miserable infidelities in Spain and Belgium with Lisa Brooke coming to Charmian's knowledge, he had been, so far, docile before all the threats and deprivations of the past winter. Mabel Pettigrew had only needed to indicate that she was in possession of the full correspondence between Lisa Brooke and Godfrey, dated 1902, 1903, and 1904, and his one immediate idea had been: Charmian must not know. Tell Eric, tell everyone. But keep it from Charmian.

Mrs. Pettigrew was aware that in this he was not displaying any special consideration for Charmian's feelings. That might have been endurable. The real reason was beyond her grasp, yet undeniably present. It was real enough to render Godfrey limp in her hands. What he seemed to fear was some superiority in Charmian and the loss of his pride before her. And, though Mabel Pettigrew indeed was doing better out of Godfrey than she had hoped, she sat in Charmian's bedroom and overwhelmingly resented the inexplicableness of Charmian's power.

'You seem to have a mild touch of asthma ,' Charmian remarked. 'Better keep as still and quiet as possible and presently I will get Godfrey to ring the doctor.'

Mrs. Pettigrew was thinking of that business scandal at Col-

ston Breweries which had been hushed up at the time, the documents of which she now had in her keeping. Now, if Godfrey
had been really frightened about her possible disclosure of these
documents she would have understood him. But all he worried
about was those letters between himself and Lisa Brooke. Charmian must not know. His pride before Charmian, Charmian,
an old wreck like Charmian.

Charmian stretched her hand towards the bell-push by her
bed. 'Godfrey will ring for the doctor,' she said.

'No, no, I'm better now,' said Mrs. Pettigrew, gradually controlling her breath, for she had the self-discipline of a nun
where business was concerned. 'It was just a little turn. Mrs.
Anthony is such a worry.'

Charmian leaned back on her pillow and moved her hand
wearily over her heart-shaped face. 'Have you had asthma
before, Mabel?'

'It is not asthma. It's just a little chest trouble.' Mrs. Pettigrew's face was less alarmingly red. She breathed slowly and
deeply after her ordeal, and lit a cigarette.

'You have great courage, Mabel,' Charmian observed, 'if only
you would employ it to the proper ends. I envy your courage.
I sometimes feel helpless without my friends around me. Very
few of my friends come to see me now. It isn't their fault.
Godfrey did not seem to want them after my stroke. When my
friends were around me every day, what courage I had!'

'You would be better off in the home,' said Mabel Pettigrew.
'You know you would. Lots of company, your friends might
even come and visit you sometimes.'

'It's true I would prefer to be in the nursing home. However,'
said Charmian, 'Godfrey needs me here.'

'That's where you're wrong,' said Mrs. Pettigrew.

Charmian wondered, once more, which of Godfrey's secrets
the woman could have got hold of. The Colston Brewery affair?
Or merely one or more of his numerous infidelities? Of course,
one was always obliged to appear to know nothing where a man
like Godfrey was concerned. His pride. It had been the only
way to live reasonably with him. For a moment, she was
tempted to go to Godfrey and say, 'There is nothing you can

tell me about your past life which would move me in the slightest. I know most of your supposed secrets, and what I do not know would still not surprise me.'

But she did not possess the courage to do this. He might—he would certainly—turn on her. He would never forgive her for having played this game, for over fifty years, of knowing nothing while at the same time knowing everything, as one might be 'not at home' while actually in the house. What new tyranny might he not exert to punish her knowledge?

And the simple idea of *facing* each other with such a statement between them was terrible. This should have been done years ago. And yet, it should not have been done. There was altogether too much candour in married life; it was an indelicate modern idea, and frequently led to upsets in a household, if not divorce . . .

And she, too, had her pride to consider. Her mind munched over the humiliations she had received from Godfrey. Never had she won a little praise or recognition but she had paid for it by some bitter, petty, disruptive action of Godfrey's.

But I could sacrifice my pride, she thought, in order to release him. It is a matter of courage. The most I can do is to stay on here at home with him. She envied Mrs. Pettigrew her courage.

Mrs. Pettigrew rose and came to stand by her bed.

'You're more of a hindrance to Godfrey here than you would be in a nursing home. It's ridiculous to say he needs you.'

'I shall not go,' said Charmian. 'Now I think I must have my nap. What is the time?'

'I came,' said Mrs. Pettigrew, 'to tell you about Mrs. Anthony. She can't do the cooking any more, we shall all have stomach trouble. I will have to take over the meals. And besides, this cold supper she leaves for us at night is not satisfactory. It doesn't agree with me, going to bed on a cold supper. I will have to take over the cooking.'

'That is very good of you,' murmured Charmian, calculating meanwhile what was behind all this, since, with Mrs. Pettigrew, something always seemed to be behind her statements.

'Otherwise,' said Mrs. Pettigrew, 'one of us might be poisoned.'

'Well, really!' said Charmian.

'*Poisoned*,' said Mrs. Pettigrew. 'Poison is so easy. Think it over.'

She left the room.

Charmian was frightened, and at the same time a long-latent faculty stirred in her mind to assess the cheap melodrama of Mrs. Pettigrew's words. But Charmian's fear predominated in the end, and, as she lay fearfully in her bed, she knew she would not put it past Mrs. Pettigrew to poison her once she took control of the food. A poisoning was not easy to accomplish, but still Mrs. Pettigrew might know of undetectable methods. Charmian thought on and on, and frightened herself more and more. Another woman, she thought, would be able to go to her husband and say 'Our housekeeper is threatening to poison me'—or to insist on an investigation by her friends, her son, the doctor. But Godfrey was craven, Eric was hostile, the doctor would attempt to soothe her down, assuming she had started to entertain those wild suspicions of the aged.

Then it is settled, Charmian thought. This is the point where my long, long duty to Godfrey comes to an end. I shall go to the nursing home.

The decision gave her a sense of latitude and relief. In the nursing home she could be a real person again, as she had been yesterday with Henry Mortimer, instead of a frightened invalid. She needed respect and attention. Perhaps she would have visitors. There, she could invite those whom she was prevented from seeing here at home through Godfrey's rudeness. The nursing home was not far from Stedrost. Perhaps Guy Leet would be driven over to see her. Guy Leet was amusing.

She heard the front door slam and then the slam of the car door. Mrs. Pettigrew's footsteps followed immediately, clicking towards the front door. Charmian heard her open the door and call, 'Godfrey, I'm coming with you. Wait.' But the car had already started and Godfrey was gone. Mrs. Pettigrew slammed the door shut once more and went to her room. A few minutes later she had descended the stairs and left the house.

*   *   *

Mrs. Pettigrew had informed Godfrey of her intention to accompany him to his solicitor. When she found he had once more given her the slip she felt pretty sure he had no intention of keeping his appointment with the lawyer. Within a few moments she had put on her hat and coat and marched up the road to find a taxi.

First of all she went to the bombed building off the King's Road. There, sure enough, was Godfrey's car. There was, however, no sign of Godfrey. She ordered the taxi to drive round the block in a hope that she would catch Godfrey before he reached his destination, wherever that might be.

Godfrey, meanwhile, was on his way to Olive's flat, about seven minutes' walk for him at his fastest pace. He turned into Tite Street, stooping his head still more than his natural stoop, against a sudden shower of rain. He hoped Olive would have tea ready. He hoped Olive would not have any other visitors today, obliging him to enquire, in that foolish way, for the address of her grandfather. Olive would be in a listening mood, she was a good consoling listener. She would probably have heard from Eric. Godfrey wondered what she had heard from Eric. Olive had promised to write and tell Eric, in strictest confidence, about his difficulties with Mrs. Pettigrew. She had promised to appeal to Eric. Eric would no doubt be only too glad to be on good terms with his parents again. Eric had been a disappointment, but now was his chance to prove himself. Eric would put everything right, and no doubt Olive had heard from Eric.

He reached the area gate and pushed it open. There was an unusual amount of litter down in the area. The dust-bin was crammed full; old shoes, handbags, and belts were sticking out beneath the lid. On the area pavement were scattered newspapers, tins, rusty kitchen utensils, empty bottles of numerous shapes, and a battered lampshade. Godfrey thought: Olive must be having a spring-clean, turning out all her things. Very wasteful and untidy. Always complaining of being hard up; no wonder.

No-one answered his ring. He walked over to the barred window of Olive's front room and it was then he noticed the curtains had gone. He peered in. The room was quite bare.

Must he not have come to the wrong house? He walked up the steps and looked carefully at the number. He walked down the steps again and peered once more into the empty room. Olive had definitely departed. And on realising this his first thought was to leave the vicinity of the house as quickly as possible. There was something mysterious about this. Godfrey could not stand anything mysterious. Olive might be involved in some scandal. She had said nothing, when he had seen her last week, about moving from her flat. As he walked away down Tite Street he feared more and more some swift, sudden scandal, and his one desire was to forget all knowledge of Olive.

He cut along the King's Road, bought an afternoon paper, and turned up the side street where his car was waiting. Before he reached it a taxi drew up beside him. Mrs. Pettigrew got out.

'Oh, there you are,' she said.

He stood with the newspaper hanging from his hand while she paid the taxi, bewildered by guilt. This guilt was the main sensation Mrs. Pettigrew touched off in him. No thought, word, or deed of his life had roused in him any feeling resembling the guilt he experienced as he stood waiting for Mrs. Pettigrew to pay the taxi and turn to ask him, 'Where have you been?'

'Buying the paper,' said Godfrey.

'Did you have to park your car here in order to walk down the road to buy the paper?'

'Wanted a walk,' said Godfrey. 'Bit stiff.'

'You'll be late for your appointment. Hurry up. I told you to wait for me. Why did you go off without me?'

'I forgot,' said Godfrey as he climbed into the car, 'that you wanted to come. I was in a hurry to get to the lawyer's.' She went round to the other side of the car and got in.

'You might have opened the door for me,' she said.

Godfrey did not at first understand what she meant, for he had long since started to use his advanced years as an excuse to omit the mannerly conformities of his younger days, and he was now automatically rude in his gestures as if by long-earned right. He sensed some new frightful upheaval of his habits behind her words, as he drove off fitfully towards Sloane Square.

She lifted the paper and glanced at the front page.

'Ronald,' she said. 'Here's Ronald Sidebottome in the paper. His photo; he's got married. No, don't look. Watch where you're going, we'll have an accident. Mind out—there's the red light.'

They were jerked forward roughly as Godfrey braked for the red light.

'Oh, do be careful,' she said, 'and a little more considerate.'

He looked down at her lap where the paper was lying. Ronald's flabby face beamed up at him. He stood with Olive simpering on his arm, under the headline, 'Widower, 79, weds girl, 24.'

'Olive Mannering!' Godfrey let out.

'Oh, you know her?'

'Grand-daughter of my friend the poet,' Godfrey said.

'The lights, Godfrey,' said Mrs. Pettigrew in a tired tone.

He shot the car forward.

' "Wealthy ex-stockbroker . . ." ' Mrs. Pettigrew read out. 'She knows what she's doing, all right. "Miss Mannering . . . film extra and B.B.C. actress . . . now given up her flat in Tite Street, Chelsea. . . ." ' The jig-saw began to piece itself together in Mrs. Pettigrew's mind. As heart is said to speak unto heart, Mrs. Pettigrew looked at Olive's photograph and understood where Godfrey had been wont to go on those afternoons when he had parked his car outside the bombed building.

'Of course, Godfrey, this will be a blow to you,' she said.

He thought: God, she knows everything. He went up to his solicitor's offices like a lamb, while Mrs. Pettigrew waited in the car below. He did not even attempt to circumvent her wishes, as he had half-hoped to do when finally forced to the alteration of his will. He did not now even think of the idea he had previously dabbled with, of confiding the facts to his lawyer. Mabel Pettigrew knew everything. She could tell Charmian everything. He instructed a new will to be drawn up leaving the minimum required by law to his son, and the bulk to Mrs. Pettigrew, and even most of Charmian's share, should she outlive him, in trust for Mrs. Pettigrew.

'Now,' said the solicitor. 'This might take some time to prepare, of course.'

'It must be done right away,' said Godfrey.

'Would you not like some time, Mr. Colston, to think it over? Mrs. Pettigrew is your housekeeper?'

'It must be done right away,' said Godfrey. 'No delay, if you please.'

'Disgusting,' said Godfrey later that evening to Charmian. 'A man going on eighty marrying a girl of twenty-four. Absolutely disgusting. And he's deaf as a post.'

'Godfrey,' she said, 'I am going to the nursing home on Sunday morning. I have made arrangements with the doctor and the bank. Universal Aunts are coming tomorrow to pack my things. Janet Sidebottome will accompany me. I do not wish to put you out, Godfrey. It might distress you to take me yourself. I am afraid I simply can't stand these anonymous telephone calls any longer. They will bring me speedily to my grave. I must be protected from the sight of the telephone. I have spoken to Lettie, and she approves my decision. Mrs. Pettigrew thinks, too, it will be the best course—don't you, Mabel? Everyone is agreed. I must say, I feel most sad. However, it had to be eventually. You yourself have often said——'

'But you don't mind the telephone calls!' he shouted. 'You don't care about them at all.'

'Oh yes, I do, I do. I can't put up with them any longer.'

'She does mind them,' said Mrs. Pettigrew.

'But you don't need to answer the phone,' he shouted.

'Oh but every time the telephone rings I feel it must be *him*.' Charmian gave a little shudder.

'She feels so bad about the telephone,' said Mrs. Pettigrew.

He knew he could not refute their words.

Chapter Thirteen

'What surprised me, I must confess,' Alec Warner said to Miss Taylor, 'was that, for a moment or two, I felt positively jealous. Olive, of course, was a friendly type of girl, and most conscientious in giving me all the information she could gather. I shall miss her. But the curious thing was this pang, this envy of Ronald, my first reaction to the news. Not that Olive, at any time, would have been my type.'

'Did you make a note of your reaction?'

'Oh, I made a note.'

I bet he did, thought Miss Taylor.

'Oh, I made a note. I always record these surprise deviations from my High Churchmanship.'

His 'High Churchmanship' was a figure of speech he had adopted from Jean Taylor when, at some buoyant time past, she had applied it to him, merely on account of the two occasions when he had darkened the doors of a church, to observe, with awe and curiosity, a vicar of his acquaintance conducting the service of evensong all by himself in the empty building—Alec's awe and curiosity being directed exclusively towards the human specimen with his prayer book and splendid persistence in vital habits.

'Granny Green has gone,' said Miss Taylor.

'Ah yes, I noticed a stranger occupying her bed. Now what was Granny Green?'

'Arterio-sclerosis. It affected her heart in the end.'

'Yes, well, it is said we are all as old as our arteries. Did she make a good death?'

'I don't know.'

'You were asleep at the time,' he said.

'No, I was awake. There was a certain amount of fuss.'

'She didn't have a peaceful end?'

'No, not peaceful for us.'

'I always like to know,' he said, 'whether a death is a good or bad one. Do keep a look-out.'

For a moment she utterly hated him. 'A good death,' she said, 'doesn't reside in the dignity of bearing but in the disposition of the soul.'

Suddenly he hated her. 'Prove it,' he said.

'Disprove it,' she said wearily.

'I'm afraid,' he said, 'I've forgotten to ask how you are keeping. How are you keeping, Jean?'

'A little stronger, but the cataract is a trouble.'

'Charmian is gone to the nursing home in Surrey at last. Would you not like to join her there?'

'Godfrey is left alone with Mrs. Pettigrew, then.'

'You would like to be with Charmian, surely.'

'No,' she said.

He looked round the ward and up to the noisy end. There the senile cases were grouped round the television and so were less noisy than usual, but still emitting, from time to time, a variety of dental and guttural sounds and sometimes a whole, well-intentioned speech. Those who were mobile would occasionally leave their chairs and wander up the ward, waving or talking to the bedridden. One tall patient poured herself a beaker of water and began to raise it to her lips, but forgetting the purpose before the act was accomplished, poured the water into another jug; then she turned the beaker upside down on her head so that a little water, left in the beaker, splashed over her forehead. She seemed pleased with this feat. On the whole, the geriatrics were keen on putting objects on their heads.

'Interesting,' said Alec. 'The interesting thing is, senility is somewhat different from insanity. The actions of these people, for instance, differ in many particulars from those of the aged people whom I visit at St. Aubrey's Home in Folkestone. There, some of the patients have been mad most of their lives. In some ways they are more coherent, much more methodical than those who merely turn strange in their old age. The really mad old people have had more practice in irrational behaviour, of course. But all this,' said Alec, 'cannot be of much interest to you. Unless one is interested in gerontology, I cannot see that their company, day and night, can be pleasant to you.'

'Perhaps I'm a gerontologist at heart. They are harmless. I don't mind them, now. Alec, I am thinking of poor Godfrey Colston. What can have possessed Charmian to go away just when her health was improving?'

'The anonymous telephone calls were worrying her,' she said.

'Oh no. Mrs. Pettigrew must have forced her to go. And Mrs. Pettigrew,' said Miss Taylor, 'will most certainly make Godfrey's remaining years a misery.'

He reached for his hat. 'Think over,' he said, 'the idea of

joining Charmian in the nursing home. It would so please me
if you would.'

'Now Alec, I can't leave my old friends. Miss Valvona, Miss
Duncan——'

'And this?' He nodded towards the senile group.

'That is our memento mori. Like your telephone calls.'

'Goodbye then, Jean.'

'Oh Alec, I wish you wouldn't leave just yet. I have something important to say, if you will just sit still for a moment and
let me get my thoughts in order.'

He sat still. She leaned back on her pillow, removed her
glasses, and dabbed lightly with her handkerchief at one eye
which was inflamed. She replaced her glasses.

'I shall have to think,' she said. 'It involves a question of dates.
I have them in my memory but I shall have to think for a few
minutes. While you are waiting you may care to speak to the
new patient in Granny Green's bed. Her name is Mrs. Bean.
She is ninety-nine and will be a hundred in September.'

He went to speak to Mrs. Bean, tiny among the pillows, her
small toothless mouth open like an 'O', her skin stretched thin
and white over her bones, her huge eye-sockets and eyes in a
fixed infant-like stare, and her sparse white hair short and
straggling over her brow. Her head nodded faintly and con-
tinuously. If she had not been in a female ward, Alec thought,
one might not have been sure whether she was a very old man
or a woman. She reminded him of one of his mental patients
at Folkestone, an old man who, since 1918, had believed he was
God. Alec spoke to Mrs. Bean and received a civil and coherent
answer which came, as it seemed, from a primitive reed instrument in her breast-bone, so thin and high did she breathe, in
and out, when answering him.

He stepped over to Miss Valvona, paid his respects, and heard
from her his horoscope for the day. He nodded to Mrs. Reewes-
Duncan, and waved to various other occupants of the ward
familiar to him. One of the geriatric set came and shook hands
with him and said she was going to the bank, and, having departed from the ward, was escorted back by a nurse who said
to her, 'Now you've been to the bank.'

Alec carefully watched the patient's happy progress back to
the geriatric end, reflected on the frequency with which the
senile babble about the bank, and returned to Jean Taylor who
said:

'You must inform Godfrey Colston that Charmian was un-
faithful to him repeatedly from the year after her marriage. That
is starting in the summer of 1902 when Charmian had a villa
on Lake Geneva, and throughout that year, when Charmian
used often to visit the man at his flat in Hyde Park Gate. And
this went on throughout 1903 and 1904 and also, I recall, when
Charmian was up in Perthshire in the autumn—Godfrey could
not leave London at the time. There were also occasions at
Biarritz and Torquay. Have you got that, Alec? Her lover was
Guy Leet. She continued to see him at his flat in Hyde Park
Gate through most of 1905—up to September. Listen carefully,
Alec, you are to give Godfrey Colston all the facts. Guy Leet.
So she gave him up in the September of 1907, I well remember,
I was with them in the Dolomites, and Charmian became ill
then. You must remember Guy is ten years younger than Charmian. Then in 1926 the affair began again, and it went on for
about eighteen months. That was about the time I met you,
Alec. Guy wanted her to leave Godfrey, and I know she thought
of doing so quite often. But then she knew Guy had so many
other women—Lisa Brooke, of course, and so on. Charmian
couldn't really trust Guy. Charmian missed him, he did so
amuse her. After that she entered the Church. Now I want you
to give these facts to Godfrey. He has never suspected Charmian, she managed everything so well. Have you got a pencil on
you, Alec? Better write it down. First occasion, 1902——'

'You know, Jean,' he said, 'this might be serious for poor
Godfrey and Charmian. I mean, I can't think you really want to
betray Charmian after all those years.'

'I don't want to,' she said, 'but I will, Alec.'

'Godfrey probably knows already,' he said.

'The only people who know about this are Charmian, Guy,
and myself. Lisa Brooke knew, and in fact she blackmailed
Charmian quite cruelly. That was when Charmian had her nervous breakdown. And in fact the main reason Guy married Lisa

was to keep her quiet, and save Charmian from the threat of scandal. It was never a proper marriage, but, however, as I say, Guy did marry Lisa for Charmian's sake. I will say that for him. Of course, Guy Leet did have charm.'

'He still has charm,' said Alec.

'Has he? Well, I don't doubt it. Now, Alec, write this down, will you?'

'Jean, you would regret it.'

'Alec, if you won't give Godfrey this information I shall have to ask Dame Lettie to do so. She would make the matter far more unpleasant for Charmian. I see it is necessary that Godfrey Colston should stop being morally afraid of Charmian—at least it is worth trying. I think, if he knows of Charmian's infidelity, he won't fear any disclosures about his. Let him go and gloat over Charmian. Let him——'

'Charmian will be shocked. She trusts you.' He put the case for the opposition, but she knew he was stirred and excited by her suggestion. He had never, in the past, hesitated to make mischief if it served his curiosity: now he could serve her ends.

'There is a time for loyalty and a time when loyalty comes to an end. Charmian should know that by now,' she said.

He looked at her curiously as if to find in her face something that he had previously overlooked, some latent jealousy.

'The more religious people are, the more perplexing I find them. And I think Charmian would be hurt by your action.'

'Charmian herself is a religious woman.'

'No, only a woman with a religion.' He had always found it odd that Miss Taylor, having entered the Church only to please Charmian, should have become the more addicted of the two.

He made notes of the information Miss Taylor gave to him. 'Make it clear,' she said, 'that this is a message from me. If my hands were in use I would write to him myself. Tell him from me he has nothing to fear from Mrs. Pettigrew. Poor old man.'

'Were you ever jealous of Charmian?' he said.

'Of course I was,' she said, 'from time to time.'

Alec was wondering as he wrote down the details of Charmian's love-affair, if Godfrey Colston would be agreeable to taking his pulse and temperature before and after the telling.

On the whole, he thought not. Guy Leet had been obliging in this respect, but then Guy was a sport. Still, one might try.

* * *

'You know, Taylor,' said Dame Lettie, 'I do not feel I can continue to visit you. These creatures are too disturbing, and now that I am not getting my proper sleep my nerves are not up to these decrepit women here. One wonders, really, what is the purpose of keeping them alive at the country's expense.'

'For my part,' said Miss Taylor, 'I would be glad to be let die in peace. But the doctors would be horrified to hear me say it. They are so proud of their new drugs and new methods of treatment—there is always something new. I sometimes fear, at the present rate of discovery, I shall never die.'

Dame Lettie considered this statement, uncertain whether it was frivolous or not. She shifted bulkily in her chair and considered the statement with a frown and a downward droop of her facial folds.

Miss Taylor supplied obligingly: 'Of course the principle of keeping people alive is always a good one.'

Dame Lettie glanced along the ward at the geriatrics who were, at that moment, fairly docile. One old lady sat up in her cot singing a song or something; a few were being visited by relatives who spoke little but for the most part simply sat out the visiting time with their feeble forebears, occasionally breaking the silence with some piece of family news, spoken loudly into the half-comprehending faces, and accepting with blank calm the response, whether this were a cluck or a crow, or something more substantial. The rest of the geriatric patients were grouped at the television corner, watching and commenting. Really, there was nothing one could complain of in them.

But Lettie had been, in any case, jittery beyond the usual when she arrived. She had not answered Miss Taylor's greeting, but had scraped the bedside chair closer to Miss Taylor and started talking immediately.

'Taylor, we all went to see Mortimer. It was utterly futile——'

'Oh, yes, Mr. Warner told me yesterday——'

'Quite useless. Mortimer is not to be trusted. The police are, of course, shielding him. He must have accomplices—one of them is apparently a young man, another a middle-aged man with a lisp, and then there is a foreigner, and also——'

'Chief Inspector Mortimer,' said Miss Taylor, 'always used to seem to me rather sane.'

'Sane, of course he's sane. I am not saying he isn't sane. I made the great mistake, Taylor, of letting him know I had re-membered him in my will. He always appeared to be so helpful on the committees, so considerate. But I see now, he has been a schemer. He did not expect me to live so long, and he is using these methods to frighten me to death. Of course I have now taken him out of my will, and I took steps to make this fact known to him, hoping his persecution would then cease. But now, in his rage, he has intensified his efforts. The others who received the anonymous calls are merely being used as a blind, a cover, you see, Taylor, a blind. And Eric, I believe, is working in with him. I have written to Eric, but have received no reply, which alone is suspicious. I am their main objective and victim. Now, a further development. A few weeks ago, you remember I arranged to have my telephone disconnected.'

'Oh yes,' said Miss Taylor, closing her eyes to rest them.

'Well, shortly after that, as I was going to bed, I could swear I heard a noise at my bedroom window. As you know, my win-dow looks out on the . . .'

Dame Lettie had, in the past few weeks, got into the habit of searching the house every night before going to bed. One could not be too careful. She searched the house from top to bottom, behind sofas, in cupboards, under beds. And even then there were creaks and unaccountable noises springing up all over the place. This nightly search of the house and the garden took three-quarters of an hour, by the end of which Dame Lettie was in no condition to deal with her maid's hysterics. After a week of this routine Gwen had declared the house to be haunted and Dame Lettie to be a maniac, and had left.

Thus, Dame Lettie was not in the mood for the geriatrics when she visited Miss Taylor in the Maud Long Ward.

'I suppose,' ventured Miss Taylor, 'you have informed the

police of your suspicions. If someone is trying to get into the
house, surely the police——'

'The police,' Dame Lettie explained with long-tried em-
phasis, 'are shielding Mortimer and his accomplices. The police
always stick together. Eric is in with them. They are all in it
together.'

'Perhaps a little rest in a country nursing home would do you
good. All this must be very exhausting.'

'Not me,' said Dame Lettie. 'Oh no, Taylor, no nursing home
for me while I have my faculties and am able to get about on my
feet. I am looking for another maid. An older woman. They are
so difficult to come by, they all want their television.' She
looked over to the senile patients gathered round their television
receiver. 'Such an expense to the country. An abominable invention.'

'Really, in cases like theirs, it is an entirely suitable invention.
It does hold their attention.'

'Taylor, I cannot come here again. It is too distressing.'

'Go away for a holiday, Dame Lettie. Forget about the house
and the phone calls.'

'Even the private detective whom I employed is in league with
Mortimer. Mortimer is behind it all. Eric is . . .'

Miss Taylor dabbed her sore eye under her glasses. She
wanted to close her eyes, and longed for the bell to ring which
marked the end of the visiting hour.

'Mortimer . . . Mortimer . . . Eric,' Dame Lettie was going
on. Miss Taylor felt reckless.

'In my belief,' she said, 'the author of the anonymous telephone calls is Death himself, as you might say. I don't see, Dame
Lettie, what you can do about it. If you don't remember Death,
Death reminds you to do so. And if you can't cope with the
facts the next best thing is to go away for a holiday.'

'You have taken leave of your senses, Taylor,' said Dame
Lettie, 'and I can do no more for you.' She stopped at the outer
office and, demanding to speak to the ward sister, registered her
opinion that Miss Taylor was off her head and should be
watched.

*   *   *

When Gwen had left Dame Lettie's employment she quite understandably told her boy friend all about the nightly goings-on, how the mad Dame would go round the house, poking into all the cupboards and corners, and the garden, poking into the shrubberies with an electric torch, no wonder her eyesight was failing.

'And she wouldn't let me tell the police,' said Gwen. 'She doesn't trust the police. No wonder, they'd have laughed at her. Oh, but it gave me the creeps because when you're looking for noises, you keep hearing them all over the house and you think you see shapes in the darkness, and half the time it was herself I bumped into in the garden. Oh, but that house is just about haunted. I couldn't stand it a minute longer.'

Gwen's boy friend thought it a good story and recounted it at his work which was in a builder's yard.

'My girl was in with an old girl, some dame or countess or other up Hampstead way . . . went round the place every night . . . kept hearing burglars . . . wouldn't get the police . . . My girl walked out on her a week past, too much of it. . . .'

'There's some cranky ones going about,' commented one of his friends, 'I'll tell you. I remember during the war when I was a batman to a colonel, he . . .'

So it was that a labourer, new to the yard, picked up Gwen's story—a youth who would not have considered himself a criminal type, but who knew a window cleaner who would give two or perhaps three pounds an item for likely information. But you had to have an address.

'Where'd you say this countess was living?' he said to Gwen's boy. 'I know all up Hampstead and round the Heath.'

Gwen's boy said, 'Oh, this is a posh part, Hackleton Rise. My girl says the old woman'll be carted off looney in the end. She's one of them, did you see in the papers?—about the phone-call hoax. She's cut off her phone now . . .'

The young labourer took his information to the window cleaner, who did not pay him immediately. 'I got to check the address with my contact.'

The window cleaner himself never actually touched a job like this, but there was money in information. In a few days' time his contact expressed himself satisfied, and paid over ten pounds, remarking that the old girl in question wasn't a countess after all. The window cleaner duly paid a small share to the young labourer remarking that the information was a bit faulty, and that he'd better not be leaky with his mouth the next few days.

So it came about that Dame Lettie's house and nocturnal searchings fell under scrutiny.

On the day of her last visit to Miss Taylor she returned to Hampstead by taxi shortly after five. She called in at the employment agency to see if they had found her a woman yet, a middle-aged woman, clean with good references, to live in. No, they had found no-one yet, Dame Lettie, but they were keeping their eyes open. She walked the rest of the way home.

Gloomily she made a pot of tea and drank a cup standing in the kitchen. She then puffed her way into her study and started writing a letter to Eric. Her fountain-pen ran out of ink. She refilled it and continued,

> . . . I am thinking only of your poor mother put away in a home, & your poor old father who has done so much for you, and who is rapidly failing in health, when I demand that at least you should write & explain your silence. There has been bitterness between your parents and yourself, I know. But the time is come, surely, in their declining years, for you to make what amends you can. Your father was telling me only the other day, that, for his part, he is willing to let bygones be bygones. In fact, he asked me to write to you in this vein.

She stopped and looked out of the window. An unfamiliar car had pulled up at the house opposite. Someone visiting the Dillingers, apparently, not knowing the Dillingers were away. She began to feel chilly and got up to draw the curtain. A man was sitting waiting in the car. As she drew the curtains, he drove off. She returned to her desk and continued,

> Do not suppose I am not aware of your activities in London and your attempts to frighten me. Do not suppose I am in the least alarmed.

She scored these last sentences through with her pen. That was not what she had meant to write. She had, at first, thought of

writing in this manner, but her second thoughts, she now recalled, had decided her to write something more in the nature of
an appeal. One had to employ cunning with a man like Eric. She
took a fresh sheet and began again, stopping once to look over
her shoulder at a potential noise.

> I am thinking only of your poor mother put away in a home,
> & your poor old father, enfeebled and rapidly failing in health,
> when I . . .

She finished the letter, addressed and sealed it, and called Gwen
to catch the six o'clock post. Then she remembered Gwen had
left.

Dame Lettie laid the letter helplessly on the hall table and
pulled herself together so far as to think of supper and to switch
on the news.

She prepared her supper of steamed fish, ate it, and washed
up. She listened to the wireless till half-past nine. Then she
turned it off and went into the hall where she stood for about five
minutes, listening, Eventually, various sounds took place, coming successively from the kitchen quarters, the dining-room on
her right, and upstairs.

She spent the next forty-five minutes in a thorough search of
the house and the garden, front and back. Then she locked and
bolted the front door and the back door. She locked every room
and took away the keys. Finally she climbed slowly up to bed,
stopping every few steps to regain her breath and to listen.
Certainly, there was somebody on the roof.

She locked her bedroom door behind her and tilted a chair
under the door-knob. Certainly, there was someone down there
in the garden. She must get in touch with the Member tomorrow.
He had not replied to her previous letter which she had posted on
Monday, or was it Tuesday? Well, there had been time for a
reply. Corruption in the police force was a serious matter. There
would have to be a question in the House. One was entitled to
one's protection. She put her hand out to feel the heavy walking-
stick securely propped by her bed. She fell asleep at last. She
woke suddenly with the noise in her ears, and after all, was
amazed by the reality of this.

She switched on the light. It was five past two. A man was standing over by her dressing-table, the drawers of which were open and disarranged. He had turned round to face her. Her bedroom door was open. There was a light in the passage and she heard someone else padding along it. She screamed, grabbed her stick, and was attempting to rise from her bed when a man's voice from the passage outside said, 'That's enough, let's go.' The man by the dressing-table hesitated nervily for a moment, then swiftly he was by Lettie's side. She opened wide her mouth and her yellow and brown eyes. He wrenched the stick from the old woman's hand and, with the blunt end of it, battered her to death. It was her eighty-first year.

Chapter Fourteen

FOUR days passed before the milkman reported an accumulation of four pints of milk on Dame Lettie's doorstep, and the police entered her house to find the body, half in, half out of her bed.

Meanwhile Godfrey did not wonder, even vaguely, why he had not heard from Lettie. Now that her telephone was disconnected he seldom heard from her. In any case, he had other things to think about that morning. Alec Warner had been to see him with that extraordinary, disturbing, impudent, yet life-giving message from Taylor. He had, of course, ordered Warner out of the house. Alec had seemed to expect this and had departed with easy promptitude to Godfrey's 'Get out', like an actor who had rehearsed the part. He had, however, left a slip of paper behind him, bearing a series of dates and place-names. Godfrey examined the document and felt unaccountably healthier than he had been for some months. He went out and bought himself a whisky and soda while he decided what to do. And, over his drink, he despised Guy Leet yet liked the thought of him, since he was associated with his new sense of wellbeing. He had another whisky, and chuckled to himself to think of

Guy bent double over his two sticks. An ugly fellow; always had been, the little rotter.

*   *   *

Guy Leet sat in his room at the Old Stable, Stedrost, Surrey, laboriously writing his memoirs which were being published by instalments in a magazine. The laboriousness of the task resided in the physical, not the mental effort. His fingers worked slowly, clutched round the large barrel of his fountain-pen. His fingers were good for perhaps another year—if you could call these twisted, knobble-knuckled members good. He glanced reproachfully at them from time to time—perhaps good for another year, depending on the severity of the intervening winter. How primitive, Guy thought, life becomes in old age, when one may be surrounded by familiar comforts and yet more vulnerable to the action of nature than any young explorer at the Pole. And how simply the physical laws assert themselves, frustrating all one's purposes. Guy suffered from an internal disorder of the knee-joints which caused one leg to collapse across the other whenever he put his weight on it. But although he frequently remarked, 'The law of gravity, the beast,' he was actually quite cheerful most of the time. He also suffered from a muscular rheumatism of the neck which caused his head to be perpetually thrust forward and askew. However, he adapted his eyesight and body as best he could to these defects, looking at everything sideways and getting about with the aid of his servant and his car, or on two sticks. He had in his service a pious, soft-spoken, tip-toeing unmarried middle-aged Irishman for whom Guy felt much affection, and whom he called Tony to his face and Creeping Jesus behind his back.

Tony came in with his morning coffee and the mail, which always arrived late. Tony placed two letters beside the paper-knife. He placed the coffee before Guy. He stroked the fronts of his trousers, wriggled, and beamed. He was doing a Perpetual Novena for Guy's conversion, even though Guy had told him, 'The more you pray for me, Tony, the more I'm a hardened sinner. Or would be, if I had half a chance.'

He opened the larger envelope. Proofs of the latest instalment
of his memoirs. 'Here, Tony,' he said, 'check these proofs.'

'Ah, ye know I can't read without me glasses.'

'That's a euphemism, Tony.' For Tony's reading capacity
was not too good, though he managed when necessary by following each word with his finger.

'Indeed, sir, 'tis a pity.' Tony disappeared.

Guy opened the other letter and gave a smile which might
have appeared sinister to one who did not realise that this was
only another consequence of his neck being twisted. The letter
was from Alec Warner.

Dear Guy,

I'm afraid I sent Percy Mannering the last instalment of
your *memoirs*. He would have seen it in any case. I'm afraid
he is a trifle upset about your further reference to Dowson.

Mannering in replying to thank me for sending him the
article, tells me he is coming down to see you, no doubt to
talk things over. I hope he will not prove too difficult and
that you will make all allowances.

Now, dear fellow, you will, I know, assist me by taking the
old fellow's pulse and temperature as soon as it can con-
veniently be done after he has discussed the article with you.
Preferably, of course, *during* the discussion, but this may prove
difficult. Any further observations as to his colour, speech
(clarity of, etc.) and general bearing *during* the little discussion
will be most welcome, as you know.

Mannering will be with you tomorrow, i.e. the day on which
you will, I expect, receive this letter—at about 3.40 p.m. I
have supplied him with train times and all necessary directions.

My dear Fellow,

I am, most gratefully,

Alec Warner.

Guy put the letter back into its envelope. He telephoned to
the nursing home where Charmian was now resident and asked
if he might call and see her that afternoon, and was informed,
after the nurse had been to make enquiries, that he might. He
then told Tony to have the car ready at three-fifteen.

He had intended to see Charmian, in any case. And today was warm and bright, though clouds came over at intervals. He held no resentment against Alec Warner. The chap was a born mischief-maker; but he didn't know it, that was the saving grace. He was sorry poor Percy would have to undergo the journey for nothing that afternoon.

When he left at a quarter past three he left a message on the door of his Old Stable, 'Away for a few days.' Quite improbable it sounded, but Percy would have to take it or leave it.

'''Tis a lie,' commented Tony, sliding into the car to drive his master off.

*   *   *

Charmian liked her new room. It was large and furnished with bright old-fashioned chintzes. It reminded her of her head-mistress's room at school in those times when the days were always, somehow, sunny, and everyone seemed to love each other. She had been quite eighteen years of age before she had realised that everyone did not love each other; this was a fact which she had always found it difficult to convey to others. 'But surely, Charmian, you must have come across spitefulness and hatred before you were eighteen?'

'Only in retrospect,' she would reply, 'did I discern discord in people's actions. At the time, all seemed harmony. Everyone loved each other.'

Some said she was colouring the past with the rosy glow of nostalgia. But she plainly remembered her shock when, at the age of eighteen, she became conscious of evil—a trifling occasion; her sister had said something detrimental about her—but it was only then that Charmian discovered the reality of words like 'sin' and 'calumny' which she had known, as words, for as long as she could remember.

The window of her room looked out on a lawn in the centre of which stood a great elm. She could sit at her window and watch the other patients walking in the grounds, and they might have been the girls at her old school sauntering at their recreation period, and she with her headmistress taking tea by the window.

'Everything,' she said to Guy some time after he had made his difficult way across the room, 'has an innocent air in this place. I feel almost free from Original Sin.'

'How dull for you, dear,' said Guy.

'It's an illusion, of course.'

A young nurse brought in tea and placed it between them. Guy winked at her. The nurse winked back, and left them.

'Behave yourself, Guy.'

'And how,' he said, 'did you leave Godfrey?'

'Oh, he was most depressed. These anonymous telephone calls worry him.' She gestured towards her white telephone receiver. The civil young man had vaguely assumed in her mind the shape of a telephone receiver. At home he had been black; here he was white. 'Does he worry you, Guy?'

'Me? No. I don't mind a bit of fun.'

'They worry Godfrey. It is surprising how variously people react to the same thing.'

'Personally,' said Guy, 'I tell the young fellow to go to hell.'

'Well, he vexes Godfrey. And then we have an unsuitable housekeeper. She also worries him. Godfrey has a lot of worries. You would see a change in him, Guy. He is failing.'

'Doesn't like this revival of your books?'

'Guy, I don't like talking against Godfrey, you know. But, between ourselves, he *is* rather jealous. At his age, one would have thought he had no more room for these feelings, somehow. But there it is. He was so rude, Guy, to a young critic who came to see me.'

'Fellow has never understood you,' said Guy. 'But still I perceive you have a slight sense of guilt concerning him.'

'Guilt? Oh no, Guy. As I was saying, I feel unusually innocent in this place.'

'Sometimes,' he said, 'a sense of guilt takes a self-righteous turn. I see no cause for you to feel either in the right or in the wrong where Godfrey's concerned.'

'I have regular visits from a priest,' she said, 'and if I want moral advice, Guy, I shall consult him.'

'Oh quite, quite.' Guy placed his gnarled hand on her lap; he was afraid he was forgetting how to handle women.

'And then,' said Charmian, 'you know he has estranged Eric. It is really Godfrey's fault, Guy. I do not like to say these things, and of course Eric was a disappointment, but I can't help feeling Godfrey's attitude——'

'Eric,' said Guy, 'is a man of fifty-five.'

'Fifty-seven,' said Charmian, 'next month.'

'Fifty-seven,' said Guy. 'And he has had time to acquire a sense of responsibility.'

'That,' sighed Charmian, 'Eric has never possessed. But I did think at one time he might have been a painter. I never had much hope of his writing, but his paintings—he did seem to have talent. At least, to me. But Godfrey was so mean about money, and Godfrey——'

'If I remember,' said Guy, 'it was not until Eric was past forty-five that Godfrey refused to give him any more money.'

'And then Lettie,' said Charmian, 'has been so cruel about her wills. Always promising Eric the earth, and then retracting her promises. I don't know why she doesn't do something for Eric while she is still alive.'

'Do you think,' said Guy, 'that money would make Eric any less spiteful?'

'Well, no,' said Charmian, 'I don't. I have been sending Eric sums of money for some years, secretly, through Mrs. Anthony who is our daily woman. But he is still spiteful. Of course he disapproves of my books.'

'They are beautiful books,' said Guy.

'Eric doesn't approve the style. I'm afraid Godfrey has never handled Eric tactfully, that is the trouble.'

'Beautiful,' said Guy. 'I have just been re-reading *The Seventh Child*. I love particularly that scene at the end with Edna in her mackintosh standing at the cliff's edge on that Hebridean coast being drenched by the spray, and her hair blown about her face. And then turning to find Karl by her side. One thing about your lovers, Charmian, they never required any preliminary discussions. They simply looked at each other and *knew*.'

'That,' said Charmian, 'is one of the things Eric cannot stand.'

'Eric is a realist. He has no period-sense, no charity.'

'Oh my dear Guy, do you think these new young men read my books from charity?'

'Not from indulgence and kindness. But charity elevates the mind and governs the inward eye. If a valuable work of art is rediscovered after it has gone out of fashion, that is due to some charity in the discoverer, I believe. But I say, without a period-sense as well, no-one can appreciate your books.'

'Eric has no charity,' she said.

'Well, perhaps it is just that he is middle-aged. The really young are so much pleasanter,' said Guy.

She was not listening. 'He is like Godfrey in so many ways,' she said. 'I can't help remembering how much I had to shut my eyes to in Godfrey. Lipstick on his handkerchiefs——'

'Stop feeling guilty about Godfrey,' Guy said. He had expected a livelier meeting with Charmian. He had never known Charmian to complain so much. He wished he had not enquired after Godfrey in the first place. Her words depressed him. They were like spilt sugar; however much you swept it up some grains would keep grinding under your feet.

'About your novels,' he said. 'The plots are so well-laid. For instance in *The Seventh Child*, although of course one feels that Edna will never marry Gridsworthy, you have this tension between Anthony Garland and Colonel Yeoville, and until of course their relationships to Gabrielle are revealed, there is every likelihood that Edna will marry one or the other. And yet, of course, all along one is aware of a kind of *secret life* within Edna, especially at that moment when she is alone in the garden at Neuflette, and then comes unexpectedly upon Karl and Gabrielle. And then one feels sure she will marry Gridsworthy after all merely for his kindness. And really, right up to the last page one does not know Karl's true feelings. Or rather, one knows them—but does *he* know them? I must admit, although I remembered the story well, I felt the same enormous sense of relief, when I read it again the other day, that Edna did not throw herself over the cliff. The suspense, the plot alone, quite apart from the prose, are superb.'

'And yet,' said Charmian, smiling up at the sky through the window, 'when I was halfway through writing a novel I always got into a muddle and didn't know where it was leading me.'

Guy thought: She is going to say—dear Charmian—she is going to say 'The characters seemed to take on a life of their own.'

'The characters,' said Charmian, 'seemed to take control of my pen after a while. But at first I always got into a tangle. I used to say to myself,

> Oh what a tangled web we weave
> When first we practise to deceive!

Because,' she said, 'the art of fiction is very like the practice of deception.'

'And in life,' he said, 'is the practice of deception in life an art too?'

'In life,' she said, 'everything is different. Everything is in the Providence of God. When I think of my own life . . . Godfrey . . .'

Guy wished he had not introduced the question of life, but had continued discussing her novels. Charmian was upset about Godfrey, that was plain.

'Godfrey has not been to visit me yet. He is to come next week. If he is able. But he is failing. You see, Guy, he is his own worst enemy. He . . .'

How banal and boring, Guy thought, do the most interesting people become when they are touched by a little bit of guilt.

He left at five. Charmian watched him from the window being helped into his car. She was vexed with herself for going on so much about Godfrey. Guy had never been interested in her domestic affairs. He was such an amusing companion. The room, with its chintzes, felt empty.

Guy waved out of his car window, a stiff, difficult wave. It was only then that Charmian noticed the other car which had drawn up while Guy had been helped into his seat. Charmian peered down; it looked like Godfrey's car. It was, and Godfrey was climbing out, in his jerky way. She supposed he had come on an impulse to escape Mrs. Pettigrew. If only he could go to live in a quiet private hotel. But as he walked across the path, she noticed he looked astonishingly bright and healthy. She felt rather tired.

*   *   *

Guy Leet considered, as he was driven home, whether in fact he was enjoying that sense of calm and freedom that is supposed to accompany old age or whether he was not. Yesterday he had been an old, serene man. Today he felt younger and less peaceful. How could one know at any particular moment what one's old age finally amounted to? On the whole, he thought, he must be undergoing the experience of calm and freedom, although it was not like anything he would have anticipated. He was, perhaps, comparatively untroubled and detached, mainly because he became so easily exhausted. He was amazed at Charmian's apparent energy—and she ten years his senior. He supposed he must be a dear old thing. He was fortunate in possessing all his material needs, and now that Lisa's will was being proved, he might possibly spend the winter in a really warm climate. And he had earned Lisa's money. And he bore no grudge against Charmian for her ingratitude. Not many men would have married Lisa simply to keep her quiet for Charmian's sake. Not many would have endured the secrecy of such a marriage, a mere legal bond necessary to Lisa's full sensual enjoyment of her many perversions. 'I've got to be married,' she would say in that hoarse voice, 'my dear, I don't want the man near me, but I've got to know I'm married or I can't enjoy myself.'

Foolishly, they had exchanged letters on the subject, which might have upset his claim on Lisa's money. He did not think Tempest's suit would have succeeded, but it would have been unpleasant. But that eventuality had come to nothing. He would get Lisa's money; he had earned it. He had given satisfaction to Lisa and safety to Charmian.

He doubted if Charmian ever thought with gratitude of his action. Still, he adored Charmian. She had been wonderful, even when he had met her a year ago at a time when her mind was failing. Now that she was so greatly improved, what a pity she had this Godfrey trouble on her mind. However, he adored Charmian for what she had been and what she still really was.

And he had earned Lisa's money. Trinidad might be delightful next winter. Or Barbados. He must write for some information.

When they drew up at the Old Stable Percy Mannering appeared out of the back garden and approached the car waving a magazine in the direction of the front door where Guy's message was pinned up.

'Away for a few days,' shouted Percy.

'I have just returned,' said Guy. 'Tony will give me a hand, and then we will go indoors for a drink. Meanwhile let us not alarm the lilies of the field.'

'Away for a few days,' shouted Percy, 'my foot.'

Tony trotted round the car and took Guy by the arms.

'I've been waiting,' shouted Percy, 'for you.'

Guy, as he was helped to his feet, was trying to recall what exactly he had written about Ernest Dowson in the latest published instalment of his memoirs which so enraged Percy. Guy was not a moment inside the door before he found out, for Percy then started to inform him.

'You quote from the poem about Cynara,

'"I have been faithful to thee, Cynara! in my fashion."

'You then comment, "Yes, that was always Dowson's way, even to the point of dying in the arms of another man's wife— his best friend!"—That's what you wrote, is it not?'

'It must be,' said Guy, sinking into his chair, 'if you say so.'

'And yet you know as well as I do,' shouted Percy, 'that Sherard rescued Dowson from a pub and took him home to be nursed and fed. And Dowson did indeed die in Mrs. Sherard's arms, you utter snake; she was sustaining and comforting him in a sudden last spasm of his consumption. You know that as well as I do. And yet you write as if Dowson and she——'

'I am but a hardened old critic,' said Guy.

Percy banged his fist on the table. 'Critic—— You're an unutterable rat.'

'A hardened old journalist,' said Guy.

'A steaming scorpion. Where is your charity?'

'I know nothing of charity,' said Guy. 'I have never heard of the steaming properties of the scorpion. I never cared for Dowson's verse.'

'You're a blackguard—you've slandered his person. This has nothing to do with verse.'

'What I wrote is the sort of thing, in my opinion, that *might* have happened,' said Guy. 'It is as near enough my meaning.'

'A cheap jibe,' yelled Percy. 'Anything for a cheap joke, you'd say anything——'

'It was quite cheap, I admit,' said Guy. 'I am underpaid for these essays of mine.'

Percy grabbed one of Guy's sticks which were propped beside his chair. Guy grabbed the other stick and, calling out for Tony, looked up with his schoolboy face obliquely at Percy.

'You will write a retraction,' said Percy Mannering with his wolf-like look, 'or I'll knock your mean little brains out.'

Guy aimed weakly with his stick at Percy's stick, and almost succeeded in knocking it out of the old man's quivering hand. Percy adjusted his stick, got it in both hands and with it knocked Guy's stick to the floor, just as Tony came in with a tray and a rattle of glasses.

'Jesus, Mary,' said Tony and put down the tray.

'Tony, will you kindly recover my walking stick from Mr. Mannering.'

Percy Mannering stood fiercely displaying his two greenish teeth and gripping the stick ready to strike, it seemed, anyone.

Tony slithered cautiously round the room until Guy's desk was between him and Percy. He lowered his head, rolled up his eyes, and glared at them from beneath his sandy eyebrows like a bull about to charge, except that he did not really look like a bull. 'Take care what ye do,' he said to them both.

Percy removed one of his hands from the shaking stick and took up the offensive journal. He fluttered this at Tony.

'Your master,' he declared, 'has uttered a damnable lie about a dead friend of mine.'

''Tis within the realm of possibility,' said Tony, clutching the edge of the desk.

'If you will lay a piece of writing paper on the desk, Tony,' said Guy, 'Mr. Mannering wishes to write a letter of protest to the editor of the magazine which he holds in his hand.'

The poet grinned wildly. The telephone, which was on a side table beside Guy's chair, mercifully rang out.

'Come and answer the phone,' said Guy to Tony.

But Tony was looking at Percy Mannering who still clung to the stick.

The telephone rang on.

'If ye will lift the instrument I'll lay out the paper as requested,' said Tony, 'for a man can do but one thing at a time.' He opened a drawer and extracted a sheet of paper.

'Oh, it's you,' Guy was saying. 'Well, now, sonny, I'm busy at the moment. I have a poet friend here with me and we are just about to have a drink.'

Guy heard the clear boyish voice continue: 'Is it Mr. Percy Mannering who's with you?'

'That's right,' said Guy.

'I'd like to talk to him.'

'For you,' said Guy, offering the receiver to Percy.

'Me? Who wants me, what?'

'For you,' said Guy, 'a youngster of school age I should think.'

Percy bawled suspiciously into the telephone, 'Hallo, who's there?'

'Remember you must die,' said a man's voice, not at all that of a young person.

'This is Mannering here. Percy Mannering.'

'That's correct,' said the voice, and rang off.

Percy looked round the room with a bewildered air. 'That's the chap they're talking about,' he said.

'Drinks, Tony,' said Guy.

'That's the man,' roared Percy, his eyes gleaming as with some inner greed.

'Nice youngster, really. I suppose he's been over-working at his exams. The cops will get him, of course.'

'That wasn't a youngster,' said Percy, lifting his drink and draining it off, 'it was a strong mature voice, very noble, like W. B. Yeats.'

'Fill Mr. Mannering's glass, Tony,' said Guy. 'Mr. Mannering will be staying for dinner.'

Percy took his drink, laid down the stick, and sank into a chair.

'What an experience!' he said.

'Intimations of immortality,' commented Guy.

Percy looked at Guy and pointed to the telephone. 'Are you behind this?'

'No,' Guy said.

'No.' The old man drained his glass, looked at the clock and rose from his chair. 'I'll miss my train,' he said.

'Stop the night,' said Guy. 'Do stay.'

Percy walked uncertainly about the room. He picked up the magazine, and said,

'Look here——'

'There is a sheet of paper laid out for you to write your protest to the editor,' Guy said.

'Yes,' said the old man. 'I'll do that tomorrow.'

'There is a passage in *Childe Harold*,' said Guy, 'I would like to discuss with you. It——'

'No-one,' stated Percy, 'in the past fifty years has understood *Childe Harold*. You have to *begin* with the last two cantos, man. That is the SECRET of the poem. The episodes——'

Tony put his head round the door. 'Did ye call me?'

'No, but while you're here, Mr. Mannering will be stopping the night.'

Percy stayed the night and wrote his letter of protest to the editor next morning. He stayed for three weeks during which time he wrote a Shakespearean sonnet entitled 'Memento Mori', the final couplet of the first version being,

> Out of the deep resounds the hollow cry,
> *Remember—oh, remember you must die!*

The second version being,

> But slowly the reverberating sigh
> Sounds in my ear: *Remember you must die!*

The third being,

And from afar the Voices mingle and cry
O mortal Man, *remember you must die!*

and there were many other revisions and versions.

*   *   *

Eric Colston and Mrs. Pettigrew were waiting for Godfrey's return.

'There's something funny going on in the old man's mind today,' Mrs. Pettigrew said. 'I should judge it was something to do with a visit from old Warner this morning. He couldn't have stayed long. I had just gone across the road for cigarettes and when I got back there was Warner on the doorstep. I asked him if he wanted to see Godfrey. He said, "I've seen Godfrey, thanks." But I'll find out what it's all about—you just wait, I'll find out. Then, when I got indoors Godfrey gave me a really wild grin and then *he* went out. I was too late to catch him. He didn't come back to lunch, there's his fish fingers lying on the table. Oh, I'll find out.'

'Has he signed the will yet?' said Eric.

'No, the lawyers are taking their time.'

Eric thought: I'll bet they are taking their time. He had taken the first train to London on receiving that letter from Olive. His first action had been to call on the solicitor. His next was to get in touch with Mrs. Pettigrew.

Mrs. Pettigrew filled Eric's glass. She noticed, as she had done earlier in the day, his little hands, and she felt quite frightened.

Eric was a stocky man, rather resembling his mother in appearance except that the feminine features and build looked odd in him. His hips were broad, his head was large. He had Charmian's wide-spaced eyes, pointed chin, and small neat nose. His mouth was large like that of Dame Lettie whose battered body was later that evening to be discovered.

But, Mrs. Pettigrew told herself, she was experienced with men like Eric. Not that she had ever encountered quite the same details of behaviour in any other man. But she was familiar with the general pattern; she knew he was not normal, for though he greatly desired money he yet seemed willing to sacrifice

quantities of it to gain some more intense and sinuous satisfaction. She had in her life before met men prepared to sacrifice
the prospect of money in order to gain, for instance, a social
ambition.

To that extent she felt she knew her man. She felt it was not
surprising that such a man would sacrifice anything for revenge.
And yet, could she trust him?

'I am doing this,' he told her, 'for moral reasons. I believe—I
firmly believe, it will do the old man good. Teach him a lesson.'

Oh, but Eric was a mess! She looked at his little hands and
the feminine setting of the eyes like Charmian's and felt perhaps
she was foolish to trust him.

*   *   *

Eric was a mess. Olive's letter had told him his father was
being blackmailed by 'a certain Mrs. Pettigrew' into bequeathing a large portion of his fortune to her. Eric had acted promptly
and without a moment's thought. Even in the train up from
Cornwall he had not taken thought but had flirted all the way
with delicious ideas—the discomfiture of Godfrey; the under-
mining of Charmian; the possible sympathetic-bosomed qualities of this Mrs. Pettigrew under her possibly tough exterior;
the thrill of being able to expose everyone to everyone if it
proved expedient to do so; and the thrill of obtaining sufficient
immediate cash to enable him to go and tell his Aunt Lettie
what he really thought of her.

Not that he knew what he thought of her. He retained in his
mind an axiom from his youth: the family had let him down
badly. Everyone, even the family, had agreed upon that in the
years when Eric was between twenty-two and twenty-eight, and
the century was between twenty-three and twenty-nine years
old. He had rejected every idea his family had ever held except
this one idea, 'Somehow or other we have let Eric down. How
did it happen? Poor Eric, Charmian has mothered him too much.
Charmian has not been a mother enough to him. Godfrey has
been too occupied, has never taken any notice of the boy. Godfrey has been too lenient, too strict, too mean, has given him too
much money.' The elders had grown out of these sayings when

the fashion changed, but by then Eric had taken them for his creed. Lettie bore him off on consoling holidays. He robbed her, and the hotel staff got the blame. She tried to get him interested in prison-visiting. He started smuggling letters and tobacco into Wormwood Scrubs. 'Poor Eric, he hasn't had a chance. He should never have been sent to that crank school. How could he ever be expected to pass an exam? I blame Charmian . . . I blame Lettie . . . Godfrey has never cared . . .' He went to an art school and was caught stealing six tubes of paint. They sent him to a Freudian analyst whom he did not like. They sent him to an Adlerian, and subsequently to an individualist. Meanwhile, there was an incident with a junior porter of a club, in the light of which he was sent to another psychiatrist of sympathetic persuasion. He was so far cured that he got one of the maids into trouble. Charmian was received into the Church.

'Eric will grow out of this phase,' said Charmian. 'My grandfather was wild as a youth.'

But Eric was amazed when his elders eventually stopped blaming themselves for his condition. He thought them hypocritical and callous to go back on their words. He longed for them to start discussing him again in the old vein; but by the time he was thirty-seven they had said quite bitter things to him. He had bought a cottage in Cornwall, where he drank their money. He was in a home for inebriates when the war broke out. He emerged to be called up by the military, but was turned down on account of his psychological history. He loathed Charmian, Godfrey, and Lettie. He loathed his cousin Alan who was doing so well as as engineer and who, as a child, had always been considered dull in comparison with Eric. He married a negress and got divorced six months later, a settlement being made on her by Godfrey. From time to time he wrote to Charmian, Godfrey, and Lettie, to tell them that he loathed them. When, in 1947, Godfrey refused him any more money, he made it up with Lettie and obtained small revenues and larger promises from her. But Lettie, when she saw so little return for her cash by way of his company, reduced her bounty to mere talk about her will. Eric wrote a novel, and got it published on the strength of Charmian's name. It bore a similarity to Charmian's writing. 'Poor

Eric,' said Charmian, 'has not much originality. But I do think, Godfrey, now that he is really doing some work, we ought to assist him.' She sent him, over a period of two years, all she possessed. Eric thought her mean, he thought her envious of his novel, and said so. Godfrey refused to write to him. Charmian had confided to Guy Leet, 'I suspect that Godfrey has a secret horror of another novelist in the family.' And she added, what was not strictly true, but was a neat conclusion, 'Of course, Godfrey always wanted Eric to join that dreary firm.'

By the time he was fifty Eric began to display what looked like a mind of his own. That is, instead of sending wild vituperative accusations to his family, he now sent cold reasoned denunciations. He proved, point by point, that they had let him down badly from the time of his first opening his eyes.

'In his middle-age Eric is becoming so like Godfrey,' said Charmian, 'though of course Godfrey does not see it.'

Eric no longer called Charmian's novels lousy muck. He analysed them piece by piece, he ridiculed the spare parts, he demolished the lot. He had some friends who applauded his efforts.

'But he takes my work so seriously,' said Charmian. 'Nobody ever wrote of it like that.'

Charmian's health had failed by the mid-fifties. The revival of her novels astonished Eric, for he had by some fractional oversight misjudged an element in the temper of his age. He canvassed his friends and was angered and bewildered to find so many had fallen for the Charmian Piper period-cult.

Charmian's remittances, smuggled through Mrs. Anthony, were received with silence. His second book had secretly appealed to Dame Lettie. It had been described as 'realistic and brutally frank', but the energy which he might have put into developing his realistic and brutally frank talents was now dispersed in resentment against Charmian. The revival of her novels finished him off and he found he could no longer write.

Even the reports in the papers that Godfrey, Charmian, and Lettie had been recipients of threatening telephone calls failed to stimulate him.

Throughout the war, and since, he had been mainly living on

women of means, the chief of whom had been Lisa Brooke. He had found it hard, after Lisa's death, to replace her. Everyone was hard up, and Eric put on weight with the worry of it all, which did not help. His difficulties were approaching a climax at the moment he had received Olive's letter. 'Your father is being cruelly blackmailed by a certain Mrs. Pettigrew, the housekeeper. I think he would be willing to make up the past differences, if there was anything you could do without letting your mother know. . . .'

He took the first train up to London, in a state of excitement, and spent the journey visualising the possibilities before him.

When he arrived at Paddington at a quarter to six he had no idea what he was going to do. He went into the bar and had a drink. At seven he emerged and saw a telephone box. He telephoned to the home of his father's solicitor, and on the strength of his communication, obtained an interview that evening. He got from the solicitor an assurance that preparations for the new will would be delayed as long as possible. He received some additional advice to which he did not listen.

He went to call on Olive, but found her flat deserted. He stayed the night with some reluctant acquaintances in Notting Hill Gate. At eleven next morning he telephoned to Mrs. Pettigrew and met her for lunch in a café in Kensington.

'I wish you to know, Mrs. Pettigrew,' he said, 'that I'm with you. The old man deserves a lesson. I take the moral point of view, and I'm quite willing to forgo the money.'

'I'm sure,' said Mrs. Pettigrew at first, 'I don't know what you mean, Mr. Eric.' She wiped the corners of her mouth with her handkerchief, pulling her lower lip askew in the process.

'He would die,' said Eric, 'rather than my poor mother got to know about his gross infidelities. And so would I. In fact, Mrs. Pettigrew,' he said with his smile which had long ceased to be winning, 'you have us both in your hands, my father and I.'

Mrs. Pettigrew said, 'I've done a lot for your parents. Your poor mother, before she was taken away, I had to do *everything* for her. There aren't many that would have put up with so much. Your mother was inclined to be—well, you know what old people are. I suppose I'm old myself, but——'

'Not a bit,' said Eric. 'You don't look a day older than sixty.'

'Well, I felt my years while I had your mother to attend to.'

'I'm sure you did. She's impossibly conceited,' said Eric; 'impossible.'

'Quite impossible. And, now, your father——'

'He's impossible,' said Eric, 'an old brute.'

'What exactly,' said Mrs. Pettigrew, 'had you in mind, Mr. Eric?'

'Well, I felt it my duty to stand behind you. And here I am. Money,' he said, 'means hardly anything to me.'

'Ah, you can't go far without money, Mr. Eric——'

'Do call me Eric,' he said.

'Eric,' she said, 'your best friend's your pocket.'

'Well, of course, a little cash at the right time is always useful. At the right time. It's surprising, really, my father has lived so long after the life he's led.'

'Eric, I would never let you go short. I mean, until the time comes. . . .'

'You can always get ready cash out of him?'

'Oh yes.'

Eric thought: I bet you can.

'I think we should see him together,' said Eric.

She looked at his little hands. Can I trust him? she wondered. The will was not yet signed and sealed.

'Trust me,' said Eric. 'Two heads are better than one.'

'I would like to think it over,' she said.

'You would prefer to work alone?'

'Oh, don't say that. I mean, this plan of yours is rather sudden, and I feel, after all I've done for Godfrey and Charmian, I'm entitled to——'

'Perhaps, after all,' said Eric, 'it is my duty to go down to Surrey to see Mother and inform her of her husband's little indiscretions. Distasteful as that course might be, in fact, it might save a lot of trouble. It would take a load off my father's mind, and there would then be no need for you to take any further interest in him. It must be a strain on you.'

She came back on him sharply: 'You don't know the details

of your father's affairs. I do. You have no evidence. I have.
Written proof.'

'Oh yes,' he said, 'I have evidence.'

Is it bluff? she wondered.

'When do you want to come and see him?' she said.

'Now,' he said.

But when they got back, Godfrey was still out. Mrs. Anthony
had left. Mrs. Pettigrew felt quite frightened. And when Eric
started roaming about the house, picking up the china ornaments
and turning them upside down to look at them, she felt quite
vexed. But she held her peace. She felt she knew her man. At
least she ought to, with all her experience.

When he sat down, eventually, in Charmian's old chair, she
ruffled his hair, and said, 'Poor Eric. You've had a raw deal from
them, haven't you?' He leaned his large head against her bosom
and felt quite nice.

After tea Mrs. Pettigrew had a slight attack of asthma and
withdrew to the garden, where she got it under control. On her
return she thought she saw Godfrey in the chair where she had
left Eric. But it was Eric all right. He was asleep, his head lolling
sideways; although in features he most resembled Charmian, he
looked remarkably like Godfrey in this pose.

*   *   *

Charmian's impression of Godfrey's brightness and health,
when she saw him from her window, became more pronounced
when he was shown into her room.

'Cheerful place,' he said, looking round.

'Come and sit down, Godfrey. Guy Leet has just gone. I'm
afraid I'm rather tired.'

'Yes, I saw him leaving.'

'Yes, poor soul. It was kind of him to visit me. He has such
difficulty getting about.'

'So different,' said Godfrey, leaning back in his chair like a
satisfied man, and stretching his legs apart, 'from the way he
got about in the summer of 1902 in the villa on Lake Geneva,
up to 1907 at his flat in Hyde Park Gate, in Scotland and Biarritz and Torquay and then in the Dolomites when you were

taken ill. Then nineteen years later when he was living in Ebury Street, up to the time of——'

'I should like a cigarette,' said Charmian.

'What?' said Godfrey.

'Give me a cigarette, Godfrey, or I shall ring and ask the nurse to fetch one.'

'Look here, Charmian, you'd better stay off cigarettes. I mean——'

'I would like to smoke a cigarette before I die. As to Guy Leet —you yourself, Godfrey, have hardly any room to talk. You yourself. Lisa Brooke. Wendy Loos. Eleanor——'

'The little rotter,' said Godfrey. 'Well, just look what he's come to and only seventy-five. Bent double over two sticks.'

'Jean Taylor must have talked,' she said. She stretched out her hand and said, 'A cigarette, Godfrey.' He gave her one and lit it.

'I'm getting rid of Mrs. Pettigrew,' he said. 'A most domineering bitch. Always upsetting Mrs. Anthony.'

Charmian inhaled her cigarette. 'Any other news?' she said.

'Alec Warner,' he said, 'is losing control of his faculties. He came to see me this morning and wanted me to take my pulse and temperature. I ordered him out of the house.'

Charmian began to laugh, and could not stop, and eventually had to be put to bed, while Godfrey was taken away and given a soft-boiled egg with thin bread and butter, and sent home.

* * *

At eight o'clock they had finished supper. Mrs. Pettigrew said, 'If he isn't home by nine I'd better ring the police. He might have had an accident. That car, it isn't safe. He's a menace on the road.'

'I shouldn't worry,' said Eric, reflecting that, after all, the new will was not signed.

'Oh, I always worry about him,' she said. 'That's what I mean when I say that I'm entitled to. . . .'

Godfrey drove more carefully than usual. Having satisfied himself that Warner's information was accurate he felt that life was worth taking care of. Not that one had doubted Warner's information. Poor Charmian. At any rate, she had no call, now,

to be uppish and righteous. Not that she really had been prig-
gish; but she had always assumed that air of purity which made
one feel such a swine. Poor Charmian; it was very catty of Taylor to gossip about her after all these years. Still, Taylor had
done one a good turn without knowing it. . . .

Here he was at home. A long drive for an old man.

Godfrey came in with his glasses in his hand, rubbing his eyes.

'Where on earth have you been?' said Mrs. Pettigrew. 'Eric
is here to see you.'

'Oh, good evening, Eric,' said Godfrey. 'Have a drink.'

'I've got one,' said Eric.

'I'm keeping quite well, thank you,' said Godfrey, raising his
voice.

'Oh, really?' said Eric.

'Eric wishes to speak to you, Godfrey.'

'Mrs. Pettigrew and I are in this together, Father.'

'In what?'

'The question of the new will. And in the meantime, I expect
to be remunerated according to the situation.'

'You're growing a paunch,' said Godfrey. 'I haven't got a
paunch.'

'Otherwise we shall really have to present Mother with the
facts.'

'Be reasonable, Godfrey,' said Mrs. Pettigrew.

'Get to hell out of my house, Eric,' said Godfrey. 'I give you
ten minutes or I call the police.'

'I think we're a little tired,' said Mrs. Pettigrew, 'aren't we?'

'And you leave tomorrow morning,' he said to her.

The door bell rang.

'Who can that be?' said Mrs. Pettigrew. 'Did you forget to
leave the car lights on, Godfrey?'

Godfrey ignored the bell. 'You can't tell Charmian anything,'
he said, 'that she doesn't know already.'

'What did you say?' said Mrs. Pettigrew.

The door bell rang again.

Godfrey left them and went to open it. Two men stood on
the doorstep.

'Mr. Colston?'

'That's right.'

'Could we have a word with you? It's the C.I.D.'

'The car lights are on,' said Godfrey.

'It's about your sister,' said the senior-looking of the men, 'Dame Lettie Colston, I'm afraid.'

Next day was Sunday. 'Hoax Caller Strikes at Last' declared the headlines. 'Aged Welfare Worker killed in bed. Jewellery and valuables missing.'

Chapter Fifteen

'IF you look for one thing,' said Henry Mortimer to his wife, 'you frequently find another.'

Mrs. Mortimer was opening and closing her mouth like a bird. This was because she was attempting to feed a two-year-old boy with a spoon, and as he opened his mouth to take each spoonful of soft egg, she involuntarily opened hers. This child was her grandson whom she was minding while her daughter was confined with a second child.

Mrs. Mortimer wiped the infant's mouth and pushed a jug of milk out of his reach.

'Look for one thing and you find another,' said Henry Mortimer. 'They found twenty-two different wills among Lettie Colston's papers, dated over the past forty years.'

'Silly woman,' said Emmeline Mortimer, 'to change her mind so often.' She tickled the cheek of her grandson and clucked into his face, and while his mouth was open in laughter she popped in the last spoonful of egg, most of which he spluttered out. 'I was sorry for poor old Godfrey breaking down at the inquest. He must have been fond of his sister,' she said.

She gave the child his mug of milk which he clutched in both hands and drank noisily, his eyes bright above the rim, darting here and there.

When the child was settled in a play-pen in the garden Mrs. Mortimer said to her husband,

'What's that you were saying about poor Lettie Colston's wills?'

'The chaps were checking upon her papers in the course of routine, in case they should provide any clue to the murder, and of course they checked up on all her beneficiaries. Quite a list out of twenty-two consecutive wills.'

'The murderer wasn't known to her, was he?'

'No—oh no, this was before they got him. They were checking up, and . . .'

Dame Lettie's murderer had been caught within three weeks of her death and was now awaiting trial. In those three weeks, however, her papers had been thoroughly examined, and those of the beneficiaries of her twenty-two wills who were still alive had been quietly traced, checked, and dismissed from suspicion. Only one name had proved a very slight puzzle; Lisa O'Brien of Nottingham, whose name appeared in a bequest dated 1918. The records, however, showed that Lisa Brooke, née Sidebottome, aged 33, had married a man named Matthew O'Brien aged 40 at Nottingham in that year. The C.I.D. did not look much further. Lisa O'Brien in the will must be a woman of advanced years by now, and in fact, it emerged that she was dead; O'Brien himself, if still alive, would be beyond the age of the suspect. The police were no longer interested, and ticked the name O'Brien off their list.

Henry Mortimer, however, as one acquainted with the murdered woman and her circle, had been approached, and had undertaken to investigate any possible connection between the murder and the anonymous telephone calls. Not that the police believed these calls had taken place; every possible means of detection had failed, and they had concluded with the support of their psychologists that the old people were suffering from hallucinations.

The public, however, had to be satisfied. Henry Mortimer was placed in charge of this side of the case. The police were able to announce:

The possibility of a connection between the murder and the anonymous telephone calls which the murdered woman was reported to receive from time to time before her death is being investigated.

Mortimer fulfilled his duties carefully. Like his colleagues, he suspected the murderer to be a chance criminal. Like his colleagues, he knew the anonymous voice would never be traced in flesh and blood. Nevertheless, he examined the police documents, and finally sent in a report which enabled the police to issue a further statement:

The authorities are satisfied that there is no connection between the murder of Dame Lettie Colston and the anonymous telephone calls of which she had been complaining some months before her death.

Meantime, however, Henry had noticed the details of Lisa O'Brien, and was interested.

'You look for one thing and you find another,' he had said to himself. For he had never before heard of this marriage of Lisa's. Her first marriage with rich old Brooke had been dissolved in 1912. Her secret marriage with Guy Leet had recently come to light, when Guy had claimed her fortune. But Matthew O'Brien —Henry did not recall any Matthew O'Brien. He must be quite old now, probably dead.

He had requested the C.I.D. to check further on Matthew O'Brien. And they had found him quite quickly, in a mental home in Folkestone where he had been resident for more than forty years.

'And so,' said Mortimer to his wife, 'you look for one thing and you find another.'

'Do Janet and Ronald Sidebottome know anything of this husband?' said Mrs. Mortimer.

'Yes, they remember him quite well. Lisa went touring Canada with him. They didn't hear from her for a year. When she turned up again she told them he had been killed in an accident.'

'How long has he been in this mental home?'

'Since 1919—a few months after their marriage. Janet is going down to identify him tomorrow.'

'That will be difficult after all these years.'

'It is only a formality. The man is undoubtedly Matthew O'Brien whom Lisa Brooke married in 1918.'

'And she said he was dead?'

'Yes, she did.'

'Well, what about Guy Leet? Didn't she marry him? That makes them bigamists, doesn't it?'

'I shouldn't think for a moment Guy knew the man was still alive. Everyone, apparently, believed he was dead.'

'The police won't trouble poor Guy about it?'

'Oh, the police won't bother him now. Especially at his age.'

'What a woman,' said Mrs. Mortimer, 'that Lisa Brooke was. Well, I expect her money—— Oh, what will happen to her money, now? Guy Leet is surely——'

'That's a question, indeed. Lisa's fortune belongs to Matthew O'Brien by rights, sane or insane.'

Henry went out into the garden and said to his squealing grandson,

'What's all this racket going on?' He rolled him over and over on the warm stubbly grass. He picked up the child and threw him into the blue sky and caught him again.

'He'll throw up his breakfast,' remarked Emmeline, who stood with her head on one side, and smiled proudly at the child.

'Up-up-ee,' demanded the child.

Henry rolled him over and over, left him yelling for more, and went indoors to catch Alec Warner on the telephone before he should go out.

'You're interested in the St. Aubrey's Home at Folkestone?' Henry said.

'Yes. But only in the older patients. I've been visiting them on private research for ten years.'

'Do you know a man there called Matthew O'Brien?'

'Matt O'Brien, oh yes, a private patient. A dear old chap, nearly eighty. He's bedridden now. Quite batty, of course, but he always knows me.'

'Were you thinking,' said Henry, 'of going down there any time this week?'

'Well, I only go once a month, as a rule, and I went last week. Is there anything special?'

'Only,' said Henry, 'that Janet Sidebottome has agreed to go down to Folkestone tomorrow to identify Matthew O'Brien. I won't go into details, but if you would care to accompany her, since you are acquainted with the Home, it would be a kindness to Janet who will probably be distressed. Ronald can't go with her, he's in bed with a chill.'

'What has Janet Sidebottome to do with Matt O'Brien?'

'Can you go?' said Henry.

'Yes,' said Alec.

'Then Janet will explain everything. Do you know her number?'

'Yes,' said Alec.

'And one of our men will be there to meet you.'

'A copper?' said Alec.

'A detective,' said Mortimer. 'The affair might be of some incidental interest to you.'

'That's just what I was thinking,' said Alec.

*   *   *

Janet said, 'It is all most distressing. Ronald should have been here to assist me. He met Matthew several times. I can't think why Ronald should have a chill in this fine weather.'

Alec shouted above the rattle of the taxi.

'No need to be distressed. I shall do my best to replace Ronald.'

'Oh, no, don't distress Ronald,' she said. 'I only meant——'

He gave her a smile. She sadly adjusted her hearing equipment, and said, 'My hearing is rather poor.'

'You may not be able to recognise Matt O'Brien,' he articulated. 'He's an old man, and the years of insanity may have changed him beyond recognition. They get drugs, you know, and then the drugs have an effect on the appearance. But don't worry if his features are not familiar to you. I think the authorities already have evidence that he's Lisa's husband. They have Lisa's signature, for instance, from the time of his admission.'

'I will do my best,' said Janet. 'But it is a distressing experience.'

'He is gentle,' shouted Alec. 'He thinks he is God. He has never been violent.'

'I am distressed about my late sister,' Janet said. 'I don't like to admit it, but I must; Lisa was never straight in her dealings. It is a blessing she was never found out in this business.'

'It would have been bigamy,' said Alec.

'It was bigamy,' she said. 'There was no excuse for Lisa, she had every opportunity in life. But it was the same when she was a girl. She caused our dear father a great deal of sorrow. And when Simon Brooke divorced her, there was all that scandal. Scandal was serious in those days.'

'What did you think of Matt O'Brien at the time?'

'Well, he was an Irishman, a lawyer. He talked a great deal, but then he was an Irishman, and he was quite charming. And do you know, when Lisa told me he was dead, I could hardly believe it. He had seemed to me so lively. Of course, we did not suspect the truth. It is very distressing.'

'It will soon be over,' said Alec. 'We shall not be with him for long.'

The interview with Matt O'Brien was soon over. The detective met them in the hall and a nurse took them up to Matt's room where he lay on his pillow among his loose white hair.

'Hallo, Matt,' said Alec, 'I've brought two friends of mine to see you.'

The detective nodded to the old man and stood back discreetly and formally beside the nurse.

Janet approached his bedside and lifted his limp hand in greeting. He raised his other hand in benediction.

The old man moved his pale eyes towards Alec.

'It's you, Alec,' he said in a blurred voice, as if his tongue were in the way.

'I was wondering,' said Alec, 'if you remember a lady called Lisa at all? Lisa Brooke. Lisa Sidebottome.'

'Lisa,' said the old man.

'You don't remember Lisa—a red-haired lady?' said Alec.

'Lisa,' said the old man, looking at Janet.

'No, this isn't Lisa. This is her sister, Janet. She's come to see you.'

The old man was still looking at Janet.

'Don't you remember Lisa?—Well, never mind,' said Alec.

The old man shook his head. 'I recollect all creatures,' he said.

'Lisa died last year,' Alec said. 'I just thought you might know of her.'

'Lisa,' said the old man and looked out at the sky through the window. It was a bright afternoon, but he must have seen a night sky full of stars. 'My stars are shining in the sky,' he said. 'Have I taken her to Myself?'

Janet was served with tea downstairs and invited to put her feet up for a while.

She put away her handkerchief. 'I did not,' she said, 'at first find any resemblance. I thought there must be a mistake. But as he turned his head aside to the window, I saw the profile, I recognised his features quite plainly. Yes, I am sure he is the same Matthew O'Brien. And his manner, too, when he spoke of the stars. . . .'

Alec declined tea. He took a notebook from his pocket and tore a page from it.

'Will you excuse me if I scribble a note to a friend?—I have to catch the post.' He was already scribbling away when Miss Sidebottome gave him leave to do so.

*   *   *

Dear Guy—I believe I shall be the first to give you the following information.

A man named Matthew O'Brien has been discovered, who was already married to Lisa when you married her.

Mortimer will give you the details, which have now been fully established.

As it happened, I have been visiting this man, in the course of research, at St. Aubrey's Home for mental cases, for the past ten years, without suspecting any such association.

I imagine there will be no blame imputed to you. But of course, as your marriage with Lisa was invalid, you will not

now benefit from her estate. Lisa's money, or at least the great
bulk of it, will, of course, go to her legal husband—I fancy it
will be kept in trust for him as he is mentally incapacitated.

Be a good fellow, and, immediately on reading this letter,
take your pulse and temperature, and let me know. . . .

Alec begged an envelope from the receptionist. He slipped
in his note, and addressed and stamped it. He slid the letter into
the post-box in the hall, and returned to comfort Janet.

*   *   *

Alec felt, when he left Janet Sidebottome's hotel after escort-
ing her painfully home, that he had had a fruitful though exhausting day.

Reflecting on Matt O'Brien's frail and sexless flesh and hair on
his pillow, and how the old man had looked back and forth
between Janet and himself, he was reminded of that near-cen-
tenarian, Mrs. Bean, who had replaced Granny Green in the
Maud Long Ward. So different from each other in features, they
yet shared this quality, that one would not know what was their
sex from first impressions. He resolved to make a note of this in
Matt O'Brien's case-history.

He felt suddenly tired and stopped a taxi. As it drove him
home he ruminated on the question why scientific observation
differed from humane observation, and how the same people
observed in these respective senses, actually seemed to be different people. He had to admit that Mrs. Bean, for instance, to
whom he had not paid close attention, had none the less re-
warded him with one of those small points of observation that
frequently escaped him when he was deliberately watching his
object. However, the method he had evolved was, on the whole,
satisfactory.

A fire-engine clanged past. Alec leaned in his corner and
closed his eyes. The taxi turned a corner. Alec shifted his position and looked out into the evening. The taxi was purring along
the Mall towards St. James's Street.

The driver leaned back and opened the communicating
window.

'A fire somewhere round here,' he said.

Alec found himself on the pavement outside his block of chambers, in a crowd. There were policemen everywhere, smoke, people, firemen, water, then suddenly a cry from the crowd and everyone looking up as a burst of flame shot from the top of the building.

Alec pushed through to the inner edge of the crowd. A policeman barred his way with a strong casual arm. 'I live here,' Alec explained. 'Let me pass, please.'

'Can't go in there,' said the policeman. 'Stand back, please.'

'Get back,' shouted the crowd.

Alec said, 'But I live there. My things. Where's the porter?'

'The building is on fire, sir,' said the policeman.

Alec made a rush advance and got past the policeman into the smoke and water at the entrance to the building. Someone hit him on the face. The crowd fell back as a wave of smoke and flame issued from a lower window. Alec stood and looked into the interior while another policeman from the opposite side of the crowd walked over to him.

'Come back,' said the policeman, 'you're obstructing the firemen.'

'My papers are up there,' Alec said.

The policeman took him by the arm and pulled him away. 'There is a cat,' Alec said desperately, 'in my rooms. I can't let pussy burn. Let me dash up and let her out. I'll take the risk.'

The policeman did not reply, but continued to propel Alec away from the fire.

'There's a dog up there. A beautiful husky from a polar expedition,' Alec haggled. 'Top floor, first door.'

'Sorry, too late, guvnor,' said one of the firemen. 'Your dog must have had it by now. The top storey's burnt out.'

One of the residents among the crowd said, 'There are no pets in those flats. Pets are not allowed.'

Alec walked away; he went to his club and booked a room for the night.

Chapter Sixteen

THE summer had passed and it was Granny Bean's birthday for which the ward had been preparing for some days.

There was a huge cake with a hundred candles. Some men from the newspapers came in with their cameras. Others talked a while to Granny Bean, who was propped up in a new blue bed-jacket.

'Yes,' Granny Bean answered them in her far-away flute, 'I've lived a long time.'

'Yes,' said Granny Bean, 'I'm very happy.'

'That's right,' she agreed, 'I seen Queen Victoria once as a girl.'

'What does it feel like to be a hundred, Mrs. Bean?'

'All right,' she said weakly, nodding her head.

'You mustn't tire her,' Sister Lucy who had put on her service medal for the occasion, told the news men.

The men took down notes from the sister. 'Seven children, only one now alive, in Canada. Started life as a seamstress hand at the age of eleven. . . .'

The matron came in at three o'clock and read out the telegram from the Queen. Everyone applauded. Granny Valvona commented, ' ". . . on your hundredth birthday," doesn't sound quite right. Queen Mary always used to say, "on the occasion of your centenary." ' But everyone said it came to the same thing.

The matron stood proxy for Granny Bean in blowing out the candles. She was out of breath by the twenty-third. The nurses took turns to blow out the rest.

They were cutting the cake. One of the news men called, 'Three cheers for Granny Bean.'

The hilarity was dying down and the men had gone by the time the normal visitors started to arrive. Some of the geriatrics were still eating or doing various things with their slice of cake.

Miss Valvona adjusted her glasses and reached for the newspaper. She read out for the third time that day: ' "September 21st—today's birthday. Your year ahead: *You can expect an eventful year. Controversial matters may predominate from December to March. People associated with music, transport, and the fashion industry will find the coming year will bring a marked progress.*' Now, were you not connected with the fashion industry, Granny Bean? It says here in black and white. . . .'

But Mrs. Bean had dropped asleep on her pillow after the nurse had given her a warm drink. Her mouth was formed once more into a small 'O' through which her breath whistled faintly.

'Festivities going on?' said Alec Warner, looking around at the party decorations.

'Yes, Mrs. Bean is a hundred today.'

The deep lines on Alec's face and brow showed deeper. It was four months since he had lost his entire notes and records in the fire.

Jean Taylor had said, 'Try to start all over again, Alec. You will find a lot of it will come back to your mind while you work.'

'I could never trust my memory,' he had said, 'as I trusted those notes.'

'Well, you must start all over again.'

'I haven't got it in me,' he said, 'to do that at my age. It was an accumulation of years of labour. It was invaluable.'

He had seldom, since then, referred to his loss. He felt, sometimes, he said once, that he was really dead, since his records had ceased to exist.

'That's rather a metaphysical idea for you, Alec,' she said. 'For in fact you are not dead, but still alive.'

He told her, it was true he frequently went over his vast notebooks in his mind, as through a card index. 'But never,' he said, 'shall I make another note. I read instead. It is in some ways a better thing.'

She caught him looking with an almost cannibal desire at Granny Bean on her hundredth birthday. He sighed and looked away.

'We all appear to ourselves frustrated in our old age, Alec, because we cling to everything so much. But in reality we are still fulfilling our lives.'

'A friend of mine fulfilled his yesterday.'

'Oh, who was that?'

'Matt O'Brien in Folkestone. He thought he was God. He died in his sleep. He has left a fortune, but never knew about it. Lisa's money of course. No relatives.'

'Will Guy Leet——?'

'No, Guy has no claim. I think Lisa's estate will now go according to her will to Mrs. Pettigrew.'

'In that case,' said Miss Taylor, 'she will, after all, have her reward.'

*　　*　　*

'Mrs. Pettigrew had her reward. Lisa's will was proved in her favour and she inherited all her fortune. After her first stroke Mrs. Pettigrew went to live in a hotel at South Kensington. She is still to be seen at eleven in the morning at Harrods' Bank where she regularly meets some of the other elderly residents to discuss the shortcomings of the hotel management, and to plan various campaigns against the staff. She can still be seen in the evening jostling for a place by the door of the hotel lounge before the dinner gong sounds.

Charmian died one morning in the following spring, at the age of eighty-seven.

Godfrey died the same year as the result of a motor accident, his car having collided with another at a bend in Kensington Church Street. He was not killed outright, but died a few days later of pneumonia which had set in from the shock. It was the couple in the other car who were killed outright.

Guy Leet died at the age of seventy-eight.

Percy Mannering is in an old men's home, where he is known as 'The Professor' and is treated with special respect, having his bed put in an alcove at the far corner of the dormitory—a position reserved for patients who have known better days. His granddaughter, Olive, sometimes visits him. She takes away his poems and letters addressed to editors; she types them out, and despatches them according to Percy's directions.

Ronald Sidebottome is allowed up in the afternoons but is not expected to last another winter.

Janet Sidebottome died of a stroke following an increase in blood pressure, at the age of seventy-seven.

Mrs. Anthony, now widowed, had a legacy from Charmian, and has gone to live at a seaside town, near her married son. Sometimes, when she hears of old people receiving anonymous telephone calls, she declares it is a good thing, judging by what she has seen, that she herself is hard of hearing.

Chief Inspector Mortimer died suddenly of heart-failure at the age of seventy-three, while boarding his yacht *The Dragonfly* Mrs. Mortimer spends most of her time looking after her numerous grandchildren.

Eric is getting through the Colston money which came to him on the death of his father.

Alec Warner had a paralytic stroke following a cerebral haemorrhage. For a time he was paralysed on one side and his speech was incoherent. In time he regained the use of his limbs; his speech improved. He went to live permanently in a nursing home and frequently searched through his mind, as through a card index, for the case-histories of his friends, both dead and dying.

What were they sick, what did they die of?

Lettie Colston, he recited to himself, comminuted fractures of the skull; Godfrey Colston, hypostatic pneumonia; Charmian Colston, uraemia; Jean Taylor, myocardial degeneration; Tempest Sidebottome, carcinoma of the cervix; Ronald Sidebottome, carcinoma of the bronchus; Guy Leet, arteriosclerosis; Henry Mortimer, coronary thrombosis. . . .

Miss Valvona went to her rest. Many of the grannies followed her. Jean Taylor lingered for a time, employing her pain to magnify the Lord, and meditating sometimes confidingly upon Death, the first of the four last things to be ever remembered.

THE END

THE GIRLS
OF SLENDER MEANS

For
ALAN MACLEAN

Chapter One

LONG ago in 1945 all the nice people in England were poor, allowing for exceptions. The streets of the cities were lined with buildings in bad repair or in no repair at all, bomb-sites piled with stony rubble, houses like giant teeth in which decay had been drilled out, leaving only the cavity. Some bomb-ripped buildings looked like the ruins of ancient castles until, at a closer view, the wallpapers of various quite normal rooms would be visible, room above room, exposed, as on a stage, with one wall missing; sometimes a lavatory chain would dangle over nothing from a fourth- or fifth-floor ceiling; most of all the staircases survived, like a new art-form, leading up and up to an un-specified destination that made unusual demands on the mind's eye. All the nice people were poor; at least, that was a general axiom, the best of the rich being poor in spirit.

There was absolutely no point in feeling depressed about the scene, it would have been like feeling depressed about the Grand Canyon or some event of the earth outside everybody's scope. People continued to exchange assurances of depressed feelings about the weather or the news, or the Albert Memorial which had not been hit, not even shaken, by any bomb from first to last.

The May of Teck Club stood obliquely opposite the site of the Memorial, in one of a row of tall houses which had endured, but barely; some bombs had dropped nearby, and in a few back gardens, leaving the buildings cracked on the outside and shakily-hinged within, but habitable for the time being. The shattered windows had been replaced with new glass rattling in loose frames. More recently, the bituminous black-out paint had been removed from landing and bathroom windows. Windows were important in that year of final reckoning; they told at a glance whether a house was inhabited or not; and in the course of the past years they had accumulated much meaning, having been the main danger-zone between domestic life and the war going on outside: everyone had said, when the sirens sounded, 'Mind the windows. Keep away from the windows. Watch out for the glass.'

The May of Teck Club had been three times window-shattered since 1940, but never directly hit. There the windows of the upper bedrooms overlooked the dip and rise of treetops in Kensington Gardens across the street, with the Albert Memorial to be seen by means of a slight craning and twist of the neck. These upper bedrooms looked down on the opposite pavement on the park side of the street, and on the tiny people who moved along in neat-looking singles and couples, pushing little prams loaded with pin-head babies and provisions, or carrying little dots of shopping bags. Everyone carried a shopping bag in case they should be lucky enough to pass a shop that had a sudden stock of something off the rations.

From the lower-floor dormitories the people in the street looked larger, and the paths of the park were visible. All the nice people were poor, and few were nicer, as nice people come, than these girls at Kensington who glanced out of the windows in the early mornings to see what the day looked like, or gazed out on the green summer evenings, as if reflecting on the months ahead, on love and the relations of love. Their eyes gave out an eager-spirited light that resembled near-genius, but was youth merely. The first of the Rules of Constitution, drawn up at some remote and innocent Edwardian date, still applied more or less to them:

> The May of Teck Club exists for the Pecuniary Convenience and Social Protection of Ladies of Slender Means below the age of Thirty Years, who are obliged to reside apart from their Families in order to follow an Occupation in London.

As they realised themselves in varying degrees, few people alive at the time were more delightful, more ingenious, more movingly lovely, and, as it might happen, more savage, than the girls of slender means.

*   *   *

'I've got something to tell you,' said Jane Wright, the woman columnist.

At the other end of the telephone, the voice of Dorothy Markham, owner of the flourishing model agency, said, 'Darling, where have you been?' She spoke, by habit since her debutante days, with the utmost enthusiasm of tone.

'I've got something to tell you. Do you remember Nicholas Farringdon? Remember he used to come to the old May of Teck just after the war, he was an anarchist and poet sort of thing. A tall man with——'

'The one that got on to the roof to sleep out with Selina?'

'Yes, Nicholas Farringdon.'

'Oh rather. Has he turned up?'

'No, he's been martyred.'

'What-ed?'

'Martyred in Haiti. Killed. Remember he became a Brother——'

'But I've just been to Tahiti, it's marvellous, everyone's marvellous. Where did you hear it?'

'Haiti. There's a news paragraph just come over Reuters. I'm sure it's the same Nicholas Farringdon because it says a missionary, former poet. I nearly died. I knew him well, you know, in those days. I expect they'll hush it all up, about those days, if they want to make a martyr story.'

'How did it happen, is it gruesome?'

'Oh, I don't know, there's only a paragraph.'

'You'll have to find out more through your grapevine. I'm shattered. I've got heaps to tell you.'

*   *   *

The Committee of Management wishes to express surprise at the Members' protest regarding the wallpaper chosen for the drawing room. The Committee wishes to point out that Members' residential fees do not meet the running expenses of the Club. The Committee regrets that the spirit of the May of Teck foundation has apparently so far deteriorated that such a protest has been made. The Committee refers Members to the terms of the Club's Foundation.

Joanna Childe was a daughter of a country rector. She had a good intelligence and strong obscure emotions. She was training to be a teacher of elocution and, while attending a school of drama, already had pupils of her own. Joanna Childe had been drawn to this profession by her good voice and love of poetry which she loved rather as it might be assumed a cat loves birds; poetry, especially the declamatory sort, excited and possessed her; she would pounce on the stuff, play with it quivering in her mind, and when she had got it by heart, she spoke it forth with devouring relish. Mostly, she indulged the habit while giving elocution lessons at the club where she was highly thought of for it. The vibrations of Joanna's elocution voice from her room or from the recreation room where she frequently rehearsed, were felt to add tone and style to the establishment when boy-friends called. Her taste in poetry became the accepted taste of the club. She had a deep feeling for certain passages in the authorised version of the Bible, besides the Book of Common Prayer, Shakespeare, and Gerard Manley Hopkins, and had newly discovered Dylan Thomas. She was not moved by the poetry of Eliot and Auden, except for the latter's lyric:

> *Lay your sleeping head, my love,*
> *Human on my faithless arm;*

Joanna Childe was large, with light shiny hair, blue eyes, and deep-pink cheeks. When she read the notice signed by Lady Julia Markham, chairwoman of the committee, she stood with the other young women round the green baize board and was given to murmur:

'He rageth, and again he rageth, because he knows his time is short.'

It was not known to many that this was a reference to the Devil, but it caused amusement. She had not intended it so. It was not usual for Joanna to quote anything for its aptitude, and at conversational pitch.

Joanna, who was now of age, would henceforth vote conservative in the elections, which at that time in the May of Teck Club was associated with a desirable order of life that none of the members was old enough to remember from direct experience. In principle they all approved of what the committee's notice stood for. And so Joanna was alarmed by the amused reaction to her quotation, the hearty laugh of understanding that those days were over when the members of anything whatsoever might not raise their voices against the drawing-room wallpaper. Principles regardless, everyone knew that the notice was plain damned funny. Lady Julia must be feeling pretty desperate.

'He rageth and again he rageth, because he knows his time is short.'

Little dark Judy Redwood who was a shorthand typist in the Ministry of Labour said, 'I've got a feeling that as members we're legally entitled to a say in the administration. I must ask Geoffrey.' This was the man Judy was engaged to. He was still in the forces, but had qualified as a solicitor before being called up. His sister, Anne Baberton, who stood with the notice-board group, said, 'Geoffrey would be the last person I would consult.' Anne Baberton said this to indicate that she knew Geoffrey better than Judy knew him; she said it to indicate affectionate scorn; she said it because it was the obvious thing for a nicely brought-up sister to say, since she was proud of him; and besides all this, there was an element of irritation in her words, 'Geoffrey would be the last person I would consult', for she knew there was no point in members taking up this question of the drawing-room wallpaper.

Anne trod out her cigarette-end contemptuously on the floor of the large entrance hall with its pink and grey Victorian tiles. This was pointed to by a thin middle-aged woman, one of the few older, if not exactly the earliest members. She said, 'One is not permitted to put cigarette-ends on the floor.' The words did not appear to impress themselves on the ears of the group, more than the ticking of the grandfather clock behind them. But Anne said, 'Isn't one permitted to spit on the floor, even?' 'One certainly isn't,' said the spinster. 'Oh, I thought one was,' said Anne.

The May of Teck Club was founded by Queen Mary before her marriage to King George the Fifth, when she was Princess

May of Teck. On an afternoon between the engagement and the marriage, the Princess had been induced to come to London and declare officially open the May of Teck Club which had been endowed by various gentle forces of wealth.

None of the original Ladies remained in the club. But three subsequent members had been permitted to stay on past the stipulated age-limit of thirty, and were now in their fifties, and had resided at the May of Teck Club since before the First World War at which time, they said, all members had been obliged to dress for dinner.

Nobody knew why these three women had not been asked to leave when they had reached the age of thirty. Even the warden and committee did not know why the three remained. It was now too late to turn them out with decency. It was too late even to mention to them the subject of their continuing residence. Successive committees before 1939 had decided that the three older residents might, in any case, be expected to have a good influence on the younger ones.

During the war the matter had been left in abeyance, since the club was half empty; in any case members' fees were needed, and bombs were then obliterating so much and so many in the near vicinity that it was an open question whether indeed the three spinsters would remain upright with the house to the end. By 1945 they had seen much coming of new girls and going of old, and were generally liked by the current batch, being subject to insults when they interfered in anything, and intimate confidences when they kept aloof. The confidences seldom represented the whole truth, particularly those revealed by the young women who occupied the top floor. The three spinsters were, through the ages, known and addressed as Collie (Miss Coleman), Greggie (Miss Macgregor), and Jarvie (Miss Jarman). It was Greggie who had said to Anne by the notice-board:

'One isn't permitted to put cigarette-ends on the floor.'

'Isn't one permitted to spit on the floor, even?'

'No, one isn't.'

'Oh, I thought one was.'

Greggie effected an indulgent sigh and pushed her way through the crowd of younger members. She went to the open door, set in a wide porch, to look out at the summer evening like a shopkeeper waiting for custom. Greggie always behaved as if she owned the club.

The gong was about to sound quite soon. Anne kicked her cigarette-stub into a dark corner.

Greggie called over her shoulder, 'Anne, here comes your boy-friend.'

'On time, for once,' said Anne, with the same pretence of scorn that she had adopted when referring to her brother Geoffrey: 'Geoffrey would be the last person I would consult.' She moved, with her casual hips, towards the door.

A square-built high-coloured young man in the uniform of an English captain came smiling in. Anne stood regarding him as if he was the last person in the world she would consult.

'Good evening,' he said to Greggie as a well-brought-up man would naturally say to a woman of Greggie's years standing in the doorway. He made a vague nasal noise of recognition to Anne, which if properly pronounced would have been 'Hallo'. She said nothing at all by way of greeting. They were nearly engaged to be married.

'Like to come in and see the drawing-room wallpaper?' Anne said then.

'No, let's get cracking.'

Anne went to get her coat off the banister where she had slung it. He was saying to Greggie, 'Lovely evening, isn't it?'

Anne returned with her coat slung over her shoulder. 'Bye, Greggie,' she said. 'Goodbye,' said the soldier. Anne took his arm.

'Have a nice time,' said Greggie.

The dinner-gong sounded and there was a scuffle of feet departing from the notice-board and a scamper of feet from the floors above.

*   *   *

On a summer night during the previous week the whole club, forty-odd women, with any young men who might happen to have called that evening, had gone like swift migrants into the dark cool air of the Park, crossing its wide acres as the crow

flies in the direction of Buckingham Palace, there to express
themselves along with the rest of London on the victory in the
war with Germany. They clung to each other in twos and threes,
fearful of being trampled. When separated, they clung to, and
were clung to by, the nearest person. They became members of
a wave of the sea, they surged and sang until, at every half-
hour interval, a light flooded the tiny distant balcony of the
Palace and four small straight digits appeared upon it: the King,
the Queen, and the two Princesses. The royal family raised
their right arms, their hands fluttered as in a slight breeze, they
were three candles in uniform and one in the recognisable fur-
trimmed folds of the civilian queen in wartime. The huge
organic murmur of the crowd, different from anything like the
voice of animate matter but rather more a cataract or a geological
disturbance, spread through the parks and along the Mall.
Only the St. John's Ambulance men, watchful beside their vans,
had any identity left. The royal family waved, turned to go,
lingered and waved again, and finally disappeared. Many
strange arms were twined round strange bodies. Many liaisons,
some permanent, were formed in the night, and numerous
infants of experimental variety, delightful in hue of skin and
racial structure, were born to the world in the due cycle of nine
months after. The bells pealed. Greggie observed that it was
something between a wedding and a funeral on a world scale.

The next day everyone began to consider where they personally stood in the new order of things.

Many citizens felt the urge, which some began to indulge, to
insult each other, in order to prove something or to test their
ground.

The government reminded the public that it was still at war.
Officially this was undeniable, but except to those whose rela-
tions lay in the Far-Eastern prisons of war, or were stuck in
Burma, that war was generally felt to be a remote affair.

A few shorthand-typists at the May of Teck Club started to
apply for safer jobs—that is to say, in private concerns, not
connected with the war like the temporary Ministries where
many of them had been employed.

Their brothers and men friends in the forces, not yet demobilized, by a long way, were talking of vivid enterprises for the exploitation of peace, such as buying a lorry and building up from it a transport business.

*   *   *

'I've got something to tell you,' said Jane.

'Just a minute till I shut the door. The kids are making a row,' Anne said. And presently, when she returned to the telephone, she said, 'Yes, carry on.'

'Do you remember Nicholas Farringdon?'

'I seem to remember the name.'

'Remember I brought him to the May of Teck in 1945, he used to come often for supper. He got mixed up with Selina.'

'Oh, Nicholas. The one who got up on the roof? What a long time ago that was. Have you seen him?'

'I've just seen a news item that's come over Reuters. He's been killed in a local rising in Haiti.'

'Really? How awful! What was he doing there?'

'Well, he became a missionary or something.'

'No!'

'Yes. It's terribly tragic. I knew him well.'

'Ghastly. It brings everything back. Have you told Selina?'

'Well, I haven't been able to get her. You know what Selina's like these days, she won't answer the phone personally, you have to go through thousands of secretaries or whatever they are.'

'You could get a good story for your paper out of it, Jane,' Anne said.

'I know that. I'm just waiting to get more details. Of course it's all those years ago since I knew him, but it would be an interesting story.'

*   *   *

Two men—poets by virtue of the fact that the composition of poetry was the only consistent thing they had so far done— beloved of two May of Teck girls and, at the moment, of nobody else, sat in their corduroy trousers in a café in Bayswater with their silent listening admirers and talked about the new future as they flicked the page-proofs of an absent friend's novel. A copy of *Peace News* lay on the table between them. One of the men said to the other:

> *And now what will become of us without Barbarians? Those people were some sort of a solution.*

And the other smiled, bored-like, but conscious that very few in all the great metropolis and its tributary provinces were as yet privy to the source of these lines. This other who smiled was Nicholas Farringdon, not yet known or as yet at all likely to be.

'Who wrote that?' said Jane Wright, a fat girl who worked for a publisher and who was considered to be brainy but somewhat below standard, socially, at the May of Teck.

Neither man replied.

'Who wrote that?' Jane said again.

The poet nearest her said, through his thick spectacles, 'An Alexandrian poet.'

'A new poet?'

'No, but fairly new to this country.'

'What's his name?'

He did not reply. The young men had started talking again. They talked about the decline and fall of the anarchist movement on the island of their birth in terms of the personalities concerned. They were bored with educating the girls for this evening.

Chapter Two

JOANNA CHILDE was giving elocution lessons to Miss Harper, the cook, in the recreation room. When she was not giving lessons she was usually practising for her next examination. The house frequently echoed with Joanna's rhetoric. She got six shillings an hour from her pupils, five shillings if they were May of Teck members. Nobody knew what her arrangements were with Miss Harper, for at that time all who kept keys of food-cupboards made special arrangements with all others.

Joanna's method was to read each stanza herself first and make her pupil repeat it.

Everyone in the drawing room could hear the loud lesson in progress beating out the stresses and throbs of *The Wreck of the Deutschland*.

> *The frown of his face*
> *Before me, the hurtle of hell*
> *Behind, where, where was a, where was a place?*

The club was proud of Joanna Childe, not only because she chucked up her head and recited poetry, but because she was so well built, fair and healthy looking, the poetic essence of tall, fair rectors' daughters who never used a scrap of make-up, who had served tirelessly day and night in parish welfare organisations since leaving school early in the war, who before that had been Head Girl and who never wept that anyone knew or could imagine, being stoical by nature.

What had happened to Joanna was that she had fallen in love with a curate on leaving school. It had come to nothing. Joanna had decided that this was to be the only love of her life.

She had been brought up to hear, and later to recite,

> *. . . Love is not love*
> *Which alters when it alteration finds,*
> *Or bends with the remover to remove:*

All her ideas of honour and love came from the poets. She was vaguely acquainted with distinctions and sub-distinctions of human and divine love, and their various attributes, but this was picked up from rectory conversations when theologically-minded clerics came to stay; it was in a different category of instruction from ordinary household beliefs such as the axiom, 'People are holier who live in the country', and the notion that a nice girl should only fall in love once in her life.

It seemed to Joanna that her longing for the curate must have been unworthy of the name of love, had she allowed a similar longing, which she began to feel, for the company of a succeeding curate, more suitable and even handsomer, to come to anything. Once you admit that you can change the object of a

strongly-felt affection, you undermine the whole structure of
love and marriage, the whole philosophy of Shakespeare's
sonnet: this had been the approved, though unspoken, opinion
of the rectory and its mental acres of upper air. Joanna pressed
down her feelings for the second curate and worked them off in
tennis and the war effort. She had not encouraged the second
curate at all but brooded silently upon him until the Sunday
she saw him standing in the pulpit and announce his sermon
upon the text:

> . . . if thy right eye offend thee, pluck it out, and cast it
> from thee: for it is profitable for thee that one of thy members
> should perish, and not that thy whole body should be cast
> into hell.
> And if thy right hand offend thee, cut it off, and cast it
> from thee: for it is profitable for thee that one of thy members
> should perish, and not that thy whole body should be cast
> into hell.

It was the evening service. Many young girls from the district
had come, some of them in their service uniforms. One particular Wren looked up at the curate, her pink cheeks touched by
the stained-glass evening light; her hair curled lightly upwards
on her Wren hat. Joanna could hardly imagine a more handsome man than this second curate. He was newly ordained, and
was shortly going into the Air Force. It was spring, full of preparations and guesses, for the second front was to be established
against the enemy, some said in North Africa, some said
Scandinavia, the Baltic, France. Meantime, Joanna listened
attentively to the young man in the pulpit, she listened obses-
sively. He was dark and tall, his eyes were deep under his
straight black brows, he had a chiselled look. His wide mouth
suggested to Joanna generosity and humour, that type of
generosity and humour special to the bishop sprouting within
him. He was very athletic. He had made it as clear that he
wanted Joanna as the former curate had not. Like the rector's
eldest daughter that she was, Joanna sat in her pew without
seeming to listen in any particular way to this attractive fellow.
She did not turn her face towards him as the pretty Wren was

doing. The right eye and the right hand, he was saying, means that which we hold most precious. What the scripture meant, he said, was that if anything we hold most dear should prove an offence—as you know, he said, the Greek word here was σκάνδαλον, frequently occurring in Scripture in the connotation of scandal, offence, stumbling-block, as when St. Paul said. . . . The rustics who predominated in the congregation looked on with their round moveless eyes. Joanna decided to pluck out her right eye, cut off her right hand, this looming offence to the first love, this stumbling-block, the adorable man in the pulpit.

'For it is profitable for thee that one of thy members should perish, and not that thy whole body should be cast into hell,' rang the preacher's voice. 'Hell, of course,' he said, 'is a negative concept. Let us put it more positively. More positively, the text should read, "It is better to enter maimed into the Kingdom of Heaven than not to enter at all." ' He hoped to publish this sermon one day in a Collected Sermons, for he was as yet inexperienced in many respects, although he later learned some reality as an Air Force chaplain.

Joanna, then, had decided to enter maimed into the Kingdom of Heaven. By no means did she look maimed. She got a job in London and settled at the May of Teck Club. She took up elocution in her spare time. Then, towards the end of the war, she began to study and make a full-time occupation of it. The sensation of poetry replaced the sensation of the curate, and she took on pupils at six shillings an hour pending her diploma.

> *The wanton troopers riding by*
> *Have shot my fawn, and it will die.*

Nobody at the May of Teck Club knew her precise history, but it was generally assumed to be something emotionally heroic. She was compared to Ingrid Bergman, and did not take part in the argument between members and staff about the food, whether it contained too many fattening properties, even allowing for the necessities of war-time rationing.

Chapter Three

LOVE and money were the vital themes in all the bedrooms and dormitories. Love came first, and subsidiary to it was money for the upkeep of looks and the purchase of clothing coupons at the official black-market price of eight coupons for a pound.

The house was a spacious Victorian one, and very little had been done to change its interior since the days when it was a private residence. It resembled in its plan most of the women's hostels, noted for cheapness and tone, which had flourished since the emancipation of women had called for them. No one at the May of Teck Club referred to it as a hostel, except in moments of low personal morale such as was experienced by the youngest members only on being given the brush-off by a boy-friend.

The basement of the house was occupied by kitchens, the laundry, the furnace, and fuel-stores.

The ground floor contained staff offices, the dining room, the recreation room and, newly papered in a mud-like shade of brown, the drawing room. This resented wallpaper had un-fortunately been found at the back of a cupboard in huge quantities, otherwise the walls would have remained grey and stricken like everyone else's.

Boy-friends were allowed to dine as guests at a cost of two-and-sixpence. It was also permitted to entertain in the recreation room, on the terrace which led out from it, and in the drawing room whose mud-brown walls appeared so penitential in tone at that time—for the members were not to know that within a few years many of them would be lining the walls of their own homes with paper of a similar colour, it then having become smart.

Above this, on the first floor, where, in the former days of private wealth, an enormous ball-room had existed, an enor-mous dormitory now existed. This was curtained off into numerous cubicles. Here lived the very youngest members, girls between the ages of eighteen and twenty who had not long moved out of the cubicles of school dormitories throughout the English countryside, and who understood dormitory life from start to finish. The girls on this floor were not yet experienced in discussing men. Everything turned on whether the man in question was a good dancer and had a sense of humour. The Air Force was mostly favoured, and a D.F.C. was an asset. A Battle of Britain record aged a man in the eyes of the first-floor dormitory, in the year 1945. Dunkirk, too, was largely something that their fathers had done. It was the air heroes of the Normandy landing who were popular, lounging among the cushions in the drawing room. They gave full entertainment value:

'Do you know the story of the two cats that went to Wimble-don?—Well, one cat persuaded another to go to Wimbledon to watch the tennis. After a few sets one cat said to the other, "I must say, I'm bloody bored. I honestly can't see why you're so interested in this game of tennis." And the other cat replied, "Well, my father's in the racquet!" '

'No!' shrieked the girls, and duly doubled up.

'But that's not the end of the story. There was a colonel sitting behind these two cats. He was watching the tennis because the war was on and so there wasn't anything for him to do. Well, this colonel had his dog with him. So when the cats started talking to each other the dog turned to the colonel and said, "Do you hear those two cats in front of us?" "No, shut up," said the colonel, "I'm concentrating on the game." "All right," said the dog—very happy this dog, you know—"I only thought you might be interested in a couple of cats that can talk." '

'Really,' said the voice of the dormitory later on, a twittering outburst, 'what a wizard sense of humour!' They were like birds waking up instead of girls going to bed, since 'Really, what a wizard sense of humour' would be the approximate collective euphony of the birds in the park five hours later, if anyone was listening.

On the floor above the dormitory were the rooms of the staff and the shared bedrooms of those who could afford shared bedrooms rather than a cubicle. Those who shared, four or two to a room, tended to be young women in transit, or temporary members looking for flats and bed-sitting rooms. Here, on the second floor, two of the elder spinsters, Collie and Jarvie, shared a room as they had done for eight years, since they were saving money now for their old age.

But on the floor above that, there seemed to have congregated, by instinctive consent, most of the celibates, the old maids of settled character and various ages, those who had decided on a spinster's life, and those who would one day do so but had not yet discerned the fact for themselves.

This third-floor landing had contained five large bedrooms, now partitioned by builders into ten small ones. The occupants ranged from prim and pretty young virgins who would never become fully-wakened women, to bossy ones in their late twenties who were too wide-awake ever to surrender to any man. Greggie, the third of the elder spinsters, had her room on this floor. She was the least prim and the kindest of the women there.

On this floor was the room of a mad girl, Pauline Fox, who was wont to dress carefully on certain evenings in the long dresses which were swiftly and temporarily reverted to in the years immediately following the war. She also wore long white gloves, and her hair was long, curling over her shoulders. On these evenings she said she was going to dine with the famous actor, Jack Buchanan. No one disbelieved her outright, and her madness was undetected.

Here, too, was Joanna Childe's room from which she could be heard practising her elocution at times when the recreation room was occupied.

> *All the flowers of the spring*
> *Meet to perfume our burying;*

At the top of the house, on the fourth floor, the most attractive, sophisticated and lively girls had their rooms. They were filled with deeper and deeper social longings of various kinds, as peace-time crept over everyone. Five girls occupied the five top rooms. Three of them had lovers in addition to men-friends with whom they did not sleep but whom they cultivated with a view to marriage. Of the remaining two, one was almost engaged to be married, and the other was Jane Wright, fat but intellectually glamorous by virtue of the fact that she worked for a publisher. She was on the look-out for a husband, meanwhile being mixed up with young intellectuals.

Nothing but the roof-tops lay above this floor, now inaccessible by the trap-door in the bathroom ceiling—a mere useless square since it had been bricked up long ago before the war after a girl had been attacked by a burglar or a lover who had entered by it— attacked or merely confronted unexpectedly, or found in bed with him as some said; as the case might be, he left behind him a legend of many screams in the night and the skylight had been henceforth closed to the public. Workmen who, from time to time, were called in to do something up above the house had to approach the roof from the attic of a neighbouring hotel. Greggie claimed to know all about the story, she knew everything about the club. Indeed it was Greggie who, inspired by a shaft of remembrance, had directed the warden to the hoard of mud-coloured wallpaper in the cupboard which now defiled the walls of the drawing room and leered in the sunlight at everyone. The top-floor girls had often thought it might be a good idea to sun-bathe on the flat portion of the roof and had climbed up on chairs to see about the opening of the trap-door. But it would not budge, and Greggie had once more told them why. Greggie produced a better version of the story every time.

'If there was a fire, we'd be stuck,' said Selina Redwood who was exceedingly beautiful.

'You've obviously been taking no notice of the emergency instructions,' Greggie said. This was true. Selina was seldom in to dinner and so she had never heard them. Four times a year the emergency instructions were read out by the warden after dinner, on which nights no guests were allowed. The top floor was served for emergency purposes by a back staircase leading down two flights to the perfectly sound fire-escape, and by the fire-equipment which lay around everywhere in the club. On these evenings of no guests the members were also reminded about putting things down lavatories, and the difficulties of plumbing systems in old houses, and of obtaining plumbers these days. They were reminded that they were expected to put everything back in place after a dance had been held in the club. Why some members unfortunately just went off to night clubs with their men friends and left everything to others, said the warden, she simply did not know.

Selina had missed all this, never having been in to dinner on the warden's nights. From her window she could see, level with the top floor of the house, and set back behind the chimney pots, the portion of flat roof, shared by the club with the hotel next door, which would have been ideal for sun-bathing. There was no access to any part of the roof from the bedroom windows, but one day she noticed that it was accessible from the lavatory window, a narrow slit made narrower by the fact that the wall in which it was set had been sub-divided at some point in the house's history when the wash-rooms had been put in. One had to climb up on the lavatory seat to see the roof. Selina measured the window. The aperture was seven inches wide by fourteen inches long. It opened casement-wise.

'I believe I could get through the lavatory window,' she said to Anne Baberton who occupied the room opposite hers.

'Why do you want to get through the lavatory window?' said Anne.

'It leads out to the roof. There's only a short jump from the window.'

Selina was extremely slim. The question of weight and measurement was very important on the top floor. The ability or otherwise to wriggle sideways through the lavatory window would be one of those tests that only went to prove the club's food policy to be unnecessarily fattening.

'Suicidal,' said Jane Wright who was miserable about her fatness and spent much of her time in eager dread of the next meal, and in making resolutions what to eat of it and what to leave, and in making counter-resolutions in view of the fact that her work at the publishers' was essentially mental, which meant that her brain had to be fed more than most people's.

Among the five top-floor members only Selina Redwood and Anne Baberton could manage to wriggle through the lavatory window, and Anne only managed it naked, having made her body slippery with margarine. After the first attempt, when she had twisted her ankle on the downward leap and grazed her skin on the return clamber, Anne said she would in future use her soap ration to facilitate the exit. Soap was as tightly rationed as margarine, but more precious, for margarine was fattening, anyway. Face cream was too expensive to waste on the window venture.

Jane Wright could not see why Anne was so concerned about her one inch and a half on the hips more than Selina's, since Anne was already slender and already fixed up for marriage. She stood on the lavatory seat and threw out Anne's faded green dressing gown for her to drape round her slippery body and asked what it was like out there. The two other girls on the floor were away for the week-end on this occasion.

Anne and Selina were peeping over the edge of the flat roof at a point where Jane could not see them. They returned to report that they had looked down on the back garden where Greggie was holding her conducted tour of the premises for the benefit of two new members. She had been showing them the spot where the bomb had fallen and failed to go off, and had been removed by a bomb-squad, during which operation everyone had been obliged to leave the house. Greggie had also been showing them the spot where, in her opinion, an unexploded bomb still lay.

The girls got themselves back into the house.

'Greggie and her sensations': Jane felt she could scream. She added, 'Cheese pie for supper tonight, guess how many calories?'

The answer, when they looked up the chart, was roughly 350 calories. 'Followed by stewed cherries,' said Jane, '94 calories normal helping unless sweetened by saccharine, in which case 64 calories. We've had over a thousand calories today already. It's always the same on Sundays. The bread-and-butter pudding alone was——'

'I didn't eat the bread-and-butter pudding,' said Anne. 'Bread-and-butter pudding is suicidal.'

'I only eat a little bit of everything,' Selina said. 'I feel starved all the time, actually.'

'Well, I'm doing brain-work,' said Jane.

Anne was walking about the landing sponging off all the

margarine. She said, 'I've had to use up soap and margarine as well.'

'I can't lend you any soap this month,' Selina said. Selina had a regular supply of soap from an American Army officer who got it from a source of many desirable things, called the P.X. But she was accumulating a hoard of it, and had stopped lending.

Anne said, 'I don't want your bloody soap. Just don't ask for the taffeta, that's all.'

By this she meant a Schiaparelli taffeta evening dress which had been given to her by a fabulously rich aunt, after one wearing. This marvellous dress, which caused a stir wherever it went, was shared by all the top floor on special occasions, excluding Jane whom it did not fit. For lending it out Anne got various returns, such as three clothing coupons or a half-used piece of soap.

Jane went back to her brain-work and shut the door with a definite click. She was rather tyrannous about her brain-work, and made a fuss about other people's wirelesses on the landing, and about the petty-mindedness of these haggling bouts that took place with Anne when the taffeta dress was wanted to support the rising wave of long-dress parties.

'You can't wear it to the Milroy. It's been twice to the Milroy . . . it's been to Quaglino's, Selina wore it to Quags, it's getting known all over London.'

'But it looks altogether different on me, Anne. You can have a whole sheet of sweet-coupons.'

'I don't want your bloody sweet-coupons. I give all mine to my grandmother.'

Then Jane would put out her head. 'Stop being so petty-minded and stop screeching. I'm doing brain-work.'

Jane had one smart thing in her wardrobe, a black coat and skirt made out of her father's evening clothes. Very few dinner jackets in England remained in their original form after the war. But this looted outfit of Jane's was too large for anyone to borrow; she was thankful for that, at least. The exact nature of her brain-work was a mystery to the club because, when asked about it, she reeled off fast an explanation of extreme and alien detail about costing, printers, lists, manuscripts, galleys, and contracts.

'Well, Jane, you ought to get paid for all that extra work you do.'

'The world of books is essentially disinterested,' Jane said. She always referred to the publishing business as 'The world of books'. She was always hard up, so presumably ill paid. It was because she had to be careful of her shillings for the meter which controlled the gas-fire in her room that she was unable, so she said, to go on a diet during the winter, since one had to keep warm as well as feed one's brain.

Jane received from the club, on account of her brain-work and job in publishing, a certain amount of respect which was socially offset by the arrival in the front hall, every week or so, of a pale, thin foreigner, decidedly in his thirties, with dandruff on his dark overcoat, who would ask in the office for Miss Jane Wright, always adding, 'I wish to see her privately, please.' Word also spread around from the office that many of Jane's incoming telephone calls were from this man.

'Is that the May of Teck Club?'

'Yes.'

'May I speak to Miss Wright privately, please?'

At one of these moments the secretary on duty said to him, 'All the members' calls are private. We don't listen in.'

'Good. I would know if you did, I wait for the click before I speak. Kindly remember.'

Jane had to apologise to the office for him. 'He's a foreigner. It's in connection with the world of books. It isn't my fault.'

But another and more presentable man from the world of books had lately put in an appearance for Jane. She had brought him into the drawing room and introduced him to Selina, Anne, and the mad girl Pauline Fox who dressed up for Jack Buchanan on her lunatic evenings.

This man, Nicholas Farringdon, had been rather charming, though shy. 'He's thoughtful,' Jane said. 'We think him brilliant but he's still feeling his way in the world of books.'

'Is he something in publishing?'

'Not at the moment. He's still feeling his way. He's writing something.'

Jane's brain-work was of three kinds. First, and secretly, she wrote poetry of a strictly non-rational order, in which occurred, in about the proportion of cherries in a cherry-cake, certain words that she described as 'of a smouldering nature', such as loins and lovers, the root, the rose, the seawrack, and the shroud. Secondly, also secretly, she wrote letters of a friendly tone but with a business intention, under the auspices of the pale foreigner. Thirdly, and more openly, she sometimes did a little work in her room which overlapped from her day's duties at the small publisher's office.

She was the only assistant at Huy Throvis-Mew Ltd. Huy Throvis-Mew was the owner of the firm, and Mrs. Huy Throvis-Mew was down as a director on the letter heading. Huy Throvis-Mew's private name was George Johnson, or at least it had been so for some years, although a few very old friends called him Con and older friends called him Arthur or Jimmie. However, he was George in Jane's time, and she would do anything for George, her white-bearded employer. She parcelled up the books, took them to the post or delivered them, answered the telephone, made tea, minded the baby when George's wife, Tilly, wanted to go and queue for fish, entered the takings into ledgers, entered two different versions of the petty cash and office expenses into two sets of books, and generally did a small publisher's business. After a year George allowed her to do some of the detective work on new authors, which he was convinced was essential to the publishing trade, and to find out their financial circumstances and psychologically weak points so that he could deal with them to a publisher's best advantage.

Like the habit of changing his name after a number of years, which he had done only in the hope that his luck would turn with it, this practice of George's was fairly innocent, in that he never really succeeded in discovering the whole truth about an author, or in profiting by his investigations at all. Still, it was his system, and its plot-formation gave him a zest for each day's work. Formerly George had done these basic investigations himself, but lately he had begun to think he might have more luck by leaving the new author to Jane. A consignment of books, on their way to George, had recently been seized at the port of

Harwich and ordered to be burnt by the local magistrates on the grounds of obscenity, and George was feeling unlucky at this particular time.

Besides, it saved him all the expense and nervous exhaustion involved in the vigilant lunching with unpredictable writers, and feeling his way with them as to whether their paranoia exceeded his. It was better altogether to let them talk to Jane in a café, or bed, or wherever she went with them. It was nerve-racking enough to George to wait for her report. He fancied that many times in the past year she had saved him from paying out more ready money for a book than necessary—as when she had reported a dire need for ready cash, or when she had told George exactly what part of the manuscript he should find fault with— it was usually the part in which the author took a special pride— in order to achieve the minimum resistance, if not the total collapse, of the author.

George had obtained a succession of three young wives on account of his continuous eloquence to them on the subject of the world of books, which they felt was an elevating one—he had deserted the other two, not they him—and he had not yet been declared bankrupt although he had undergone in the course of the years various tangled forms of business recon- struction which were probably too much for the nerves of his creditors to face legally, since none ever did.

George took a keen interest in Jane's training in the handling of a writer of books. Unlike his fireside eloquence to his wife Tilly, his advice to Jane in the office was furtive, for he half believed, in the twilight portion of his mind, that authors were sly enough to make themselves invisible and be always floating under the chairs of publishers' offices.

'You see, Jane,' said George, 'these tactics of mine are an essential part of the profession. All the publishers do it. The big firms do it too, they do it automatically. The big fellows can afford to do it automatically, they can't afford to acknowledge all the facts like me, too much face to lose. I've had to work out every move for myself and get everything clear in my mind where authors are concerned. In publishing, one is dealing with a temperamental raw material.'

He went over to the corner curtain which concealed a coat-rail, and pulled aside the curtain. He peered within, then closed the curtain again and continued, 'Always think of authors as your raw material, Jane, if you're going to stay in the world of books.' Jane took this for fact. She had now been given Nicholas Farringdon to work on. George had said he was a terrible risk. Jane judged his age to be just over thirty. He was known only as a poet of small talent and an anarchist of dubious loyalty to that cause; but even these details were not at first known to Jane. He had brought to George a worn-out-looking sheaf of typewritten pages, untidily stacked in a brown folder. The whole was entitled *The Sabbath Notebooks*.

Nicholas Farringdon differed in some noticeable respects from the other writers she had come across. He differed, un-noticeably so far, in that he knew he was being worked on. But meantime she observed he was more arrogant and more impatient than other authors of the intellectual class. She noticed he was more attractive.

She had achieved some success with the very intellectual author of *The Symbolism of Louisa May Alcott*, which George was now selling very well and fast in certain quarters, since it had a big lesbian theme. She had achieved some success with Rudi Bittesch, the Rumanian who called on her frequently at the club.

But Nicholas had produced a more upsetting effect than usual on George, who was moreover torn between his attraction to a book he could not understand and his fear of its failure. George handed him over to Jane for treatment and meanwhile complained nightly to Tilly that he was in the hands of a writer, lazy, irresponsible, insufferable, and cunning.

Inspired by a brain-wave, Jane's first approach to a writer had been, 'What is your raison d'être?' It had worked marvellously. She tried it on Nicholas Farringdon when he called to the office about his manuscript one day when George was 'at a meeting', which was to say, hiding in the back office. 'What is your raison d'être, Mr. Farringdon?'

He frowned at her in an abstract sort of way, as if she were a speaking machine that had gone wrong.

Inspired by another brain-wave Jane invited him to dine at the May of Teck Club. He accepted with a special modesty, plainly from concern for his book. It had been rejected by ten publishers already, as had most of the books that came to George.

His visit put Jane up in the estimation of the club. She had not expected him to react so eagerly to everything. Sipping black Nescafé in the drawing room with Jane, Selina, dark little Judy Redwood and Anne, he had looked round with a faint, contented smile. Jane had chosen her companions for the evening with the instinct of an experimental procuress which, when she perceived the extent of its success, she partly regretted and partly congratulated herself on, since she had not been sure from various reports whether Nicholas preferred men, and now she concluded that he at least liked both sexes. Selina's long unsurpassable legs arranged themselves diagonally from the deep chair where she lolled in the distinct attitude of being the only woman present who could afford to loll. There was something about Selina's lolling which gave her a queenly eminence. She visibly appraised Nicholas, while he continued to glance here and there at the several groups of chattering girls in other parts of the room. The terrace doors stood wide open to the cool night and presently from the recreation room there came, by way of the terrace, the sound of Joanna in the process of an elocution lesson.

> *I thought of Chatterton, the marvellous Boy,*
> *The sleepless Soul that perished in his pride;*
> *Of Him who walked in glory and in joy*
> *Following his plough, along the mountain-side;*
> *By our own spirits are we deified:*
> *We Poets in our youth begin in gladness;*
> *But thereof come in the end despondency and madness.*

'I wish she would stick to *The Wreck of the Deutschland*,' Judy Redwood said. 'She's marvellous with Hopkins.'

Joanna's voice was saying, 'Remember the stress on Chatterton and the slight pause to follow.'

Joanna's pupil recited:

I thought of Chatterton, the marvellous Boy,

*   *   *

The excitement over the slit window went on for the rest of the afternoon. Jane's brainwork proceeded against the background echoes of voices from the large wash-room where the lavatories were. The two other occupants of the top floor had returned, having been to their homes in the country for the week-end: Dorothy Markham, the impoverished niece of Lady Julia Markham who was chairwoman of the club's management committee, and Nancy Riddle, one of the club's many clergymen's daughters. Nancy was trying to overcome her Midlands accent, and took lessons in elocution from Joanna with this end in view.

Jane, at her brain-work, heard from the direction of the wash-room the success of Dorothy Markham's climb through the window. Dorothy's hips were thirty-six and a half inches; her bust measurement was only thirty-one, a fact which did not dismay her, as she intended to marry one of three young men out of her extensive acquaintance who happened to find themselves drawn to boyish figures, and although she did not know about such things as precisely as did her aunt, Dorothy knew well enough that her hipless and breastless shape would always attract the sort of young man who felt at home with it. Dorothy could emit, at any hour of the day or night, a waterfall of débutante chatter, which rightly gave the impression that on any occasion between talking, eating, and sleeping, she did not think, except in terms of these phrase-ripples of hers: 'Filthy lunch.' 'The most gorgeous wedding.' 'He actually raped her, she was amazed.' 'Ghastly film.' 'I'm desperately well, thanks, how are you?'

Her voice from the wash-room distracted Jane: 'Oh hell, I'm black with soot, I'm absolutely filthington.' She opened Jane's door without knocking and put in her head. 'Got any soapyjo?' It was some months before she was to put her head round Jane's door and announce, 'Filthy luck. I'm preggers. Come to the wedding.'

Jane said, on being asked for the use of her soap, 'Can you lend me fifteen shillings till next Friday?' It was her final resort for getting rid of people when she was doing brain-work.

Evidently, from the sound of things, Nancy Riddle was stuck in the window. Nancy was getting hysterical. Finally, Nancy was released and calmed, as was betokened by the gradual replacement of Midlands vowels with standard English ones issuing from the wash-room.

Jane continued with her work, describing her effort to herself as pressing on regardless. All the club, infected by the Air Force idiom current among the dormitory virgins, used this phrase continually.

She had put aside Nicholas's manuscript for the time being, as it was a sticky proposition; she had not yet, in fact, grasped the theme of the book, as was necessary before deciding on a significant passage to cast doubt upon, although she had already thought of the comment she would recommend George to make: 'Don't you think this part is a bit derivative?' Jane had thought of it in a brain-wave.

She had put the book aside. She was at work, now, on some serious spare-time work for which she was paid. This came into the department of her life that had to do with Rudi Bittesch whom she hated, at this stage in her life, for his unattractive appearance. He was too old for her, besides everything else. When in a depressed state of mind, she found it useful to remember that she was only twenty-two, for the fact cheered her up. She looked down Rudi's list of famous authors and their respective addresses to see who still remained to be done. She took a sheet of writing paper and wrote her great-aunt's address in the country, followed by the date. She then wrote:

Dear Mr. Hemingway,
    I am addressing this letter to you care of your publisher in the confidence that it will be sent on to you.

This was an advisable preliminary, Rudi said, because sometimes publishers were instructed to open authors' letters and throw them away if not of sufficient business importance, but this approach, if it got into the publishers' hands, 'might touch their heart'. The rest of the letter was entirely Jane's province. She paused to await a small brain-wave, and after a moment continued:

I am sure you receive many admiring letters, and have hesitated to add yet another to your post-bag. But since my release from prison, where I have been for the past two years and four months, I have felt more and more that I want you to know how much your novels meant to me during that time. I had few visitors. My allotted weekly hours of leisure were spent in the Library. It was unheated alas, but I did not notice the cold as I read on. Nothing I read gave me so much courage to face the future and to build a new future on my release as *For Whom The Bell Tolls*. The novel gave me back my faith in life.

I just want you to know this, and to say 'Thank you'.

Yours sincerely

(Miss) J. Wright.

PS. This is not a begging letter. I assure you I would return any money that was sent to me.

If this succeeded in reaching him it might bring a hand-written reply. The prison letter and the asylum letter were more liable to bring replies in the author's own hand than any other type of letter, but one had to choose an author 'with heart', as Rudi said. Authors without heart seldom replied at all, and if they did it was a typewritten letter. For a typewritten letter signed by the author, Rudi paid two shillings if the autograph was scarce, but if the author's signature was available every-where, and the letter a mere formal acknowledgment, Rudi paid nothing. For a letter in the author's own handwriting Rudi paid five shillings for the first page and a shilling thereafter. Jane's ingenuity was therefore awakened to the feat of composing the sort of letters which would best move the recipient to reply in total holograph.

Rudi paid for the writing paper and the postage. He told her he only wanted the letters 'for sentimental purpose of my collec-tion'. She had seen his collection. But she assumed that he was collecting them with an eye to their increasing value year by year.

'If I write myself it does not ring true; I do not get interesting replies. By the way, my English is not like the English of an English girl.'

She would have made her own collection if only she had not needed the ready money, and could afford to save up the letters for the future.

'Never ask for money in your letters,' Rudi had warned her. 'Do not mention the subject of money. It makes criminal offence under false pretences.' However, she had the brainwave of adding her postscript, to make sure.

Jane had worried, at first, lest she should be found out and get into some sort of trouble. Rudi reassured her. 'You say you only make a joke. It is not criminal. Who would check up on you, by the way? Do you think Bernard Shaw is going to write and make questions about you from the old aunt? Bernard Shaw is a Name.'

Bernard Shaw had in fact proved disappointing. He had sent a type-written postcard:

> Thank you for your letter in praise of my writings. As you say they have consoled you in your misfortunes, I shall not attempt to gild the lily by my personal comments. As you say you desire no money I shall not press upon you my holograph signature which has some cash value. G.B.S.

The initials, too, had been typed.

Jane learned by experience. Her illegitimate-child letter brought a sympathetic reply from Daphne du Maurier, for which Rudi paid his price. With some authors a scholarly question about the underlying meaning worked best. One day, on a brain-wave, she wrote to Henry James at the Athenaeum Club.

'That was foolish of you because James is dead, by the way,' Rudi said.

'Do you want a letter from an author called Nicholas Farringdon?' she said.

'No, I have known Nicholas Farringdon, he's no good, he is not likely to be a Name ever. What has he written?'

'A book called *The Sabbath Notebooks*.'

'Is it religious?'

'Well, he calls it political philosophy. It's just a lot of notes and thoughts.'

'It smells religious. He will finish up as a reactionary Catholic, to obey the Pope. Already I have predicted this before the war.'

'He's jolly good-looking.'

She hated Rudi. He was not at all attractive. She addressed and stamped her letter to Ernest Hemingway and ticked off his name on the list, writing the date beside it. The girls' voices had disappeared from the wash-room. Anne's wireless was singing:

> *There were angels dining at the Ritz*
> *And a nightingale sang in Berkeley Square.*

It was twenty minutes past six. There was time for one more letter before supper. Jane looked down the list.

Dear Mr. Maugham,
    I am addressing this letter to you at your club. . . .

Jane paused for thought. She ate a square of chocolate to keep her brain going till supper-time. The prison letter might not appeal to Maugham. Rudi had said he was cynical about human nature. On a brain-wave she recalled that he had been a doctor. It might be an idea to make up a sanatorium letter. . . . She had been ill for two years and four months with tuberculosis. After all, this disease was not attributable to human nature, there was nothing in it to be cynical about. She regretted having eaten the chocolate, and put the rest of the bar right at the back of a shelf in her cupboard where it was difficult to reach, as if hiding it from a child. The rightness of this action and the wrongness of her having eaten any at all were confirmed by Selina's voice from Anne's room. Anne had turned off the wireless and they had been talking. Selina would probably be stretched out on Anne's bed in her languid manner. This became certain as Selina began to repeat, slowly and solemnly, the Two Sentences.

The Two Sentences were a simple morning and evening exercise prescribed by the Chief Instructress of the Poise Course which Selina had recently taken, by correspondence, in twelve lessons for five guineas. The Poise Course believed strongly in auto-suggestion and had advised, for the maintenance of poise in the working woman, a repetition of the following two sentences twice a day:

> Poise is perfect balance, an equanimity of body and mind, complete composure whatever the social scene. Elegant dress, immaculate grooming, and perfect deportment all contribute to the attainment of self-confidence.

Even Dorothy Markham stopped her chatter for a few seconds every morning at eight-thirty and evening at six-thirty, in respect for Selina's Sentences. All the top floor was respectful. It had cost five guineas. The two floors below were indifferent. But the dormitories crept up on the landings to listen, they could hardly believe their ears, and saved up each word with savage joy to make their boyfriends in the Air Force laugh like a drain, which was how laughter was described in those circles. At the same time, the dormitory girls were envious of Selina, knowing in their hearts they would never quite be in the Selina class where looks were concerned.

The Sentences were finished by the time Jane had shoved her remaining piece of chocolate well out of sight and range. She returned to the letter. She had T.B. She gave a frail cough and looked round the room. It contained a wash-basin, a bed, a chest-of-drawers, a cupboard, a table and lamp, a wicker chair, a hard chair, a bookcase, a gas fire and a meter-box with a slot to measure the gas, shilling by shilling. Jane felt she might easily be in a room in a sanatorium.

'One last time,' said Joanna's voice from the floor below. She was now rehearsing Nancy Riddle, who was at this moment managing her standard English vowels very well.

'And again,' said Joanna. 'We've just got time before supper. I'll read the first stanza, then you follow on.'

> *At the top of the house the apples are laid in rows,*
> *And the skylight lets the moonlight in, and those*
> *Apples are deep-sea apples of green. There goes*
> *A cloud on the moon in the autumn night.*

Chapter Four

IT was July 1945, three weeks before the general election.

> They are lying in rows there, under the gloomy beams;
>   On the sagging floor; they gather the silver streams
>   Out of the moon, those moonlit apples of dreams
>   And quiet is the steep stair under.

'I wish she would stick to *The Wreck of the Deutschland*.'
'Do you? I rather like *Moonlit Apples*.'

We come now to Nicholas Farringdon in his thirty-third year. He was said to be an anarchist. No-one at the May of Teck Club took this seriously as he looked quite normal; that is to say, he looked slightly dissipated, like the disappointing son of a good English family that he was. That each of his brothers—two accountants and one dentist—said of him from the time he left Cambridge, in the mid 1930's, 'Nicholas is a bit of a misfit, I'm afraid,' would not have surprised anyone.

Jane Wright applied for information about him to Rudi Bittesch who had known Nicholas throughout the 1930's. 'You don't bother with him. He is a mess by the way,' Rudi said. 'I know him well, he is a good friend of mine.' From Rudi she gathered that before the war he had been always undecided whether to live in England or France, and whether he preferred men or women, since he alternated between passionate intervals with both. Also, he could never make up his mind between suicide and an equally drastic course of action known as Father D'Arcy. Rudi explained that the latter was a Jesuit philosopher who had the monopoly for converting the English intellectuals. Nicholas was a pacifist up to the outbreak of war, Rudi said, then he joined the army. Rudi said, 'I have met him one day in Piccadilly wearing his uniform, and he said to me the war has brought him peace. Next thing he is psycho-analysed out of the army, a wangle, and he is working for the Intelligence. The anarchists have given him up but he calls himself an anarchist, by the way.'

Far from putting Jane against Nicholas Farringdon, the scraps of his history that came to her by way of Rudi gave him an irresistible heroism in her mind, and, through her, in the eyes of the top-floor girls.

'He must be a genius,' said Nancy Riddle.

Nicholas had a habit of saying, 'When I'm famous . . .' when referring to the remote future, with the same cheerful irony that went into the preface of the bus conductor on the No. 73 route to his comments on the law of the land: 'When I come to power . . .'

Jane showed Rudi *The Sabbath Notebooks*, so entitled because Nicholas had used as an epigraph the text 'The Sabbath was made for Man, not Man for the Sabbath'.

'George must be out of his mind to publish this,' Rudi said when he brought it back to Jane. They sat in the recreation room at the other end of which, cornerwise by the open french window, a girl was practising scales on the piano with as much style as she could decently apply to the scales. The music-box tinkle was far enough away, and sufficiently dispersed by the Sunday morning sounds from the terrace, not to intrude too strongly on Rudi's voice, as he read out, in his foreign English, small passages from Nicholas's book in order to prove something to Jane. He did this as a cloth merchant, perhaps wishing to persuade a customer to buy his best quality of goods, might first produce samples of inferior stuff, feel it, invite comment, shrug, and toss it away. Jane was convinced that Rudi was right in his judgment of what he was reading, but she was really more fascinated by what small glimpses of Nicholas Farringdon's personality she got from Rudi's passing remarks. Nicholas was the only presentable intellectual she had met.

'It is not bad, not good,' said Rudi, putting his head this way, that way, as he said it. 'It is mediocrity. I recall he composed this in 1938 when he had a freckled bed-mate of the female sex; she was an anarchist and pacifist. Listen, by the way . . .' He read out:

X is writing a history of anarchism. Anarchism properly has no history in the sense that X intends—i.e. in the sense of continuity and development. It is a spontaneous movement of people in particular times and circumstances. A history of anarchism would not be in the nature of political history, it would be analogous to a history of the heartbeat. One may make new discoveries about it, one may compare its reactions under varying conditions, but there is nothing new of itself.

Jane was thinking of the freckled girl-friend whom Nicholas had slept with at the time, and she almost fancied they had taken *The Sabbath Notebooks* to bed together. 'What happened to his girl-friend?' Jane said. 'There is nothing wrong with this,' Rudi said, referring to what he had just read, 'but it is not so magnificent a great truth that he should like a great man place it on the page, by the way, in a paragraph alone. He makes *pensées* as he is too lazy to write the essay. Listen . . .'

Jane said, 'What happened to the girl?'

'She went to prison for pacifism maybe, I don't know. If I would be George I would not touch this book. Listen . . .'

Every communist has a fascist frown; every fascist has a communist smile.

'Ha!' said Rudi.

'I thought that was a very profound bit,' Jane said, as it was the only bit she could remember.

'That is why he writes it in, he counts that the bloody book has got to have a public, so he puts in some little bit of aphorism, very clever, that a girl like you likes to hear, by the way. It means nothing, this, where is the meaning?' Most of Rudi's last words were louder-sounding than he had intended, as the girl at the piano had paused for rest.

'There's no need to get excited,' said Jane loudly.

The girl at the piano started a new set of rippling tinkles.

'We move to the drawing room,' said Rudi.

'No, everyone's in the drawing room this morning,' Jane said. 'There's not a quiet corner in the drawing room.' She did not particularly want to display Rudi to the rest of the club.

Up and down the scales went the girl at the piano. From a window above, Joanna, fitting in an elocution lesson with Miss

Harper, the cook, in the half-hour before the Sunday joint was ready to go in the oven, said, 'Listen':

> *Ah! Sun-flower! weary of time,*
> *Who countest the steps of the Sun;*
> *Seeking after that sweet golden clime,*
> *Where the traveller's journey is done;*

'Now try it,' said Joanna. 'Very slowly on the third line. Think of a sweet golden clime as you say it.'

> *Ah! Sun-flower! . . .*

The dormitory girls who had spilled out of the drawing room on to the terrace chattered like a parliament of fowls. The little notes of the scales followed one another obediently. 'Listen,' said Rudi:

> Everyone should be persuaded to remember how far, and with what a pathetic thump, the world has fallen from grace, that it needs must appoint politicians for its keepers, that its emotions, whether of consolation at breakfast-time or fear in the evening . . .

Rudi said, 'You notice his words, that he says the world has fallen from grace? This is the reason that he is no anarchist, by the way. They chuck him out when he talks like a son of the Pope. This man is a mess that he calls himself an anarchist; the anarchists do not make all that talk of original sin, so forth; they permit only anti-social tendencies, unethical conduct, so forth. Nick Farringdon is a diversionist, by the way.'

'Do you call him Nick?' Jane said.

'Sometimes in the pubs, the *Wheatsheaf* and the *Gargoyle*, so on, he was Nick in those days. Except there was a barrow-boy called him Mr. Farringdon. Nicholas said to him, "Look, I wasn't christened Mister," but was no good; the barrow-boy was his friend, by the way.'

'Once more,' said Joanna's voice.

> *Ah! Sun-flower! weary of time,*

'Listen,' said Rudi:

Nevertheless, let our moment or opportunity be stated. We do not need a government. We do not need a House of Commons. Parliament should dissolve forever. We could manage very well in our movement towards a complete anarchist society, with our great but powerless institutions: we could manage with the monarchy as an example of the dignity inherent in the free giving and receiving of precedence and favour without power; the churches for the spiritual needs of the people; the House of Lords for purposes of debate and recommendation; and the universities for consultation. We do not need institutions with power. The practical affairs of society could be dealt with locally by the Town, Borough, and Village Councils. International affairs could be conducted by variable representatives in a non-professional capacity. We do not need professional politicians with an eye to power. The grocer, the doctor, the cook, should serve their country for a term as men serve on a jury. We can be ruled by the corporate will of men's hearts alone. It is Power that is defunct, not as we are taught, the powerless institutions.

'I ask you a question,' Rudi said. 'It is a simple question. He wants monarchy, he wants anarchism. What does he want? These two are enemies in all of history. Simple answer is, he is a mess.'

'How old was the barrow-boy?' Jane said.

'And again,' said Joanna's voice from the upper window.

Dorothy Markham had joined the girls on the sunny terrace. She was telling a hunting story. '. . . the only one time I've been thrown, it shook me to the core. What a brute!'

'Where did you land?'

'Where do you think?'

The girl at the piano stopped and folded her scale-sheet with seemly concentration.

'I go,' said Rudi, looking at his watch. 'I have an appointment to meet a contact for a drink.' He rose and once more, before he handed over the book, flicked through the typewritten pages. He said, sadly, 'Nicholas is a friend of mine, but

I regret to say he's a non-contributive thinker, by the way. Come here, listen to this:'

> There is a kind of truth in the popular idea of an anarchist as a wild man with a homemade bomb in his pocket. In modern times this bomb, fabricated in the back workshops of the imagination, can only take one effective form: Ridicule.

Jane said, ' "Only take" isn't grammatical, it should be "take only". I'll have to change that, Rudi.'

*　　　*　　　*

So much for the portrait of the martyr as a young man as it was suggested to Jane on a Sunday morning between armistice and armistice, in the days of everyone's poverty, in 1945. Jane, who lived to distort it in many elaborate forms, at the time merely felt she was in touch with something reckless, intellectual, and Bohemian by being in touch with Nicholas. Rudi's contemptuous attitude bounded back upon himself in her estimation. She felt she knew too much about Rudi to respect him; and was presently astonished to find that there was indeed a sort of friendship between himself and Nicholas, lingering on from the past.

Meantime, Nicholas touched lightly on the imagination of the girls of slender means, and they on his. He had not yet slept on the roof with Selina on the hot summer nights—he gaining access from the American-occupied attic of the hotel next door, and she through the slit window—and he had not yet witnessed that action of savagery so extreme that it forced him involuntarily to make an entirely unaccustomed gesture, the signing of the cross upon himself. At this time Nicholas still worked for one of those left-hand departments of the Foreign Office, the doings of which the right-hand did not know. It came under Intelligence. After the Normandy landing he had been sent on several missions to France. Now there was very little left for his department to do except wind-up. Winding-up was arduous, it involved the shuffling of papers and people from office to office; particularly it involved considerable shuffling between the

British and American Intelligence pockets in London. He had a
bleak furnished room at Fulham. He was bored.

*　　　*　　　*

'I've got something to tell you, Rudi,' said Jane.

'Hold on please, I have a customer.'

'I'll ring you back later, then, I'm in a hurry. I only wanted
to tell you that Nicholas Farringdon's dead. Remember that
book of his he never published—he gave you the manuscript.
Well, it might be worth something now, and I thought——'

'Nick's dead? Hold on please, Jane. I have a customer waiting
here to buy a book. Hold on.'

'I'll ring you later.'

*　　　*　　　*

Nicholas came, then, to dine at the club.

>   *I thought of Chatterton, the marvellous Boy,*
>   *The sleepless Soul that perished in his Pride;*

'Who is that?'

'It's Joanna Childe, she teaches elocution, you must meet
her.'

The twittering movements at other points in the room,
Joanna's singular voice, the beautiful aspects of poverty and
charm among these girls in the brown-papered drawing room,
Selina, furled like a long soft sash, in her chair, came to Nicholas
in a gratuitous flow. Months of boredom had subdued him to
intoxication by an experience which, at another time, might
itself have bored him.

Some days later he took Jane to a party to meet the people
she longed to meet, young male poets in corduroy trousers and
young female poets with waist-length hair, or at least females
who typed the poetry and slept with the poets, it was nearly
the same thing. Nicholas took her to supper at Bertorelli's;
then he took her to a poetry reading at a hired meetinghouse in
the Fulham Road; then he took her on to a party with some of
the people he had collected from the reading. One of the poets
who was well thought of had acquired a job at Associated News

in Fleet Street, in honour of which he had purchased a pair of luxurious pigskin gloves; he displayed these proudly. There was an air of a resistance movement against the world at this poetry meeting. Poets seemed to understand each other with a secret instinct, almost a kind of prearrangement, and it was plain that the poet with the gloves would never show off these poetic gloves so frankly, or expect to be understood so well in relation to them, at his new job in Fleet Street or anywhere else, as here.

Some were men demobilised from the non-combatant corps. Some had been unfit for service for obvious reasons—a nervous twitch of the facial muscles, bad eyesight, or a limp. Others were still in battle dress. Nicholas had been out of the army since the month after Dunkirk, from which he had escaped with a wound in the thumb; his release from the army had followed a mild nervous disorder in the month after Dunkirk.

Nicholas stood noticeably aloof at the poets' gathering, but although he greeted his friends with a decided reserve, it was evident that he wanted Jane to savour her full joy of it. In fact, he wanted her to invite him again to the May of Teck Club, as dawned on her later in the evening.

The poets read their poems, two each, and were applauded. Some of these poets were to fail and fade into a no-man's-land of Soho public houses in a few years' time, and become the familiar messes of literary life. Some, with many talents, faltered, in time, from lack of stamina, gave up, and took a job in advertising or publishing, detesting literary people above all. Others succeeded and became paradoxes; they did not always continue to write poetry, or even poetry exclusively.

One of these young poets, Ernest Claymore, later became a mystical stockbroker of the 1960's, spending his weekdays urgently in the City, three week-ends each month at his country cottage—an establishment of fourteen rooms, where he ignored his wife and, alone in his study, wrote Thought—and one week-end a month in retreat at a monastery. In the 1960's Ernest Claymore read a book a week in bed before sleep, and sometimes addressed a letter to the press about a book review: 'Sir, Maybe I'm dim. I have read your review of . . .'; he was to publish three short books of philosophy which everyone could easily understand indeed; at the moment in question, the summer of 1945, he was a dark-eyed young poet at the poetry recital, and had just finished reading, with husky force, his second contribution:

> *I in my troubled night of the dove clove brightly my*
> *Path from the tomb of love incessantly to redress my*
> *Articulate womb, that new and necessary rose, exposing my . . .*

He belonged to the Cosmic school of poets. Jane, perceiving that he was orthosexual by definition of his manner and appearance, was uncertain whether to cultivate him for future acquaintance or whether to hang on to Nicholas. She managed to do both, since Nicholas brought along this dark husky poet, this stockbroker to be, to the party which followed, and there Jane was able to make a future assignment with him before Nicholas drew her aside to enquire further into the mysterious life of the May of Teck Club.

'It's just a girls' hostel,' she said, 'that's all it boils down to.'

Beer was served in jam-jars, which was an affectation of the highest order, since jam-jars were at that time in shorter supply than glasses and mugs. The house where the party was held was in Hampstead. There was a stifling crowd. The hosts, Nicholas said, were communist intellectuals. He led her up to a bedroom where they sat on the edge of an unmade bed and looked, with philosophical exhaustion on Nicholas's side, and on hers the enthusiasm of the neophyte Bohemian, at the bare boards of the floor. The people of the house, said Nicholas, were undeniably communist intellectuals, as one could see from the variety of dyspepsia remedies on the bathroom shelf. He said he would point them out to her on the way downstairs when they rejoined the party. By no means, said Nicholas, did the hosts expect to meet their guests at this party. 'Tell me about Selina,' said Nicholas.

Jane's dark hair was piled on top of her head. She had a large face. The only attractive thing about her was her youth and those mental areas of inexperience she was not yet conscious of. She had forgotten for the time being that her job was to reduce Nicholas's literary morale as far as possible, and was treacherously behaving as if he were the genius that, before the week was out, he claimed to be in the letter he got her to forge for him in Charles Morgan's name. Nicholas had decided to do everything nice for Jane, except sleep with her, in the interests of two projects: the publication of his book and his infiltration of the May of Teck Club in general and Selina in particular. 'Tell me more about Selina.' Jane did not then, or at any time, realise that he had received from his first visit to the May of Teck Club a poetic image that teased his mind and pestered him for details as he now pestered Jane. She knew nothing of his boredom and social discontent. She did not see the May of Teck Club as a microcosmic ideal society; far from it. The beautiful heedless poverty of a Golden Age did not come into the shilling-meter life which any sane girl would regard only as a temporary one until better opportunities occurred.

> *A damsel with a dulcimer*
> *In a vision once I saw:*
> *It was an Abyssinian maid,*

The voice had wafted with the night breeze into the drawing room. Nicholas said, now, 'Tell me about the elocution teacher.'

'Oh, Joanna—you must meet her.'

'Tell me about the borrowing and lending of clothes.'

Jane pondered as to what she could barter for this information which he seemed to want. The party downstairs was going on without them. The bare boards under her feet and the patchy walls seemed to hold out no promise of becoming memorable by tomorrow. She said, 'We've got to discuss your book some time. George and I've got a list of queries.'

Nicholas lolled on the unmade bed and casually thought he would probably have to plan some defence measures with George. His jam-jar was empty. He said, 'Tell me more about Selina. What does she do apart from being secretary to a pansy?'

Jane was not sure how drunk she was, and could not bring

herself to stand up, this being the test. She said, 'Come to lunch on Sunday.' Sunday lunch for a guest was two-and-sixpence extra; she felt she might be taken to more of these parties by Nicholas, among the inner circle of the poets of today; but she supposed he wanted to take Selina out, and that was that; she thought he would probably want to sleep with Selina, and as Selina had slept with two men already, Jane did not envisage any obstacle. It made her sad to think, as she did, that the whole rigmarole of his interest in the May of Teck Club, and the point of their sitting in this bleak room, was his desire to sleep with Selina. She said, 'What bits would you say were the most important?'

'What bits?'

'Your book,' she said. '*The Sabbath Notebooks.* George is looking for a genius. It must be you.'

'It's all important.' He formed the plan immediately of forging a letter from someone crudely famous to say it was a work of genius. Not that he believed it to be so one way or the other, the idea of such an unspecific attribute as genius not being one on which his mind was accustomed to waste its time. However, he knew a useful word when he saw it, and, perceiving the trend of Jane's question, made his plan. He said, 'Tell me again that delightful thing Selina repeats about poise.'

'Poise is perfect balance, an equanimity of body and mind, complete composure whatever the social scene. Elegant dress, immaculate . . . Oh, Christ,' she said, 'I'm tired of picking crumbs of meat out of the shepherd's pie, picking with a fork to get the little bits of meat separated from the little bits of potato. You don't know what it's like trying to eat enough to live on and at the same time avoid fats and carbohydrates.'

Nicholas kissed her tenderly. He felt there might be a sweetness in Jane, after all, for nothing reveals a secret sweetness so much as a personal point of misery bursting out of a phlegmatic creature.

Jane said, 'I've got to feed my brain.'

He said he would try to get her a pair of nylon stockings from the American with whom he worked. Her legs were bare and dark-haired. There and then he gave her six clothing coupons out of his coupon book. He said she could have his next week's egg. She said, 'You need your egg for your brain.'

'I have breakfast at the American canteen,' he said. 'We have eggs there, and orange juice.'

She said she would take his egg. The egg-ration was one a week at this time, it was the beginning of the hardest period of food-rationing, since the liberated countries had now to be supplied. Nicholas had a gas-ring in his bed-sitting room on which he cooked his supper when he was at home and remembered about supper. He said, 'You can have all my tea, I drink coffee. I get it from the Americans.'

She said she would be glad of his tea. The tea-ration was two ounces one week and three ounces the next, alternately. Tea was useful for bartering purposes. She felt she would really have to take the author's side, where Nicholas was concerned, and somehow hoodwink George. Nicholas was a true artist and had some feelings. George was only a publisher. She would have to put Nicholas wise to George's fault-finding technique of business.

'Let's go down,' Nicholas said.

The door opened and Rudi Bittesch stood watching them for a moment. Rudi was always sober.

'Rudi!' said Jane with unusual enthusiasm. She was glad to be seen to know somebody in this milieu who had not been introduced by Nicholas. It was a way of showing that she belonged to it.

'Well, well,' Rudi said. 'How are you doing these days, Nick, by the way?'

Nicholas said he was on loan to the Americans.

Rudi laughed like a cynical uncle and said himself, he too could have worked for the Americans if he had wanted to sell out.

'Sell out what?' Nicholas said.

'My integrity to work only for peace,' said Rudi. 'By the way, come and join the party and forget it.'

On the way down he said to Nicholas, 'You're publishing a book with Throvis-Mew? I hear this news by Jane.'

Jane said quickly, in case Rudi should reveal that he had already seen the book, 'It's a sort of anarchist book.'

Rudi said to Nicholas, 'You still like anarchism, by the way?'
'But not anarchists by and large, by the way,' Nicholas said.

* * *

'How has he died, by the way?' said Rudi.
'He was martyred, they say,' said Jane.
'In Haiti? How is this?'
'I don't know much, except what I get from the news sources. Reuters says a local rising. Associated News has a bit that's just come in . . . I was thinking of that manuscript *The Sabbath Notebooks*.'
'I have it still. If he is famous by his death, I find it. How has he died . . . ?'
'I can't hear you, it's a rotten line . . .'
'I say I can't hear, Rudi . . .'
'How has he died . . . By what means?'
'It will be worth a lot of money, Rudi.'
'I find it. This line is bad by the way, can you hear me? How has he died . . . ?'
'. . . a hut . . .'
'I can't hear . . .'
'. . . in a valley . . .'
'Speak loud.'
'. . . in a clump of palms . . . deserted . . . it was market day, everyone has gone to market.'
'I find it. There is maybe a market for this Sabbath book. They make a cult of him, by the way?'
'He was trying to interfere with their superstitions, they said. They're getting rid of a lot of Catholic priests.'
'I can't hear a word. I ring you tonight, Jane. We meet later.'

Chapter Five

SELINA came into the drawing room wearing a high hoop-brimmed blue hat and shoes with high block wedges; these fashions from France, it was said, were symbols of the Resistance. It was late on Sunday morning. She had been for a seemly walk along the pathways of Kensington Gardens with Greggie.

Selina took off her hat and laid it on the sofa beside her. She said, 'I've got a guest for lunch, Felix.' Felix was Colonel G. Felix Dobell who was head of a branch of the American Intelligence Service which occupied the top floor of the hotel next door to the club. He had been among a number of men invited to one of the club's dances, and there had selected Selina for himself.

Jane said, 'I'm having Nicholas Farringdon for lunch.'

'But he was here during the week.'

'Well, he's coming again. I went to a party with him.'

'Good,' said Selina. 'I like him.'

Jane said, 'Nicholas works with the American Intelligence. He probably knows your Colonel.'

It was found that the men had not met. They shared a table for four with the two girls, who waited on them, fetching the food from the hatch. Sunday lunch was the best meal of the week. Whenever one of the girls rose to fetch and carry, Felix Dobell half-rose in his chair, then sat down again, for courtesy. Nicholas lolled like an Englishman possessed of droits de seigneur while the two girls served him.

The warden, a tall grey-skinned woman habitually dressed in grey, made a brief announcement that 'the Conservative M.P. was coming to give a pre-election discussion' on the following Tuesday.

Nicholas smiled widely so that his long dark face became even more good-looking. He seemed to like the idea of *giving* a discussion, and said so to the Colonel who amiably agreed with him. The Colonel seemed to be in love with the entire club,

Selina being the centre and practical focus of his feelings in this respect. This was a common effect of the May of Teck Club on its male visitors, and Nicholas was enamoured of the entity in only one exceptional way, that it stirred his poetic sense to a point of exasperation, for at the same time he discerned with irony the process of his own thoughts, how he was imposing upon this little society an image incomprehensible to itself.

The grey warden's conversational voice could be heard addressing grey-haired Greggie who sat with her at table, 'You see, Greggie, I can't be everywhere in the club at once.'

Jane said to her companions, 'That's the one fact that makes life bearable for us.'

'That is a very original idea,' said the American Colonel, but he was referring to something that Nicholas had said before Jane had spoken, when they were discussing the political outlook of the May of Teck Club. Nicholas had offered: 'They should be told not to vote at all, I mean persuaded not to vote at all. We could do without the government. We could manage with the monarchy, the House of Lords, the . . .'

Jane looked bored, as she had several times read this bit in the manuscript, and she rather wanted to discuss personalities, which always provided her with more real pleasure than any impersonal talk, however light and fantastic, although she did not yet admit this fact in her aspiring brain. It was not till Jane had reached the apex of her career as a reporter and interviewer for the largest of women's journals that she found her right role in life, while still incorrectly subscribing to a belief that she was capable of thought—indeed, was demonstrating a capacity for it. But now she sat at table with Nicholas and longed for him to stop talking to the Colonel about the happy possibilities inherent in the delivery of political speeches to the May of Teck girls, and the different ways in which they might be corrupted. Jane felt guilty about her boredom. Selina laughed with poise when Nicholas said, next, 'We could do without a central government. It's bad for us, and, what's worse, it's bad for the politicians . . .' but that he was as serious about this as it was possible for his self-mocking mind to be about anything, seemed to be apparent to the Colonel, who amazingly assured

Nicholas, 'My wife Gareth also is a member of the Guild of Ethical Guardians in our town. She's a hard worker.'

Nicholas, reminding himself that poise was perfect balance, accepted this statement as a rational response. 'Who are the Ethical Guardians?' said Nicholas.

'They stand for the ideal of purity in the home. They keep a special guard on reading material. Many homes in our town will not accept literature unstamped by the Guardians' crest of honour.'

Nicholas now saw that the Colonel had understood him to hold ideals, and had connected them with the ideals of his wife Gareth, these being the only other ideals he could immediately lay hands on. It was the only explanation. Jane wanted to put everything straight. She said, 'Nicholas is an anarchist.'

'Ah no, Jane,' said the Colonel. 'That's being a bit hard on your author-friend.'

Selina had already begun to realise that Nicholas held unorthodox views about things to the point where they might be regarded as crackpot to the sort of people she was used to. She felt his unusualness was a weakness, and this weakness in an attractive man held desirability for her. There were two other men of her acquaintance who were vulnerable in some way. She was not perversely interested in this fact, so far as she felt no urge to hurt them; if she did so, it was by accident. What she liked about these men was that neither of them wished to possess her entirely. She slept with them happily because of this. She had another man friend, a business-man of thirty-five, still in the Army, very wealthy, not weak. He was altogether possessive; Selina thought she might marry him eventually. In the meantime she looked at Nicholas as he conversed in this mad sequence with the Colonel, and thought she could use him.

They sat in the drawing room and planned the afternoon which had developed into a prospective outing for four in the Colonel's car. By this time he had demanded to be called Felix.

He was about thirty-two. He was one of Selina's weak men. His weakness was an overwhelming fear of his wife, so that he took great pains not to be taken unawares in bed with Selina on their country week-ends, even although his wife was in California. As he locked the door of the bedroom Felix would say, very worried, 'I wouldn't like to hurt Gareth,' or some such thing. The first time he did this Selina looked through the bathroom door, tall and beautiful with wide eyes, she looked at Felix to see what was the matter with him. He was still anxious and tried the door again. On the late Sunday mornings, when the bed was already uncomfortable with breakfast crumbs, he would sometimes fall into a muse and be far away. He might then say, 'I hope there's no way Gareth could come by knowledge of this hideout.' And so he was one of those who did not want to possess Selina entirely; and being beautiful and liable to provoke possessiveness, she found this all right provided the man was attractive to sleep with and be out with, and was a good dancer. Felix was blond with an appearance of reserved nobility which he must have inherited. He seldom said anything very humorous, but was willing to be gay. On this Sunday afternoon in the May of Teck Club he proposed to drive to Richmond, which was a long way by car from Knightsbridge in those days when petrol was so scarce that nobody went driving for pleasure except in an American's car, in the vague mistaken notion that their vehicles were supplied by 'American' oil, and so were not subject to the conscience of British austerity or the reproachful question about the necessity of the journey displayed at all places of public transport.

Jane, observing Selina's long glance of perfect balance and equanimity resting upon Nicholas, immediately foresaw that she would be disposed in the front seat with Felix while Selina stepped, with her arch-footed poise, into the back, where Nicholas would join her; and she foresaw that this arrangement would come about with effortless elegance. She had no objection to Felix, but she could not hope to win him for herself, having nothing to offer a man like Felix. She felt she had a certain something, though small, to offer Nicholas, this being her literary and brain-work side which Selina lacked. It was in fact a misunderstanding of Nicholas—she vaguely thought of him as a more attractive Rudi Bittesch—to imagine he would receive more pleasure and reassurance from a literary girl than simply a girl. It was the girl in Jane that had moved him to kiss her at the party; she might have gone further with Nicholas without her literary leanings. This was a mistake she continued to make in her relations with men, inferring from her own preference for men of books and literature their preference for women of the same business. And it never really occurred to her that literary men, if they like women at all, do not want literary women but girls.

But Jane was presently proved right in her prediction about the seating arrangements in the car; and it was her repeated accuracy of intuition in such particulars as these which gave her confidence in her later career as a prophetic gossip-columnist.

Meantime the brown-lined drawing room began to chirp into life as the girls came in from the dining room bearing trays of coffee cups. The three spinsters, Greggie, Collie, and Jarvie, were introduced to the guests, as was their accustomed right. They sat in hard chairs and poured coffee for the young loungers. Collie and Jarvie were known to be in the process of a religious quarrel, but they made an effort to conceal their differences for the occasion. Jarvie, however, was agitated by the fact that her coffee cup had been filled too full by Collie. She laid the cup and swimming saucer on a table a little way behind her, and ignored it significantly. She was dressed to go out, with gloves, bag, and hat. She was presently going to take her Sunday-school class. The gloves were made of a stout green-brown suède. Jarvie smoothed them out on her lap, then fluttered her fingers over the cuffs, turning them back. They revealed the utility stamp, two half-moons facing the same way, which was the mark of price-controlled clothes and which, on dresses, where the mark was merely stamped on a tape sewn on the inside, everyone removed. Jarvie surveyed her gloves' irremovable utility mark with her head at a slight angle, as if considering some question connected with it. She then smoothed out the gloves again and jerkily adjusted her spectacles. Jane felt in a great panic to get married. Nicholas, on hearing that Jarvie was about to go to teach a Sunday-school class, was solicitous to enquire about it.

'I think we had better drop the subject of religion,' Jarvie said, as if in conclusion of an argument long in progress. Collie said, 'I thought we *had* dropped it. What a lovely day for Richmond!'

Selina slouched elegantly in her chair, untouched by the threat of becoming a spinster, as she would never be that sort of spinster, anyway. Jane recalled the beginning of the religious quarrel overheard on all floors, since it had taken place in the echoing wash-room on the second landing. Collie had at first accused Jarvie of failing to clean the sink after using it to wash up her dishes of stuff, which she surreptitiously cooked on her gas-ring where only kettles were lawfully permitted. Then, ashamed of her outburst, Collie had more loudly accused Jarvie of putting spiritual obstacles in her path 'just when you know I'm growing in grace'. Jarvie had then said something scornful about the Baptists as opposed to the true spirit of the Gospels. This religious row, with elaborations, had now lasted more than two weeks but the women were doing their best to conceal it. Collie now said to Jarvie, 'Are you going to waste your coffee with the milk in it?' This was a moral rebuke, for milk was on the ration. Jarvie turned, smoothed, patted, and pulled straight the gloves on her lap and breathed in and out. Jane wanted to tear off her clothes and run naked into the street, screaming. Collie looked with disapproval at Jane's bare fat knees.

Greggie, who had very little patience with the two other elder members, had been winning her way with Felix, and had enquired what went on 'up there, next door', meaning in the hotel, the top floor of which the American Intelligence was using, the lower floors being strangely empty and forgotten by the requisitioners.

'Ah, you'd be surprised, ma'am,' Felix said.

Greggie said she must show the men round the garden before they set off for Richmond. The fact that Greggie did practically all the gardening detracted from its comfort for the rest of the girls. Only the youngest and happiest girls could feel justified in using it to sit about in, as it was so much Greggie's toiled-at garden. Only the youngest and happiest could walk on the grass with comfort; they were not greatly given to scruples and consideration for others, by virtue of their unblighted spirits.

Nicholas had noticed a handsome bright-cheeked fair-haired girl standing, drinking down her coffee fairly quickly. She left the room with graceful speed when she had drunk her coffee.

Jane said, 'That's Joanna Childe who does elocution.'

Later, in the garden, while Greggie was conducting her tour, they heard Joanna's voice. Greggie was displaying her various particular items, rare plants reared from stolen cuttings, these being the only objects that Greggie would ever think of stealing. She boasted, like a true gardening woman, of her thefts and methods of acquiring snips of other people's rare plants. The sound of Joanna's afternoon pupil lilted down from her room.

Nicholas said, 'The voice is coming from up there, now. Last time, it came from the ground floor.'

'She uses her own room at week-ends when the recreation room is used a lot. We're very proud of Joanna.'

Joanna's voice followed her pupil's.

Greggie said, 'This hollow shouldn't be there. It's where the bomb dropped. It just missed the house.'

'Were you in the house at the time?' said Felix.

'I was,' said Greggie. 'I was in bed. Next moment I was on the floor. All the windows were broken. And it's my suspicion there was a second bomb that didn't go off. I'm almost sure I saw it drop as I picked myself up off the floor. But the disposal squad found only the one bomb and removed it. Anyway, if there's a second it must have died a natural death by now. I'm talking about the year 1942.'

Felix said, with his curious irrelevancy, 'My wife Gareth talks of coming over here with U.N.R.R.A. I wonder if she could put up at your Club in transit for a week or two? I have to be back and forth, myself. She would be lonely in London.'

'It would have been lying underneath the hydrangeas on the right if I was correct,' Greggie said.

> *The sea of faith*
> *Was once, too, at the full, and round earth's shore*
> *Lay like the folds of a bright girdle furled.*
> *But now I only hear*
> *Its melancholy, long, withdrawing roar,*
> *Retreating to the breath*
> *Of the night-wind, down the vast edges drear*
> *And naked shingles of the world.*

'We'd better be on our way to Richmond,' Felix said.

'We're awfully proud of Joanna,' said Greggie.

'A fine reader.'

'No, she recites from memory. But her pupils read, of course. It's elocution.'

Selina gracefully knocked some garden mud off her wedge shoes on the stone step, and the party moved inside.

The girls went to get ready. The men disappeared into the dark little downstairs cloakroom.

'That is a fine poem,' said Felix, for Joanna's voices were here, too, and the lesson had moved to *Kubla Khan*.

Nicholas almost said, 'She is orgiastical in her feeling for poetry. I can hear it in her voice,' but refrained in case the Colonel should say 'Really?' and he should go on to say, 'Poetry takes the place of sex for her, I think.'

'Really? She looked sexually fine to me.'

Which conversation did not take place, and Nicholas kept it for his notebooks.

They waited in the hall till the girls came down. Nicholas read the notice-board, advertising second-hand clothes for sale, or in exchange for clothing coupons. Felix stood back, a re-frainer from such intrusions on the girls' private business, but tolerant of the other man's curiosity. He said, 'Here they come.'

The number and variety of muted noises-off were consider-able. Laughter went on behind the folded doors of the first-floor dormitory. Someone was shovelling coal in the cellar, having left open the green baize door which led to those quarters. The telephone desk within the office rang distantly shrill with boy-friends, and various corresponding buzzes on the landings summoned the girls to talk. The sun broke through as the fore-cast had promised.

> *Weave a circle round him thrice,*
> *And close your eyes with holy dread,*
> *For he on honey-dew hath fed,*
> *And drunk the milk of Paradise.*

Chapter Six

'DEAR Dylan Thomas,' wrote Jane.

Downstairs, Nancy Riddle, who had finished her elocution lesson, was attempting to discuss with Joanna Childe the common eventualities arising from being a clergyman's daughter.

'My father's always in a filthy temper on Sundays. Is yours?'

'No, he's rather too occupied.'

'Father goes on about the Prayer Book. I must say, I agree with him there. It's out of date.'

'Oh, I think the Prayer Book's wonderful,' said Joanna. She had the Book of Common Prayer practically by heart, including the Psalms—especially the Psalms—which her father repeated daily at Matins and Evensong in the frequently empty church. In former years at the rectory Joanna had attended these services every day, and had made the responses from her pew, as it might be on 'Day 13', when her father would stand in his lofty meekness, robed in white over black, to read:

Let God arise, and let his enemies be scattered:

whereupon without waiting for pause Joanna would respond:

let them also that hate him flee before him.

The father continued:

Like as the smoke vanisheth, so shalt thou drive them away:

And Joanna came in swiftly:

and like as wax melteth at the fire, so let the ungodly perish at the presence of God.

And so on had circled the Psalms, from Day 1 to Day 31 of the months, morning and evening, in peace and war; and often the first curate, and then the second curate, took over the office, uttering as it seemed to the empty pews, but by faith to the congregations of the angels, the Englishly rendered intentions of the sweet singer of Israel.

Joanna lit the gas-ring in her room in the May of Teck Club
and put on the kettle. She said to Nancy Riddle:

'The Prayer Book is wonderful. There was a new version
got up in 1928, but Parliament put it out. Just as well, as it
happened.'

'What's the Prayer Book got to do with them?'

'It's within their jurisdiction funnily enough.'

'I believe in divorce,' Nancy said.

'What's that got to do with the Prayer Book?'

'Well, it's all connected with the C. of E. and all the arguing.'

Joanna mixed some powdered milk carefully with water from
the tap and poured the mixture upon two cups of tea. She passed
a cup to Nancy and offered saccharine tablets from a small tin
box. Nancy took one tablet, dropped it in her tea, and stirred it.
She had recently got involved with a married man who talked
of leaving his wife.

Joanna said, 'My father had to buy a new cloak to wear over
his cassock at funerals, he always catches cold at funerals. That
means no spare coupons for me this year.'

Nancy said, 'Does he wear a cloak? He must be High. My
father wears an overcoat; he's Low to Middle, of course.'

*   *   *

All through the first three weeks of July Nicholas wooed Selina
and at the same time cultivated Jane and others of the May of
Teck Club.

The sounds and sights impinging on him from the hall of
the club intensified themselves, whenever he called, into one
sensation, as if with a will of their own. He thought of the lines:

> *Let us roll all our strength, and all*
> *Our sweetness up into one ball;*

And I would like, he thought, to teach Joanna that poem or
rather demonstrate it; and he made spasmodic notes of all this
on the back pages of his *Sabbath* manuscript.

Jane told him everything that went on in the Club. 'Tell me
more,' he said. She told him things, in her clever way of intuition, which fitted his ideal of the place. In fact, it was not an

unjust notion, that it was a miniature expression of a free society, that it was a community held together by the graceful attributes of a common poverty. He observed that at no point did poverty arrest the vitality of its members but rather nourished it. Poverty differs vastly from want, he thought.

*　　　*　　　*

'Hallo, Pauline?'

'Yes?'

'It's Jane.'

'Yes?'

'I've got something to tell you. What's the matter?'

'I was resting.'

'Sleeping?'

'No, resting. I've just got back from the psychiatrist, he makes me rest after every session. I've got to lie down.'

'I thought you were finished with the psychiatrist. Are you not very well again?'

'This is a new one. Mummy found him, he's marvellous.'

'Well, I just wanted to tell you something, can you listen? Do you remember Nicholas Farringdon?'

'No, I don't think so. Who's he?'

'Nicholas . . . remember that last time on the roof at the May of Teck . . . Haiti, in a hut . . . among some palms, it was market day, everyone had gone to the market centre. Are you listening?'

*　　　*　　　*

We are in the summer of 1945 when he was not only enamoured of the May of Teck Club as an aesthetic and ethical conception of it, lovely frozen image that it was, but he presently slept with Selina on the roof.

> *The mountains look on Marathon*
> *And Marathon looks on the sea;*
> *And musing there an hour alone,*
> *I dream'd that Greece might still be free;*
> *For standing on the Persians' grave,*
> *I could not deem myself a slave.*

Joanna needs to know more life, thought Nicholas, as he loitered in the hall on one specific evening, but if she knew life she would not be proclaiming these words so sexually and matriarchally as if in the ecstatic act of suckling a divine child.

At the top of the house the apples are laid in rows.

She continued to recite as he loitered in the hall. No-one was about. Everyone was gathered somewhere else, in the drawing room or in the bedrooms, sitting round wireless sets, tuning in to some special programme. Then one wireless, and another, roared forth louder by far than usual from the upper floors; others tuned in to the chorus, justified in the din by the voice of Winston Churchill. Joanna ceased. The wirelesses spoke forth their simultaneous Sinaitic predictions of what fate would befall the freedom-loving electorate should it vote for Labour in the forthcoming elections. The wirelesses suddenly started to reason humbly:

We shall have Civil Servants . . .

The wireless changed their tones, they roared:

No longer civil . . .

Then they were sad and slow:

No longer . . .
. . . *servants.*'

Nicholas imagined Joanna standing by her bed, put out of business as it were, but listening, drawing it into her bloodstream. As in a dream of his own that depicted a dream of hers, he thought of Joanna in this immovable attitude, given up to the cadences of the wireless as if it did not matter what was producing them, the politician, or herself. She was a proclaiming statue in his mind.

A girl in a long evening dress slid in the doorway, furtively. Her hair fell round her shoulders in a brown curl. Through the bemused mind of the loitering, listening man went the fact of a girl slipping furtively into the hall; she had a meaning, even if she had no meaningful intention.

She was Pauline Fox. She was returning from a taxi-ride

round the park at the price of eight shillings. She had got into the taxi and told the driver to drive round, round anywhere, just drive. On such occasions the taxi-drivers suspected at first that she was driving out to pick up a man, then as the taxi circled the Park and threepences ticked up on the meter, the drivers suspected she was mad, or even, perhaps, one of those foreign royalties still exiled in London: and they concluded one or the other when she ordered them back to the door to which she had summoned them by carefully pre-arranged booking. It was dinner with Jack Buchanan which Pauline held as an immovable idea to be established as fact at the May of Teck Club. In the day-time she worked in an office and was normal. It was dinner with Jack Buchanan that prevented her from dining with any other man, and caused her to wait in the hall for half an hour after the other members had gone to the dining room, and to return surreptitiously half an hour later when nobody, or few, were about.

At times, when Pauline had been seen returning within so short a time, she behaved quite convincingly.

'Goodness, back already, Pauline! I thought you'd gone out to dinner with——'

'Oh! Don't talk to me. We've had a row.' Pauline, with one hand holding a handkerchief to her eye, and the other lifting the hem of her dress, would run sobbing up the stairs to her room.

'She must have had a row with Jack Buchanan again. Funny she never brings Jack Buchanan here.'

'Do you believe it?'

'What?'

'That she goes out with Jack Buchanan?'

'Well, I've wondered.'

Pauline looked furtive, and Nicholas cheerfully said to her, 'Where have *you* been?'

She came and gazed into his face and said, 'I've been to dinner with Jack Buchanan.'

'You've missed Churchill's speech.'

'I know.'

'Did Jack Buchanan get rid of you the moment you had finished your dinner?'

'Yes. He did. We had a row.'

She shook back her shining hair. For this evening, she had managed to borrow the Schiaparelli dress. It was made of taffeta, with small side panniers stuck out with cleverly curved pads over the hips. It was coloured dark blue, green, orange and white in a floral pattern as from the Pacific Islands.

He said, 'I don't think I've ever seen such a gorgeous dress.'

'Schiaparelli,' she said.

He said, 'Is it the one you swap among yourselves?'

'Who told you that?'

'You look beautiful,' he replied.

She picked up the rustling skirt and floated away up the staircase.

Oh, girls of slender means!

The election speech having come to an end, everybody's wireless was turned off for a space, as if in reverence to what had just passed through the air.

He approached the office door which stood open. The office was still empty. The warden came up behind him, having deserted her post for the duration of the speech.

'I'm still waiting for Miss Redwood.'

'I'll ring her again. No doubt she's been listening to the speech.'

Selina came down presently. Poise is perfect balance, an equanimity of body and mind. Down the staircase she floated, as it were even more realistically than had the sad communer with the spirit of Jack Buchanan a few moments ago floated up it. It might have been the same girl, floating upwards in a Schiaparelli rustle of silk with a shining hood of hair, and floating downwards in a slim skirt with a white-spotted blue blouse, her hair now piled high. The normal noises of the house began to throb again. 'Good evening,' said Nicholas.

> *And all my days are trances,*
> *And all my nightly dreams*
> *Are where thy dark eye glances,*
> *And where thy footstep gleams—*
> *In what ethereal dances,*
> *By what eternal streams!*

'Now repeat,' said Joanna's voice.

'Come on then,' said Selina, stepping ahead of him into the evening light like a racer into the paddock, with a high disregard of all surrounding noises.

Chapter Seven

'HAVE you got a shilling for the meter?' said Jane.

'Poise is perfect balance, an equanimity of body and mind, complete composure whatever the social scene. Elegant dress, immaculate grooming, and perfect deportment all contribute to the attainment of self-confidence.'

'Have you got a shilling for two sixpences?'

'No. Anne's got a key that opens the meters, though.'

'Anne, are you in? What about a loan of the key?'

'If we all start using it too often we'll be found out.'

'Only this once. I've got brain-work to do.'

Now sleeps the crimson petal, now the white;

*   *   *

Selina sat, not yet dressed, on the edge of Nicholas's bed. She had a way of glancing sideways beneath her lashes that gave her command of a situation which might otherwise place her in a weakness.

She said, 'How can you bear to live here?'

He said, 'It does till one finds a flat.'

In fact he was quite content with his austere bed-sitting room. With the reckless ambition of a visionary, he pushed his passion for Selina into a desire that she, too, should accept and exploit the outlines of poverty in her life. He loved her as he loved his native country. He wanted Selina to be an ideal society personified among her bones, he wanted her beautiful limbs to obey her mind and heart like intelligent men and women, and for these to possess the same grace and beauty as her body. Whereas Selina's desires were comparatively humble, she only wanted,

at that particular moment, a packet of hair-grips which had just
then disappeared from the shops for a few weeks.

It was not the first instance of a man taking a girl to bed with
the aim of converting her soul, but he, in great exasperation,
felt that it was, and poignantly, in bed, willed and willed the
awakening of her social conscience. After which, he sighed softly
into his pillow with a limp sense of achievement, and presently
rose to find, with more exasperation than ever, that he had not
in the least conveyed his vision of perfection to the girl. She sat
on the bed and glanced around beneath her lashes. He was
experienced in girls sitting on his bed, but not in girls as cool
as Selina about their beauty, and such beauty as hers. It was
incredible to him that she should not share with him an understanding of the lovely attributes of dispossession and poverty,
her body was so austere and economically furnished.

She said, 'I don't know how you can live in this place, it's
like a cell. Do you cook on that thing?' She meant the gas
grill.

He said, while it dawned upon him that his love affair with
Selina remained a love affair on his side only, 'Yes, of course.
Would you like some bacon and egg?'

'Yes,' she said, and started to dress.

He took hope again, and brought out his rations. She was
accustomed to men who got food from the black market.

'After the twenty-second of this month,' said Nicholas, 'we
are to get two and a half ounces of tea—two ounces one week and
three ounces the next.'

'How much do we get now?'

'Two ounces every week. Two ounces of butter; margarine,
four ounces.'

She was amused. She laughed for a long time. She said, 'You
sound so funny.'

'Christ, so I do!' he said.

'Have you used all your clothing coupons?'

'No, I've got thirty-four left.'

He turned the bacon in the pan. Then, on a sudden thought,
he said, 'Would you like some clothing coupons?'

'Oh yes, please.'

He gave her twenty, ate some bacon with her, and took her home in a taxi.

He said, 'I've arranged about the roof.'

She said, 'Well, see and arrange about the weather.'

'We can go to the pictures if it's raining,' he said.

*   *   *

He had arranged to have access to the roof through the top floor of the hotel next door, occupied as it was by American Intelligence, which organisation he served in another part of London. Colonel Dobell, who, up to ten days ago, would have opposed this move, now energetically supported it. The reason for this was that his wife Gareth was preparing to join him in London and he was anxious to situate Selina in another context, as he put it.

In the north of California, up a long drive, Mrs. G. Felix Dobell had not only resided, but held meetings of the Guardians of Ethics. Now she was coming to London, for she said that a sixth sense told her Felix was in need of her presence there.

Now sleeps the crimson petal, now the white;

Nicholas greatly desired to make love to Selina on the roof, it needs must be on the roof. He arranged everything as precisely as a practised incendiary.

The flat roof of the club, accessible only by the slit window on the top floor, was joined to a similar flat roof of the neighbouring hotel by a small gutter. The hotel had been requisitioned and its rooms converted into offices for the use of the American Intelligence. Like many other requisitioned premises in London, it had been overcrowded with personnel during the war in Europe, and now was practically unoccupied. Only the top floor of this hotel, where uniformed men worked mysteriously day and night, and the ground floor, which was guarded day and night by two American servicemen, and served by night- and day-porters who worked the lift, were in use. Nobody could enter this house without a pass. Nicholas obtained a pass quite easily, and he also by means of a few words and a glance obtained the ambivalent permission of

Colonel Dobell, whose wife was already on her journey, to move into a large attic office which was being used as a typing pool. Nicholas was given a courtesy desk there. This attic had a hatch door leading to the flat roof.

*   *   *

The weeks had passed, and since in the May of Teck Club they were weeks of youth in the ethos of war, they were capable of accommodating quick happenings and reversals, rapid formations of intimate friendships, and a range of lost and discovered loves that in later life and in peace would take years to happen, grow, and fade. The May of Teck girls were nothing if not economical. Nicholas, who was past his youth, was shocked at heart by their week-by-week emotions.

'I thought you said she was in love with the boy.'

'So she was.'

'Well, wasn't it only last week he died? You said he died of dysentery in Burma.'

'Yes, I know. But she met this naval type on Monday, she's madly in love with him.'

'She can't be in love with him,' said Nicholas.

'Well, they've got a lot in common she says.'

'A lot in common? It's only Wednesday now.'

> *Like one, that on a lonesome road*
> *Doth walk in fear and dread,*
> *And having once turned round, walks on,*
> *And turns no more his head;*
> *Because he knows a frightful fiend*
> *Doth close behind him tread.*

'Joanna's marvellous at that one, I love it.'

'Poor Joanna.'

'Why do you say poor Joanna?'

'Well, she never gets any fun, no men friends.'

'She's terribly attractive.'

'Frightfully attractive. Why doesn't someone do something about Joanna?'

*   *   *

Jane said, 'Look here, Nicholas, there's something you ought to know about Huy Throvis-Mew as a firm and George himself as a publisher.'

They were sitting in the offices of Throvis-Mew, high above Red Lion Square; but George was out.

'He's a crook,' said Nicholas.

'Well, that would be putting it a bit strongly,' she said.

'He's a crook with subtleties.'

'It's not quite that, either. It's a psychological thing about George. He's got to get the better of an author.'

'I know that,' Nicholas said. 'I had a long emotional letter from him making a lot of complaints about my book.'

'He wants to break down your confidence, you see, and then present you with a rotten contract to sign. He finds out the author's weak spot. He always attacks the bit the author likes best. He——'

'I know that,' said Nicholas.

'I'm only telling you because I like you,' Jane said. 'In fact, it's part of my job to find out the author's weak spot, and report to George. But I like you, and I'm telling you all this because——'

'You and George,' said Nicholas, 'draw me a tiny bit closer to understanding the Sphinx's inscrutable smile. And I'll tell you another fact.'

Beyond the grimy window rain fell from a darkening sky on the bomb-sites of Red Lion Square. Jane had looked out in an abstract pose before making her revelation to Nicholas. She now actually noticed the scene, it made her eyes feel miserable and her whole life appeared steeped in equivalent misery. She was disappointed in life, once more.

'I'll tell you another fact,' said Nicholas. 'I'm a crook, too. What are you crying for?'

'I'm crying for myself,' said Jane. 'I'm going to look for another job.'

'Will you write a letter for me?'

'What sort of a letter?'

'A crook-letter. From Charles Morgan to myself. Dear Mr. Farringdon, When first I received your manuscript I was tempted to place it aside for my secretary to return to you with some polite excuse. But as happy chance would have it, before passing your work to my secretary, I flicked over the pages and my eyes lit on . . .'

'Lit on what?' said Jane.

'I'll leave that to you. Only choose one of the most concise and brilliant passages when you come to write the letter. That will be difficult, I admit, since all are equally brilliant. But choose the piece you like best. Charles Morgan is to say he read that one piece, and then the whole, avidly, from start to finish. He is to say it's a work of genius. He congratulates me on a work of genius, you realise. Then I show the letter to George.'

Jane's life began to sprout once more, green with possibility. She recalled that she was only twenty-three, and smiled.

'Then I show the letter to George,' Nicholas said, 'and I tell him he can keep his contract, and——'

George arrived. He looked busily at them both. Simultaneously, he took off his hat, looked at his watch, and said to Jane, 'What's the news?'

Nicholas said, 'Ribbentrop is captured.'

George sighed.

'No news,' said Jane. 'Nobody's rung at all. No letters, nobody's been, nobody's rung us up. Don't worry.'

George went into his inner office. He came out again immediately.

'Did you get my letter?' he said to Nicholas.

'No,' said Nicholas, 'which letter?'

'I wrote, let me see, the day before yesterday, I think. I wrote——'

'Oh, that letter,' said Nicholas. 'Yes, I believe I did receive a letter.'

George went away into his inner office.

Nicholas said to Jane, in a good, loud voice, that he was going for a stroll in the Park now that the rain had stopped, and that it was lovely having nothing to do but dream beautiful dreams all the day long.

'Yours very sincerely and admiringly, Charles Morgan,' wrote Jane. She opened the door of her room and shouted, 'Turn down the wireless a bit, I've got to do some brain-work before supper.'

On the whole, they were proud of Jane's brain-work and her connection with the world of books. They turned down all the wirelesses on the landing.

She read over the first draft of the letter, then very carefully began again, making an authentic-looking letter in a small but mature hand such as Charles Morgan might use. She had no idea what Charles Morgan's handwriting looked like; and had no reason to find out, since George would certainly not know either, and was not to be allowed to retain the document. She had an address at Holland Park which Nicholas had supplied. She wrote this at the top of her writing paper, hoping that it looked all right, and assuring herself that it did since many nice people did not attempt to have their letter-heads printed in war-time and thus make unnecessary demands on the nation's labour.

She had finished by the time the supper-bell rang. She folded the letter with meticulous neatness, having before her eyes the pencil-line features of Charles Morgan's photograph. Jane calculated that this letter by Charles Morgan which she had just written was worth at least fifty pounds to Nicholas. George would be in a terrible state of conflict when he saw it. Poor Tilly, George's wife, had told her that when George was persecuted by an author, he went on and on about it for hours.

Nicholas was coming to the club after supper to spend the evening, having at last persuaded Joanna to give a special recital of *The Wreck of the Deutschland*. It was to be recorded on a tape-machine that Nicholas had borrowed from the news-room of a Government office.

Jane joined the throng in its descent to supper. Only Selina loitered above, finishing off her evening's disciplinary recitation:

... Elegant dress, immaculate grooming, and perfect deportment all contribute to the attainment of self-confidence.

The warden's car stopped piercingly outside as the girls reached the lower floor. The warden drove a car as she would have driven a man had she possessed one. She strode, grey, into her office and shortly afterwards joined them in the dining room, banging on the water-jug with her fork for silence, as she always did when about to make an announcement. She announced that an American visitor, Mrs. G. Felix Dobell, would address the club on Friday evening on the subject, 'Western Woman: her Mission'. Mrs. Dobell was a leading member of the Guardians of Ethics and had recently come to join her husband who was serving with the United States Intelligence Service stationed in London.

After supper Jane was struck by a sense of her treachery to the establishment of Throvis-Mew, and to George with whom she was paid to conspire in the way of business. She was fond of old George, and began to reflect on his kindly qualities. Without the slightest intention of withdrawing from her conspiracy with Nicholas, she gazed at the letter she had written and wondered what to do about her feelings. She decided to telephone to his wife, Tilly, and have a friendly chat about something.

Tilly was delighted. She was a tiny redhead of lively intelligence and small information, whom George kept well apart from the world of books, being experienced in wives. To Tilly, this was a great deprivation, and she loved nothing better than to keep in touch, through Jane, with the book business and to hear Jane say, 'Well, Tilly, it's a question of one's raison d'être.' George tolerated this friendship, feeling that it established himself with Jane. He relied on Jane. She understood his ways.

Jane was usually bored by Tilly, who, although she had not exactly been a cabaret dancer, imposed on the world of books, whenever she was given the chance, a high leg-kicker's spirit which played on Jane's nerves, since she herself was newly awed by the gravity of literature in general. She felt Tilly was altogether too frivolous about the publishing and writing scene, and moreover failed to realise this fact. But her heart in its treachery now swelled with an access of warmth for Tilly. She telephoned and invited her to supper on Friday. Jane had already calculated that, if Tilly should be a complete bore, they would be able to fill in an hour with Mrs. G. Felix Dobell's lecture. The club was fairly eager to see Mrs. Dobell, having already seen a certain amount of her husband as Selina's escort, rumoured to be her lover. 'There's a talk on Friday by an American woman on the Western Woman's Mission, but we won't listen to that, it would be a bore,' Jane said, contradicting her resolution in her effusive anxiety to sacrifice anything, anything to George's wife, now that she had betrayed and was about to deceive George.

Tilly said, 'I always love the May of Teck. It's like being back at school.' Tilly always said that, it was infuriating.

* * *

Nicholas arrived early with his tape-recorder, and sat in the recreation room with Joanna waiting for the audience to drift in from supper. She looked to Nicholas very splendid and Nordic, as from a great saga.

'Have you lived here long?' said Nicholas sleepily, while he admired her big bones. He was sleepy because he had spent most of the previous night on the roof with Selina.

'About a year. I daresay I'll die here,' she said with the conventional contempt of all members for the club.

He said, 'You'll get married.'

'No, no.' She spoke soothingly, as to a child who had just been prevented from spooning jam into the stew.

A long shriek of corporate laughter came from the floor immediately above them. They looked at the ceiling and realised that the dormitory girls were as usual exchanging those R.A.F. anecdotes which needed an audience hilariously drunken, either with alcohol or extreme youth, to give them point.

Greggie had appeared, and cast her eyes up to the laughter as she came towards Joanna and Nicholas. She said, 'The sooner that dormitory crowd gets married and gets out of the club, the better. I've never known such a rowdy dormitory crowd in all my years in the club. Not a farthing's worth of intelligence between them.'

Collie arrived and sat down next to Nicholas. Greggie said, 'I was saying about the dormitory girls up there: they ought to get married and get out.'

This was also, in reality, Collie's view. But she always opposed

Greggie on principle and, moreover, in company she felt that a contradiction made conversation. 'Why should they get married? Let them enjoy themselves while they're young.'

'They need marriage to enjoy themselves properly,' Nicholas said, 'for sexual reasons.'

Joanna blushed. Nicholas added, 'Heaps of sex. Every night for a month, then every other night for two months, then three times a week for a year. After that, once a week.' He was adjusting the tape-recorder, and his words were like air.

'If you're trying to shock us, young man, we're unshockable,' said Greggie, with a delighted glance round the four walls which were not accustomed to this type of talk, for, after all, it was the public recreation room.

'I'm shockable,' said Joanna. She was studying Nicholas with an apologetic look.

Collie did not know what attitude she should take up. Her fingers opened the clasp of her bag and snapped it shut again; then they played a silent tip-tap on its worn bulging leather sides. Then she said, 'He isn't trying to shock us. He's very realistic. If one is growing in grace—I would go so far as to say when one *has* grown in grace—one can take realism, sex, and so forth in one's stride.'

Nicholas beamed lovingly at this.

Collie gave a little half-cough, half-laugh, much encouraged in the success of her frankness. She felt modern, and continued excitedly, 'It's a question of what you never have you never miss, of course.'

Greggie put on a puzzled air, as if she genuinely did not know what Collie was talking about. After thirty years' hostile fellowship with Collie, of course she did quite well understand that Collie had a habit of skipping several stages in the logical sequence of her thoughts, and would utter apparently disconnected statements, especially when confused by an unfamiliar subject or the presence of a man.

'Whatever do you mean?' said Greggie. '*What* is a question of what you never have you never miss?'

'Sex, of course,' Collie said, her voice unusually loud with the effort of the topic. 'We were discussing sex and getting married.

I say, of course, there's a lot to be said for marriage, but if you never have it you never miss it.'

Joanna looked at the two excited women with meek compassion. To Nicholas she looked stronger than ever in her meekness, as she regarded Greggie and Collie at their rivalry to be uninhibited.

'What do you mean, Collie?' Greggie said.

'You're quite wrong there, Collie. One does miss sex. The body has a life of its own. We do miss what we haven't had, you and I. Biologically. Ask Sigmund Freud. It is revealed in dreams. The absent touch of the warm limbs at night, the absent——'

'Just a minute,' said Nicholas, holding up his hand for silence, in the pretence that he was tuning-in to his empty tape-machine. He could see that the two women would go to any lengths, now they had got started.

'Open the door, please.' From behind the door came the warden's voice and the rattle of the coffee tray. Before Nicholas could leap up to open it for her she had pushed into the room with some clever manoeuvring of hand and foot like a business-like parlourmaid.

'The Beatific Vision does not appear to *me* to be an adequate compensation for what we miss,' Greggie said conclusively, getting in a private thrust at Collie's religiosity.

While coffee was being served and the girls began to fill the room, Jane entered, fresh from her telephone conversation with Tilly, and, feeling somewhat absolved by it, she handed over to Nicholas her brain-work letter from Charles Morgan. While reading it, he was handed a cup of coffee. In the process of taking the cup he splashed some coffee on the letter.

'Oh, you've ruined it!' Jane said. 'I'll have to do it all over again.'

'It looks more authentic than ever,' Nicholas said. 'Naturally, if I've received a letter from Charles Morgan telling me I'm a genius, I am going to spend a lot of time reading it over and over, in the course of which the letter must begin to look a bit worn. Now, are you sure George will be impressed by Morgan's name?'

'Very,' said Jane.

'Do you mean you're very sure or that George will be very impressed?'

'I mean both.'

'It would put me off, if I were George.'

The recital of *The Wreck of the Deutschland* started presently. Joanna stood with her book ready.

'Not a hush from anybody,' said the warden, meaning, 'Not a sound.'—'Not a hush,' she said, 'because this instrument of Mr. Farringdon's apparently registers the drop of a pin.'

One of the dormitory girls, who sat mending a ladder in a stocking, carefully caused her needle to fall on the parquet floor, then bent and picked it up again. Another dormitory girl who had noticed the action snorted a suppressed laugh. Otherwise there was silence but for the quiet purr of the machine waiting for Joanna.

> *Thou mastering me*
> *God! giver of breath and bread;*
> *World's strand, sway of the sea;*
> *Lord of living and dead;*
> *Thou hast bound bones and veins in me, fastened me flesh,*
> *And after it almost unmade . . .*

Chapter Eight

A SCREAM of panic from the top floor penetrated the house as Jane returned to the club on Friday afternoon, the 27th of July. She had left the office early to meet Tilly at the club. She did not feel that the scream of panic meant anything special. Jane climbed the last flight of stairs. There was another more piercing scream, accompanied by excited voices. Screams of panic in the club might relate to a laddered stocking or a side-splitting joke.

When she reached the top landing, she saw that the commotion came from the wash-room. There, Anne and Selina, with two of the dormitory girls, were attempting to extricate from the little slit window another girl who had evidently been attempting to climb out and had got stuck. She was struggling and kicking without success, exhorted by various instructions from the other girls. Against their earnest advice, she screamed aloud from time to time. She had taken off her clothes for the attempt and her body was covered with a greasy substance; Jane immediately hoped it had not been taken from her own supply of cold cream which stood in a jar on her dressing table.

'Who is it?' Jane said, with a close inspective look at the girl's unidentifiable kicking legs and wriggling bottom which were her only visible portions.

Selina brought a towel which she attempted to fasten round the girl's waist with a safety-pin. Anne kept imploring the girl not to scream, and one of the others went to the top of the stairs to look over the banister in the hope that nobody in authority was being unduly attracted upward.

'Who is it?' Jane said.

Anne said, 'I'm afraid it's Tilly.'

'Tilly!'

'She was waiting downstairs and we brought her up here for a lark. She said it was like being back at school, here at the club, so Selina showed her the window. She's just half an inch too large, though. Can't you get her to shut up?'

Jane spoke softly to Tilly. 'Every time you scream,' she said, 'it makes you swell up more. Keep quiet, and we'll work you out with wet soap.'

Tilly went quiet. They worked on her for ten minutes, but she remained stuck by the hips. Tilly was weeping. 'Get George,' she said at last, 'get him on the phone.'

Nobody wanted to fetch George. He would have to come upstairs. Doctors were the only males who climbed the stairs, and even then they were accompanied by one of the staff.

Jane said, 'Well, I'll get somebody.' She was thinking of Nicholas. He had access to the roof from the Intelligence Headquarters; a hefty push from the roof-side of the window might be successful in releasing Tilly. Nicholas had intended to come

to the club after supper to hear the lecture and observe, in a
jealous complex of curiosity, the wife of Selina's former lover.
Felix himself was to be present.

Jane decided to telephone and beg Nicholas to come immediately and help with Tilly. He could then have supper at the
club, his second supper, Jane reflected that week. He might
now be home from work, he usually returned to his room at
about six o'clock.

'What's the time?' said Jane.

Tilly was weeping, with a sound that threatened a further
outburst of screams.

'Just on six,' said Anne.

Selina looked at her watch to see if this was so, then walked
towards her room.

'Don't leave her, I'm getting help,' Jane said. Selina opened
the door of her room, but Anne stood gripping Tilly's ankles.
As Jane reached the next landing she heard Selina's voice.

'Poise is perfect balance, an equanimity . . .'

Jane laughed foolishly to herself and descended to the telephone boxes as the clock in the hall struck six o'clock.

*   *   *

It struck six o'clock on that evening of July 27th. Nicholas had
just returned to his room. When he heard of Tilly's predicament he promised eagerly to go straight to the Intelligence
Headquarters, and on to the roof.

'It's no joke,' Jane said.

'I'm not saying it's a joke.'

'You sound cheerful about it. Hurry up. Tilly's crying her
eyes out.'

'As well she might, seeing Labour have got in.'

'Oh, hurry up. We'll all be in trouble if——'

He had rung off.

At that hour Greggie came in from the garden to hang about
the hall, awaiting the arrival of Mrs. Dobell who was to speak
after supper. Greggie would take her into the warden's sitting

room, there to drink dry sherry till the supper-bell went. Greggie hoped also to induce Mrs. Dobell to be escorted round the garden before supper.

A distant anguished scream descended the staircase.

'Really,' Greggie said to Jane, who was emerging from the telephone box, 'this club has gone right down. What are visitors to think? Who's screaming up there on the top floor? It sounds exactly as it must have been when this house was in private hands. You girls behave exactly like servant girls in the old days when the master and mistress were absent. Romping and yelling.'

> Make me thy lyre, even as the forest is:
> What if my leaves are falling like its own!
> The tumult of thy mighty harmonies

'George, I want George,' Tilly wailed thinly from far above. Then someone on the top floor thoughtfully turned on the wireless to an all-drowning pitch:

> There were angels dining at the Ritz
> And a nightingale sang in Berkeley Square.

And Tilly could be heard no more. Greggie looked out of the open front door and returned. She looked at her watch. 'Six-fifteen,' she said. 'She should be here at six-fifteen. Tell them to turn down the wireless up there. It looks so vulgar, so bad . . .'

'You mean it sounds so vulgar, so bad.' Jane was keeping an eye out for the taxi which she hoped would bring Nicholas, at any moment, to the functional hotel next door.

'Once again,' said Joanna's voice clearly from the third floor to her pupil. 'The last three stanzas again, please.'

> Drive my dead thoughts over the universe
> Like withered leaves to quicken a new birth!

Jane was suddenly overcome by a deep envy of Joanna, the source of which she could not locate exactly at that hour of her youth. The feeling was connected with an inner knowledge of

Joanna's disinterestedness, her ability, a gift, to forget herself and her personality. Jane felt suddenly miserable, as one who has been cast out of Eden before realising that it had in fact been Eden. She recalled two ideas about Joanna that she had gathered from various observations made by Nicholas: that Joanna's enthusiasm for poetry was limited to one kind, and that Joanna was the slightest bit melancholy on the religious side; these thoughts failed to comfort Jane.

Nicholas arrived in a taxi and disappeared in the hotel entrance. As Jane started to run upstairs another taxi drew up. Greggie said, 'Here's Mrs. Dobell. It's twenty-two minutes past six.'

Jane bumped into several of the girls who were spilling in lively groups out of the dormitories. She thrust her way through their midst, anxious to reach Tilly and tell her that help was near.

'Jane-ee!' said a girl. 'Don't be so bloody rude, you nearly pushed me over the banister to my death.'

But Jane was thumping upward.

Now sleeps the crimson petal, now the white;

Jane arrived at the top floor to find Anne and Selina frantically clothing Tilly's lower half to make her look decent. They had got as far as the stockings. Anne was holding a leg while Selina, long-fingered, smoothed the stocking over it.

'Nicholas has come. Is he out on the roof yet?'

Tilly moaned, 'Oh, I'm dying. I can't stand it any more. Fetch *George*, I want George.'

'Here's Nicholas,' said Selina, tall enough to see him emerging from the low doorway of the hotel attic, as he had lately done on the calm summer nights. He stumbled over a rug which had been bundled beside the door. It was one of the rugs they had brought out to lie on. He recovered his balance, started walking quickly over towards them, then fell flat on his face. A clock struck the half-hour. Jane heard herself say in a loud voice, 'It's half past six.' Suddenly, Tilly was sitting on the bathroom floor beside her. Anne, too, was on the floor, crumpled with her arm over her eyes as if trying to hide her presence. Selina lay stunned against the door. She opened her mouth to scream, and probably did scream, but it was then that the rumbling began to assert itself from the garden below, mounting swiftly to a mighty crash. The house trembled again, and the girls who had tried to sit up were thrown flat. The floor was covered with bits of glass, and Jane's blood flowed from somewhere in a trickle, while some sort of time passed silently by. Sensations of voices, shouts, mounting footsteps, and falling plaster brought the girls back to various degrees of responsiveness. Jane saw, in an unfocused way, the giant face of Nicholas peering through the open slit of the little window. He was exhorting them to get up quick.

'There's been an explosion in the garden.'

'Greggie's bomb,' Jane said, grinning at Tilly. 'Greggie was right,' she said. This was a hilarious statement, but Tilly did not laugh, she closed her eyes and lay back. Tilly was only half-dressed and looked very funny indeed. Jane then laughed loudly at Nicholas, but he too had no sense of humour.

*　　*　　*

Down in the street the main body of the club had congregated, having been in one of the public rooms on the ground floor at the time of the explosion, or else lingering in the dormitories. There, the explosion had been heard more than it was felt. Two ambulances had arrived and a third was approaching. Some of the more dazed among the people were being treated for shock in the hall of the neighbouring hotel.

Greggie was attempting to assure Mrs. Felix Dobell that she had foreseen and forewarned the occurrence. Mrs. Dobell, a handsome matron of noticeable height, stood out on the edge of the pavement, taking little notice of Greggie. She was looking at the building with a surveyor's eye, and was possessed of that calm which arises from a misunderstanding of the occasion's true nature, for although she was shaken by the explosion, Mrs. Dobell assumed that belated bombs went off every day in Britain, and, content to find herself intact, and slightly pleased to have shared a war experience, was now curious as to what routine would be adopted in the emergency. She said, 'When do you calculate the dust will settle?'

Greggie said, yet once more, 'I knew that live bomb was in that garden. I knew it. I was always saying that bomb was there. The bomb-disposal squad missed it, they missed it.'

Some faces appeared at an upper bedroom. The window opened. A girl started to shout, but had to withdraw her head; she was choking with the dust that was still surrounding the house in clouds.

It was difficult to discern the smoke, when it began to show, among the dust. A gas-main had, in fact, been ruptured by the explosion and a fire started to crawl along the basement from the furnaces. It started to crawl and then it flared. A roomful of flame suddenly roared in the ground-floor offices, lapping against the large window-panes, feeling for the woodwork, while Greggie continued to shrill at Mrs. Dobell above the clamour of the girls, the street-crowd, the ambulances, and the fire engines. 'It was ten chances to one we might have been in the garden when the bomb went off. I was going to take you round the garden before supper. We would have been buried, dead, killed. It was ten to one, Mrs. Dobell.'

Mrs. Dobell said, as one newly enlightened, 'This is a terrible incident.' And being more shaken than she appeared to be, she added, 'This is a time that calls for the exercise of discretion, the woman's prerogative.' This saying was part of the lecture she had intended to give after supper. She looked round in the crowd for her husband. The warden, whose more acute shock-effects had preceded Mrs. Dobell's by a week, was being carried off through the crowd on a stretcher.

'Felix!' yelled Mrs. Dobell. He was coming out of the hotel adjoining the club, with his olive-greenish khaki uniform dusky with soot and streaked as with black oil. He had been investigating the back premises of the club. He said: 'The brick-work of the walls looks unsteady. The top half of the fire escape has collapsed. There are some girls trapped up there. The firemen are directing them up to the top floor; they'll have to be brought through the skylight on to the roof.'

*　　*　　*

'Who?' said Lady Julia.

'Jane Wright speaking. I rang you last week to see if you could find out some more about——'

'Oh yes. Well, I'm afraid there's very little information from the F.O. They never comment officially, you know. From what I can gather, the man was making a complete nuisance of himself, preaching against the local superstitions. He had several warnings and apparently he got what he asked for. How did you come to know him?'

'He was friendly with some of the girls at the May of Teck Club when he was a civilian, I mean before he joined this Order. He was there on the night of the tragedy, in fact, and——'

'It probably turned his brain. Something must have affected his brain, anyhow, because what I gather unofficially he was a complete . . .'

*   *   *

The skylight, although it had been bricked up by someone's hysterical order, at that time in the past when a man had penetrated the attic-floor of the Club to visit a girl, was not beyond being unbricked by the firemen. It was all a question of time.

Time was not a large or present fact to those girls of the May of Teck Club, thirteen of them, who, with Tilly Throvis-Mew, remained in the upper stories of the building when, following the explosion in the garden, fire broke out in the house. A large portion of the perfectly safe fire-escape which had featured in so many safety-instruction regulations, so many times read out to the members at so many supper-times, now lay in zigzag fragments among the earthy mounds and upturned roots of the garden.

Time, which was an immediate onward-rushing enemy to the onlookers in the street and the firemen on the roof, was only a small far-forgotten event to the girls; for they were stunned not only by the force of the explosion, but, when they recovered and looked round, still more by the sudden dislocation of all familiar appearances. A chunk of the back wall of the house gaped to the sky. There, in 1945, they were as far removed from the small fact of time as weightless occupants of a space-rocket. Jane got up, ran to her room, and with animal instinct snatched and gobbled a block of chocolate which remained on her table. The sweet stuff assisted her recovery. She turned to the wash-rooms where Tilly, Anne, and Selina were slowly rising to their feet. There were shouts from the direction of the roof. An unrecognised face looked in the slit window, and a large hand wrenched the loose frame away from it.

But the fire had already started to spread up the main staircase, preceded by heraldic puffs of smoke, the flames sidling up the banisters.

The girls who had been in their rooms on the second and third floors at the time of the explosion had been less shaken than those at the top of the house, since there some serious defect in the masonry had been caused indirectly by a bombardment early in the war. The girls on the second and third floors were cut and bruised, but were stunned by the sound of the blast rather than the house-shaking effects of it.

Some of the second-floor dormitory girls had been quick and alert enough to slip down the staircase and out into the street, in the interval between the explosion of the bomb and the start of the fire. The remaining ten, when they variously attempted to escape by that route, met the fire and retreated upward.

Joanna and Nancy Riddle, having finished their elocution lesson, had been standing at the door of Joanna's room when the bomb went off, and so had escaped the glass from the window. Joanna's hand was cut, however, by the glass from a tiny travelling clock which she had been winding at the time. It was Joanna who, when the members shrieked at the sight of the fire, gave the last shriek, then shouted: 'The fire-escape!' Pauline Fox fled behind her, and the others followed along the second-floor corridors and up the narrow back staircase to the third-floor passage-way where the fire-escape window had always stood. This was now a platform open to the summer evening sky, for here the wall had fallen away and the fire-escape with it. Plaster tumbled from the bricks as the ten women crowded to the spot that had once been the fire-escape landing. They were still looking in a bewildered way for the fire-escape stairway. Voices of firemen shouted at them from the garden. Voices came from the direction of the flat roof above, and then one voice clearly through a megaphone ordered them back, lest the piece of floor they stood on should collapse.

The voice said, 'Proceed to the top floor.'

'Jack will wonder what's happened to me,' said Pauline Fox. She was first up the back stairs to the wash-rooms where Anne, Selina, Jane, and Tilly were now on their feet, having steadied themselves on learning of the fire. Selina was taking off her skirt.

Above their heads, set in a sloping ceiling, was the large square outline of the old, bricked-in skylight. Men's voices, the scrabble of ladders and loud thumps of bricks being tested, came down from this large square. The men were evidently trying to find a means of opening the skylight to release the girls, who meanwhile stared up at the square mark in the ceiling. Tilly said, 'Won't it open?' Nobody answered, because the girls of the club knew the answer. Everyone in the club had heard the legend of the man who had got in by the skylight and, some said, been found in bed with a girl.

Now Selina stood on the lavatory seat and jumped up to the slit window. She slid through it to the roof with an easy diagonal movement. There were now thirteen women in the wash-room. They stood in the alert, silent attitude of jungle-danger, listening for further instruction from the megaphone on the roof outside.

Anne Baberton followed Selina through the slit window, with difficulty, because she was flustered. But a man's two hands came up to the window to receive her. Tilly Throvis-Mew began to sob. Pauline Fox ripped off her dress and then her underclothes until she was altogether naked. She had an undernourished body; there would have been no difficulty for her in getting through the slit window fully clothed, but she went naked as a fish.

Only Tilly sobbed heavily, but the rest of the girls were trembling. The noises from the sloping roof ceased as the firemen jumped down from investigating the skylight on to the flat roof area; footsteps beat and shuffled there, beyond the slit window where throughout the summer Selina had lain with Nicholas, wrapped in rugs, under Orion's Belt and the Plough, which constituted the only view in Greater London that remained altogether intact.

Within the wash-room the eleven remaining women heard a fireman's voice addressing them through the window, against the simultaneous blare of megaphone instructions to the firemen. The man at the window said, 'Stay where you are. Don't panic. We're sending for tools to uncover the brickwork over the skylight. We won't be long. It's a question of time. We are doing everything we can to get you out. Remain where you are. Don't panic. It's just a question of time.'

The question of time opened now as a large thing in the lives of the eleven listeners.

*   *   *

Twenty-eight minutes had passed since the bomb had exploded in the garden. Felix Dobell joined Nicholas Farringdon on the flat roof after the fire started. They assisted the three slim girls through the window. Anne and naked Pauline Fox had been huddled into the two blankets of variable purpose, and hustled through the roof-hatch of the neighbouring hotel, the back windows of which had been smashed by the blast. Nicholas was as fleetingly impressed as was possible in the emergency, by the fact that Selina allowed the other girls to take the blankets. She lingered, shivering a little, but with an appealing grace, like a wounded roe deer, in her white petticoat and bare feet. Nicholas thought she was lingering for his sake, since Felix had disappeared with the two other girls to help them down to the first-aid ambulances. He left Selina standing thoughtfully on the hotel side of the roof, and returned to the slit window of the club to see for himself if any of the remaining girls were slim enough to escape by that way. It had been said by the firemen that the building might collapse within the next twenty minutes.

As he approached the slit window Selina slipped past him and, clutching the sill, heaved herself up again.

'Come down, what are you doing?' Nicholas said. He tried to grasp her ankles, but she was quick and, crouching for a small second on the narrow sill, she dipped her head and sidled through the window into the wash-room.

Nicholas immediately supposed she had done this in an attempt to rescue one of the girls, or assist their escape through the window.

'Come back out here, Selina,' he shouted, heaving himself up to see through the slit. 'It's dangerous. You can't help anybody.'

Selina was pushing her way through the standing group. They moved to give way without resistance. They were silent, except for Tilly, who now sobbed convulsively without tears, her eyes, like the other eyes, wide and fixed on Nicholas with the importance of fear.

Nicholas said, 'The men are coming to open the skylight. They'll be here in a moment. Are there any others of you would be able to get through the window here? I'll give them a hand. Hurry up, the sooner the better.'

Joanna held a tape-measure in her hand. At some time in the interval between the firemen's discovery that the skylight was firmly sealed and this moment, Joanna had rummaged in one of these top bedrooms to find this tape-measure, with which she had measured the hips of the other ten trapped with herself, even the most helpless, to see what were their possibilities of escape by the seven-inch window slit. It was known all through the club that thirty-six and a quarter inches was the maximum for hips that could squeeze themselves through it, but as the exit had to be effected sideways with a manœuvring of shoulders, much depended on the size of the bones, and on the texture of the individual flesh and muscles, whether flexible enough to compress easily or whether too firm. The latter had been Tilly's case. But apart from her, none of the women now left on the top floor was slim in anything like the proportions of Selina, Anne, and Pauline Fox. Some were plump. Jane was fat. Dorothy Markham, who had previously been able to slither in and out of the window to sunbathe, was now two months pregnant; her stomach was taut with an immovable extra inch. Joanna's efforts to measure them had been like a scientific ritual in a hopeless case, it had been a something done, it provided a slightly calming distraction.

Nicholas said, 'They won't be long. The men are coming

now.' He was hanging on to the ledge of the window with his toes dug into the brickwork of the wall. He was looking towards the edge of the flat roof where the fire ladders were set. A file of firemen were now mounting the ladders with pickaxes, and heavy drills were being hauled up.

Nicholas looked back into the wash-room.

'They're coming now. Where did Selina go?'

No-one answered.

He said, 'That girl over there—can't she manage to come through the window?'

He meant Tilly. Jane said, 'She's tried once. She got stuck. The fire's crackling like mad down there. The house is going to collapse any minute.'

In the sloping roof above the girls' heads the picks started to clack furiously at the brickwork, not in regular rhythm as in normal workmanship, but with the desperate hackwork of impending danger. It would not be long, now, before the whistles would blow and the voice from the megaphone would order the firemen to abandon the building to its collapse.

Nicholas had let go his hold to observe the situation from the outside. Tilly appeared at the slit window, now, in a second attempt to get out. He recognised her face as that of the girl who had been stuck there at the moment before the explosion, and whom he had been summoned to release. He shouted at her to get back lest she should stick again, and jeopardise her more probable rescue through the skylight. But she was frantic with determination, she yelled to urge herself on. It was a successful performance after all. Nicholas pulled her clear, breaking one of her hip-bones in the process. She fainted on the flat roof after he had set her down.

He pulled himself up to the window once more. The girls huddled, trembling and silent, round Joanna. They were looking up at the skylight. Some large thing cracked slowly on a lower floor of the house and smoke now started to curl in the upper air of the wash-rooms. Nicholas then saw, through the door of the wash-room, Selina approaching along the smoky passage. She was carrying something fairly long and limp and evidently light in weight, enfolding it carefully in her arms. He thought it was a body. She pushed her way through the girls coughing delicately from the first waves of smoke that had reached her in the passage. The others stared, shivered only with their prolonged apprehension, for they had no curiosity about what she had been rescuing or what she was carrying. She climbed up on the lavatory seat and slid through the window, skilfully and quickly pulling her object behind her. Nicholas held up his hand to catch her. When she landed on the roof-top she said, 'Is it safe out here?' and at the same time was inspecting the condition of her salvaged item. Poise is perfect balance. It was the Schiaparelli dress. The coat-hanger dangled from the dress like a headless neck and shoulders.

'Is it safe out here?' said Selina.

'Nowhere's safe,' said Nicholas.

Later, reflecting on this lightning scene, he could not trust his memory as to whether he then involuntarily signed himself with the cross. It seemed to him, in recollection, that he did. At all events, Felix Dobell, who had appeared on the roof again, looked at him curiously at the time, and later said that Nicholas had crossed himself in superstitious relief that Selina was safe.

She ran to the hotel hatch. Felix Dobell had taken up Tilly in his arms, for although she had recovered consciousness she was too injured to walk. He bore her to the roof-hatch, following Selina with her dress; it was now turned inside-out for safe-keeping.

From the slit window came a new sound, faint, because of the continuous tumble of hose-water, the creak of smouldering wood and plaster in the lower part of the house, and, above, the clamour and falling bricks of the rescue work on the skylight. This new sound rose and fell with a broken hum between the sounds of desperate choking cough. It was Joanna, mechanically reciting the evening psalter of Day 27, responses and answers.

The voice through the megaphone shouted, 'Tell them to stand clear of the skylight in there. We'll have it free any minute now. It might collapse inwards. Tell those girls to stand clear of the skylight.'

Nicholas climbed up to the window. They had heard the instructions and were already crowding in to the lavatory by the slit window, ignoring the man's face that kept appearing in it. As if hypnotised, they surrounded Joanna, and she herself stood as one hypnotised into the strange utterances of Day 27 in the Anglican order, held to be applicable to all sorts and conditions of human life in the world at that particular moment, when in London homing workers plodded across the Park, observing with curiosity the fire-engines in the distance, when Rudi Bittesch was sitting in his flat at St. John's Wood trying, without success, to telephone to Jane at the club to speak to her privately, the Labour Government was new-born, and elsewhere on the face of the globe people slept, queued for liberation-rations, beat the tom-toms, took shelter from the bombers or went for a ride on a dodgem at the fun-fair.

Nicholas shouted, 'Keep well away from the skylight. Come right in close to the window.'

The girls crowded into the lavatory space. Jane and Joanna, being the largest, stood up on the lavatory seat to make room for the others. Nicholas saw that every face was streaming with perspiration. Joanna's skin, now close to his eyes, seemed to him to have become suddenly covered with large freckles as if fear had acted on it like the sun; in fact it was true that the pale freckles on her face, which normally were almost invisible, stared out in bright gold spots by contrast with her skin, which was now bloodless with fear. The versicles and responses came from her lips and tongue through the din of demolition.

> *Yea, the Lord hath done great things for us already; whereof, we rejoice.*
> *Turn our captivity, O Lord: as the rivers in the south.*
> *They that sow in tears: shall reap in joy.*

Why, and with what intention, was she moved to indulge in this? She remembered the words, and she had the long habit of recitation. But why, in this predicament and as if to an audience? She wore a dark green wool jersey and a grey skirt. The other girls, automatically listening to Joanna's voice as they had always done, were possibly less frantic and trembled less, because of it, but they turned their ears more fearfully and attentively to the meaning of the skylight noises than they did to the actual meaning of her words for Day 27.

Except the Lord build the house: their labour is but lost that build it.
Except the Lord keep the city: the watchman waketh but in vain.
It is but lost labour that ye haste to rise up early, and so late take rest, and eat the bread of carefulness: for so he giveth his beloved sleep.
Lo, children . . .

Any Day's liturgy would have been equally mesmeric. But the words for the right day was Joanna's habit. The skylight thudded open with a shower of powdery plaster and some lop-sided bricks. While the white dust was still falling the firemen's ladder descended. First up was Dorothy Markham, the chattering débutante whose bright life, for the past forty-three minutes, had gone into a bewildering darkness like illuminations at a sea-side town when the electricity system breaks down. She looked haggard and curiously like her aunt, Lady Julia, the chairman of the club's committee who was at that moment innocently tying up refugee parcels at Bath. Lady Julia's hair was white, and so now was the hair of her niece Dorothy, covered as it was by falling plaster-dust, as she clambered up the fire-ladder to the sloping tiles and was assisted to the safe flat roof-top. At her heels came Nancy Riddle, the daughter of the Low-Church Midlands clergyman, whose accents of speech had been in process of improvement by Joanna's lessons. Her elocution days were over now, she would always speak with a Midlands accent. Her hips looked more dangerously wide than they had ever noticeably been, as she swung up the ladder behind Dorothy. Three girls then attempted to follow at once; they had been occupants of a four-bed dormitory on the third floor, and were all newly released from the Forces; all three had the hefty, built-up appearance that five years in the Army was apt to give to a woman. While they were sorting themselves out, Jane grasped the ladder and got away. The three ex-warriors then followed.

Joanna had jumped down from the lavatory seat. She was now circling round, vaguely wobbling, like a top near the end of its spin. Her eyes shifted from the skylight to the window in a puzzled way. Her lips and tongue continued to recite compulsively the litany of the day, but her voice had weakened and she stopped to cough. The air was full of powdered plaster and smoke. There were three girls left beside herself. Joanna groped for the ladder and missed. She then stopped to pick up the tape-measure which was lying on the floor. She groped for it as if she were partially blind, still intoning:

> So that they who go by say not so much as, The Lord prosper you:
> we wish you good luck in the Name of the Lord.
> Out of the deep have I called . . .

The other three took the ladder, one of them, a surprisingly slender girl called Pippa, whose non-apparent bones had evidently been too large to have allowed her escape through the window, shouted back, 'Hurry up, Joanna.'

'Joanna, the ladder!'

And Nicholas shouted from the window, 'Joanna, get up the ladder.'

She regained her senses and pressed behind the last two girls, a brown-skinned heavily-sinewed swimmer and a voluptuous Greek exile of noble birth, both of whom were crying with relief. Joanna promptly started to clamber after them, grasping in her hand a rung that the last girl's foot had just left. At that moment, the house trembled and the ladder and wash-room with it. The fire was extinguished, but the gutted house had been finally thrown by the violence of the work on the skylight. A whistle sounded as Joanna was half-way up. A voice from the megaphone ordered the men to jump clear. The house went down as the last fireman waited at the skylight for Joanna to emerge. As the sloping roof began to cave in, he leapt clear, landing badly and painfully on the flat roof-top. The house sank into its centre, a high heap of rubble, and Joanna went with it.

Chapter Nine

THE tape-recording had been erased for economy reasons, so that the tape could be used again. That is how things were in 1945. Nicholas was angry in excess of the occasion. He had wanted to play back Joanna's voice to her father who had come up to London after her funeral to file in forms as to the effects of the dead. Nicholas had written to him, partly with an urge to impart his last impressions of Joanna, partly from curiosity, partly, too, from a desire to stage a dramatic play-back of Joanna doing *The Wreck of the Deutschland*. He had mentioned the tape-recording in his letter.

But it was gone. It must have been wiped out by someone at his office.

> *Thou hast bound bones and veins in me, fastened*
> *   me flesh,*
> *And after it almost unmade, what with dread,*
> *   Thy doing: and dost thou touch me afresh?*

*   *   *

Nicholas said to the rector, 'It's infuriating. She was at her best in *The Wreck of the Deutschland*. I'm terribly sorry.'

Joanna's father sat, pink-faced and white-haired. He said, 'Oh, please don't worry.'

'I wish you could have heard it.'

As if to console Nicholas in his loss, the rector murmured with a nostalgic smile:

> *It was the schooner* Hesperus
> *That sailed the wintry sea,*

'No, no, the *Deutschland*. *The Wreck of the Deutschland*.'

'Oh, the *Deutschland*.' With a gesture characteristic of the English aquiline nose, his seemed to smell the air for enlightenment.

Nicholas was moved by this to a last effort to regain the lost recording. It was a Sunday, but he managed to get one of his colleagues on the telephone at home.

'Do you happen to know if anyone removed a tape from that box I borrowed from the office? Like a fool I left it in my room at the office. Someone's removed an important tape. Something private.'

'No, I don't think . . . just a minute . . . yes, in fact, they've wiped out the stuff. It was poetry. Sorry, but the economy regulations, you know . . . What do you think of the news? Takes your breath away, doesn't it?'

Nicholas said to Joanna's father, 'Yes, it really has been wiped out.'

'Never mind. I remember Joanna as she was in the rectory. Joanna was a great help in the parish. Her coming to London was a mistake, poor girl.'

Nicholas refilled the man's glass with whisky and started to add water. The clergyman signed irritably with his hand to convey the moment when the drink was to his taste. He had the mannerisms of a widower of long years, or of one unaccustomed to being in the company of critical women. Nicholas perceived that the man had never seen the reality of his daughter. Nicholas was consoled for the blighting of his show; the man might not have recognised Joanna in the *Deutschland*.

> *The frown of his face*
> *Before me, the hurtle of hell*
> *Behind, where, where was a, where was a place?*

'I dislike London. I never come up unless I've got to,' the clergyman said, 'for convocation or something like that. If only Joanna could have settled down at the Rectory . . . She was restless, poor girl.' He gulped his whisky like a gargle, tossing back his head.

Nicholas said, 'She was reciting some sort of office just before she went down. The other girls were with her, they were listening in a way. Some psalms.'

'Really? No-one else has mentioned it.' The old man looked embarrassed. He swirled his drink and swallowed it down, as if Nicholas might be going on to tell him that his daughter had gone over to Rome at the last, or somehow died in bad taste.

Nicholas said violently, 'Joanna had religious strength.'

'I know that, my boy,' said the father, surprisingly.

'She had a sense of Hell. She told a friend of hers that she was afraid of Hell.'

'Really? I didn't know that. I've never heard her speak morbidly. It must have been the influence of London. I never come here, myself, unless I've got to. I had a curacy once, in Balham, in my young days. But since then I've had country parishes. I prefer country parishes. One finds better, more devout, and indeed in some cases, quite holy souls in the country parishes.'

Nicholas was reminded of an American acquaintance of his, a psycho-analyst who had written to say he intended to practise in England after the war, 'away from all these neurotics and this hustling scene of anxiety'.

'Christianity is all in the country parishes these days,' said this shepherd of the best prime mutton. He put down his glass as if to seal his decision on the matter, his grief for the loss of Joanna turning back, at every sequence, on her departure from the rectory.

He said, 'I must go and see the spot where she died.'

Nicholas had already promised to take him to the demolished house in Kensington Road. The father had reminded Nicholas of this several times as if afraid he might inattentively leave London with this duty unfulfilled.

'I'll walk along with you.'

'Well, if it's not out of your way I'll be much obliged. What do you make of this new bomb? Do you think it's only propaganda stuff?'

'I don't know, sir,' said Nicholas.

'It leaves one breathless with horror. They'll have to make an armistice if it's true.' He looked around him as they walked towards Kensington. 'These bomb-sites look tragic. I never come up if I can help it, you know.'

Nicholas said, presently, 'Have you seen any of the girls who were trapped in the house with Joanna, or any of the other members of the club?'

The rector said, 'Yes, quite a few. Lady Julia was kind enough to have a few to tea to meet me yesterday afternoon. Of course, those poor girls have been through an ordeal, even the onlookers among them. Lady Julia suggested we didn't discuss the actual incident. You know, I think that was wise.'

'Yes. Do you recall the girls' names at all?'

'There was Lady Julia's niece, Dorothy, and a Miss Baberton, who escaped, I believe, through a window. Several others.'

'A Miss Redwood? Selina Redwood?'

'Well, you know, I'm rather bad at names.'

'A very tall, very slender girl, very beautiful. I want to find her. Dark hair.'

'They were all charming, my dear boy. All young people are charming. Joanna was, to me, the most charming of all, but there I'm partial.'

'She was charming,' said Nicholas, and held his peace.

But the man had sensed his pursuit with the ease of the pastoral expert on home ground, and he enquired solicitously, 'Has this young girl disappeared?'

'Well, I haven't been able to trace her. I've been trying for the past nine days.'

'How odd. She couldn't have lost her memory, I suppose? Wandering the streets . . .?'

'I think she would have been found in that case. She's very conspicuous.'

'What does her family report?'

'Her family are in Canada.'

'Perhaps she's gone away to forget. It would be understandable. Was she one of the girls who were trapped?'

'Yes. She got out through a window.'

'Well, I don't think she was at Lady Julia's from your description. You could telephone and ask.'

'I have telephoned, in fact. She hasn't heard anything of Selina and neither have any of the other girls. But I was hoping they might be mistaken. You know how it is.'

'Selina . . .' said the rector.

'Yes, that's her name.'

'Just a moment. There was a mention of a Selina. One of the

girls, a fair girl, very young, was complaining that Selina had gone off with her only ball dress. Would that be the girl?'

'That's the girl.'

'Not very nice of her to pinch another girl's dress, especially when they've all lost their wardrobes in the fire.'

'It was a Schiaparelli dress.'

The rector did not intrude on this enigma. They came to the site of the May of Teck Club. It looked now like one of the familiar ruins of the neighbourhood, as if it had been shattered years ago by a bomb-attack, or months ago by a guided missile. The paving stones of the porch lay crookedly leading nowhere. The pillars lay like Roman remains. A side wall at the back of the house stood raggedly at half its former height. Greggie's garden was a heap of masonry with a few flowers and rare plants sprouting from it. The pink and white tiles of the hall lay in various aspects of long neglect, and from a lower part of the ragged side wall a piece of brown drawing-room wallpaper furled more raggedly.

Joanna's father stood holding his wide black hat.

At the top of the house the apples are laid in rows,

The rector said to Nicholas, 'There's really nothing to see.'

'Like my tape-recording,' said Nicholas.

'Yes, it's all gone, all elsewhere.'

*   *   *

Rudi Bittesch lifted and flicked through a pile of notebooks that lay on Nicholas's table. He said, 'Is this the manuscript of your book, by the way?'

He would not have taken this liberty in the normal course, but Nicholas was under a present obligation to him. Rudi had discovered the whereabouts of Selina.

'You can have it,' said Nicholas, meaning the manuscript. He said, not foreseeing the death he was to die, 'You can keep it. It might be valuable one day when I'm famous.'

Rudi smiled. All the same, he tucked the books under his arm and said, 'Coming along?'

On the way to pick up Jane to go and see the fun at the Palace,

Nicholas said, 'Anyway, I've decided not to publish the book. The typescripts are destroyed.'

'I have this bloody big lot of books to carry, and now you tell me this. What value to me if you don't publish?'

'Keep them, you never know.'

Rudi had a caution about these things. He kept *The Sabbath Notebooks*, eventually to reap his reward.

'Would you like a letter from Charles Morgan to me saying I'm a genius?' Nicholas said.

'You're bloody cheerful about something or other.'

'I know,' said Nicholas. 'Would you like to have the letter, though?'

'What letter?'

'Here it is.' Nicholas brought Jane's letter from his inside pocket, crumpled like a treasured photograph.

Rudi glanced at it. 'Jane's work,' he said, and handed it back. 'Why are you so cheerful? Did you see Selina?'

'Yes.'

'What did she say?'

'She screamed. She couldn't stop screaming. It's a nervous reaction.'

'The sight of you must have brought all back to her. I advised to keep away.'

'She couldn't stop screaming.'

'You frightened her.'

'Yes.'

'I said keep away. She's no good, by the way, with a crooner in Clarges Street. You see him?'

'Yes, he's a perfectly nice chap. They're married.'

'So they say. You want to find a girl with character. Forget her.'

'Oh, well. Anyway, he was very apologetic about her screaming, and I was very apologetic, of course. It made her scream more. I think she'd have preferred to see a fight.'

'You don't love her that much, to fight a crooner.'

'He was quite a decent crooner.'

'You heard him croon?'

'No, of course, that's a point.'

Jane was restored to her normal state of unhappiness and hope, and was now established in a furnished room in Kensington Church Street. She was ready to join them.

Rudi said, 'You don't scream when you see Nicholas?'

'No,' she said, 'but if he goes on refusing to let George publish his book I will scream. George is putting the blame on me. I told him about the letter from Charles Morgan.'

'You should fear him,' Rudi said. 'He makes ladies scream by the way. Selina got a fright from him today.'

'I got a fright from her last time.'

'Have you found her then?' said Jane.

'Yes, but she's suffering from shock. I must have brought all the horrors back to her mind.'

'It was hell,' Jane said.

'I know.'

'Why is he in love with Selina by the way?' Rudi said. 'Why doesn't he find a woman of character or a French girl?'

*   *   *

'This is a toll call,' Jane said, rapidly.

'I know. Who's speaking?' said Nancy, the daughter of the Midlands clergyman, now married to another Midlands clergyman.

'It's Jane. Look, I've just got another question to ask you, quickly, about Nicholas Farringdon. Do you think his conversion had anything to do with the fire? I've got to finish this big article about him.'

'Well, I always like to think it was Joanna's example. Joanna was very High Church.'

'But he wasn't in love with Joanna, he was in love with Selina. After the fire he looked for her all over the place.'

'Well, he couldn't have been converted by Selina. Not converted.'

'He got a note in his manuscript that a vision of evil may be as effective to conversion as a vision of good.'

'I don't understand these fanatics. There's the pips, Jane. I think he was in love with us all, poor fellow.'

*   *   *

The public swelled on V.J. night of August as riotously as on the victory night of May. The little figures appeared duly on the balcony every half-hour, waved for a space and disappeared.

Jane, Nicholas, and Rudi were suddenly in difficulties, being pressed by the crowd from all sides. 'Keep your elbows out if possible,' Jane and Nicholas said to each other, almost simultaneously; but this was useless advice. A seaman, pressing on Jane, kissed her passionately on the mouth; nothing whatsoever could be done about it. She was at the mercy of his wet beery mouth until the crowd gave way, and then the three pressed a path to a slightly healthier spot, with access to the park.

Here, another seaman, observed only by Nicholas, slid a knife silently between the ribs of a woman who was with him. The lights went up on the balcony, and a hush anticipated the Royal appearance. The stabbed woman did not scream, but sagged immediately. Someone else screamed through the hush, a woman, many yards away, some other victim. Or perhaps that screamer had only had her toes trodden upon. The crowd began to roar again. All their eyes were at this moment fixed on the Palace balcony, where the royal family had appeared in due order. Rudi and Jane were busy yelling their cheers.

Nicholas tried unsuccessfully to move his arm above the crowd to draw attention to the wounded woman. He had been shouting that a woman had been stabbed. The seaman was shouting accusations at his limp woman, who was still kept upright by the crowd. These private demonstrations faded in the general pandemonium. Nicholas was borne away in a surge that pressed from the Mall. When the balcony darkened, he was again able to make a small clearing through the crowd, followed by Jane and Rudi towards the open park. On the way, Nicholas was forced to a standstill and found himself close by the knifer. There was no sign of the wounded woman. Nicholas, waiting to move, took the letter to Charles Morgan from his pocket and thrust it down the seaman's blouse, and then was borne onwards. He did this for no apparent reason and to no effect, except that it was a gesture. That is the way things were at that time.

They walked back through the clear air of the park, stepping round the couples who lay locked together in their path. The park was filled with singing. Nicholas and his companions sang too. They ran into a fight between British and American service-men. Two men lay unconscious at the side of the path, being tended by their friends. The crowds cheered in the distance, behind them. A formation of aircraft buzzed across the night sky. It was a glorious victory.

Jane mumbled, 'Well, I wouldn't have missed it, really.' She had halted to pin up her straggling hair, and had a hair-pin in her mouth as she said it. Nicholas marvelled at her stamina, re-calling her in this image years later in the country of his death—how she stood, sturdy and bare-legged on the dark grass, occu-pied with her hair—as if this was an image of all the May of Teck establishment in its meek, unselfconscious attitudes of poverty, long ago in 1945.

THE END

park was filled with saplings. Nicholas and his companions soon
lost. They arrived at a point between British and American service-
men. They were late-comers at the side of the path, being
landed by their friends. This crowd cheered in the distance
around them. A fountain of aircraft burned across the night
finally was a glorious vision.

Jane mounted. "Well, I wouldn't have missed it, really." She
had settled up in her dreadful hair, and had a hat-pin in her
mouth as she said it. Nicholas marvelled at her stamina, re-
calling her in this line a year later in the country of his death,
how she stood, sturdy and bare-legged on the stony grass, occupied with her hair—and if this was an image of all the May of
life's carnal Innocent in its most... permutational attitudes of
perpetuity, long after in...